Other Titles by TW Brown

The DEAD Series:

DEAD: The Ugly Beginning
DEAD: Revelations
DEAD: Fortunes & Failures
DEAD: Winter
DEAD: Siege & Survival
DEAD: Confrontation
DEAD: Reborn
DEAD: Darkness Befc
DEAD: Spring
DEAD: Reclamation

DEAD Special Edition

DEAD: Perspectives Story (Vols. 1 & 2)
DEAD: Vignettes (Vols. 1 & 2)
DEAD: The Geeks (Vols. 1 & 2)

Zomblog

Zomblog
Zomblog II
Zomblog: The Final Entry
Zomblog: Snoe
Zomblog: Snoe's War
Zomblog: Snoe's Journey

Miscellaneous

Gruesomely Grimm Zombie Tales Vol. I
That Ghoul Ava: Her First Adventures
That Ghoul Ava & The Queen of the Zombies
That Ghoul Ava Kick Some Faerie A**
Next, on a very special That Ghoul Ava
Dakota

Reclamation

(Book 10 of the *DEAD* series)

TW Brown

Portland, Oregon, USA

DEAD: Reclamation
Book 10 of the *DEAD* series
©2014 May December Publications LLC

Printed in the U.S.A.

ISBN 978-1-940734-30-9

The World of the *DEAD* expands with:

Snaphot—**Portland, Oregon**
(Coming in the spring of 2015)
To see your town die in the *DEAD* world, email TW Brown at:
twbrown.maydecpub@gmail.com

A moment with the author...

I love what I do. I appreciate each and every one of you that have come this far in the journey. So before you go forward, let me send you on your way with a warning: sometimes, bad things happen.

Of course I won't be sharing any spoilers, but I wanted to let you know ahead of time that this final three book arc has the potential to be upsetting. Am I going to kill off every character and end it with the zombies bringing down the last living human? No. Did I consider it? Sure. I mean, don't we all see that as an eventuality?

Why would they wipe out over ninety percent of humanity in the first year and then just stop? Sure, the pickings would get slim, but don't you think there is a likelihood that the zombies win? I know I do. However, I will say that you will not find that ending here.

On the other side of that coin, some of the stories will take a final bow. I have actually considered pulling a *Wayne's World Super Ultimate Happy Alternate Ending* and writing it for the *DEAD: Special Edition* collection that I do after each three books. Maybe if enough people ask for it...I will do just that. After all, the Special Editions are written based on fan feedback of what they would have liked to know more about. So why couldn't I devote an alternate final chapter to a few of the stories? That is the cool thing about my job...I can do whatever I want! So start banging that drum if you want to be heard.

I wanted to actually share something about the way this book came about. Many of you know that I hate using outlines. That is why things often happen that I find myself wondering how the characters will possibly escape it alive. And then...they don't.

A few examples, I never intended for the Geeks to drop so damn fast. They just kept getting into trouble that I could not save them from. And then there was Steve. Steve was actually supposed to be part of the *DEAD: Spring* finale. I do actually reach a point with myself that I say, "Enough already!" However, in writing this particular book, I hit a few spots that had me concerned. And as it got deeper, I tried to alter the direction, but then the words would not come. The only way things would move forward was for me to either delete several chapters worth of work (with no guarantee that I would not end up stumbling down the same rabbit hole) or to just surrender to the words that come.

I have always trusted in the latter. I feel it makes the story more "real." It is when I start trying to make things happen that my work becomes forced and loses some of its tension. That is also when it stops feeling like me. Let's face it, we came this far because the story did not follow conventional plans. You are invested in these very real people because they act like we would, not like supermen and women…trained in all matters of survival and who happen to always stumble upon just what they need in that final second to escape their ugly demise.

MY CHARACTERS DIE!

This is a zombie apocalypse, not *Adventures in Happyland*. (Although a zombie version of that might be fun.) The world is a dangerous place, and even with careful planning and a lot of luck, chances for survival are sketchy at best.

So, buckle in, this might get messy. Also, I have included an excerpt from the first book in the *DEAD: Snapshot* series, *DEAD: Snapshot—**Portland, Oregon***. So, while the characters that you have come to know and love might be sailing off into the sunset very soon, the *DEAD* world has many untold tales of horror, salvation, and yes…even some human depravity.

A few quick thank you mentions are in order. They may seem silly to some, but these are our way of trying to make the people who matter realize that we know they are out there. Heck, must people skip this part anyway.

To the firefighters of the world who go into a real Hell on Earth every wildfire season and put it all on the line to try and save the homes of people they don't know and will probably never meet formally…you are freakin' Rock Stars. To the men and women of the armed forces, home and abroad, you are overworked, underpaid, and often under-appreciated—thank you for standing the midwatch. My Beta readers—Sophie, Tammy, and Vix—you make my book so much better Last but not least, my wife. Denise has been through hell and back this year, but she still finds time to do all the computer stuff that make my books available…thank you, Hunny Bunny.

In conclusion, I hope you enjoy the ride. I hope that, either way, you will take the few moments out of your day to post a review on Amazon and any other venue where reviews are accepted. And never feel shy about reaching out and letting me know what you think. I don't have "people" who read my emails and reply for me. I do that every morning over coffee as I sit down to the day's work. I love hearing from you. And I am always happy to be interviewed for blogs or just asked random questions.

Warriors…come out to play-yay!!!
TW Brown
October 2014

George A. Romero & Stephen King
Two men who don't even know I exist
And both changed my life

Contents

1

Thalia

Billy Haynes once told me that you can get somebody to talk just by leaving them in a room full of items that look like they would cause a great deal of pain. I hope it works.

"Is he secured, Thalia?" Dr. Zahn asked.

"Yes, ma'am," I said as I shut the door behind me.

"Then you should get up to HQ. Billy is setting the roster for the next patrol. And don't forget that your little brother is over at the garden. You are supposed to pick him up on the way home."

"I know." I sure hope I didn't sound as annoyed as I felt.

My name is Thalia Rosa Hobart. I am little Stevie Hobart's big sister…daughter of Steve, and I can't remember a time when zombies did not exist.

***

"No activity has been seen in the La Grande valley for three months," Billy was saying as he stood at the head of the huge room in front of the heavily notated and hand drawn map on the wall.

"And when did the wind turbines around Island City get yanked down?" a voice from somewhere in front of me asked.

1

"Best guess is within the last two weeks." Billy did not hide his grimace of annoyance.

Seriously, this was stuff that the rumor mill had been spitting out for the past ten days. Why would anybody ask that question? The only person that stupid—

"So why have we waited this long to send a team down?" Kayla Brockhouse asked as she stood up, probably so that people could see that stupid look on her face...and her boobs. She thought those were the answer to everything.

I fought the urge to yank her back down into her chair by that curly blond hair of hers that she grew out well beyond regulation. Just another example of how those stupid bumps on her chest acted like some sort of male brain damage inducer. Her squad leader apparently found his eyes unable to go high enough up her body to see that she had at least three inches past the collar. I wonder if zombies are that stupid.

Mroar...oh...you have boobs? Well, never mind then, I'll go eat somebody else.

"Something funny, Miss Hobart?" Billy's voice snapped me out of my daydream.

"Uhh...no?" *Damn, had that sounded like a question?*

He gave me a nasty glare and I patted myself on the back for not sticking my tongue out. Billy had never been the same since losing Katrina. She'd been on a routine security patrol a few years ago. Her team had never returned. There had been some frantic searching that revealed nothing. Eventually, Billy disappeared. He returned almost a month later...different.

It did not take a genius to know what he'd found out there. Still, he never talked about it...ever. At least not to anybody who might leak anything. I am pretty sure that he told Dr. Zahn. She would go to the grave with whatever it was he had said in those few days that he stayed in the doc's office.

"As I was saying..." Billy gave me one more tight lipped grimace, and then continued, "...the reason we have not gone down there is because ZH-Seven was in the area between us and them."

ZH-Seven wasn't the largest zombie herd, but it did number

2

well over a half a million. You did not want that crossing between you and home if you could help it. Herds were really the only thing about zombies that anybody was concerned about these days. In fact, most times, if you passed a single or a small group, you just ignored it. It wasn't worth the time or the energy.

The reality was that zombies were still very dangerous. You only went head-to-head with one if you absolutely had no choice. The logic was that you couldn't get bitten if you were not within range of their mouths. The hope that those things would fall over had long since vanished. Nobody could explain it. It defied biology (according to people that knew about that sort of thing).

"The route is now clear, and we want to send a full field team down *to observe only.*" He really emphasized those last three words and practically shouted that last one.

There was a ripple in the room. We seldom sent full field teams anymore. That was a relic from the days when you could still scavenge from abandoned homes and such. Those cupboards had been bare for a long time. If it wasn't already cleaned out, then it was well past its expiration date.

Full field teams had a six person squad with a complete armament load out, two scouts, and a medic. We almost never allowed a medical person to leave on a run these days. While the danger was slim, the mindset was that it was stupid to risk such a valuable resource like a medically trained individual. As it was, the first actual class had just graduated, swelling our number of trained medical persons from five to eight.

Dr. Zahn had put together a program and was in charge of making sure the medics knew what they were doing. She had help from Sunshine, a lady who knew her stuff when it came to herbs and natural remedies. Also, there was this other lady named Cynthia Bird. She had been a veterinarian. Dr. Zahn relied on her a lot when it came to training—mostly because the doc did not have the patience (see what I did there?).

The other two medical people in the community had been EMTs. One was this man named Greg Carrigan. Greg was one of the immune. He had lost his right hand in the early days. He never smiled much, but he always had a nice word to say.

"The team will leave just before dawn tomorrow," Billy announced. "Jim Sagar will be leading. The patrol list is posted. Check it on your way out. If you are on it, then you are excused from any tower watch you might have been assigned. That is all."

Everybody got up and started for the door. I was falling in, ready to go pick up my brother when Billy called.

"Thalia, a word please."

I sighed. He was probably going to give me a bunch of grief about not paying attention. He was always riding me and giving me a hard time. Sometimes I wondered if I had ticked him off when I was little and this was some form of revenge. I let everybody pass, but I noticed Kayla give me a nasty look on the way out. One of these days I was going to catch her alone…and when I did…

"I wanted to tell you instead of you seeing it on the board," Billy said by way of greeting. "You are on the team for this run."

I was suddenly struck dumb. I had never been on anything more than perimeter patrols despite being one of the best in hand-to-hand, knife and axe throwing, and the crossbow. I was not only the winner of my age bracket at the annual Establishment Festival, but I had won the overall against people twice, three, and four times my age.

"Are you serious?" My voice came out a bit squeaky, and I felt my face flush.

"There is nobody better if we need a sharpshooter," Billy said. I swear I saw the slightest hint of a smile.

"But if this is an observe only mission—" I began. He cut me off.

"It is, but we have reports that there may be some raiders in the area."

I had a million questions, but I was scared to ask any just in case that might be the one question that made him change his mind. I had wanted to go out there for as long as I could remember. It wasn't that I was anxious to kill zombies or anything, it was just the simple fact that I wanted to see what was outside of the little area that we called home.

And I guess that is not entirely accurate either. Our community has stretched and expanded to cover quite a lot of space. I think somebody said that it was almost a mile long and two miles wide. We had stayed close to the creek in order to have our regular source of water, but we had pushed the forest back a ways up into the mountains.

I remember playing here...I remember snow...and I remember that zombie that got Emily. I shoved that horrible memory aside.

"Jim will keep you close to him, and I don't want to hear that you did anything to make me regret my decision." Billy folded his big arms across his massive chest and stared down at me with a raised eyebrow.

I imagine it would almost look funny, the two of us standing almost toe-to-toe. I had not even realized how close he was until it dawned on me that I could barely see his face.

Taking a step back, I swallowed once to make sure that my throat was clear. "I promise to make you proud, but I do have one tiny question." He nodded for me to continue. "Does Melissa know?"

"I talked with her last night." I opened my mouth, but he kept talking. "And I made her promise that she would not say anything. I did not want the word to get around and have you hear it from another source."

He had a point. There was no such thing as a secret in our community. We numbered just over three hundred men, women, and children; and everybody seemed to always be in each other's business.

"Hey, Cupcake!" a voice called from the doorway behind me.

"Hey there, See-gar." I spun to see Jim Sagar stroll into the room.

You could not tell by looking at him, but Jim was a genius when it came to explosives. He was the only one who had free reign to slip out on his own. He would always come back with a full backpack of stuff and then vanish into his apartment for a few days. The rumor was that if his place ever caught fire, it would level the entire compound.

I still thought the name of this place was a bit corny. There had been a vote years back. The choice had been a strange one. I guess there used to be these schools called colleges. The big two in the state of Oregon had sports teams; one was called the Ducks, and the other was called the Beavers. As you enter our walled community, you pass under a sign that reads: Welcome to Platypus Creek.

"Making your first big run," Jim said with his ever-present crooked smile as he reached over and tousled my short, black hair.

"It's not like I have never been outside the walls," I grumbled, finally pulling my head away when he did not seem inclined to stop.

"It is an entirely different thing when you lose sight of those walls," Billy said in his usual gruff tone. "And that is also why I wanted to talk to you alone. If you want, I can send Paula. If it gets a bit too much, you can come back. Nobody would think badly of you."

I looked back and forth between the two men. Even Jim had lost that smile. I am certain that was the first time that I had ever seen his face when he wasn't at least sporting a lopsided grin.

"What am I missing?" I wasn't getting scared if that was their intention. Actually, I was more curious than ever.

"You have been in this place for the majority of your lifetime. I am willing to bet that you don't remember too much about what it was like out there," Billy said, his voice now had a very uncharacteristic softness. "Once you get away from this place, it is an entirely different world. The closest community was Island City. Something took that place down. If it was a herd, that is one thing. However, we do not believe that it was zombies."

"If it was people," Jim picked up the narrative, "then they are bad…real bad. It has been a while since any of us had to kill a living person, but those of us who have done so…it sticks with you forever."

6

"And you think this is living people who took out Island City?"

I had never been there, but I had heard the stories. While we were certainly advanced as far as communities were concerned, Island City was like a fairy tale. If you believed the stories, they had electric lights that ran night *and* day. There was a market that was rumored to be almost the size of five of ours lined up.

Sometimes the trade caravan would arrive and you could get this stuff called ice cream. Melissa had surprised me with some chocolate ice cream on my fifteenth birthday. That had been the first time (at least as far as I can recall) that I'd ever had chocolate...much less chocolate ice cream.

"We are almost positive," Billy said.

"So, if you guys were going to get all worked up and try to scare me, why put me on this run in the first place?" I snapped. I mean, it was obvious what they were trying to do, and it was really making me angry.

"Because I told them you were ready," another voice called from the doorway. I turned to see Paula Yin standing there.

Paula had very pretty Asian features that made her look almost delicate. She wasn't. More than one guy had learned that the hard way. She was dressed in cutoff jeans, but it was the faded and tattered tee shirt that had the picture of (of all things) a zombie on it that got my attention.

"*Dawn of the Dead*?" I asked with a tilt of the head.

"Huh?" Paula seemed confused for a second, and then she looked down at what might have once been a dark green shirt. Now it was sort of pale, and even threadbare in spots. Also, there was a nasty stain on the left shoulder. "Oh!" Her eyes brightened and she had a wicked smile when she looked up.

"That movie was hilarious," Jim muttered. "Didn't much care for the remake. Thank God those things can't run. I still love that opening scene when that little girl goes skidding down the hallway and then pops up to her feet."

I noticed him shiver just a bit, and I tried to imagine a zombie that could run...much less pop up to its feet. That would suck.

"As I was saying," Paula spoke up, breaking the mood and bringing things back to where they belong, "you are ready."

"So why are these two trying to scare me...or whatever the heck that was they were pulling with the whole thing about the outside world being so full of danger?"

"Oh...don't get me wrong." Paula pulled a withered piece of unidentifiable dried fruit from her pocket and nibbled on it, washing it down with a swig from her canteen. "It can be hellish out there at the best of times. Every single time I come back from one, I swear it is my last field mission."

"But we stopped doing full field missions a long time ago," I pointed out. The looks on everybody's faces told me that might not be entirely true.

"We stopped announcing them," Billy said.

He looked around the room like he expected somebody to pop out from behind something. I could not ever recall seeing him this...jumpy. Paula's face was as emotionless as always, and Jim...well, you could never trust what you saw on his face.

"Then how have you been doing it?" I asked. "And how have you kept it a secret? People here know how many times their neighbor uses the toilet. I find it a little hard to believe you could pull off sending out groups on full field missions without it being common knowledge."

"Where do you think I go?" Jim asked with a straight face. "And how many times have you heard that Sunshine is out collecting herbal samples?"

"The key is to send folks out separately and have them meet up at a pre-determined location," Billy said.

"Then why is this one different?" The room was suddenly so silent that my own breathing sounded loud in my ears.

"We think there may be something seriously wrong in Island City. If we are correct, and if the reports from the initial observations are accurate, it could mean trouble." Billy was pacing now, and I was officially nervous. "If our suspicions are true, then we will need the validation from an announced field mission."

"I am coming with you," Paula said as she came to stand beside me and put an arm around my shoulder. "I need to know now if you think you can kill a living person."

I thought about that for a long moment. I looked from one face to the other. I really wanted to just say yes. My fear was that, if I said that I couldn't, they would take me off the mission. It wasn't that I was looking forward to killing a living person; it was just that I really wanted to go out there and see what the world was like outside of these walls.

Sometimes I had dreams. In those dreams, I saw this city...Seattle, Washington. I knew the icons like the Space Needle from some of the books in our library. I wondered what it would be like to go up in such a thing and be able to look around.

There are rumors that a small community of survivors turned that thing into a fortress and that they live there now. Of course, there are lots of rumors. You have to be able to separate the tiny slivers of truth from all of the garbage.

"Well?" Billy asked, snapping me out of my thoughts.

I could actually feel my shoulders slump just a little as the air leaked from my body and deflated me when the realization came that I had to tell the truth or risk the lives of other people...people like Paula.

"I don't know." It was the truth. I really could not say that I could kill another living person, but I could not say that I couldn't either.

"Perfect," Paula said as she gave me a hug. "Get your field gear prepped and ready, we leave early in the morning."

I did not know what to say. And apparently they did not really care, because the three of them headed out the door. A rectangle of sunlight shone, and then it was gone. I stood there for who knows how long as I tried to make sense out of everything.

"Crap!" I blurted.

I had to get over to the garden to pick up Stevie. I hurried out the door and into the bustle that was everyday life here in Platypus Creek.

***

"Thalia!" Stevie called, a big smile on his face.

He was filthy from head to toe, his face smeared with enough mud that I knew a mud ball fight had to have taken place at some point in his day. I tried not to smile back, but it was just too hard to keep it in.

Folks that remember him say that little Stevie is the spitting image of his dad...our dad. Steve Hobart rescued me when the world fell apart. I wish I would have been a little older so that I could remember him better. I get flashes sometimes, but nothing more. Sadly, I get flashes of a lot of faces. All of them gone. All of them dead.

Steve and Melissa got married here. In fact, the hill where he proposed is where they built a little arch. That is where weddings are held. Most of the folks don't know why, and some even complain because it is such a hike, but the view is amazing and provides an excellent backdrop for a wedding.

"Are you ready to go?" I called.

Stevie looked around at the rows stretched out for several yards beyond him. He was working in the potato patch. Those made up a good portion of our diet since they were easy to grow out here and were filling.

"Sure." He gave a shrug and patted a few of his fellow field workers on the shoulder as he passed.

"So...is it true?" he asked as he climbed over the small fence and made a futile effort to wipe his hands on his pants.

"Is what true?" I replied, jumping back as he tried to swipe at me with his muddy hands.

"Are you going on a field run?" I guess standing there with my mouth open was a good enough answer for him. "Promise to bring me back something?"

"Whoa!" I held my hands up. "How do you know about this?"

"Jenna Haynes overheard. She told me at lunch."

That was a sad story. Unfortunately, it was a common one. Jenna was Billy and Katrina's daughter. She is only eight years old.

She couldn't have been much more than a year old when her mom went on a run and never returned. I think that would be a little worse just because you don't really know. I at least know that Steve died. I know there was a funeral. I am pretty sure that I was there, but I have been to so many that I can't pick his out from all the others.

Billy is not allowed to make a field run. The rule is that if you are a single parent, that you would only be considered for field runs in an emergency. If a child is lucky enough to have both parents, then only one can be out at a time. I think that bothers Billy the most…Katrina filled in for him because he was sick or something. That run where she disappeared was supposed to be him.

"And how did Jenna just happen to hear?" I asked.

"Because I was faking asleep," a voice said from behind me, making me jump.

I turned to see a big, round face staring up at me with bright hazel eyes and hair cut in an almost boyish bowl cut. Jenna looked too much like her dad and would probably not ever be called cute or pretty. However, she also sported her dad's body type. Most ten- or twelve-year-olds would not mess with Jenna Haynes. She was going to be a monster if she kept growing in this manner.

She had one other distinction. She was one of a handful of children born from two immune parents. Both Billy and Katrina had endured the horror of a zombie bite and survived. She was now part of a study being run by Dr. Zahn. Nobody really knew what the doc was looking for, much less if she had found anything up to this point, but she endured a monthly blood draw along with a few other things.

"So?" Stevie prodded, wanting to hear me confirm what he apparently already knew.

"It's true," I admitted.

"That is so cool!" the boy crowed. "You finally get to go out there like you always wanted. Promise you will bring me back something!"

"If I find anything cool, I will bring it back." I glanced over to Jenna. "Yes, I will bring you back something also."

The girl smiled big. I'd seen pictures of these things called Jack-o-lanterns. Why anybody would waste good pumpkin by carving it up like that, I have no idea. However, her smile immediately made me think of just exactly that. It was worse at the moment since she was currently missing two teeth: one top and one bottom.

"When do you go?" Stevie asked as the pair fell in beside me as I started towards home.

"You tell me," I shot back. Jenna giggled.

"Does mom know?" Stevie ignored my response.

That was a good question. I know that Melissa had been pretty upset when I had enlisted. She and Paula had almost gotten into a fight that day. I was glad that hadn't happened. Melissa was a great mom, but she was not much of a fighter.

"I guess we will find out."

We walked down the trail that led to what had been the very first two-story apartments built within the compound. It had five upper and five lower units. I remember the day we moved in. I had my very own room for the first time ever. I think I stayed in there with the door shut for hours, just looking at the four empty walls, the footlocker, and the sleeping bag. It was like a castle to me.

I reached the gate and waved up to Gladys Rennard. She was three years older than me, but she acted like she was ten years younger. You could always hear her and her mom yelling at each other over one thing or another. I know she absolutely hated the fact that she had to stand gate watch.

Even though our apartment is within the main walls, it (just like the other ten that have been built so far) has its own perimeter wall. It is not as tall as the outer walls are, coming just to about my eye level, but the hope is that it would stand up to a wave of zombies should the perimeter ever be breached.

The gate swung open after a moment. Stevie, Jenna, and I exchanged secret smirks as he listened to Gladys struggle with the crank that had to be turned manually to open the gate. As we walked in, I instantly spotted Melissa on the side of the apartment fussing with the garden. She couldn't grow mold in a damp dark room, but she sure gave it her best effort.

"You better tell Mom alone," Stevie whispered. "I gotta go see what she did to my squash and beans."

Just then, her head popped up and she saw us. Rising to her feet, she wiped her hands on her coveralls and started in our direction.

"Kids!" she called with a big smile.

Her face was etched with a lot of what people called worry lines, but it was still easy to tell that she had been pretty—and still was when she smiled. Her dark hair was starting to show streaks of white that stood out and looked like strands of silver in the sunlight. I have been told that people used to put stuff in their hair to hide that sort of thing. Seems rather silly.

"Hi, Mom!" Stevie and I called back.

"Jenna Haynes, you are getting to be so big!" Melissa wrapped us all in a hug as soon as we were in range.

"Thank you, ma'am," the girl managed, her face smooshed into Melissa's side.

As soon as the hug was over, Stevie slipped away towards the garden. I doubted that I would ever understand what he found so fascinating about dirt and plants, but I envied his ability to grow things.

"Are you staying for dinner, Jenna?" Melissa asked as she herded us towards the stairs.

That was another thing that was cool. Since we had been the first family to move in to these apartments, we'd had first choice. We took the apartment at the far left on the second floor. It was the largest one of all the other apartments. My room even had a small, round window that I could look out from and see the creek.

"No, ma'am," Jenna answered. "Daddy said he will be by to collect me before dinner."

Billy lived on the ground floor at the opposite end from us. His apartment only had two rooms and was the smallest of the bunch.

"I am going on my first field run!" I blurted.

I really wish that I was better at that sort of thing. Sometimes, my mouth just opens and stuff falls out of it before I have a chance to decide if whatever it was would be a good idea to say out loud or not. I knew by the way that Melissa's face froze and her eyes went wide that I probably should have not broken the news quite like this. My biggest problem was that I just did not believe in beating around the bush, as the old saying goes. Much like a Band-Aid, I think it is simply better to give one sharp rip and be done with it.

When Melissa turned around, I took a step back. It wasn't because she looked really angry, or that I thought she would hit me or something. Actually, it was because her face was totally blank. She was just looking at me, and there was nothing on her face or in her eyes that gave away how she felt in that instant. For her, that was pretty major. She had the worst time trying to hide her feelings because they were always so clear in her expression...even when (and actually, especially when) she tried to hide them.

"Is this why all of those people have been coming in and out of Billy's place at all hours of the day and night?" she finally asked, breaking the most uncomfortable silence that I think I had ever experienced.

"I guess." That was news to me. I hadn't noticed to be honest.

"And when you say you are going on a field run..." Her voice had grown softer until it eventually faded and I actually stood there for a few seconds before I realized that she had basically asked her entire question.

"Billy says that it is a full team, complete with scouts and a medic. We are going to check on Island City."

It might have just been for a second, or it might have been just my imagination, but I thought I saw something flash across Melissa's face. I knew she hated the idea of me going out there. She had not stepped outside of these walls since they'd gone up. Even more telling, once they finished our apartment and we moved in, she had not gone out of the walls to this place either except for community meetings.

When I had started going to classes, I always walked with some of the other children and their parents. I do have memories of her waking me up with her crying in the middle of the night. And I saw the way people looked at her when they did not think anybody was watching them.

I'd asked Billy about it one day. He told me that Melissa had been pretty messed up when Daddy Steve and his group found her. I guess it was Daddy Steve that helped her come back to normal. When he died, Billy said that Melissa never recovered.

"What is wrong with Island City?" she asked, but if her face was missing any emotion, her voice was even worse. It didn't even sound human.

It sounded like that weird doll that I got for my birthday one year. I still have it, mostly just because of how creepy it sounds. It has blond hair and blue eyes that stare at you no matter where you stand. I know that the only reason I actually still have it is because I shoved it in the back of my closet after my birthday party and didn't find it for almost three years. To this day, when it says, "Will you be my fwend?" the hairs on the back of my neck stand up.

"It sounds like it is wiped out." There I go again, not filtering what I say. *Thalia! Stop being such a ninny!* Mentally I slapped myself, but I doubt it did any good.

"What do you mean…wiped out?"

I tried to think if there was any way that I could tell her stuff without it sounding worse.

"The wind turbines have been pulled down, and there may be some band of living humans behind it. Billy doubts that it is zombies." So, apparently the answer to my "Can I make it sound any worse?" question is a big fat YES!

"Anybody home?"

If Billy could have picked a worse time to show up at the house, I sure couldn't think of it. Melissa was past me and to the door faster than I'd ever seen her move in my life.

I imagine the neighbors got quite a show. Here is Billy, a

few inches over six feet, and easily over two hundred and fifty pounds. Then you have Melissa...almost five feet even and maybe a hundred pounds if you dunked her in the creek fully clothed in patrol gear.

She was yelling louder than I'd ever heard and threatening Billy with things that I did not think a human body could physically do to itself. But, to his credit, Billy simply stood there and took it. Once, during the entire scene, his eyes met mine and I was able to mouth the words "I'm so sorry."

Of all people, it was actually little Stevie that broke it up. He came walking up from the garden, face smeared with dirt, hands absolutely filthy. He was holding a handful of green beans in one hand.

"Hey, Mom?" he said, acting like his mother was not screaming at the top of her lungs, tears streaming down her face. "Can you make these for dinner tonight?"

It was just so completely random.

Melissa froze with her mouth open and just looked at Stevie like he had fallen from the sky. Then, she looked up at Billy and invited him to dinner.

I helped in the kitchen and sat down that night to the oddest and most awkward meal ever. Stevie and Jenna laughed and joked like there was nothing going on. By the time the Hayneses left, I was exhausted.

So, now I am in my bed, staring up at the ceiling...and I can't get my eyes to shut. I can't believe that I am finally going to get to leave the compound in the morning. I keep looking over by my door to where all my gear is piled up. Melissa even helped me check my field pack.

She actually sat down with me in my room and we sharpened knives together. I kept thinking she was going to make some sort of speech, but in the end, she simply kissed me on the forehead like she has every evening since I can remember after tucking me in for the night. I know she will not be out of her room when I leave in the morning, and that's okay. In some ways, I think I am glad. I don't want to show up at the muster point with my eyes all red from crying.

Thalia

Stevie doesn't think that I saw him slip a note in one of the side pouches on my pack. I think he is almost as excited for me as I am for myself.

Almost.

Dead: Reclamation

2

Vignettes LV

Juan set the axe down beside the tree and wiped the sweat from his face. The ground might be covered with a foot or so of snow, but he was sweating like this was the beaches of California or Florida.

The sound of laughter came in a rush as two figures bounded for him. Juan knelt and opened his arms to catch the twins as they leapt.

"Daddy!" the girl in the pink coat squealed.

As usual it was Della who made all the noise. Denita was the quiet one, and other than a sigh of contentment when her dad gave her a squeeze, she made almost no sound.

"Mama says that it is time for dinner." Della cocked her hip and crossed her arms in that same way her mother had when she was disapproving of something, but would not actually voice the sentiment.

"Something wrong, *hija*?" Juan shot a glance at Denita. He already knew that he would get no answers there. He felt a momentary pang at her withdrawn countenance.

"You smell icky," Della scolded, not having any problems at all expressing what was on her mind.

"That is because I have been working hard," Juan said with a sly slowness. Without warning, he lunged at Della and the two rolled in the snow, Juan making a point of squeezing his daughter tight to his chest. The squeals of laughter were a welcome reward and the two engaged in some playful wrestling before Denita made a soft cough that signaled she had stood in the snow long enough and wished to return to the cabin.

Juan stood, dusting off the snow—making sure to send a shower of it Della's direction. Once he got most of it brushed away, he grasped each daughter by the hand and started back to the cabin.

Today was the girls' seventh birthday. As he crossed the gently rolling, snow-covered hills, he reflected on how good his life was compared to how it had been before the deaders.

He had a wonderful wife that he loved with all his heart. He had a few good friends that he knew he could trust with his life; and had done so on more than one occasion the past several years. He had beautiful twin daughters. Sadly, he'd also had a son. That was why Denita almost never spoke. She had been four when she witnessed the death of her brother.

"Yo, Juan!" a familiar voice called in greeting.

"Hey, Keith," Juan hollered back, giving a nod to one of the men he trusted not only with his own life, but that of his family as well.

"We'll be over shortly." Keith gave a wave of his hand, indicating the heavily bundled woman holding an equally swaddled infant.

"See you then."

Juan opened his gate and ushered the girls inside. Mackenzie was standing in the open doorway, hand on her hip in almost the exact same pose of disapproval that Della had struck only moments before. Lips pressed tight, somebody unfamiliar with the woman would think that she was absolutely furious. She was simply annoyed. Juan knew the furious Mackenzie and this was not even close.

"Are you deliberately trying to avoid this, Mister Juan Hoya?" Mackenzie gave him a light backhand to the chest.

"Maybe," Juan replied honestly.

"Well you don't have much choice if you want to be anywhere near me." The woman reached into her apron and produced a set of well sharpened scissors. "You can grow that nasty beard as much as you want when you are out hunting, but when you come home to me—"

Mackenzie was giving the familiar speech. The last line was known well enough that Della was able to cut her off and finish it.

"You will be the baby smooth hunk I fell in love with." Della covered her mouth with her hands, stifling a giggle as her parents turned their attention her way, each with raised eyebrow and the hint of a smile.

Juan had been out with the hunting party for almost five weeks. They had returned with enough meat to get a good start on stocking the larders for all the families of their little community. Moose, bear, salmon, and snowshoe hare were plentiful.

They had even been able to stop in at the native village of the Kluti Kaah. It was always good to check in and see if there was any news. There had been. Fortunately, it was the same news they had been getting for the past three years.

No deaders.

"So, have you given my suggestion any thought?" Mackenzie asked as Juan slipped out of his clothes and stepped into the wash basin.

"About striking out for Anchorage?" Juan gave the cord a tug and allowed the lukewarm water to pour over him.

"If we are going to do it this year, it needs to be in the next few weeks, otherwise we risk being caught out there in the weather."

Juan sighed. He had wanted to punch that damn caravan driver in the face. All his talk about how the lights were on in Anchorage had gotten Mackenzie all worked up. She wasn't the only one to get the itch in their little community, but she was the only one that mattered.

"Why do you want to do this?" Juan asked as he soaped up.

"Because I want our children to have a shot at a normal life."

Juan could have parroted her response. Lord knew, he'd

heard that almost more times than her line about his smooth face.

"And what is so great about normal? Look where that got us," Juan threw up his hands, indicating their current surroundings. "Besides, we got it nice here. Food is more than plentiful, the girls have plenty of friends, and they even have you as their teacher."

Mackenzie opened her mouth to respond, but the knock at the door silenced her. She gave Juan a stern look with narrowed eyes and went to answer the door.

Juan sighed a huge breath of relief. Now, if Keith and the others could keep their mouths shut for just a few more days, he could spring the surprise and make Mackenzie's face light up.

They were moving to Anchorage.

***

The woman stood on the shore. The chilled salt water washed over her feet, but she barely felt it. Truth be told, she barely felt anything…ever.

That had not always been the case. Years ago she had been a silly twit of a girl. She mooned over practically every boy she ever made eye contact with and was prone to tiny fits and tantrums when she did not get her way. Then the zombies came.

When they poured into the cinema on that fateful night, Gemma's life had changed. It would be almost a year into that nightmare when she would discover that things could actually be worse.

Gemma had been travelling with a woman named Vix and a young man named Harold who was just a year or so older than she. They had gone through all sorts of hell, but they kept finding ways to cheat death at the last second or escape by the slightest margin.

That all came to an end one day.

She and Harold had insisted on checking out a fort that promised sanctuary. It had been the single most violent and horrible day of her life. Those men had held her while they beat

22

poor Harold to death with metal batons. She had heard the snapping of bones along with the howls and yelps of pain despite the fact that they had shoved a large stone into his mouth and then bound it into place with a leather strap. Then they produced a zombie head from a bag and after cutting away his trousers, they shoved that head between his legs.

They cut off both his feet with saws. When he passed out from the pain, they threw water on his face and went back to work. She had no idea when he finally died, but she had been glad if only because his sounds of absolute agony finally ceased.

They brought her back to camp and passed her around, doing horrible things to her. When they finished, she was thrown in a cage with nine other women. She had curled up in a ball and cried.

That night, there was a series of screams and the sounds of fighting could be heard. In the morning, it was learned that several of the men had fallen victim to the zombie plague. Over a dozen men had to be executed because they showed the symptoms of those dark tracers in the eyes.

"You are one of the resistant," a woman whispered in Gemma's ear. Gemma turned to see an Indian woman who would have probably been beautiful enough to star in one of those Bollywood movies before all the abuse she had obviously suffered.

The woman's name was Chaaya Kapoor. She explained to Gemma that she had been a biologist before what she referred to as "the unclean" arose and wiped out humanity. She went on to explain that before being captured, she had been with a small pack of survivors in Gillingham. They had discovered the fact that a person who was bitten and did not die could still infect a healthy person through fluid exchange much like HIV was transmitted.

It took Gemma a moment to understand what the woman was getting at. When she did, a ripple of fear tore through her.

"They're going to kill me," Gemma whimpered. The moment she said it, a sense of calm seemed to pour over her soul and put her at peace.

"Why are you smiling?" Chaaya asked.

"Because." Gemma closed her eyes and let out a sigh that came from the greatest relief that she could remember feeling since this nightmare had begun. "I will never have to endure a night like that again. It is over."

There was a moment of silence, and then Gemma's eyes flew open as a prick of pain shot up her arm. Chaaya had grabbed her arm and brought it to her mouth. Gemma jerked away, but it was too late.

"What are you doing?" Gemma hissed.

"I will either die and become one of the unclean, or I will become like you and the next time those animals take me…they will pay the price," Chaaya replied with a wicked smile that was made all the more sinister by the smear of blood at the corners of her mouth and the dark stains on her teeth.

Two other women sitting nearby had obviously overheard. Both begged to be next. While it all seemed perfectly horrific, Gemma understood their desire and nodded. Within minutes all the other women in the cage had heard and asked to take some of her tainted blood as well.

Sadly, not all of the women were immune. However, Gemma was amazed to discover that Chaaya and one other woman showed no signs of the zombie plague after several minutes had passed.

Sure enough, it was not long before a dozen men came stalking to the cage. They were wielding those wicked batons. However, they had simply not prepared themselves for a handful of women who knew that they were about to die, along with a trio that had nothing to lose.

The men were ambushed. Gemma and Chaaya both had the same idea; flee. They bolted past the chaotic melee that had erupted, made worse when the men saw the black tracers in the eyes of their victims-turned-attackers.

Gemma, Chaaya, and the other woman ran as fast as they could. The fort was massive, and Gemma had been a little surprised to discover that there were less than fifty men total within it walls.

24

She only knew of one possible escape route. A stone staircase kitty-corner across the immense open square from where their cage sat would lead up to the walls. From there, they would have to make a leap of faith into the Thames.

She heard yelling and commands for them to stop, but the three women led by Gemma only ran that much faster; each one knowing that the slightest misstep would seal their fate.

They reached the top of the rampart and actually had to follow it another twenty or so yards before they arrived at a spot where they could jump and have the best chance of landing in the water.

Gemma landed with a splash.

***

Chad yanked the axe free and glanced over at his daughter. Ronni was carrying an armload of branches over to add to the pile. He could hear the sound of a saw working back and forth in rhythmic fashion.

It had been nearly a decade since he had packed up and left Dustin Miller and his compound. It had been bittersweet, but in the end, Dustin understood. Chad had simply lost faith in people. The only thing in his life that had any meaning was his daughter. And while he could not give her a "normal" life, he could give her a peaceful one.

His experience ever since the nightmare of the dead coming back and feeding on the living had been that the zombies were the least of their problems. People were lousy when there was no deterrent to whatever whim struck their fancy.

He and his daughter had headed north. After almost a year on the move, they came to an area in the foothills on the eastern side of Mount Shasta. The sign above the entrance to the empty parking lot read: Spinner Fall Lodge.

They had ventured in and discovered the place empty. It had also been thoroughly cleaned out. To Chad, considering the remoteness of the location, he had to figure that somebody was either very nearby, or had been.

His guess proved correct.

He and Ronni had decided that the place was large and sturdy enough to act as a place to set up camp and at least catch their breath and rest their feet for a while. Plus, the nearby stream was visibly teaming with fish. It took less than an hour for Chad to hook a half dozen very large trout.

They were cooking the fish over a fire when a voice called out, "Coming out of the woods!"

Chad and Ronni looked up to see a figure with a cap pulled low and a scarf wrapped around the lower half of the face. That, along with the heavy, bulky clothing, made it impossible to determine gender visually. However, the voice clued Chad in right away.

"If this is your place, we didn't mean anything." Chad rose to his feet, careful to keep his hands out wide. He stepped over just enough to put his body between the stranger and his daughter.

"Actually, I have a camp on that island." The stranger hiked a thumb over her shoulder.

Chad craned his neck and nodded. That island would be a good choice if a person was alone or only with a couple of others. If he had any plans of settling here, that would be an ideal location.

"Still, if we have imposed or trespassed, we will be on our way." Chad brought his eyes back to the stranger.

"Actually, I'd really like to join you for dinner if I could." Making a show of being very cautious, the woman brought a small bag off her shoulder and opened it. She produced a handful of blackberries. "I'll supply dessert."

Chad had glanced at Ronni. His daughter gave a noncommittal shrug. That is how they met Caroline Hardin.

Caroline had been with a group of seven. Together, the group had fortified a small settlement just north of the lodge. They had considered staying in the lodge itself, but they preferred the idea of being away from anyplace that might attract attention—living or otherwise. What they had done instead was to strip the lodge of anything they could use as they built their own little settlement in the woods.

They had fared well until one of them contracted a virus of some sort. It had spread fast with fever and the inability to keep anything in or down. Two died quick, but the others lingered. At some point, Caroline had slipped out of consciousness. She awoke having no idea how much time had passed. She was also the only one to survive.

Not wanting to venture from a location that had seen so little traffic of the undead, much less the living, Caroline had decided that she would make camp on the island. She had been slowly bringing what she needed from her old camp when Chad and Ronni arrived.

They had stayed in the area for years. With it only being the three of them, Chad had agreed that the island would be the best place for them to settle. Then a drought hit, and with it, the land became a tinderbox waiting for that one spark. It came in the form of lighting. The wildfires raged in the hills and Chad made the decision for them to move. Taking what they could salvage, the trio moved on.

They had been on the go for the better part of five months when they found a place that a faded sign identified as Hyatt Reservoir. After two days where they made a complete circuit of the massive lake, they found a hilltop that had a creek at the base.

They had found their new home. They started with a perimeter fence and cleared enough land to have a decent farm. Today marked the day they would start on the construction of their log cabin.

With winter still months away, they would have plenty of time to get in that first crop. It would be sparse as far as vegetables were concerned, but they would have no shortage of meat and fish.

He felt a little like a character from a movie he had seen when he was young. *Jeremiah Johnson* had been the title. There had been a scene where Jeremiah and the Native American woman had built a cabin together.

He shook his head as his mind allowed that part of the movie to play out. It had ended poorly.

"Are you just gonna stand there?"

The voice of his daughter snapped him back to reality. He gave a sheepish smile and moved down the length of the log to make the next notch.

***

Jody crawled forward on his stomach. After scanning the area with his binoculars, he handed them to Bill Pitts. For the briefest of moments, he had the sensation of just how surreal the situation was that he currently found himself.

Bill Pitts had been a hard-nosed sergeant back in the days before the world went haywire with the rise of the dead. Then he had been a deserter. And to round it off, he had been the leader of a superior force that could have wiped his little community off the face of the earth. Instead, there was an accord reached. It had met with some resistance, but in the end, it had actually proved to be a huge benefit for both communities.

Over the past decade, the two communities had come together. They had brought in over five thousand other survivors. In addition, they now had electricity using a combination of wind and solar energy.

It was a bit like the Old West; and there was a wildness to it that some found to be too much. However, the truth was that they were prospering as a community. And that was the current problem. There were those who wanted what the people of Swift-Hope had built.

The fact that they had built a corridor that allowed travel between the two small hubs as well as the ability of folks to settle along the length of that corridor only made them a larger target. There had been resistance to the idea of that expansion as well. Jody and his closest friend Danny O' Leary had almost come to blows over it.

The plan was to clear a straight line between Hope and Swifton. They would build a barricade, as well as place towers along the length. The idea was that, if these two communities were going to co-exist, then it would be a benefit to ensure that travel between the two was not risky. Both communities began to go to work on the project. And it was actually a surprise when people began to volunteer to take residence in the watch towers that were built along the length.

These towers were each a miniature fortress. Once completed, the person or persons who volunteered to live there became part of the community security. Flags were made to send messages much like coastal warning flags.

Over the years, there had been setbacks. Twice, massive swarms of the undead had come. Both times it had been like weathering the fury of a tsunami. You could do nothing but watch the wave of undead slam into the defenses and then do everything possible to minimize the destruction when they breached the perimeter wall.

That had also been the reason for another form of security. It was clear that the undead reacted to sound. It was for that reason that they had devised a second line of defense: turrets.

Based on the design of the rook in a chess set, they had built single stone structures in a ring around their communities and the travel corridor. These had been built about a mile out and were also manned by volunteers. The incentives for taking these isolated positions were regular supply deliveries of the finest produce and meat, along with a variety of goods created by citizens of the duo-city now known as Swift-Hope.

It was the job of these outposts to not only notify the community of impending danger, but also to commence the distraction protocol. That included the lighting of a series of huge bonfires that would hopefully alter the course of an incoming swarm. Additionally, there were a series of hand-cranked sirens that were placed in a line. Once again, these would ideally serve to lure the leading edge of a large concentration of the undead on a new course.

Three days ago, a runner from Turret Eleven arrived. Turret Ten had not raised its flag in response to the regular check in that the turrets did with each other as just another layer of security as well as to help ease some of the feelings of isolation that might set in over time.

They had sent a runner to Turret Ten. That runner had not returned. This was not the first time they had faced hostiles in the form of humans. Most of the time it was a hit-and-run style of attack. Due to the size of the Swift-Hope community, there had not really been any human threat that could truly be a danger to them. Obviously, this was different.

"I see at least a dozen," Bill said as he handed the binoculars back to Jody.

"They are either very brave or very stupid," Jody muttered as he took another look.

These invaders had obviously taken Turret Ten. People were coming and going in and out like they had no cares in the world. A huge fire had been built and what he had to assume were the bodies of the people who had once manned the post were being burned.

However, it also looked like they had taken a prisoner. A man was in a cage that had been hoisted a good twenty feet off the ground. The man looked pretty beat up and somebody had taken a blade to his chest, making an uncountable number of slices obviously meant to entice the man to give up information.

"Don't do anything stupid, Rafe," Bill warned.

Jody felt his gut twist. He focused in on the face of the man and had to force his hands to relax their grip on the glasses.

"What have you gotten yourself into, Danny?" Jody whispered.

***

The following is an excerpt from a journal found in an abandoned camp just outside of the ruins of Billings, Montana:

Entry One—
My name is Adam. I won't bore you with my last name, since, if you are reading this, you would probably mispronounce it anyway. How about just Adam V.?

I am a hunter.

That opens up the question of what I hunt. Well, in the world of the dead, most of us are hunters of some sort. We hunt for food, or we hunt for a safe place to live. Some may even hunt for the lost world that lives in our memory.

I hunt the living. Don't worry. I have a reason, and I don't just hunt any living person. I only hunt the ones who have been brought to my attention.

As many of you know, when the dead came, it changed damn near everything. Some was actually for the better. No more Hollywood tabloids for one. Seriously, who cares about if some talentless pop star's sister was banging the manager?

Although, now that I think about it...the manager might have made my list. I think the sister was only fourteen or fifteen and the manager was some skeezy old dude in his forties.

Some was for the worst. That first year, it seemed like every creep and playground lurker decided that it was open season on women and children. You could not run into a group of people that didn't have at least one sad story to tell. And you always knew which one right away. They had that haunted look nine times out of ten. Most would jump out of their skin if you tapped them on the shoulder.

Zombies were not the worst problem like the old movies, books, and television shows always made you think. Nope, it was the living. As far as I am concerned, that is still the case.

Personally, I can't be mad at zombies. That is like being mad at a great white shark or a grizzly bear. You show up in their home smelling like food and then get upset when they took a bite? Zombies are the same way. They are just doing what they do. They are the ultimate species when it comes to equal opportunity. Rich, poor, fat, skinny. You are all the same in the milky eyes of the undead.

But when it comes to people, that is different. You are making a choice to prey on those weaker than you for your own sick gratification. That is why I must wipe you off the face of the earth. With the population being reduced like it is, a single death is equal to thousands. So, the way I see it, every single time I kill one of those useless shit bags, I am actually killing thousands of the bastards.

My actual number of official kills is eighty-nine. Five escaped, and eleven I never found. I am currently hunting number ninety. He won't escape. I know this because I am sitting on a log, writing this journal entry while he sits five feet away, staked to the ground. His name does not matter, and I will not let him become some sort of legend by writing it here.

Words are power. They last for all time. Whether you write them or say them, once they are out there, they live for eternity.

I actually found this journal in his backpack. It belonged to a girl named Suzi McFarlane. Most of her pages had been torn out. I don't know why, I didn't ask. I have no idea what became of the poor girl that used to write in this book, all I do know for certain is that this guy will never do anything to anybody again.

So…why have I appointed myself the judge, jury, and executioner of these scum bags? Simple. I was a dad before the zombies came. And it wasn't zombies that took my precious little girl away from me. Death by zombie would have been a kind mercy compared to the fate my angel suffered at the hands of Ward Thomas Wilson.

Sorry…I had to stop writing for a minute. I spent a while kicking some garbage around. I am sure you get my meaning. Then I had a good cry. Not enough years will pass that I won't randomly break out into tears over losing my baby girl.

You might be wondering why I would use Ward Thomas Wilson's name, and not the name of that piece of crap that is sobbing just a few feet from me as I write this entry. Easy, Ward Thomas Wilson is a name that belongs in history. He put me into motion as the man I am today. He launched me on this quest that has no apparent ending. It is Ward Thomas Wilson that has helped bring the painful deaths I have handed out to the eighty-nine souls that now burn beside him in Hell.

Entry Two—
And now there are ninety.

He cried. Actually, he cried more than most. When I told him that he had to tell me every single thing that he did to that poor boy, he thought that I was joking. When I applied that cord to his scrotum and pulled it tight, he figured out that I was entirely serious.

I always make them spill the details, because I want to make them admit to the sick shit they have done. Most of them start crying when I ask them to tell me what they might think if I were to do those things to them. The main reason I want them to say all their crimes out loud is because I like to watch their eyes. Those are the window to the soul.

His eyes were full of guilt. That is why I took them before he died. He might have continued crying…hard to tell with all the blood.

3

Geek Surprise

"I'm so sorry, Kevin," Catie said with a sigh and the warning of tears in her voice. She leaned on him and rested her head on his shoulder.

Kevin did not know what he felt as he stood at the edge of a clearing that was being reclaimed by nature. He leaned on his walking stick and felt the months he and Catie had spent on the road sort of sink into him.

The journey had not been one that he took with any real hope; however, it was still a soul crushing experience to see what he accepted as evidence that his mother and sister had not survived.

"I want to go look inside." Kevin started forward, but Catie grabbed his arm.

"Darling, I know this is something you needed to do, but do you really think you want to see what is in there?"

Kevin turned to Catie and brushed a lock of her hair from her face. She had that look in her eyes that he knew so well. It was a look of fierce protection. While he was certainly able to fend for himself, Catie had been at his back more times than he could remember over the years.

The two of them had never intended for their relationship to blossom into what it had become—into what it was today. The funny thing was that he had Aleah to thank for the whole thing. He shook his head to clear it. Now was not the time for day-dreaming.

"I need to go in there for my own peace and closure." Kevin unshouldered his backpack, placed it on the ground beside Cat-ie's, and started forward, not bothering to look back. He knew without a doubt that Catie would be there at his side.

Reaching the dilapidated cabin, Kevin gave the door a nudge. Not surprisingly, it fell over with a loud clatter. Stepping over it, Kevin entered what had been his family's vacation re-treat. He had actually hated the place. As a teen, Kevin had been much more comfortable at his desk staring into his computer screen versus out in the wilderness doing things like fishing, splitting wood, and paddling a canoe on the lake just over the next ridge.

The inside was a shambles. It was thick with spider webs and something furry scuttled away and into the shadows in re-sponse to his sudden arrival. Still, even with the toll of time, it was clear that things had gone poorly for his mother and sister. One of the windows was gone, which, considering the amount of time that had passed, could be attributed to anything. However, the dark stain that was easily seen on the sill indicated otherwise.

Of course, there were even more obvious signs. At least five bodies had been picked clean, the bones scattered about. He could not tell if any might be his mother or sister. The skulls all had the typical trauma one would expect. One had a nasty split made by an axe most likely. Three had holes made by a small caliber weapon, and one had been decimated with little left be-sides the lower jaw. That one might have been his mother.

Kevin took in what he could and made an assumption. He knew that it was absolute fantasy to think he had the ability to reconstruct the events that had happened here over a decade ago, but he needed to do it in order to close the book.

In his mind, the zombies had come. His mother had done all she could once she accepted that they were what he had tried to tell her they were. It was just not enough. When they had broken in, she fought until she only had a single bullet in the pistol and one shell in the shotgun. After taking care of his sister, she had used the shotgun to end her own life to avoid becoming one of the walking dead.

"So this was your family's cabin?" Catie remained on the small porch, her eyes scanning the area, always alert. "I bet you hated it," Catie laughed, trying to lighten the mood.

"With a passion."

Kevin backed out of the doorway and turned to look at what had been his first proof that his mother and sister made it here. His mother's car was slowly becoming part of the landscape as vines and moss practically obscured it from view.

"What now?" Catie called as Kevin poked around in the lump that had once been a car.

"I guess we go back?"

"So you are okay?"

Kevin seemed to think about it for a few moments before nodding his head. "I didn't expect to find them alive. Now I won't have to wonder anymore."

"I am sorry, Kevin." Catie walked over and wrapped her arms around his waist, leaning her head against his back.

"Seems kinda silly now," Kevin finally said as the sounds of some distant thunder rolled through the foothills.

"Why?" Catie gripped Kevin's arms and spun him to face her. "You have carried this burden for so long, and now you at least know—"

"That I sent them to their deaths?"

Catie had been prepared for this part of the argument. She knew that it would be his initial reaction to try and take the blame.

"You could not save the world, Kevin. But look at how many people that you have saved? And those people are having babies…living the best life they can in this new world. Most of them would not have made it without you."

"But—" Kevin began, only to be silenced by Catie's finger on his lips.

"We move on and vow to try and do better," Catie parroted one of Kevin's many mantras back to him.

"So, do we head back?"

Catie had been ready for that question as well. While it was true that Aleah had been the one largely responsible for her and Kevin becoming a couple, she was not blind. She saw the looks that passed between the two when they met. And in a walled town with a population of less than two thousand, it was almost impossible for them not to cross paths daily.

"I was thinking we could try something new. You have done all you can back home. Maybe it is time that some other people benefitted from that amazing mind of yours." Catie made it a point to wriggle up against him as she spoke.

She knew every one of Kevin's weaknesses, and she was not above using them all in this instance. She wanted the two of them to start a real life together. One without Aleah's shadow cast over them.

Just as she predicted, she could feel his body react to hers. He looked down into her eyes and gazed into them with love. It was more than she ever dreamed could be possible. Hell, at one point, her luck with men had been so obviously bad, she had considered switching to women.

Kevin's hands moved down her sides and around to cup her buttocks. She threw her head back as he kissed down the side of her neck, pausing to nip playfully on her earlobe before working his way down. A soft moan escaped her lips as his teeth scraped along her collar bone.

***

"That little village we passed the day before yesterday looked kind of nice," Catie said, staring up at the dark storm clouds that threatened rain any moment.

"I guess we can take a look," Kevin agreed. "But we best get out of the open and set up camp before this storm hits. It looks like it will be a nasty one."

As if to add credence to his words, there was a flash in the sky and a sharp peal of thunder. Kevin reached for his cargo shorts and then went about securing his prosthetic foot. Meanwhile, Catie hurried about gathering wood and piling it up under the initial protection of the thick trees that provided ample coverage until she could get the tarp over them.

Kevin chuckled as he set the tent up. All his life he had hated camping as a leisure activity. He had been an avid attendee of survivalist camps in the area, but he had not seen that as camping; that had been preparation.

Just as the first heavy drops began to fall, the couple retreated under the large blue tarp and warmed their hands by the fire. By morning, the storm had passed and they broke camp with a destination in mind.

By midday, they came to the ruins of a town that was under a fine sheet of green. Several of the buildings and homes had either collapsed or were on the verge. Dark shapes littered the ground in places where bodies had fallen and been left to the elements and local carrion eaters.

Kevin marveled at how fast nature was coming back. The documentaries had it all wrong. Unchecked, nature would reclaim this place within the next five years. Sure, there would be evidence that humans once called this home, but the flora was making fast work as vines pushed into cracks and climbed over every surface.

A soft moan brought his focus back to the present. A lone walker stumbled around a corner. It paused and then oriented itself on the couple. As Catie walked over and shoved her own steel-tipped hiking stick into its face and then returned to him, he was amused at how little zombies mattered anymore.

When they had first appeared, of course the reaction had been all wrong and humanity followed the predictable path into near extinction. These days, a zombie was no more frightening than a skunk. You were not afraid of them, but you did not take them completely for granted.

As far as zombies were concerned, they were now only a problem when you encountered one of the massive herds that milled about the country. It was the living that posed the real threat these days. And towns were always something to be entered with caution. Some were full of simple, hard-working folks, but others were warlike mobs, or lawless societies where might made right.

By nightfall, they had come to a ridge that allowed them to see the distant glow of lights of three small communities. Kevin noted that they were almost in the shape of a triangle if you drew a line connecting them. The one they had seen as they arrived a couple of days ago was at the bottom of that triangle and to their right.

It was about an hour before sunrise when Catie shook Kevin. "You need to wake up!"

Kevin batted her hand away and rolled over, but she was insistent. Finally, Kevin sat up and rubbed his eyes. They were in a hammock suspended about thirty feet above the ground. It was always best to be extra secure near settlements. That would be where you found the most zombie activity since they are drawn to sound.

It did not take him long to see what the reason was behind her waking him at such an ungodly hour. The settlement that made the top point in the triangle was on fire.

"That puts things on hold," Kevin sighed.

"You think maybe the storm caused it? There was an awful lot of lightning last night." Catie scrunched in close and pulled their sleeping bag up around her shoulders.

"Anything is possible." Kevin knew that Catie didn't believe that theory any more than he, but there was no use in getting all worked up over something they had no part in or control over.

As the sun rose, Kevin and Catie sat in the perch their hammock provided and scanned the area with binoculars. Nothing looked out of order. There were no large mobs of the undead or hints of roving bands that might be raiding the area.

"Still want to go down there?" Kevin asked as he slowly swept his gaze in a wide left-to-right pattern searching for anything that might be the cause of the fire that still burned in that village.

"Maybe they need you now more than ever," Catie answered with grim determination.

Kevin was no fool. He knew why Catie was so behind this. He could even see her reasoning, but this felt too abrupt. There were plenty of smaller settlements that were not a world away from the place they had called home all these years. But then again, maybe that was precisely the point. They climbed down and rolled up their gear.

"Let's get down there and see what is what," Catie said as she slung her pack up and onto her shoulders, giving the straps a tug to cinch them up a bit.

The couple started down the hill and stopped when they reached the banks of a river. Just like the days when man first began to populate the Earth, settlements were usually next to a ready and clean water source.

The waterways had become much cleaner now that man was not dumping everything into them. Still, nobody was brave enough to risk not boiling the water first. Many of the major rivers near big cities were almost worse off now than before as the factories and such fell and sent all the toxins that remained into the water either directly or through runoff.

Still, out in what had been the sticks before the zombie apocalypse, things were noticeably cleaner. What was even more peculiar, Kevin could notice the difference in the smell of the air within an hour or so of leaving a camp or town. And, despite dismissing it at first as just his imagination, he could smell them *before* they arrived. To put it bluntly, humanity stunk.

They were just crossing the river at a flimsy rope bridge when a voice called out, freezing them in a very vulnerable spot.

"Stop where you are and state your business!" a man's voice growled from somewhere in the brush just on the other side of the gently rolling waters.

"Just a pair of travelers," Kevin called out in response, making it a point of raising his hands to show he was unarmed. Besides, whoever this was did not need to know that it was Catie who was the more dangerous of the two.

"And where you travelin' from?"

The deep southern slur in the man's voice reminded Kevin of the character from *Deliverance* that wore the cap and did those horrible things to poor Ned Beatty. There was something decidedly unfriendly sounding about this person.

"From out west, the Dakota territories," Kevin answered after deciding that it really did not make a difference if he revealed that bit of information. It wasn't like whoever this was could just up and launch an attack.

"C'mon, man, you take me for a fool?"

"Excuse me?" Kevin asked with a touch of confusion.

"Ain't nobody come all the way out here from that far. Hell, you would have to have been on the road for—"

"Just over eleven months," Kevin interrupted. "And I am not trying to take you for a fool. That is the truth."

"And what brings y'all the way out here?" the man challenged.

"My family had a cabin in these parts back in the day. I came to see if maybe my mom or sister might have made it and perhaps still be living there."

"I'm terribly sorry." A man emerged from the bushes off to Kevin's left, two more coming out as well, and then four more to the right. "I take it the place was empty."

"Sort of." Kevin let that answer hang in the air for a second to sink in. As it did, he saw knowing bobs of the head.

"Well, if'n you're tellin' the truth, I still need to ask what business brings you down here," the man finally said after a moment of silence that seemed to be more out of polite respect than anything else.

"We saw three towns from where we camped last night," Catie spoke up, deciding that she needed to assert that she was on equal footing. There was a trend in some communities to treat women almost as possessions or second-class citizens. It was always best to clear those sorts of thing up early.

"Also saw that there is a fire burning at one of them," Kevin added. The faces on the men standing on the other side of the lazy river all reacted in some manner. He saw a mix of anger, agitation...and fear. "Look, we can understand if we aren't welcome at the moment," Kevin continued when none of them spoke.

"Actually, it might be best if you were to come with us back to Falling Run...that's our little town," the man who was obviously the spokesman of the group said.

Kevin glanced at Catie who gave a slight shrug. He turned back to the man and his group. "Okay."

"Ain't you gonna take their weapons first?" a younger man asked as Kevin and Catie finished crossing the bridge.

"We can stop and go back." Kevin came to an abrupt halt just as he was about to step off the bridge. "We don't give up our things. If that is a problem, then we will gladly turn around and leave."

"Name's Clint," the man who had originally been talking to them said, casting a nasty look over his shoulder. "The youngster is Jess. And *no*," Clint said the word "no" loudly to emphasize it, "we won't be takin' your weapons."

"But—" the young man introduced as Jess began to protest.

"We ain't got time for this, boy," another man snarled.

"Follow us and we will explain on the way." Clint motioned with his arm for them to come.

Kevin was now more curious than anything else. He jumped from the bridge and turned to offer a hand to Catie. No surprise, she ignored his hand and jumped down beside him with a flip of her hair and a withering glance. The couple hurried and fell in step with the group of men.

"About three weeks ago, folks over at Rock Ridge, that's the place you saw burning, they had some sort of illness hit them pretty hard. The problem was that Rock Ridge has the highest number of immune citizens. Over half of their population is known to be immune from the bite. Actually, lots of folks from our little town and the folks at Red Hill move to Rock Ridge when they find out they are immune—" Clint explained, but then Kevin had to interrupt.

"Is that still a common occurrence? The part about finding out if you are immune? I mean, I don't know about here, but from what we have seen, the zombies are sort of coming together in larger and larger herds. The days of being bitten are almost as rare as a shark attack used to be back in the day." Kevin saw the expressions on the faces of his "hosts" as they all reacted to his question. Something was up.

"Yeah…" Clint let that word hang in the air for a moment. "You see, word got out a few months ago that the folks at Rock Ridge were offering to supposedly test folks for immunity. They said that it was a matter of a simple injection."

"Let me guess," Catie came to a stop, crossing her arms across her chest, "they were injecting people with the infection. What did they use? Zombie blood?"

"That is what we reckon," Clint agreed. "Only, I guess not everybody there was too keen on what was happening. One of the folks from Rock Ridge came down to our little town as well as well as Red Hill. They told us that there was a plan brewing at Rock Ridge to systematically wipe out all of the non-immune by infecting everybody."

"They was gonna put zombie blood in our water!" Jess blurted.

After a nasty look and somebody giving the young man an elbow to the ribs, Clint continued. "That is basically the short of it. They was gonna infect the population of both towns and then scoop up everybody that was left. Said something about wanting to create a race of folks that could actually stand a chance of survival."

"Master race," Kevin muttered.

"Yeah…that's sorta what we been sayin' around here," Clint said with a bitter tone.

"So then I take it somebody from either your town or over at Red Hill started that fire?" Catie asked.

"Actually…no." Clint stopped and turned to face the pair. "The past year, the Rock Ridge folks have been upping their security. It had reached the point where we were preparing to hightail it out of this place and find a new home."

"We're just farmers," one of the other men spoke up. "The folks at Rock Ridge are a damned army."

"Or were," Jess pointed out.

"So then what or who started the fire?" Kevin asked.

"That's just it…we don't know. A group of men arrived a

few days ago on horseback. They asked to speak to our mayor and after they left, the mayor said that we were not leaving. When we asked why, he said that he was not at liberty to say, but then he added that nobody was allowed to leave the town until further notice."

"And that notice came after the fire?" Kevin asked.

"Nope, but a few of us decided that something was afoot, so we made the decision to come out and take a look around after we heard the explosion."

Kevin hadn't heard any explosion. Obviously Catie had since she was nodding.

"So why were you down by the river?" Catie asked. "That's south...the explosion and fire is to the north."

Once again the men grew silent, and for the first time, Kevin realized that these men had formed a bit of a circle formation and the men were keeping their eyes open for something.

"We thought we saw—" Clint began, but the thunder of hooves cut him off.

Everybody froze. With the coming of dawn, a light mist was swirling, coupled with the smoke in the air from the fire less than two miles away, and it added a dreamlike quality to the vision as it unfolded.

Five black horses emerged through a small clearing in the dense foliage. The men were dressed in black as well and each had a gunnysack over his head with eye holes cut into them. A piece of coarse hemp rope was in place around their necks to complete the look.

"Whoa!" one of the men bellowed, raising his hand and bringing the group to a halt.

There was a single moment where it was as if everybody was frozen in place. Then, like a flock of quail flushed from the brush, everybody scattered. Kevin grabbed Catie's hand and dove for a steep embankment that would likely spill any rider who might try to navigate it on horseback; provided that they could actually get the animal to attempt it in the first place.

Tossing his walking stick down, Kevin allowed his body to fall sideways and at a slight feet-first angle. Catie stayed on her feet, hopping like a mountain goat as large puddles of loose earth fell away under each impact as she jumped her way to the bottom.

Once they both reached the bottom safely, Catie had Kevin's walking stick and thrust it into his hands as she led the way into some thick ferns and undergrowth that lined the edge of the river at this particular location. Kevin mistakenly thought that she intended to cross back over, but she yanked him back and down to the ground before he could exit their cover.

He turned to see her with a finger to her lips. The two of them remained still, and that allowed them to better hear what was happening just above them.

"Y'all can come out," a voice yelled. "We ain't here for none of you. We just here to take care of them freaks up in that Rock Ridge settlement."

"Yeah, y'all is plenty safe. We just finishin' God's work and takin' them 'mune folk down," another voice called.

Kevin felt his blood run cold.

He knew all too well the issues that some people had with those who showed immunity to the bite of a zombie: people like him...like Catie. If these folks were attacking the residents at Rock Ridge solely based on them being immune to the bite, then he and Catie were in the wrong place.

"Come on out, you ain't got nothin' to fear from us!" another voice shouted, this one female.

"Yeah, unless you one of them mune-ites," a voice whispered from just above where Kevin and Catie hid, the horse stomping angrily at the ground as if in support of its rider's sentiment.

That settled it for Kevin, he and Catie were getting out of here as fast as possible. Whether it was some long-standing issue, or something new brought on by the alleged plans of the people of Rock Ridge, this was no place for the two of them.

"I'm comin' out, don't kill me," Clint's voice wavered as he announced his intention.

Kevin could hear the horse above him shift just a bit. Dirt came raining down on them.

"Where's the rest of your group?" the female voice demanded. "We only make this offer one time. You come out, we make sure you ain't one of them damned mune-ites, and then you are free to go."

"What do you mean by making sure we ain't one of them…did you say 'mune-ites'?" Clint asked.

"Mune-ites, munies, call 'em what you like. You know what we are talkin' about," the first voice said with a harsh seriousness in his tone that left no room for debate or discussion.

"Ain't none of us one of them," Clint retorted, seemingly unperturbed about the severe tone with which he was being addressed.

"Then you won't mind if we are not willing to simply take your word for it," the female voice of the riders scoffed.

Gripping Catie's hand, Kevin gave a slight tug. When she resisted, he leaned in close, his lips brushing her ear.

"If we stay here…"

Catie turned, the realization of what he was hinting at suddenly putting a crease on her forehead. Kevin pointed toward an opening, and she nodded and led the way. As they reached the edge of this particular area of cover, Kevin heard somebody let out a yelp.

"That there is a bite scar!" somebody roared.

There was another series of shouts and then a cry of pain. The sounds of angry protests mixed with heated threats and warnings. However, one phrase came through loud and clear from Clint.

"Why'd you go and kill him? He weren't with them folks at Rock Ridge!"

Kevin could not hear the response, but he didn't need to; he had a good idea what these riders were all about. Catie hunched down low and clung to the edge of all the greenery that was thankfully in abundance as they followed the uneven meanderings of the river.

Once he felt that he could at least speak in a whisper without giving away their presence, Kevin tugged on Catie's hand and turned her to face him. "Our best bet is to get back over that ridge."

Catie nodded and shot a glance over Kevin's shoulder. "They killed one of those people."

Kevin knew that tone. Catie was not somebody who could let certain things go. It was in her nature to protect the weak and stand up for those who might not be able to stand up for themselves.

"This isn't our fight," Kevin warned. "We have no idea how this got started or just how bad it might be."

"But—" she protested, but it was his turn to put his finger on her lips.

"This is not our fight. And if we are going to find someplace to settle down and start *our* lives, I would just as soon it not have to start with some sort of terrible conflict."

Catie smiled and nodded. She popped up on her tiptoes and kissed him quickly before turning to lead the way. There was an area up ahead a ways that looked calm enough for them to cross. This particular spot on the river was a bit rough and rapid. She took two steps and then stopped.

"You two can just hold it right there and put your hands in the air," a familiar female voice ordered.

Kevin leaned just enough so he could see past Catie. Apparently the female rider had heard them (or heard of them from Clint and his people) and come to a spot where she had a clear view. She had her bow drawn and pointed at the two of them.

"We don't want any trouble," Kevin called back as he edged past Catie to put himself between her and the arrow pointed at them.

"Then maybe you can explain why you were sneakin' away and making such a big point of not being seen or heard?"

"Are you really asking that question?" Kevin shot back. "We heard what you did to one of those people. Would *you* stick around after hearing that?"

The woman frowned and her face scrunched up in an unflattering grimace as she tried to decipher his question. Obviously that thought had not occurred or even come close to making its presence known in what Kevin had to assume was a brain operating at minimum capacity.

"If you ain't one of them munies (when she said the word, it sounded more like ME-yoon-ees), then you got nothin' to worry about," the woman finally shot back with indignation spurred by the knowledge that this man speaking to her was making fun of her somehow.

She could not put a finger on exactly how, but she knew his sort. She really hoped he was one of those folks from Rock Ridge. She wanted this one all for herself. She would make him eat his snotty words.

"I am not going anywhere with you," Catie blurted just as Kevin opened his mouth to respond. "My husband and I have done nothing to deserve this, and all we are trying to do is find someplace peaceful where we can make a home for ourselves in time for the arrival of our baby.

"Yeah," Kevin harrumphed. And then he spun to face Catie. "Wait…what!"

"Surprise!" Catie said weakly, throwing her hands up and doing her best to smile.

This was not how she had wanted to do this. She'd almost told him last night, but she had chickened out at the last moment and decided that she wanted to just bask in the afterglow of their lovemaking. She had no doubts that Kevin loved her, or that he would be excited by the announcement. However, she also knew that he might overreact. It was for that reason alone—or at least that was what she had convinced herself of—that she had decided to wait until they found the place that he liked and agreed would be a good choice for them in their quest to settle down and start anew.

"You don't look like your fixin' to have a baby," the woman on the horse snorted. "Hell, skinny thing like you prob'ly can't even carry to term. And them hips? I'd actually almost pay to be there when you tried to squeeze a young'un out from between 'em."

"I'll be sure to send an invitation," Catie shot back.

"Well now I am really startin' to hope you is one of them damn munies. I want the pleasure of guttin' you myself."

"Let's settle down a bit, Darlene," a man's voice called as he weaved through the trees and came up beside the woman holding Kevin and Catie at bow point.

"Caught these two tryin' to sneak off without bein' checked," Darlene said proudly as if she'd just apprehended one of the world's most dangerous fugitives.

"That man Clint said they had just encountered a couple and were inviting them back to his little village just before we arrived." He turned his attention to Kevin and Catie. "He says you both claim to come from out west somewhere. Says that you all came to see if your mom and sister might have still been alive." Kevin nodded as a lump formed in his throat at the reminder.

"So that woman lied...she ain't pregnant and they ain't just out here lookin' for someplace to live!" Darlene barked.

"He says that your family had a cabin or some such up in the hills." The man shot a cold stare at Darlene and she shut her mouth with an audible click of her teeth.

"Yep, used to come when I was little. Hated it," Kevin admitted. "I was not one of those kids who wanted to go camping. Well...not unless it was someplace with hot showers and a dining hall." Kevin let loose with a light chuckle, but the man just stared at him and the mirthful sound died on his lips.

"And I am so pregnant," Catie said in a loud whisper that was meant to be heard.

"In any case, we are going to have to ask you folks to come with us," the man said.

"Why?" Kevin ground his feet into the dirt just a bit to solidify his stance in front of Catie. He was preparing himself for a fight...or death.

"Because we will be certain that you are not just more of those bastards from Rock Ridge trying to escape so that you can hide and rebuild your numbers." For the first time, the man spoke with an outward anger in his tone and an expression on his face that gushed with what could only be hatred.

"We aren't part of whatever little war you have going on." Kevin shook his head and made no effort to move. He did not like where this was going one tiny bit. "If you all want to kill each other, that is your business. We just want to be left alone and go about our business."

"And as soon as we know you are not one of the Rock Ridge munies, you can do just exactly that," the man retorted.

"And just how are you going to prove we are not one of...them?" Kevin braced himself for the answer. In his mind, it could be just about anything. He certainly did not expect the answer that came from the man's mouth.

"Because we got the mayor back there tied to a horse."

4

Education Abroad

As we moved down the slopes of the foothills, I tried really hard not to look like an idiot. My problem was that my eyes went everywhere. For one, I had no memory of things like cars and trucks. To see these things up close was actually sort of impressive.

"That was a fuel tanker," Paula said as we passed under the shadow of the hulking obstacle.

I tried to imagine how such a thing moved. I mean, I saw the wheels, so I knew the basics of how, but it was just so freaking big! The largest moving vehicle of sorts that I had seen up to this point was one of our farm wagons. And if it was loaded, it took a dozen people to haul it from one spot to the other.

I was less impressed by the wildlife. I'd seen plenty of deer, wolves, coyotes, skunks, elk, raccoons…

There was a slight rustle as the entire team came to a halt. We were just about to round a corner. And that was another thing…the roads were so big. I could not figure out how they had managed to keep them open. Landslides had washed out most areas with rocks so big that there was simply no way I could imagine that they be moved. How these things were dealt with back before zombies is something that I can only try to envision. But then, I couldn't figure out how they had built these highways in the first place.

Paula pointed and I saw why we had stopped. This was something new. I'd heard about it from the folks who had been out in the field, but to actually see it for myself...

"Slug tracks," Paula whispered.

In every herd of zombies, you get the ones that are missing legs or entire lower halves of the body. Still, they are just like any other zombie with the exception that they can't walk. In larger herds (like ZH-Seven), you can sometimes get hundreds of the creepers following along. We call them "slug tracks." They have been known to be strung out over a mile or more. Some of the larger slug tracks have actually grown into their own herd.

"Are these from ZH-Seven?" I whispered. Even though we were at least a hundred yards away and I was speaking in a voice that was little more than the act of moving my lips, it felt like I had practically screamed that question.

Paula shook her head and pulled out a map. She pointed to a spot that I had to assume was our location. Next, she showed me a green line that had been marked as the known path of ZH-Seven. This group was almost perpendicular to that one, as well as a few miles to the east.

After the signal was given, we backtracked and left the road to move through the woods for a ways. When we made camp for the evening, I listened as the scouts gave their reports. It was decided that this was a new herd. The numbers were placed at between three and four hundred creepers. Now I knew why we hadn't just waded through. In a group that size, you would always get a few of the criers. Once those things started up, any zombie for a mile in every direction would be coming your way.

The next morning, we resumed our trek. By midday, we emerged back onto the trail that had once been a highway. It was overcast, and when the first patters of rain came, it was a welcome relief. However, I also knew by the monstrous clouds starting to form that we would be in for it soon if we did not find cover.

Summer time is a mixed blessing. You can get some beautiful days that scream for you to take a dip in the creek. But it can also mean thunder and lightning. Lightning only means one thing…

"Fire!" a voice called.

Our team stopped and everybody looked off in the direction being pointed at by the person who sounded the alarm. Sure enough, a single plume of smoke was rising in the distance to the south of our location.

Looking that way, the horizon was almost as dark as night. We were a day from Island City still and would be camping for one more night out in the woods. That fire was a good many miles away, but with the dry conditions we'd seen the past few weeks and the intensity of the coming storm, we would need to be vigilant. Wildfires burned hot and could move fast.

We ducked off the main trail again and made our way down a steep off-ramp to the ruins of a small roadside area that had cryptic signs that had become unreadable over the years of neglect. Just as we entered a long building that had tattered bench seats in booths along one wall and a single long counter with round stools set on one side, the rain came.

I have always loved weather. Since I was not assigned any watch for the first shift, I took a seat by one of the large openings where a window used to be and watched the downpour. It got so heavy at times that I could barely see a few feet past the overhang of the building. Then the hail started.

The few decrepit vehicles acted as metal drums. The noise got louder and louder as the size of the hailstones grew.

"We got walkers!"

At last! I saw a few heads turn my way. Oops…I think that I said that out loud. I pulled the oiled leather bag from my pack and removed my crossbow.

Okay, yes, I've killed zombies before. Everybody who has ever been outside the safety of our community's walls has had to put one down at some time. So how is this different? The biggest thing is the fact that, if things get ugly back home, you run for the gate. Here? Unless you can run for two days straight…you gotta deal with the problem here and now.

One of the first things that you learn is to never get trapped inside a building. It does not matter if there are ten people with you; being trapped in a building that is surrounded by zombies is a death sentence.

I followed Paula and another guy, Jackson White, out the door and into the downpour that was shifting back from hail to just plain old rain. I sighted and fired, dropping the first one!

We moved as a team out into the ruined remains of the road that had run down the middle of this little stop beside the highway. I craned my neck to the right. Sure, we were out to take down these zombies, but there was a more important aspect of our job. We needed to make sure they were not the leading edge of a herd. It is more the exception than the rule to find just a couple of zombies. Sure…it happens, but not often.

"Crap!" Jackson growled.

Jackson White is a very big man. Sure, he might only be an inch or two under six feet tall, but he is broad shouldered and has arms and legs like tree trunks. I once saw him carry an elk through the gates on his shoulders and drop it at the distribution center. I then saw two guys struggle to carry it inside.

His skin is darker than anybody I have ever seen, and he has a funny accent. He was born in someplace called Jamaica, but he came to Oregon when he was just a baby. Sometimes he talks funny, and Melissa says that is his Jamaican accent. That usually only happens during the beer festival that takes place each fall when the brewers put out their new batches for folks to try. Most of the adults get kind of drunk. I don't see the fun of doing something that makes you feel so bad the next day…sometimes two.

I looked in the direction that he was staring. Sure enough, a herd was coming this way. It was too hard to get an idea of how many since they were just coming around the corner, but they were packed in tight, so the odds were that there would be at least a few hundred.

"Fall back!" Paula hissed.

We retreated into the building. Everybody was already re-packed. A few people were stuffing the last bits of whatever they had been in the process of eating into their mouths.

"How bad?" somebody called.

"Shoulder-to-shoulder and coming right down Main Street," Jackson said in his deep, rumbling voice that sounded like a giant bumblebee had learned to talk.

"Too many to risk staying," Paula announced.

That made it final. You didn't argue with Paula Yin...period. Everybody headed through an opening and past some of the biggest kitchen stoves I had ever seen. It looked like you could cook for ten or twenty people easy on the surface of those things, and there were three of them side-by-side!

We reached a doorway. Cynthia Bird was posted there as the watch. She is our medical person. The normal rule is that medics did not have to stand watch, but she had insisted, saying that, until we reached Island City, she was as useless as "tits on a boar." That had made me laugh, especially coming out of her mouth.

Cynthia Bird is Xander Bird's mom. She is one of the current council members and the only person to have been on the council for the past five years in a row. Most folks say she is Dr. Zahn's voice and presence. Melissa says that she thinks Cynthia is a young version of the doc.

Oh...and it is *Cynthia*. Nobody calls her Cindy...ever. I have no idea why, but I do know that, when a new arrival comes to our community and they are introduced to the council; it is practically part of the "welcome" speech.

"Trouble?" Cynthia asked, bringing the long sword she wore on her hip part way from the scabbard.

"We got a herd coming," Paula replied.

Our group headed out the back door and into the woods. This would be another thing that made this different from just doing a perimeter patrol back at Platypus Creek. A storm like this is cause for you to head back inside. Honestly, there is no reason to be out in this sort of weather.

I was having the time of my life!

***

"There it is," Paula said as we broke through some thick brush.

We were on a ridge looking down at what was apparently Island City. I felt a tingle in my belly. It wasn't just Island City, it was the rest of La Grande—the ruins of it—stretched out for what seemed like forever. If this was just a small town, I could only imagine and wonder what a big city looked like in person.

Melissa says that I am from Seattle. That is where Steve and I came from back in the beginning. She says that Seattle was a city of millions! I am sorry, but that is a number that I cannot even fathom when thinking about living people.

The largest herd I have ever seen with my own two eyes supposedly numbered close to a half a million. It took almost two weeks for them to pass and flow around the perimeter of our community's walls. I remember the smell, the sound. It was so loud at times that you could not hear a person unless they practically yelled in your ear—which they would not do since it would conceivably attract the attention of the herd and make them stop and gather outside our walls.

"Okay!" Paula scanned our group and seemed to be waiting for something. I did not even notice Cynthia Bird until she was actually standing right beside Paula. "Cynthia has a few things to pass on, and then we will head down."

Cynthia stepped up onto a rock so that everybody could see her. "First, I want to apologize to all of you in advance…"

That was never a good way to start things. I noticed a few nervous expressions, but nobody was saying a word.

"…we could not say anything before we left because this was something that we did not want the citizens getting all worked up about until we had more concrete details," Cynthia said in a very matter-of-fact tone that was giving away nothing.

It sounded to me like she might have practiced giving this speech a few times to be sure that she got it right. She was so calm that you almost wanted to relax, but if you were actually listening to the words, there was no way that you could not be a mix of curious and concerned.

"We are coming here to see what happened to the folks of Island City, and we believe that an outside force has been involved here in some aspect of what is likely the extermination of Island City's population. However, we also believe that there may be another factor.

"There have been reports from a few of the communities that we regularly trade and exchange with in regards to a very potent and lethal sickness."

There was a ripple of gasps and assorted profanity from almost everybody. I watched Paula. She was sort of my barometer. She was standing with her fists planted on her hips and a look of icy calm that showed no reaction at all to what had just been said.

"Then why in the fuck are we going *in* to Island City?" Antoine Clement blurted the question that seemed to be on pretty much everybody's mind. A chorus of agreements sounded, and I habitually did a scan for any zombies that might have been drawn by the noise.

Antoine was short for a guy. In fact, I was pretty sure that I was almost an inch taller, so he could not be more than an inch over five feet tall. He was from some small town in Canada called Asquith which was outside of Saskatoon. I have to admit, when he'd told me where he was from, I'd thought that he was making a joke. Seriously, who named these places? Antoine was also perhaps one of the skinniest human beings that I'd ever seen that was not a zombie.

"For one, we don't know if the reports are true—" Cynthia began, only to be cut off by Shay Fesseden.

"So we just walk in and take a few deep breaths of possibly contaminated air?" Shay's voice was hard and angry. There was a hint of a laugh when she spoke, but it was not a happy sound...more like breaking glass.

Shay had hair the color of honey. It was more than a few inches past regulation if she let that coiled braid out. I'd only seen her with her hair down once...at her wedding. Her eyes were perfectly shaped and the color of a new leaf—just the slightest shade of green.

"You should know better than that," Cynthia scolded. The growing rumble of anger went quiet just that fast. "First, the only people at this point who will be stepping foot inside the walls of Island City is me and one other. However, I have three additional filtered respirators. Unfortunately, they have only had limited testing, and so I can't vouch for what degree of protection they will provide. I can say that I have confidence in the design enough so that I have been given permission by the council to take the personal risk."

That was actually a pretty big deal. After all, like Dr. Zahn always says, "Doctors don't grow on trees." If they were allowing Cynthia to take a risk like this, then obviously any amount of testing that had been done on these filtration masks were impressive.

"Paula Yin will be one of the people joining me. The other individuals, if there are any, will be strictly voluntary. The rest of the team will be expected to make a thorough search and inspection of the surrounding area as well as catalog the breaches in the perimeter wall." Cynthia made it a point to let her gaze go from face to face as she spoke. When she made eye contact with me, I thought that I saw just the slightest arch in one eyebrow. I might have been imagining, but I didn't care and I was not going to wait and miss out.

"I'm in!" I raised a hand and stepped forward.

"And me," Jackson rumbled.

"Geez, kid," Jim Sagar said around a mouthful of some sort of rolled oat-and-honey trail bar. "Warn a fella before you just volunteer for things." He looked up to see Paula giving him a tight-lipped glare, her eyes barely slits. "Oh…yeah, I'm in."

It looked like we had our team. And then it sunk in…I was going on an actual mission. This was something that you only heard about back at the homestead around the community dinner tables. I could not wait to rub Kayla Brockhouse's nose in it.

"Okay, we go in at first light. You two get your things in order and then go ahead and start the exterior inspection. We meet back here in two days…no exceptions," Paula said as she hopped down and headed towards me and Jim. For some reason, she looked annoyed.

I watched the others re-shoulder their gear and start off. I was a little surprised that nobody grumbled or complained. I guess if you make a choice (or make no choice), then you don't get to complain about the outcome.

"Get your tree hammock set up, Thalia," Jim said as he went to work on a hole for our fire.

Out in the field, if you made a fire, you did it in what was called a Dakota Hole. I have no idea why, but that is what they call it. The hole is a couple of feet deep and maybe a foot across, and then an air flow hole is bored out at an angle.

It has been determined that zombies can see heat signatures or something, so a fire is like ringing the dinner bell. For whatever reason, the smoke is not enough to act as the same sort of lure; thus, the Dakota Hole.

Paula and Cynthia had gone down to the creek that was just at the bottom of the hill we were going to camp on for the night. I waited until I was certain that they were out of earshot before I spoke, and even then, I kept my voice to a whisper.

"Why is Paula so mad?" I asked.

Jim was silent for a while, and I actually thought that he would ignore or refuse to answer my question. Finally, he looked up from his digging and, after a quick glance over his shoulder to ensure that Paula was not yet on her way back, he answered.

"You were not supposed to be on the team to go inside," Jim said. "I was supposed to keep you quiet and we were to make the perimeter search."

"What's the big deal?"

Once more, Jim was quiet. I could tell that he was really bothered. That all by itself was enough to make me more than a little nervous. Jim was one of those guys who always seemed to be smiling and generally happy with life. Melissa said that, if this were the old days, she would be almost certain that he was on drugs.

"Look, I am in enough hot water with Knives of Death...maybe you should ask her."

I stifled a smile. "Knives of Death" was an old nickname for Paula. That is why I'd gone to her to learn blade fighting as well as some machete work. I still remember when she had called me a natural during one of our sessions; that had been one of the greatest compliments that I could ever remember receiving from anybody.

"Well then maybe I will," I said with a frown. I stuck my tongue out, but Jim was already back to digging his stupid hole.

It seemed to take forever, and by the time Paula and Cynthia had returned from gathering water, I had almost lost my nerve. However, as soon as I saw that sideways glance from Jim and his smug little smile telling me that he was fairly certain that I did not have the guts to question Paula, much less risk her annoyance, I hung from my hammock for a second to ensure that it was secure, and then I walked right up to Paula and planted myself in front of her.

"Did I do something wrong?" That was a good start.

"You are not the right person for this job," Paula replied.

Paula was not much on mincing words or trying to tell people what they wanted to hear. She scared a lot of people with her direct approach to things. However, I was not scared of her one little bit. It wasn't like she was going to pull a knife on me or something. And if she got mad…big deal. She would get over it.

"Then why did you say that I was ready for this field run?"

"You are ready for the field. I just do not think that you are the right person to send inside the walls. It might be ugly, and it might go bad really fast. You are good in a fight, I will grant you that. However, taking down a few zombies is one thing…there may be living people in there that mean to do us harm. Killing a living person is different than killing a zombie."

Well, at least now I knew her reasons. I could even see her point, but if nobody else was willing to volunteer, then was she really just going to go in there with only her and Cynthia? That seemed reckless in my opinion.

"Then you were lying," I finally said with a shrug, and turned to my hammock.

I heard somebody let out a low whistle. I am pretty sure that it was Jim. A hand grabbed my shoulder and spun me around.

"Why would you say that?" Paula's nose was just an inch or so away from mine.

"If I am ready for a field run, then I am ready for all parts of it. Not just the easy stuff or the tasks that you can handpick."

I folded my arms across my body. That could have been seen as a defensive gesture, and maybe it was considering the fact that one of the most dangerous hand-to-hand fighters in our small community of Platypus Creek was in my face. Oh…and obviously pissed. I had to fight every instinct in my body that was telling me to take a step back. I would not show weakness, and I would not back down.

"And you think you are ready to kill a living person?" I know that she was speaking in a tone just above a whisper, but it was hammering in my ears.

"I think that I am ready for the field. I think that I will do whatever the situation requires. Would I want to kill another living being? No. Would I do what I have to when the time comes…I like to think that I will."

"And that is why you are not ready," Paula replied.

I stared at her with what must have been a questioning look on my face. I know I had a questioning feeling in my gut.

"You can't simply *think* you will do something." Paula took a step back. "You have to *know* it."

She walked away and suddenly nobody would make eye contact with me. Not even Jim.

Well…I would just have to show them.

***

We climbed through the jagged remnants of what I had to say was perhaps the most impressive barricade that I'd ever seen. Okay, so I haven't seen that many, but still, this thing was amazing. There was an outer wall that was ten feet high. Next, there was the next space, but instead of it being just a huge sort of open area, it was compartmentalized. I would guess there had to be a new wall that ran between the inner and outer-most barricade walls set every twenty or so feet apart.

Up above, I could see the crisscrossing of catwalks where the residents here could just move around and pick off zombies at their leisure. Also, about every fifty feet or so was a watch tower. This place sort of made home feel vulnerable and exposed by comparison.

"What could do this?" I whispered. It was not meant as an actual question to be answered.

"Somebody packing some nasty ordinance," Jim muttered as he climbed over the charred remains of a bracing beam that was as wide as me and easily weighed a few hundred pounds. Yet, it had been snapped in half and burnt beyond belief.

We emerged on the other side and I had to stifle the urge to be just a little bit sick. There, not more than ten feet away, was a massive pile of bodies. They were all stripped naked. That made it easy to see the ravaging that their bodies had taken. Out of some sort of nervous response, I gave my mask a slight adjustment. I sure hoped that this thing worked like they said it did. I did not want whatever sickness had killed these people. Something was just not right, though. Unfortunately, I was too overwhelmed to figure out what I was missing. I only knew that it was something important.

But, back to the pile of corpses. The bodies had fist-sized boils all over them. Many had popped, leaving a dried coating of this dark, gloopy fluid that reminded me of spoiled goat's milk. There was a swelling around every single one of these people's throats. It was almost like somebody had tried to inflate a balloon just under the chin of each of these poor souls. You could see furrows in the flesh where they had clawed at their own necks, probably as they were suffocating.

"That had to suck," Jackson whispered with a mix of disgust and reverence.

Cynthia had moved in for a closer look. She had a pole with a set of pincers at the end and she was grabbing and tugging on one body or the other to move it and get a look from some other angle.

"So how does this tie in to the idea of that?" I asked, pointing to the closest pile of corpses and then the ruins of the wall where we had come through.

"Medieval warfare," Jim answered.

"Umm…what?" I had no clue what he was talking about.

"Way back when man was little more than nomadic bands hiding behind walls and such for protection from each other…" His voice trailed off, and he smiled his goofy grin. "Think of it as being just like now, except they get the bonus of no zombies back then."

He chuckled at his observation and continued. "Anyway…man was learning that illness could actually be used as a weapon. It was not uncommon for the enemy laying siege outside of a castle to chop up some infected soul and hurl the carcass over the walls with a catapult. The more virulent the sickness, the more effective it was as a weapon."

"That's disgusting," I gasped, unable to believe that such cruelty could truly exist. I think I heard Paula make a snort or cough as she moved down the alley that would open up to a large street.

I followed Paula. I was more curious than anything else. This alley ran between two long, squat buildings with doors set ever few feet.

"Holding cells," Paula answered my unasked question.

We reached the corner and that is where it just changed. If you didn't know any better, you would simply think that perhaps everybody was away at a town meeting or something.

"It looks normal," I whispered.

I had no idea why I was whispering. It just seemed like the right thing to do. I mean, it wasn't like zombies would be coming any time soon.

Of course, no sooner had I thought that when a pair came into view about three blocks away. Paula had her binoculars up and was taking a closer look. She handed her glasses to me.

"Tell me what you see."

I brought the binocs up to my eyes. In an instant, the distant walkers suddenly looked close enough to reach out and touch. I studied them. There was something odd, but I could not place it.

The harder I tried to focus and figure out exactly what it was Paula expected me to see, the more my mind seemed to go blank. Then it hit me!

"They have the same swelling around the necks…the same evidence of those boils." That last bit was made clear by the dark stains on their clothes.

"They were Immunes," Paula said, approval seeping into her voice.

"So if we encounter any zombies in here, it should be minimal," I offered.

The Immunes were a mixed blessing. I guess there was a time when people believed that the bite was an automatic death sentence. No telling how many poor people were killed out of mercy by their friends just because they had been bitten. However, even if a person is one of The Immune, they still come back as a zombie if they have been infected.

That was apparently another problem early on. I guess we lost some people because they had sex with somebody who was infected but immune. That meant anybody who is bitten and immune is still carrying the zombie virus or germ (I always get the two mixed up…I never really paid much attention in health and biology beyond the basic first aid that I knew I would need in the field). I knew one thing for sure, I did not want to find out the hard way if I was immune or not.

As it turned out, according to Dr. Zahn, the potential for immunity was much higher than many could believe. She put the chances at around twenty-five percent. Our little community of around three hundred sports thirty-five of The Immunes.

Even better, so far, there have been four children born to Immune couples. Of course we can't actually be certain, but the doc says that this whole thing has some of the same tendencies as any other illness. And if the immunity to zombies has something to do with antibodies a person possesses, then she says it is highly probable that the children of Immunes will be immune to the bite as well.

We moved in and took down the walkers and then made our way down the street. Paula seemed to know exactly where she wanted to go. After turning down a few streets, we came to one that was much wider. Up ahead was a huge building. In front of it was one of the largest open, paved areas that I had ever seen. I'd heard of parking lots, but I had no idea that they were so huge.

This large open space had been kept open, and there was a large stage-like platform in the middle. Hanging from the front of the base of the stage were the remnants of some blue and white banners that fluttered in the gentle breeze.

I felt strange being so out in the open. Can a person be afraid of wide open spaces? If so, I think I might be just a bit. I was used to my community of Platypus Creek. We were sur-rounded by trees and the only open spaces we had were the farm plots and a baseball field.

"Hear that?" Cynthia whispered, her voice sounding alien in that filtered mask.

I listened, but all I heard was my own heartbeat thudding in my ears. I was becoming more certain by the second that I did not like being out in the open like this. Then...I heard it.

"I hate crybaby-zombies," Jackson muttered.

The sound was coming from that great big building; and there was more than one. I actually preferred the crybabies. At least you could hear them. In my opinion, it beat the heck out of being surprised.

We crossed the lot and I lagged just a little when I saw a shadow move over by that stage. Or...at least I thought I saw something move.

The closer we got to that huge building, the more I was craning my neck, until, eventually, I was walking backwards. I did not want to say anything in case it was just my jitters from being out in the open. Then I saw another little bit of movement.

"Hold!" I hissed.

Just like that, Paula, Jim, Jackson and Cynthia came to a stop and turned my way. I had my crossbow ready, and so I jabbed it in the direction of the stage.

"I keep seeing something move over there...like maybe just under that platform? Whatever or whoever it is might be all the way in the back. I wasn't sure, and I might be wrong, but I think we need to check it out," I said.

"I will break wide left, Cynthia go right. Jim, you and Jackson stay put and try to keep an eye on each of us. Thalia, you move in and hold about twenty yards out directly in front," Paula instructed.

I felt a surge of adrenaline. If this turned out to be nothing more than a squirrel or something, I was going to look like an idiot.

There was a support post in the front of the stage that looked to be the middle. I lined up on that and crouched low as I began to make my approach. My finger kept tightening, and I had to take a breath a few times as I advanced in order to relax just a bit so that I did not accidentally shoot my weapon.

I reached my point and stopped, my eyes darting left and right to find Paula and Cynthia. Both women had their own crossbows drawn and were now moving so that they were actually just past the rear of the stage.

"Come out slowly," Paula called. "We are not here to hurt anybody."

Nothing happened for a handful of heartbeats, and I was starting to think that I had just made a fool out of myself. Maybe I should have just kept my mouth shut. Did I think for one second that I'd noticed something and Paula had not?

"Please don't hurt me," a shaky voice called.

At first, just a pair of hands came out from the gloom of the shadows under the stage. They were quickly followed by arms clad in heavy leather, and then the body of the young man that they belonged to. He was dressed in coarse, hemp-weave pants, and what looked like a top made from deer hide. He was missing one boot, but was still sporting one heavy wool sock. I could not imagine wearing so much in this heat. He had to be roasting.

"Come out and then I want you to lie face down on the ground," Paula said. "Thalia, once he is down, I want you to move in and frisk him. Jim, move in and cover her."

Paula had shifted her position to get back around more to the front of the stage, but I noticed that Cynthia had moved further past and now had the rear of the stage covered. I took my finger off the trigger of my crossbow since my hands were now shaking to the point where I did not trust myself. I shouldered my weapon and gave the tether a pull so the weapon did not swing around or perhaps slip out in front of me when I leaned down to check this guy.

I was less than two steps from where the man lay face down as instructed when another voice called out, "Please...don't hurt us."

Dead: Reclamation

5

Vignettes LVI

"Just one more walk-through to make sure we have everything," Mackenzie insisted.

"Babe, it's a cabin with one bedroom. I think we can be certain we got everything." Juan pulled the cinch on the draft horse and gave the creature a pat on the neck as he walked back to the wagon.

He felt like one of those pioneer types from an old western picture with John Wayne. He was actually leading a three wagon train to Anchorage. It had taken him five seasons of building up enough in trade with the Athna Athabaskan people of the Kluti Kaah village. All the while, he had been keeping tabs on the progress in Anchorage. Truthfully, he would have loved to have been able to make the trip last year, but by the time he'd finished trading, the season was late and the weather had turned. Juan had finally found something much more dangerous than the deaders: the Alaskan weather.

"Daddy, Denita took my spot in the wagon."

Juan turned to see his daughter Della staring up at him with her wide, innocent, brown eyes. He was easily suckered by his girls, but he was no idiot.

"She beat you fair and square last night playing Crazy Eights." Juan patted the girl on the head.

She obviously had not known that he heard the entire exchange where Della made the deal with her sister about who got first choice of seats in the wagon based on the outcome of their card game.

"But, Daaaa-deee," Della stomped her foot, "I don't want to sit by smelly old Rufus."

Rufus was the offspring of Tigah, a Newfoundland that Juan had rescued as a pup and presented to Mackenzie. Tigah had proved to be immune to the bite just like some people. Sadly, the day came when Tigah passed. Juan had taken the big dog out to the woods and put a splitting maul through Tigah's head. If dogs could be immune just like people, then they could also turn after dying a natural death just like people. Juan had cried when he swung that maul, but he could not have endured seeing the huge loveable dog as one of them deaders.

During the long trip to Alaska, they had come across a Golden Retriever. The poor thing had been ripped up bad, but her injuries were old enough that it seemed likely that she was immune just like Tigah. Keith had slowly enticed the frightened dog into camp and not more than three days later, the poor thing found herself hitched to Tigah. Juan had been surprised that hadn't killed the poor Golden since Tigah was easily twice her size. Only three of the nine pups survived. The assumption was that they all might be immune. It had not taken long to prove that to be partially true; at least for Tigah and Daisy's pups.

Juan had taken one of the males and named him Rufus. Dogs seemed to really hate deaders and were actually a good alarm system.

Rufus was now in his last days. In fact, Juan had struggled to allow the dog to sleep indoors at night even inside the big kennel. He had considered taking the old fella on his last walk, but every time he thought about it, he would remember some stupid moment where the big goof of a dog had done something cute or silly, and besides, Mackenzie was absolutely against it.

"Tell ya what," Juan decided to use this situation to his advantage. "You keep an eye on old Rufus for me, and I will give you a mint candy each day."

"Two." Della seemed to inherit her father's street savvy. She knew something was up, and she was not above pressing the issue for her own gain.

"Fine," Juan agreed. "But you have to do *exactly* as I tell you."

"I will, Daddy."

"You tell me every time that Rufus falls asleep. And if he stops breathing, you yell, scream, whatever it takes to get my attention right away. Understand?"

"Is that 'cause Rufus is gonna turn deader pretty soon?"

Juan sighed. This was definitely not the same world. Back in the pre-deader days, a parent would probably get reported to CPS for being so blunt about death with their children. Nowadays, death was just a part of things. He sure hoped that would change when they got to Anchorage. He wanted nothing more than to give his daughters a chance at a normal life...such as it was these days.

***

Standing here on the shore, Gemma could not help but remember. Sure, there had been many things that had happened since that day—both terrible and wonderful. Still, for the first time in her life, she had felt the burden of responsibility. The moment after her head broke through the surface and she sucked in her breath, her eyes had found the broken body of the woman that had joined her and Chaaya.

Gemma remembered the sadness she felt at seeing the woman's head turned and bent in a hideous and awkward manner. Even worse, as she got closer, she was able to see one arm bent in several places besides the elbow joint.

The two had swum with the current and let it take them away from the fort. Thankfully, nobody thought enough of the two women to actively pursue them.

It had been Chaaya who started across the river. With the current carrying them along, they were well clear of the town of Gravesend. In fact, when they finally made it ashore just before the river made a turn north, they were in a marshy field. With no weapons, they had to scurry away more than once when a creeping zombie would rise from the muck.

Just before dark, they came upon the village of Cliffe. Too tired to care, they broke into the first house they came to and searched it as quickly as they could. Between the ebbing of adrenaline from the excitement of their escape, as well as the threat of zombies, both women were absolutely exhausted.

Barricading themselves in a tiny bathroom on the second floor of the very first flat they came to, Gemma slept curled up on the tile floor and Chaaya slept in the shower basin. When they woke the next day, they searched the house for any signs of supplies. The pickings were meager and consisted of a can of kidney beans, three jars of pickles—one sweet and two gherkins—and a can of butter beans.

Beggars can't be choosers, Gemma thought as they opened the can of kidney beans. They looked at the remnants and both had to struggle not to drool at what they were seeing.

"How can so little seem like so much?" Gemma asked, not expecting any sort of response.

"When you have had nothing for such a great deal of time, even the slightest thing could seem like a treasure." Chaaya plucked a pickle from the jar and rolled her eyes in bliss as she made a noisy crunch.

That had been as satisfying of an answer as she could hope for. The rest of the day was spent systematically going from house to house in a search for more supplies. More than once, they encountered zombies inside the house they were searching.

Fortunately, Chaaya had found what would pass for a weapon until they got an opportunity to upgrade. It was a piece of pipe about two feet long and surprisingly heavy.

By the next day, they felt more confident that none of those crazies were on their tails. They had found a knapsack and an actual pack early the previous afternoon. By the end of the second day, both were full of food and they had even managed to scrounge up some bottles of water.

"My friend was going to try to make it to Queensborough,"

Gemma said as they sat in their new camp—a second floor flat with a bathroom so small that there was no way she could sleep in the room without partially tucking in her knees.

"I have heard terrible things about that place. Even worse, I know of at least twenty people who went there to check it out and never were seen or heard from again."

They sat in silence until they both eventually dozed off. Gemma had a dream about Queensborough that chilled her to the bone and made her wake with a start. In it she saw Vix being beaten and chopped up like she had seen Harold. Only, Vix did not cry out so much as once. Instead, she simply repeated the same thing over and over to the rhythm of the beating she was receiving. Even after her head was cut off and hung from the giant board, the mouth continued to move and the words rang clear as a bell.

"This is all your fault, Gemma."

***

"I see five." Chad handed the binoculars to Caroline.

She brushed her shaggy brown hair out of her face and lifted the glasses. Chad was already up and moving in a crouch to a fallen tree by the time she had scanned the area.

"Maybe they are just passing through." Caroline handed back the binoculars and peeked over the tree to where a road once ran alongside the reservoir. The harsh and changing weather of the area had done its part to crumble, wash away, and cover most of what had once been a two-lane highway.

A group was moving with obvious caution. In her experience, that never meant anything good. Still, she could not be blamed for hoping.

"Dad!" Ronni hissed.

Chad and Caroline turned as the young woman came up to their lookout point in a hurry. No longer a little girl, Ronni had grown into a woman with a fierce determination and will to survive. She was hardly the little girl that Chad had fled that FEMA shelter with so long ago.

His daughter was now a product of the new ways of the world having lived over a third of her life in the land of the undead. Her only weakness was the children who had become zombies. She insisted that they were different somehow, and therefore, should not be killed simply because they were zombies. More than once she had stayed Chad's hand.

"There is a second group." Ronni pointed back over her shoulder. "They are down by the old cabins."

"How many?" Chad asked.

"Maybe six or seven. It is obvious that they are searching for something."

A rustle in some nearby brush made them all go silent. Each pulled their weapon of choice. For Chad, it was an old cavalry officer's sword that he had stumbled upon in, of all places, a little roadside tourist trap that had a small museum as its main attraction. According to the placard, the weapon had once been the sword of George Armstrong Custer. He had no idea if that might be true, but he could not dispute the fine craftsmanship. It was easy to wield and seldom got stuck when cleaving a skull. Ronni preferred an old field machete. Its grip had practically molded to her hand from so much use over the years. Caroline had been a softball player for as long as she could remember while growing up. She had even been able to extend her years when a college scholarship had been offered. She was in her senior year when the zombies came. She had killed the first one with one of her favorite bats. She kept a duffel of bats that she had obtained over the years. Some had even been modified with spikes, but she had quickly found that spikes could get stuck. She preferred just a standard aluminum bat. Her current weapon was a twenty-nine ounce DeMARINI.

The trio instinctively fanned out to cover the front and sides of the cluster of thick brush that was shaking and rattling in fits and starts. Chad had taken the position in front, with Ronni and Caroline on either side.

When the girl came crawling out on her belly, Chad rushed in and put the point of his sword at the girl's neck. She froze, her hands going out to each side.

"P-p-please," she whimpered. "Don't kill me."

"Roll over," Chad ordered.

The girl did so, and Chad took an involuntary step back. The girl had a nasty bite on the left cheek. It had not torn the flesh away, but the area was ugly, red, puffy, and leaking blood. However, a few seconds later he was able to relax and get a clearer picture.

The girl was immune.

While still leaking blood, it was obvious that the wound was several hours old. There would be no way that she should not have the telltale black tracers in her eyes by now. Her eyes, while red-rimmed from crying, were basically clear. The blue shining through the tears was bright and healthy just as the whites were clear of any signs of infection.

"Dad," Ronni scolded as she elbowed her way in, "get that sword out of her face."

Chad stepped back as his daughter knelt down. She handed over a canteen after helping the younger girl to her feet. Chad figured the girl to be in her late teens; about the same age Ronni had been when this all started. This was one of those moments where it felt odd looking at a woman who was approaching her thirties and seeing almost nothing left of the little girl that he knew as his daughter.

"P-please don't let them get me," the stranger finally managed after taking a long drink from the canteen.

"So those people down there are looking for you?" Chad glanced back to the log where they had been watching the one group, then brought his attention back to the girl. "Why are they looking for you?"

"Because I am one of the damned."

Chad glanced at Caroline and Ronni who both returned his questioning glance with a shrug. They had no guesses.

"The damned?" Chad finally asked when the girl had not offered anything more.

"The bite did not take me." She pointed to her face. "I was bitten by one of the dead and did not change."

Chad cocked his head. The girl was telling him what happened, but he had a feeling that he was missing an important part of the story.

"So these people are hunting you down because you are immune to the bite?" Caroline voiced Chad's thoughts with an obvious tone of skepticism. "Care to tell us why?"

"They feel that those who are immune to the bite are damned souls that have committed some great sin that prevents their acceptance to Heaven."

"Melody Whittaker!" a voice shouted from much closer than Chad would like. "Come out, girl. You know how this has to end."

"I don't think they are gonna be pleased with the re-write," Caroline quipped when she saw the firm looks of determination on Chad and Ronni's face.

***

"…and we can confirm that at least one of the turret occupants was alive as of this morning," Pitts said to the group clustered around the front of the patrol barracks.

"I say we stomp a mud hole in these fucks!" George Rosamilia growled.

Jody was not surprised. The big man was perhaps Danny's best friend. While he and Danny had patched up their differences (as they always seemed to do), George and Danny had built a very strong friendship over the years.

"If George gets to go, then so do I," a female voice sounded, causing everybody that had gathered out front to turn around. Margarita Rosamilia was standing in the shadow of the nearby post office.

Margarita and George were what Jody always considered an "interesting" couple. They would have been a disaster in the old world. It was not uncommon for one or both to be sporting a black eye, busted lip, or other assorted bruises. Whether it was from their "enthusiastic" lovemaking, or a heated argument that got out of control, nobody ever knew; and what's more, nobody ever asked. The two seemed to thrive on whatever it was they had between them.

"I have not made any choices," Pitts said. He sort of choked on that last word as Margarita came to a stop directly in front of him with her arms folded across her ample bosom. "But I guess I will add you two now." He looked at the rest of those gathered around. "Any other volunteers?"

Jody was not surprised when every hand went up. Not only was this community very serious about its security—and the reality was that this was a security issue first and foremost—but Danny was a popular person in the community. You could bet the taverns would stay open late on the occasions that he came to town for one reason or another.

Jody almost felt bad that his hand was almost the last to raise. In truth, with all the people who had stepped up, he was not actually necessary. Still, Danny was a friend. The fact that they were not as close meant nothing.

His reasons for being reluctant were across the street. When Pitts announced that they would muster at the patrol barracks at four in the morning, Jody peeled away from the group and headed for the park.

"Daddy!" the little girl squealed at the sight of him.

Leaping from the swings, the little girl ran at him with her arms wide, her curly blond hair streaming behind. Jody knelt to catch her as she leaped into his arms. Looking up, he smiled as Selina came up carrying the baby.

"Hi, sweetheart." Jody stood as Selina reached them and greeted her with a kiss. "How have they been?"

"Alana has been an absolute angel. She helps mommy with changes and feedings," Selina said. "Haven't you, baby girl?"

"I'm not the baby!" Alana huffed, crossing her arms indignantly. "Jenna is the baby. I'm a big girl now!"

"Yes, you are the big girl." Selina winked at Jody. When he only managed a weak smile in return, her own expression faltered. "Go show daddy how high you can swing, okay, Alana?"

The girl wriggled from her daddy's arms and took off for the swings. Calls of "Watch me, watch me!" being hurled over her shoulder even before she had climbed onto the swing's seat and began pumping her legs furiously.

"Is it that bad?" Selina whispered as she moved to stand beside her husband after he had scooped the baby from her and cradled the infant in his own arms.

"Outriders," Jody spat the word like a curse. "They killed the Griffiths and burned the bodies. Danny must have been the runner from Turret Nine to go check on them. They have him in a cage. He looked pretty messed up. It is likely that they were torturing him. I actually almost feel sorry for whoever is doing the torturing and questioning. You know how Danny can get."

"So when do you leave?" Selina did not need to be told that her husband had volunteered. It went without saying; he was still friends with Danny despite the distance that had come between them over the years.

"We will head out at four. If we move fast, we can get there just before sunrise. That is usually when people are the most lax if they are posting a watch. For all we know, they could feel safe and think the turret is secure enough not to merit a watch. That would be the best case scenario for us."

"Just be careful."

Jody smiled as he watched Alana swing higher and higher. If not for the twenty foot high watch towers in the background and the ten foot barrier wall, he could almost be in a normal world. They had worked hard to create someplace where people could be safe, where children could grow up in a normal environment.

"I always am."

"What's the matter?" Selina asked, seeing as well as hearing something hesitant in Jody's voice. He was always so sure of himself, and she did not like the vibe she was picking up.

"I almost didn't volunteer," Jody admitted.

"Why?"

"I like what I have. I love you and the girls. I just want to be a husband and a dad now. I am tired of being a leader."

"Then don't run for re-election this time," Selina finally said after a long pause. "Lord knows that you have done enough to get things settled here. Step aside and let somebody else carry the ball for a while."

Jody opened his mouth twice before actually saying anything. He wanted to agree, but, if he was being honest with himself, he was scared of the idea of somebody else running the show. He had become accustomed to being the one to have final say on things. If he stepped down, he would just be one of the regular citizens.

"Da-deee!" Alana squealed.

Jody returned his attention to his oldest daughter. *And would that really be so bad?* he thought as he watched her swing.

***

Entry Seventeen—Met a group of people yesterday. They have a camp set up beside the Yellowstone River. There are nine men and sixteen women (if you count the two sixteen-year-olds). It was so nice to hear the laughter of children.

That is the beautiful thing about children; they have an internal radar and can sense good and bad in people much like dogs. Back in the day, if I met somebody new and my dog didn't like them, I usually let them slip out of my life. Dogs just know.

I could see the concern in a few of the women's faces when the little ones all came to me. They were like moths to a flame. By the time it started getting dark, I could see them relaxing a bit. Today, I noticed that I was not being watched as closely.

To earn my keep, I split wood, helped put up a small hut for a couple that just got married, and bagged a few quail (or at least that is what I think they were; I don't know birds very well). Nobody rides for free these days.

I also got my next job.

Entry Eighteen—He goes by the name of Darwin Goodkind. The story as I hear it is as follows. He and his little gang arrive with a small caravan of carts and wagons. They are armed to the teeth and use the excuse that it is dangerous out in the badlands.

What Darwin and his buddies don't say is that it is dangerous for the living that are unfortunate enough to encounter these monsters. They arrive in communities such as this one and bait the people with all these amazing items. Some of the "luxury" goods included Old World whiskey in sealed bottles, tools like picks, shovels, and the like—all very useful out here considering they have the old fiberglass handles that last for years before you have to craft a replacement.

They also have some other items to offer. It is then that a community is put to the test. One of the wagons apparently had a number of women in it. These folks would not go so far as to say that they were slaves, but I don't see any other way to put it. This is the post-apocalyptic version of the mail-order bride. The only thing is that these women do not have a say.

This community is one of the poorer ones that I have encountered. I guess they scraped together all they could and purchased one of the girls—the youngest of the bunch according to what I am being told—in order to set her free. The girl decided to stay on and live here.

That situation alone, while sad and vile, would probably not have been enough to put me on the trail of the Darwin Goodkind gang. However, the day after these bastards left, one of the local girls came up missing. Everybody searched, but all they found was a torn piece of her clothing and some blood.

They doubt she fell to a zombie. I guess there was not a lot of blood; also, there was an obvious scuffle according to these people.

The wagon caravan left heading east. That would be towards the direction of the Billings Ruins. If they follow the Yellowstone River, I know the route they are using.

Anybody who travels these days tends to stay close to streams and rivers. You can go a few days without food, but water is a different story altogether. Everybody still remembers the wars that broke out those first weeks in California when the water stopped coming from Colorado. Los Angeles burned to the ground less than two months in, and there was nothing that anybody could do to stop it.

I leave in the morning.

Entry Nineteen—This might be tougher than I thought. From what I have seen, there are nine of these guys. They have obviously been doing this for a while. They have four wagons of "regular" goods, and then another that they keep the women in.

Each night when they stop to make camp, they set up a perimeter with military precision and post roving guards. Part of their setup includes a series of fire barrels that they place in a ring around the camp. While not perfect, they manage to keep the area well lit. Also, they have obviously made this trip before since they seem to know exactly where to camp each night.

Once everything is done with setting up the camp, they let the women out of the wagon. It was sickening to see human beings treated worse than cattle. I did notice that they were well fed and given plenty of water. Still, they are human beings. I would never be able to live with myself if I allowed this to continue.

I realize that there may be more groups like this one…some perhaps even worse. Maybe I will cross paths with them someday, but for now, my focus is on Darwin Goodkind's gang. I will eliminate each and every one of them…or die trying.

Entry Twenty—Two more days of travel. I am still trying to figure out a way to get these guys. Anything I do as far as a simple frontal assault would not end well for me. It's not that I am scared, but I have no desire to simply throw my life away.

We stopped just outside of what is now called Oasis. It used to be the town of Columbia, Montana. The folks here did well for themselves when the zombies came. Most, if not all, were in possession of more than their fair share of guns and ammo. These were the folks the movies and books forgot about.

Rednecks.

Dead: Reclamation

Geek Interrogation

"I swear…I have never seen these two in my life," Jerold Grimes, the mayor of whatever remained of Rock Ridge whimpered.

Kevin winced as Darlene twisted her wrist enough to make the man cry out. He never understood why women always had to go for the testicles when they attacked a man. Trey Piper stood just behind Darlene, arms folded across his chest as he watched with almost no expression. He had turned out to be the leader of this little band of post-apocalyptic terrorists.

Trey looked every bit the part of a hillbilly survivalist. He had straight, greasy, dirty blond hair that clung to his forehead with the help of the molding done by the cowboy hat that currently rested on the pommel of his saddle. His face was round and he was missing a few teeth. Those that remained were not long for this world. He was skinny, but managed to have a prominent potbelly that pushed the bottom of his ill-fitting flannel shirt up enough to reveal his "outie" bellybutton.

His jeans were faded and full of plenty of patched holes; so much so that they were more patch than jeans. He wore a wide belt with the stereotypical hubcap-sized buckle. From that belt hung a variety of knives and a sword that had a Confederate flag-adorned pommel.

To complete the look were a collection of crosses that hung around his neck of varying sizes. Some were large enough to look almost awkward and others were so dainty that they looked like the chains might break if you breathed on them wrong.

Scattered about were his mobile militia. Some still sat on the backs of their horses; others had dismounted and were allowing their horses to have a break. Now that he saw what he assumed to be all of them, Kevin counted three women and eight men; although, one of the "women" was borderline. He was not entirely sure she was an actual she.

They all had bows or crossbows as well as a variety of blades. One of the men had what Kevin thought of as an executioner's axe. It was strapped to his back and had to weigh at least twenty pounds.

Standing across the open clearing where he and Catie had been taken was Clint and what was left of his group. Kevin could not be sure, but he thought there were at least three faces missing from Clint's people.

The sun was pushing away the morning haze, but the smell of smoke was a bitter reminder that a fire raged nearby; one that had been apparently set with the intention of killing an entire community.

"You know we got your daughter," Darlene hissed. "And you know what is gonna happen to her if you lie to us."

Kevin's eyes flitted briefly to the girl being held between two horses. She was manacled, and the chains from each wrist were secured to the saddles of those horses. Her head was down and a dark strand of bloody drool could be seen as it stretched and eventually broke, adding to the growing puddle at her feet.

"I am telling you the truth," Mayor Jerold Grimes sputtered between busted lips and a few broken teeth. "I swear to God."

Like a cobra, Darlene struck with her studded gloved fist. Jerold's head rocked back and fragments of more broken teeth went flying.

"You don't get to swear to God, you abomination!" she shrieked.

In Kevin's mind, there were few things more reprehensible

than a bigot. A bigot that doubled as a religious zealot was a nightmare. All the irrational ideology and fervent mania coupled with a specified intolerance made for a real piece of work.

"Okay, Darlene," Trey said. He walked over to Kevin and stared into his eyes as if he expected the man to morph into something horrific before them. "That still does not clear you."

"And what does exactly?" Kevin asked.

"Well, we are gonna have to examine you and the little lady there." He tilted his head towards Catie.

"You mean strip us naked and run your filthy hands and eyes over our bodies?" Kevin scoffed. "Hope you brought me flowers…I don't get naked for just anybody."

He wasn't surprised when the backhand came. It had been the third one he had received from this man so far. He didn't care much for it, but if it kept the focus on him and not Catie, that was fine. She had already given him an indication that she had a plan. If the focus remained on him, it would make her job that much easier.

He brought his face back around and smiled, showing off blood-stained teeth and a trickle of bright red that started to leak from one nostril. Kevin fought the urge to wipe it away and simply let it run down his face. Trey moved up so that they were almost literally nose-to-nose. Kevin could feel his hot breath and he frowned.

"You need to work on your oral hygiene." Kevin braced himself for another smack, but this time he got a fist to the gut.

He doubled over in pain and immediately tried to get air back into his lungs. He hated the wheezing sounds that were coming from him. He knew that it would upset Catie. Also, he thought he heard a chuckle come from the direction of Clint and his people. He was not sure if it was at his expense or in support of his latest quip.

"I don't understand people like you," Trey growled as he grabbed Kevin by the hair and yanked him up. "You got no chip to bargain with, yet you want to try and play games."

"Yeah?" Kevin managed with the little bit of air he could suck in. "That makes two of us…the not understanding part, I mean." Trey looked at him with an arched eyebrow, so Kevin continued. "Humanity is on its final lap. The zombies have the numbers and it is just a matter of time. Yet people like you see fit to go around and kill others for no other reason than some misguided prejudice."

"Misguided?" Trey laughed. "You mean our little war against the munies?"

"Your systematic attempt at killing off people who are immune to the bite, yes, that is to what I am referring."

"You can use all the flowery words and phrases you like, but the munies are an abomination. God sent this plague down on us to cleanse the world." Trey was building up a head of steam that reminded Kevin of a television evangelist. All this guy was missing was an ill-fitting suit, and a number to flash on the screen where the faithful could send their donations.

"Did you ever stop to think that maybe the munies, as you call them, might be the ones your God is trying to save?"

Kevin could actually see the blood rushing to Trey's cheeks, turning them a bright red. Perhaps he had struck a nerve. It reminded him of the days when the Jehovah's Witnesses came to his door. Having actually read the bible, Kevin was familiar with their favorite versus. Every single time he asked them how they thought they might be one of the one hundred and forty-four thousand supposedly saved out of all the people that had been born over the years, much less the fact that they had membership numbers over seven million, that was usually what prompted their hasty and awkward departure.

"Strip him right here," Trey ordered as he stepped back from Kevin.

Two men climbed down from their horses and approached. Kevin gave one a salacious wink as the lackey tugged at his belt. The man scowled. Whatever Catie had planned, he sure hoped it came soon; the man with the giant axe was smiling.

As if in answer to his wish, there was a yelp. Kevin fought his urge to turn his head and instead lunged forward, slamming his forehead into the bridge of the nose of the man who had been undressing him.

One of the problems (and there were many) that Kevin had with the old horror flicks was the people who just stood there and awaited their death. You knew that the bad guys or axe-wielding maniac was not going to show mercy; so, if that was the case, why on earth would you not go out at least trying to take one or two of them with you?

He and Catie were about to die. That would be a certainty as soon as their scars were revealed. So why not at least make an attempt at either getting free or killing one or two of the bastards that were about to do them in?

Trey was drawing his blade as Kevin lowered his shoulder and charged. Unfortunately for Kevin, the man side-stepped him easily and even shot out a foot to trip him as he lumbered past. Kevin went to the ground face first and got a mouthful of dirt in the process. He knew that his time was done. The blade would come down and that would be the end of things.

He was a little disappointed when he did not get that mythical "life passing before his eyes" event that he had always heard people supposedly experienced when they were about to die. Maybe his mind knew something that he was not yet fully aware of at that precise moment. There was a meaty thud and then something heavy landed on him. Kevin rolled over to find the dead eyes of Trey staring blankly at him. A split second later, he noticed the machete handle sticking up from the back of Trey's head.

Clint's face appeared. "Up you go," the man said in his backwoods drawl.

Kevin accepted the offered hand and came to his feet. The fight had been rather anti-climactic. Clint's men had obviously been paying attention. The moment Catie struck, they had leapt into action. Trey's militia was either dead, dying, or—as in Darlene's case—wounded, but being held captive at the end of a blade.

"Not so tough now, are ya?" Catie snarled at the woman. Kevin noticed that it was one of Darlene's own blades that Catie held to the woman's throat.

"Why?" Kevin asked Clint.

"While the folks at Rock Ridge might have been up to something dirty, that was really all just rumor. And how can we paint everybody with the same brush whether they are immune or not." Clint glanced over his shoulder at the rest of his men and his eyes stopped on one man in particular. The man was shaking with rage and a few of the others were actually working to calm him down. "They killed Jess, Jeb's boy, right in front of him for no other reason than he had a healed bite scar. He weren't up in Rock Ridge or nothin' of the sort. He was just a kid, dammit."

"So then..." Kevin paused, torn between gratitude and caution.

"We could care less if you and your little lady are immune. That don't mean spit to us,' Clint answered the unasked question.

"Can I correctly assume that these people are nobody you know? They aren't from your place or Red Hill?"

"Never seen any of 'em before in my life." Clint turned his head and spat. "And I don't care if I never see any of their kind again."

"So then, what sort of deal did they make with your mayor? Sounds to me like they had something arranged." Kevin went over to the horse that his pack had been strapped to and patted the animal on the neck. "And, speaking of mayors, what are you gonna do with him?" Kevin pointed to the beaten and bloody man lying on the ground in the fetal position.

"Leave him," Clint said with a shrug. "He ain't our problem. As for our own mayor...he has some explaining to do when we get back."

"What about me?" Darlene asked, defiance still strong in her voice despite her obvious disadvantage when it came to her current situation.

"What about you?" Catie snapped, pressing the tip of the sharp blade just enough to break the skin and allow a single drop of blood to well up and escape, sliding ever-so-slowly down her grime-covered flesh.

"Maybe we should bring her along and ask her a few questions," Kevin suggested. He did so with a little extra volume in order to (hopefully) get the message to Catie that he would prefer her to remain alive for the time being.

"That ain't a bad idea at all," Clint agreed. "I sure would like to know who these folks are and what brought them to these parts."

"I ain't tellin' you a damned thing!" Darlene spat with a barking laugh that matched her already unpleasant demeanor.

"Yes," Kevin nodded, "that is usually how it starts. It is my experience that a person changes that tune once their situation becomes dire enough that they wish for improvement." He glanced around and saw a wide and varying degree of confusion on the faces of everybody except Catie. That was to be expected, she had long since learned to decipher his words into their simplest forms.

"Once the torture or depravation takes enough of its toll, she'll talk," Catie said in clarification. This received nods from Clint and the others. From Darlene it was greeted with lips pressed tight and the slightest hint that she might be coming to the realization in regards to her current situation.

"You see," Kevin pulled his walking stick free from where it had been secured to his pack, "there once was a time when it was considered improper to harm a woman. These days, most of the old conventions are null. Everybody is on the same playing field. The champions of women's equality would be thrilled to know that it only took a zombie apocalypse to bring about that which they sought."

"In other words, he is not going to have one teensy problem beating the answers out of you if it becomes necessary," Catie stage-whispered with a smirk.

"However, I think we have created enough noise that it would be best if our hosts were to be so kind as to escort us back to their camp." Kevin took the reins of the horse that was still carrying his pack and turned to Clint with a nod that he should lead the way.

Catie, following Kevin's lead, swiped up the reins on the horse that had hers. Clint remained still.

"Is there a problem?" Kevin asked.

"What do we do with them that is wounded?" Clint gestured to the three men and one other woman who had not perished in the fight.

Two of the four were not even able to sit up, and one was holding his stomach where somebody had caught him good with a knife. Kevin realized that one of the individuals sitting up had been the headsman.

"Leave them." Kevin shrugged his shoulders. He saw the looks of concern that Clint and his men wore. "Is that a problem? Didn't you just say the same thing about the mayor and his daughter?"

"Well, I know they was just tryin' to kill y'all, and that they did kill a couple of ours including Jeb's boy, but I just don't think that anybody deserves to die at the hands of a zombie. Jerold and his daughter are immune, so they at least have some chance. Can't we at least end the misery of them that is hurt beyond help?"

Kevin turned to the headsman. "You want us to just kill you and end it?" The man shook his head emphatically just as Kevin guessed. He looked back at Clint with an expression of questioning.

"How about them?" Clint pointed to the pair that were unconscious and not able to answer.

Again Kevin turned to the headman. "You want us to at least take care of your buddies?" Once more the man shook his head.

"But—" Clint began. It was Catie who cut him off.

"The whole idea of folks wanting a merciful death is mostly fiction," she explained. "It seems like a good idea until it is your own death that you are sanctioning. There is no greater well of hope than that which resides within the human spirit." She shot Kevin a look as if to confirm she had gotten her lines correct. He gave her a nod and salute in response.

Over the years together, Kevin had discovered that he and Catie had a lot in common. Both were avid readers, and both were often underestimated. Him, due to his less-than-athletic stature, and hers because she was, as Kevin often put it, barely a slip of a gal.

As their relationship blossomed, Catie and Kevin spent hours talking about anything and everything. As Kevin's mother used to say, "As iron sharpens iron, so one man sharpens another." It was actually Catie that told him that was an old Proverbs verse from the Bible. Their relationship became so much more than his and Aleah's had been. In part, because Kevin never felt the need to try and save Catie from any of the horrible things out in the world. Chances were that she had already seen them and then some.

Catie's former life as a soldier in the United States Army had made her into a warrior. She had seen combat and faced down living, breathing human enemies. In fact, it was Catie who eventually taught Kevin a thing or two about fighting. An avid lover of martial arts, Catie was a force to be reckoned with in a brawl. That was something that, much as it had today, had saved their collective asses on many occasions. This was not the first time that their potential captors had ignored her to their peril.

By that same token, as she taught him to fight, he taught her about the things he had gleaned from his years as a prepper-in-training. He also spent many nights regaling her with detailed recounts of his favorite horror movies and books.

Eventually, people in the community began to notice the changes, but it was Aleah that actually voiced it. "You two are so much alike now, that it is scary. If I didn't know any better, I would say that you guys went through some sort of Freaky Friday transformation."

That was after Catie had given a speech about why it was in the community's best interest to start building a perimeter defense that had nothing to do with firepower. She had laid out a very detailed and cohesive plan involving fire and sound that would act as a distraction for any zombie herd that crossed inside a ten mile perimeter.

Kevin smiled over at Catie in approval and agreement of her statement regarding a person's instinct at self-preservation. While it was clear that Clint and his companions were still not completely at peace with the idea of leaving the three men to die in what they knew had to be a slow and painful death (made all the more likely when a chorus of low moans carried on the breeze announcing the arrival of at least a few zombies) they could not dispute that the offer for a "merciful" death had been rebuked.

"Should we at least leave them their weapons?" Clint asked, looking nervously in the direction that the sounds of approaching zombies were coming from.

"Makes no difference to me," Kevin replied with a shrug. "That axe is impressive looking, but I highly doubt it is functional against a group of the walking dead. Too unwieldy."

Catie pulled a strip of leather from a pouch that dangled from her pack and turned back to Darlene. She motioned for the woman to present her wrists. Kevin was actually surprised that the woman did not refuse. However, for all her bluster, he was willing to bet it was a lot of talk. The deeper her situation sunk in, the more likely she would be to cave and spill the beans on any others like her that may be in the area.

A few of Clint's men took hold of the other horses after cutting the mayor's daughter free and the group fell into line for the trip back to their community of Falling Run. One by one, everybody fell in single file. Catie took the second position right behind Clint with Darlene. Kevin migrated back towards the rear.

As they walked, his eyes were on constant scan mode as Kevin tried to ascertain any sorts of defenses these people might have in place. He had multiple reasons for this; the first being the fact that he wanted to know just how well-protected the place would be against an attack of either human or the zombie variety. The second reason was that, if he and Catie were actually going to consider this place as a possible home, he wanted to know what measures had been taken and what he would have to try and improve once he could do so without ruffling feathers.

That sentiment was one that he had learned from his time with Catie. On more than one occasion, she had reined him in when he started to get pushy. She never hesitated to let him know when he was making, as she so bluntly put it, "a complete horse's ass" of himself.

He was not easily impressed, but he had to admit that these people seemed prepared on multiple fronts. He spied a series of catwalks in the trees overhead. Those could be handy for either threat. Also, there were several tall berms laid out in an overlapping pattern. Most had deep trenches on the other side. Again, these would slow forces of both sorts, but it would be especially detrimental to the undead. If they did manage to climb the steep dunes made of dirt and gravel, they would most assuredly tumble into the pits on the other side. All that would remain was for people to come along and dispatch of the creatures at their leisure.

When the town proper came into view, again, Kevin was mildly impressed. The walls were built at an angle outward with towers set at regular intervals. The open ground, that looked to be kept clear via burning, was laced with coils of razor wire, barbed wire fences, more pits and berms, as well as a series of concrete bunkers with no apparent doors to allow access.

"Like those?" a man said, coming up beside Kevin.

"Tower on top for an archer as well as slits around the structure…most likely for stabbing out. I would imagine you can only access it via underground tunnel?" Kevin turned to the man who was staring at him in open-mouthed disbelief.

"I was awful proud of that…'til now anyways," the man said with a mix of disappointment that his tricks had been so easily pointed out, and awe of that very same thing.

"We have something similar back where we lived," Kevin said, making an extra effort to show appreciation in his voice just like Catie taught him. "I thought I was so smart…looks like somebody here is giving me a run for my money in that department." Sure enough, the man's disappointment turned to a beaming smile of pride.

"My idea." He hiked a thumb to indicate the squat structure.

"Nice."

The rest of the trip all the way to the gate, the two men shared details on specs and a few of the design issues they had to overcome along the way to perfecting such a solid perimeter defense construct. More than once, Kevin noticed some of those close by scowling in disapproval as a piece of their special defense measures were shared with a stranger.

"Coming in!" Clint's voice announced from the front of the column. "Lost three, bringing in one prisoner and two non-hostiles."

The sound of a massive crank being turned made its presence known. A flock of birds took flight in response with a flutter of wings and a series of angry chirps and squawks. Kevin was not surprised to see an armed reception waiting just inside the gates.

"The two newbies," a man said, stepping forward, pointing at Catie and Darlene, "step over here."

"Actually," Clint took Darlene by the elbow and pushed her forward, "this is the prisoner."

"So where is the other newbie?" The man who had stepped forward was scratching his head.

"Back here," Kevin called as he stepped up, taking his place beside Catie.

"And we need to speak to the mayor," Clint added. He leaned forward and whispered into the man's ear. Kevin watched as his expression darkened, obviously not liking what he was hearing from Clint. His eyes darted over to where Jeb stood with a forlorn expression and eyes closed in obvious sadness.

"Take the newbies to the doctor's office, take the prisoner to the holding area," the man finally ordered after Clint stepped back. "Jeb, I am damn sorry. Now…" the man's shoulders visibly slumped, "I gotta make a pair of house calls. Clint, could you come with me, please?"

A trio of the people that had been part of the armed reception committee stepped forward and ushered Kevin and Catie to a white building. As they headed for it, Kevin looked around. He was immediately reminded of Mayberry. He could not shake off the instant feeling that this was where he and Catie belonged.

They were in what made up the main part of town. There were at least a dozen buildings of varying sizes and shapes. People were going about a rather ordinary and peaceful day. He did not even see any signs of alarm about the fact that a nearby settlement was burning to the ground. Whether due to an obliviousness of the situation, or complete ambivalence, these people were acting like they did not have a care in the world. In fact, if not for the walls with roving lookouts, you would be hard pressed to see any signs that a zombie apocalypse had ever taken place.

Life was returning to normal and humanity was reclaiming their place in the order of things. For better or worse.

***

"How many times do I have to answer the same questions?" Kevin was struggling to keep his cool.

"In my experience, folks don't just up and decide to cross over half the breadth of what used to be the United States just to confirm that their family is dead. Most folks took those trips about ten or twelve years ago," the man said calmly.

Kevin was in a small room that reminded him of every questioning room he had ever seen on any television cop show. If this was how they were treating him and Catie as guests, he was really curious what sort of treatment Darlene was getting

The man sitting across from him had introduced himself as Craig. When Kevin asked "Craig what?" the man had shrugged and said, "Just Craig." Kevin had tried to make a Cher/Madonna joke, but the man had simply pointed to the chair that he wanted Kevin to sit in, and he had taken the other, effectively putting a table between them that was wide enough so that neither could actually reach the other if such an urge were to arise.

"I was having nightmares." Again, this was something that Kevin had been repeating for what felt like the better part of an hour.

"It just seems awful suspicious that you show up the same time as these other folks that allegedly burned Rock Ridge."

"Are you people really that entrenched in the past?" Kevin said with a sarcastic laugh adding a sharpness to his tone.

"Entrenched in the past?" the man asked with what had to be genuine confusion based on his expression.

"*Alleged*? Didn't we do away with that crap a long time ago? That was a construct of our ACLU-based society. The days of a person being caught with a bloody knife in his hand and claiming innocence is over, don't you think?"

"And what if that person just happened on the scene?"

"You were a lawyer back in the day, weren't you?" The man's red face confirmed Kevin's suspicions. "And so now you are...what? Head of security? Chief of police?"

"I don't see what any of this had to do with the reason we are here, which is you and your *coincidental* arrival on the heels of some sort of terrorist faction that apparently has an issue with people who express immunity."

"And you think I am part of them?" Kevin asked.

"Using your own logic, you are the one standing with a bloody knife in your hand...so to speak. Perhaps you are right, maybe *alleged* is a thing of the past. Maybe circumstance is all that is needed in lieu of actual proof." The man smiled like the cat that ate the canary. Kevin had to appreciate how his own argument was being used against him, but he still had an ace up his sleeve.

"And if I can prove categorically that I could not be associated with those lunatics?" Kevin kept his poker-face on and showed no emotion.

"I don't see how—" the man began, but Kevin cut him off.

"And you do acknowledge that these people are obviously agenda driven and seeking to wipe out any who might be immune?"

"Well...yes..." the man answered slowly, obviously sensing a trap.

Kevin stood deliberately so as not to incite the man to try and restrain him. He shrugged out of his jacket and pulled off his shirt. There on his arm was a long-healed bite scar.

"I am pretty sure that would get me kicked out of their reindeer games." Kevin pointed triumphantly at his arm.

For one of the few times, he was glad that the cat scratch

had not been his only injury. While it had been proven long ago that cats were carriers, and that a person could catch the zombie contagion through them, those little scratches had not been enough to leave any sort of scar.

"Son of a..." Craig's voice trailed off as he eyed the scar. With a grin, he stood and slung his leg up onto the table. Pulling up his pants, he turned his leg to show a horrendous scar on his calf.

"Damn," Kevin breathed, leaning over to take a closer look. "That looks like the Roger wound from the original *Dawn of the Dead*. You weren't by chance trying to hotwire a truck, were you?"

"I was trying to get over a fence," Craig admitted. Then, with a sheepish grin, he added, "That was about seventy pounds ago."

"I hear that," Kevin agreed, plopping back down into his chair. "That is something the books and movies missed unless they were trying to just make a point of showing people starve."

"What do you mean?"

"There is no more junk food. Or at least there wasn't for a few years. Our community has a few ingenious cooks that make some pretty tasty treats, but nothing like the old days."

"I'd kill my best friend for a Reese's Peanut Butter Cup." Craig got a faraway look in his eyes.

"Okay," a voice barked as the door flew open. "I think we have heard enough."

The man that had disappeared with Clint just after their arrival, entered the room. Clint was on his heels, and when Kevin craned his neck, he saw Catie standing in the hallway beyond with a tight-lipped smile on her face.

"Kevin Dreon, meet Cap Mitchell," Clint said by way of introduction.

The man extended a hand to Kevin. "Sorry to put you and the missus through all the interrogation. It's just, with all the drama that has unfolded in the past few days, we couldn't be too careful."

"No worries." Kevin made a dismissive wave with his hand.

"So, have you gotten anything from Darlene?"

"Not yet, she is a tough cookie," Cap said with a sigh. "And I gotta be honest, we ain't really got that much experience with interrogation."

"No kidding?" Kevin snorted and shot a wink at Craig who flushed just a little.

"Well, I bet I can get her to talk," Kevin said after a questioning look Catie's direction received a nod of approval. "But I need to do it my way, and you have to understand something, I have dealt with people like her before. They only speak one language. If I do this, it is my way and no interference."

Cap turned to the other two and they huddled together. While they debated in harsh whispers that made it clear there were some serious misgivings to his offer, Kevin went to Catie and pulled her close.

"They aren't ready for this," he whispered in her ear.

"Yeah, well if they say no, you and I are outta here. I won't go through that nonsense again."

Catie was referring to the time they had been captured back when it was the two of them, Aleah, Rose, and Heather. It had been by the skin of their teeth that they all survived.

"Okay," Cap finally said, stepping away from the other two.

Kevin was not surprised that Craig was unhappy with this decision. Despite their little moment of bonding over bite scars, it was clear that Craig had some antiquated ideas of how things should be.

"Besides, we got the mayor in another holding cell," Clint said, receiving nasty looks from both Cap and Craig.

"Before I go, I just got one quick question?" Kevin planted his hands on his hips. "Are all of the men here sporting names that begin with the letter 'C'?"

Clint smiled. "Nope, but we did have a Chester and a Cletus for a while."

There was a moment of silence. Catie started to giggle and it quickly spread. Before long, all of them were slapping each other on the back and sharing in a moment of levity.

***

Kevin stepped into the room and shut the door behind him. Darlene's wrists were secured, and the cuffs were attached to a large bolt in the center of the table. She sat up straight when he entered, her expression expectant. But when she saw who it was, she slumped back down in her chair.

"I gots nothin' to say to you," she huffed and blew a greasy strand of hair from her eyes.

"Maybe not yet." Kevin took the seat across from her and kept his expression and voice as neutral as possible. "But just like your friends back there would not willingly accept death because of the human nature to cling to survival, you will talk to avoid pain and possibly death."

"That supposed to scare me?" Darlene leaned forward in her seat and bared her teeth. "I can take anything you dish out and then some, you scrawny little geek."

"I am sure you think that for the moment."

"You gonna rape me? Hell, I bet you got a pencil dick, and I won't even feel a thing."

"Nothing quite so...personal." Kevin shrugged out of his coat and let it drape back over his chair. He folded his hands in front of him on the table and stared into Darlene's eyes.

"You think all your fancy talk is gonna work? Maybe you think you will trick me into saying something. Well you'd be wrong."

"Actually, I won't have to lay a hand on you. And I bet you will start talking so fast that an auctioneer would be jealous."

Darlene let go with a bray of ugly laughter. She shook her head and then pressed her lips together tight as if to visibly demonstrate her commitment to not talking.

Kevin sat still for a moment before reaching up and unbuttoning the cuff of his shirt. With deliberate slowness, he rolled the sleeve up and laid his arm out so that the scar was clearly visible. Without making eye contact, he pulled a knife from his belt and made a single slice across his forearm. A thin line of blood welled up from the cut. Kevin gave it a second before he looked up at Darlene.

Sure enough, the horror in her eyes was crystal clear. Kevin had to actually steel himself when a tear broke free from the corner of her eye and rolled down her cheek.

"P-p-please," she whispered. Despite how simple-minded she had come off as up to this point, she was very aware of the threat that was before her.

"Then start talking."

Cricket

"Whoever you are, come out slow." Okay…now I was a little bit scared.

A woman crawled out on her hands and knees. She looked up at me and I staggered back a step. Her face had one of those boils on it, and I could already see the swelling and telltale dark smudge on her throat.

"You!" I barked, taking a swift step forward and nudging the man on the ground with the toe of my boot. "Roll over."

I bit back a gasp. A boil had burst—recently, judging by the thick curd-like pus oozing from what was now nothing short of a hole in his chin. And then there was the massive swelling right under his jaw.

"Cynthia?" I called. "We got two infected people here."

"Back away from them!" Cynthia barked.

I kept my eyes on the pair as I took a step back. I could hear the sound of feet running for me, but I was too transfixed to take my eyes off of the pair.

"What happened?" I could not help but ask.

"They said they had the cure…" the man started, but he began to choke and gasp as coughs wracked his frame. I saw blood trickle from the corner of his mouth.

"Tish demanded that every citizen that had not demonstrated immunity come forward and accept the vaccine," the woman picked up the narrative. "When we loaded up the payment for these supposed doctors and their crew on the carts after the demonstration, one of the people on the work detail passed out. Nobody thought anything about it. It was treated like heat exhaustion. The person was taken to the hospital…and the team of doctors left with their payment and escort. Probably five days later, people were all coming down with this sort of flu. Then the cheeseballs started showing up—"

"The cheeseballs?" I interrupted.

The woman pointed to the boil on her cheek. "That's what folks started calling them when they burst and that thick, cheese-like crap comes out."

I nodded and she continued.

"Pretty soon, damn near everybody was incapacitated. That was when they returned…only, instead of it just being the five so-called doctors, it was a gang of thirty. They knew where we kept everything. They were either really observant when we gathered our payment, or else they had people watching. Either way, we couldn't do a damn thing to stop them.

"The handful of people who were already immune and did not need the shot had been killed in their sleep probably just before sunrise, so we had a few dozen zombies walking around inside the walls." The woman began her own coughing fit and had to stop her tale.

I looked up to see Cynthia, Jim, Jackson, and Paula all standing close enough that I knew they'd heard everything, or damn near everything. They all had very different expressions on their faces. Paula looked annoyed and on the verge of angry. Cynthia looked curious. Jim…well, he just looked like Jim with his crooked half-smile. And Jackson had his lips pressed so tight that he could have turned coal to diamonds.

"You said something about a demonstration?" Paula finally spoke once the woman looked to have regained her composure. As for the man, his eyes were closed and his breathing was coming in wet, ragged gasps for air. It was clear that he was struggling.

"One of the doctors said that he wanted one of our people to step up and accept the vaccine. Then, they had to let a zombie bite them. He said that the subject could hold a gun to the doctor's head until that person was certain that he or she was not going to turn. Also, that person and his entire family would be given their dose without having to contribute to the payment," the woman explained.

"Jip Sinatra and his boyfriend stepped forward. Most folks knew that there wasn't anything known that could scare the man, so it wasn't a surprise that he volunteered. Sure enough, over two hours passed and his eyes never changed, never got the squiggles.

"A few folks said they didn't want the vaccination...said they had no need since their jobs kept them within the walls. I guess the doctors told Tish that it was an all or nothing deal. So they got the choice of the shot...or exile. That made it a no-brainer. When the—"

The man beside this woman began to cough again, but there was something off. Then he started to claw at his throat and make the most horrific sounds I had ever heard. I took a step back and had my crossbow leveled before I even realized it.

I was embarrassed and about to apologize when my eyes came up and I saw Paula looking at me. Her eyes flicked to the man and then to my weapon. She gave just the slightest nod, but I had no doubt that I'd seen it; and I knew what she meant.

Looking down, I lined up my shot and fired. The bolt went through the left eye and I heard the tip strike the pavement. The man kicked a few times, and then he made a retching noise and a small gout of blood burst from his lips. Then he was still.

I swung my weapon to the woman as she tried to drag herself to the man who now lay dead beside her. A numbness was seeping in, and I was actually preparing myself for the lashing out that would surely be coming from the man's companion.

"Thank you," she whispered. "I could not have brought myself to do it. Please promise to make mine as quick."

"Excuse me?" I could not help it. The words just came out of my mouth before I knew it. That was absolutely not the response that I had been expecting from this person.

"Please make my death as quick and painless as you did Tim's."

We had our paths crossed somewhere. She was thanking me? And then it sunk in. They were suffering, and she knew that they were basically dead. She now wanted me to finish her off like I had her friend.

"What are you waiting for?" Cynthia whispered in my ear.

I shook my head to clear it. I had no idea how long I'd been just standing here considering the situation. However, it had been long enough for the woman to lose consciousness. I had the bolt in my hand that I'd used on the man and, after inspecting it, decided to use it as my reload. I could tell by the shaft that it was almost useless when it came to hitting a target much more than a few yards away, so I may as well get one more shot out of it that I would not have to aim or worry about.

I squeezed the trigger and then turned to see Paula and Cynthia staring at me. After a few seconds, I got nervous. Jim had taken a few steps from me and was studying his boots. Jackson had turned his back.

"What?" Seriously, both women just staring at me like I was a freaking zombie or something, and Jim seemed to want to look anywhere but at me. Then there was Jackson.

"I guess you are more ready than I thought," Paula said. "I should have trusted my instincts and believed in you from the start."

I was a little confused. After all, hadn't she been the one to push for me to make this run? Sure, we'd had a little disagreement, but it wasn't that big of a deal as far as I was concerned.

"We need to get moving." Cynthia broke the mood with a clap of her hands.

I glanced at Jim. There was a look on his face like he'd just found out something horrible. Was he mad at me? Disappointed?

"I think we know what we will find in there," Paula groused as she took a step closer to the dead couple on the pavement and gave them a nudge with the toe of her boot.

"We still need to look," Cynthia insisted.

Paula ended up being right. The place was full of dead bodies. Most were still strapped to gurneys, each showing the same symptoms. Even through the filter, the stench of death was gagging. It was made worse by the flies and vermin. I tried to ignore it, but I was getting worn thin by all of the rats scurrying away every single time that we rounded another corner. And the clouds of flies were a constant hum and buzz in my ears.

There were times that we passed bodies that looked to be moving because of the bugs crawling all over them. Also, it was very clear that it had been a while. The bodies had already passed through rigor mortis, so we were past the twenty-four hour time of death. A few of the corpses had started to bloat in the heat.

After what seemed like an eternity, we finally exited. I immediately felt the tinges of anxiety as we started across the large, open parking lot. We would check the known storage sites as well as the residences. I knew we would not be checking all of the residences, but I was curious to see inside some of them.

Houses were a thing of the past as far as our community was concerned. We lived in a more communal and close society. As we walked past some of the dark and presumably empty homes, I could not help but be inquisitive. Not only that, but I could not imagine living in so much space. It seemed like a waste. Some of these homes were large enough to hold five or six families.

At last we stopped in front of one. It was on a dead end street. Something about it seemed strangely familiar.

"Are we going to go inside?" I finally asked.

"You don't recognize it?" Paula asked.

"It seems familiar...but..." I studied the house, but nothing was coming. Then it came in a flood. "This was our house!" I was a little embarrassed by the way my voice sounded kind of squeaky.

"Let's go look inside," Paula said, passing me as she made her way up the stairs.

"You guys go ahead," Jim said. "I want to check a few things. Since it does not look like they hit the houses, I want to see if there might be anything useful."

That was Jim Sagar in a nutshell. He could make an explosive device out of just about anything.

"Fine," Paula conceded, "but you be back to the rally point on time or I will have yur ass working in the kitchen when we get home."

I think that was probably the millionth time Jim had been threatened with kitchen duty since I've known him. Funny thing...he had never spent one single day in the kitchens that I am aware of.

I scurried past and threw open the door. It was the same...but different. I ran up the stairs and opened the door to the room that I knew had been mine. Once more, there was familiarity, but still a difference that made it seem just a bit foreign.

I went to the window and could see the empty field that opened up along the back fence of all the houses on this street. I heard the thump as Paula, Cynthia, and Jackson came in behind me.

"I used to hunt rabbits in that field," I said, my voice kind of a whisper as my mind flooded with memories.

"The house is empty, but nothing was taken," Jackson said. "The people, whoever they are, that did this...they did not loot the house. I say we spot check another ten or so to confirm it, and then hit the storage silos."

"Sounds like a good idea," Paula agreed. But my mind was elsewhere.

"Billy brought us here after everything went wrong somehow," I sighed. "We had left the cabin..." I turned to face the two women and the giant of a man, "...the one the council uses now up on Lookout Hill. Then everything went wrong and we ended up here. But the people here were not very friendly. They even tried to kill Billy at least once."

I only got little flashes. I had been so young back then; it was just too long ago to remember with any clarity.

"Let's go," Cynthia said with a soft smile.

I followed them out, taking one last look at the room before closing the door and heading down the hallway. We stepped out onto the porch just as a lone walker rounded the corner. It paused, head moving back and forth like it was looking for something. Then it saw us and started our way.

I don't think I even broke stride as I walked past and jammed my spike into its head. Spikes were one of the more popular field weapons these days. They were small and easy to wield. About a foot long, spikes are fashioned from old pieces of metal.

The blacksmith of Platypus Creek probably makes twenty or more a day. Some are personalized, some are inset with precious stones. One guy even had the ashes from his dog mixed in for whatever reason.

Mine? Mine is just plain metal. It is sort of gray, sort of blue. The handle is wrapped with leather strips that have formed grooves over time and fit my grip perfectly.

We moved through this huge residential area. I had heard that Island City had swollen to a population of over two thousand. It was almost impossible to accept that there could be that many living people in one area.

It had only been the past few years that Immunes had been allowed to stay here at Island City. There was some sort of taboo involved. People were almost afraid of them. It is strange, but the people who are best suited for surviving are the outcasts of society. At least that is the case here. I wonder if there is a place for them…a place they can feel normal—

"Up ahead!" Paula hissed.

My gaze focused and my eyes immediately tracked to a huge mess of twisted metal and burnt perimeter wall. Some sort of massive cart had been driven into the barricade. This looked much worse than where we had entered.

"This is obviously the main point of entry," Cynthia said as we moved in for a closer look.

I glanced around and could see five long warehouse buildings. All of them had their huge double doors open wide. I headed over, knowing what I would see before I looked in and confirmed that a good many of the floor-to-ceiling shelves were bare.

"They were really thorough," I called over my shoulder.

Looking back in the warehouse, you could actually make out the tracks from where they walked in and out as they stripped the place.

"Why would anybody do this?" I asked it out loud, and I was not surprised when silence was my answer. It did not make sense.

We were all making a walkthrough of the warehouse district. We knew what we would find, but it was still important to make the confirmation. We were two buildings away from being finished when a distant pop sounded, causing all of us to freeze and scan the sky.

"Bat Signal," Jackson pointed.

It was sort of an inside joke. I have no idea how it started, and I don't know what other folks call them, but we have caves full of bats not too far from Platypus Creek. One of the more unpleasant jobs is going to that cave and gathering the bat poop. Mixed with some other stuff and rolled into these tubes made from dried and pressed leaves, a slingshot can fire one in the air. On a field run, they are used as a distress beacon.

"Cynthia, you and Thalia head that way," Paula ordered as she pointed back towards the residential area that we had hopscotched through while confirming that the houses had been left mostly untouched. "Jackson and I will move west and then hook south once we reach the wall. Meet up at the wind farm."

A few of the turbine towers were still standing like the skeletal remains of some giant beast. Cynthia and I took off at an easy jog. We passed more than one body burn pile. I imagine they tried early on to deal with this epidemic in any way they could think might help.

There was an eerie silence that was unsettling; not as bad as that whole "being out in wide open spaces" thing, but it was starting to gnaw on my nerves. I was only briefly aware of how disappointing this run was turning out. I had expected to see and experience a large community. Instead, I was really just walking through a giant graveyard. This was not very exciting at all. I don't know what I'd been thinking.

"Stop!" Cynthia hissed, grabbing my arm and pulling me up short as I was about to jog out into an intersection.

I was instantly on alert and scolded myself for letting my mind drift during such an important time. I vowed not to let it happen again.

At least on this mission.

It took a few seconds, but then I felt more than heard what had caught Cynthia's attention. It was a low rumble that came in regular intervals. Only, it was just so completely foreign, I could not even give a guess as to what the source might be.

I did not have long to wait for that answer.

We made it to the ridge of a hill that overlooked what had once been a pretty cool park. We had a park at Platypus, but it was nothing like this one. There was this huge wooden structure that had a ship jutting from one end and a huge multi-colored series of odd shapes connected by tubes with bubble-shaped windows. This structure was larger than the apartment complex that I called home.

Just past the park was a two-lane dirt road. It was running parallel to a series of deep ditches and then the perimeter wall. From our little ridge, we could see the plains that stretched out until they reached the foothills and then the Blue Mountains.

"Did you know there was another community to the west of Island City?" I asked Cynthia.

"I heard that one had started up, but that was a couple of years ago and then I guess I just forgot when I never heard anything else."

I brought up my binoculars and took a better look. On the open fields were a row of war machines: catapults. There were twelve of them, and there was a team at each that had obviously drilled this evolution until it ran with clock-like precision.

Whump!

Whump!

Whump!

They fired in groups of four. The second time around, I counted. Five seconds between each group.

"That is a freakin' army!" Cynthia breathed.

I had to agree. That lady had made it seem like maybe just a few people might have been involved, but what we saw made me beg to differ. Granted…perhaps our idea of a lot of people, compared to that of the residents of Island City were likely to be at odds. For me, a few hundred people was a big number. There were easily a few hundred people in this so-called army.

"What do we do?" I asked.

"We hook up with Paula and the others and get back to the rally point," Cynthia replied. I had to admire how calm she sounded.

"But the Bat Signal," I reminded.

"It was just south of here, scan the area and see if you can locate them." Cynthia started down the hill. "If you can't find them in the next ten minutes or so, you make for the rally point. If nobody arrives within an hour, you start back for home."

"Wait!"

"Do what I said, Thalia." Cynthia's voice was firm, ending any questions or discussion on whatever concerns that I might have. Oh, and there were a few.

I watched as she made her way down the hill, having to hop every so often when it got really steep. She reached the bottom and looked back once. I had the strangest feeling that I would not ever see her again.

I brought my glasses up and started to scan the general area where we had noticed the Bat Signal coming from. It was difficult, because the entire time that I was doing that, the bombardment of that distant settlement continued.

I knew there were a few other settlements in the area, but other than Island City, I had been led to believe that they were all very small. Most were nowhere near the size of Platypus Creek. This one looked to actually be a bit larger than ours. Maybe it was because it was so spread out. These people had obviously taken the time to fence off a good amount of farmland and even a pasture where I'd seen horses and cows. Of course all of those animals had bolted to the farthest corner away from the bombardment.

I was feeling my anxiety start to spike. I was not seeing any signs of movement.

Time is a funny thing. When you are having fun, it zooms past and you wonder where it went. When you are scared or things are going bad, it just stops so that every single second is a spike of agony sent to force the body to burn through all of its adrenaline stores.

I waited for what could have been ten minutes, an hour, or twenty seconds. Honestly, I had no idea. A watch is a standard item on a patrol. My problem is that I hate wearing them. I don't like any type of jewelry, and that includes watches. Nobody had bothered to check since it is a relatively minor and unimportant part of gear. It's not like it is a spike or a blade.

I took one more look at the distant massing of people that were laying siege to that poor town. I have heard people say that perhaps we did not deserve to survive the zombie apocalypse as a species. It was times like this that I thought they might have a valid point.

I was about to turn and make my way to the rally point when something grabbed my attention. A detachment had broken off from the main body. It was coming our way!

"Crap!" I whispered.

"You got that right," a voice said from behind me, making me jump.

I spun to see a man standing about thirty feet away. He had a crossbow in his hands and it was leveled at me. I had binoculars in my hand; that gave him a distinct advantage. I shoved down my desire to say anything. One of the things Paula taught me about an encounter with a stranger while out in the field was to let them talk first. They would usually tip their hand as to whether they were hostile or friendly.

"And what would a little girl like you be doing out here all by herself?" the man asked. When he smiled, I could see that he was missing several teeth, and the ones that remained did not look like they would be hanging around much longer.

I let my binoculars fall, making it a point to keep my hands out from my body so he would not think that I was going for a weapon. I also kept my mouth shut. It was not looking like this guy was going to be of the friendly sort.

"And how about that other gal that was with you," the man pressed. "Where did she go and run off to?"

That was good and bad. The bad being that he obviously knew about Cynthia, the good was that he did *not* know about Paula or any of the others.

"You deaf, girly?" the man barked, jabbing my direction with his crossbow for emphasis.

"Nope." Just giving him that one word answer might buy me some time while I tried to figure out what to do about either escaping, or at least not getting shot. My hopes that this guy was not bad had evaporated.

"Then maybe you start answering some questions."

"I thought they were rhetorical."

"Ret...ree...what the hell are you talking about?"

Oh good. The dumb ones were always the most fun. "I did not realize you were actually wanting an answer. I just sort of figured you already knew and were just toying with me."

"Toying with you?" the man barked with an ugly laugh. "Why would I want to do something like that?"

I was almost certain that did not require an answer, so I just folded my arms across my stomach and stared at the guy. His face went a little bit slack for a second, and then his eyes grew wide.

"You think I'm one of them damn rapers!" the man gasped, taking a step back and actually lowering his weapon. "Then I reckon you ain't one of them cursed raiders." The man took a moment to shift his weapon in order to let it hang from the shoulder strap, and then wiped his right hand on his pants; not that it made much difference since his clothes were filthy. "My name is Ken Ross. Folks call me Cricket."

I guess the look on my face invited him to explain. He pursed his lips and made a chirping sound that was spot on as far as cricket impersonations go.

"My name is Thalia," I answered, deciding that we were possibly fighting for the same team if not exactly wearing the same uniform. (That was a saying that Billy used all the time when he referred to encountering friendlies out in the field.) "And I am not with that…army." I hiked my thumb over my shoulder.

"Talleeya?" Cricket squinted his eyes as he butchered the pronunciation of my name. "Can I just call ya Girly?"

I shrugged my shoulders. What did it matter?

"Just here to skim through the pickings, Girly?" Cricket made a distasteful grimace, but his eyes drifted over my shoulder at the distant thumping from another volley from the row of catapults. "Then give it a few days and you can sift through whatever is left of Rendezvous."

"Rendezvous? Is that the name of that little town?" I asked, keeping my eyes on this guy. Just as it was possible that I had judged this book by its cover and been wrong, he could still turn out to be trouble.

"Yeah…folks had themselves a really nice thing going, too. I guess it was a whole bunch of college kids from Oregon State University. They arrived about two years ago and set up camp. In less than a year, they had the best farms you ever did see." Cricket shook his head and whistled through his few remaining teeth. "Come out here to escape the Valley Strip. I guess it is still a war zone from Seattle all the way down the I-5 corridor, clear to the California Border. Seems kind of sad when you think about it."

I caught a hint of movement in the shadows of the trees just behind and to the left of Cricket. Give the man credit; for being so raggedy looking, he was very observant.

"If'n you are with Girly here…I would not be hasty to do anything foolish." The crossbow had swung up and into the man's hands in a flash. Then he gave me a nod indicating my own weapon. When I reached slowly, he gave the slightest of nods and I brought my crossbow up and to the ready. "And if'n you ain't, you got trouble since I don't think the little girl is likely to be an easy target."

Paula stepped from the shadows, her hands raised, but a blade in each. The man might have believed that he had the advantage, but I'd seen her throw those knives before. He was well within her range. And Jackson was nowhere to be seen, so odds had definitely shifted to favor me and mine.

"Did some tavern have a ladies' night?" Cricket grumbled.

"Are you kidding me?" Paula said in that way that is supposed to seem like she said it under her breath, but was obviously loud enough for me and Cricket to hear very clearly.

"I think he was a resident of Island City," I said, craning my neck just a bit so that Paula could see me more clearly.

"Was?" Cricket scrunched up his face in a way that would be funny if not for the seriousness of the situation. "Girly, I still live here no matter what them yay-hoos done to my home. And before you go askin' some fool question, I don't intend on leavin' this place. I was born and raised here…reckon I'll die here if it comes to it."

"Maybe you could fill us in on exactly what happened. We got a bit of a rundown from a poor couple, but I do not know how much accuracy can be given to what was said considering how sick they both were when we spoke." Paula made a show of bringing her arms wide and then tucking her blades away in their sheathes.

"Not much to tell." Cricket sighed and shrugged his shoulders, lowering his own weapon as he did. "Damn snake oil salesmen is what they were…and I told everybody just exactly that when they come here."

The man went on to relate pretty much the same story that we had already heard. There were a few more colorful details and descriptions, but mostly the same.

"Never did trust 'em, nope, surely did not. If I'm lyin' then I'ma dyin'." Cricket had fallen in with Paula and me as we walked back towards the rally point. "And soon as the whole community got sick, you just knew something even worse was around the corner. Ain't bad enough that we had to survive a damned zombie apocalypse…gangs of idiot raiders and ne'er-do-well soldiers that thunk we was easy pickin's just 'cuz we ain't city folk. Heard it said in a movie once…Country don't mean dumb."

"So you didn't get the shot?" Paula asked.

"Hell no!" Cricket made almost a crowing sound. "Never had one when I was growin' up. Damn skippy I wouldn't just let somebody stick a needle in me and pump God knows what in my body."

"But I heard it was mandatory," I spoke up.

"Sure...but it don't take much to get somebody to cross your name off'n a list. A few jars of this or that...some knives always need sharpening, and lots of folks don't want to take the time anymore. Folks is slippin' back to the old ways where laziness just kind of takes hold. If you can get somebody else to do it for ya...why bother doin' it your damn self. So, zip-zip, pretty as you please, and old Cricket is marked as having done took his place in line."

"So you aren't immune?" I asked.

"Don't know...ain't never been bit." Cricket shrugged his shoulders, but a frown put a dent in his smile. "Seen it happen too many times to count. And once folks knew that immunity might be possible, I think it made things even worse. That disappointment when the eyes changed and told the world you was gonna be one of them nasty creatures."

"A zombie," I said with a sigh.

"Ha!" Cricket laughed. "I got news for ya, Girly...a zombie is what them voodoo folks made poor people into down in the Caribbean islands. What we got here ain't zombies. They are flesh eaters...and the young'uns...well...they are something else altogether. But I won't never call 'em zombies no matter what other folks say."

"Can we argue semantics later?" Paula hissed.

We had come to the rally point. I was not surprised to see that we were the only ones to make it so far. The problem was that whoever fired that flare should definitely be here by now since we'd had to go all the way to the other side of Island City and then back.

"You waitin' on them other folks who come with you?" Cricket asked as he hopped up onto a barrel that sat in front of what looked like some sort of garden shop. There were flowers—all wilted by now since nobody had tended them in a while—as well as rows of empty box planters. From the smell, I had to guess that the barrels were all full of compost.

"Just how long have you been following us?" Paula asked.

"I weren't really following y'all. I saw you arrive and went to someplace where I could keep a good eye on you. When you split up, that was when I thought you might be a group sent by the folks that raided us. Seein' as how they had emptied out the warehouses but left all the homes and shops, I figured they was comin' back to finish the job."

"And you were just going to watch?" I asked.

"The odds were against me. But when you all split up, it gave me a chance to move in. Only…you went into a few houses and didn't take nothin' when you come out. That made me think you might just be from one of the smaller communities in the area. I know of at least ten smaller groups that come in and do business with us. You can bet your bippy that if I showed up and the place was empty, I sure as heck would have to take a look."

I shook my head. This guy was too weird.

"Paula!" It was Jackson, and he had the rest of the folks who had gone on perimeter search hot on his heels.

They came at a sprint, and that meant trouble. It was like, the closer they got, the drier my mouth became.

"We need to get the hell out of here," Jackson said, his massive chest heaving as he tried to get his air back. The others pulled up as well, but they were all bent at the waist, hands on knees as they tried to catch their breath.

"Tell me." It was amazing how calm Paula sounded. I had to fight to keep from dancing from one foot to the other.

"You saw the flare?" Shay asked.

"Yes, and we made for it immediately, but we missed you along the way somehow." Paula was curt and to the point.

"We had to retreat down to the river and follow it back," Shay explained. "That group laying siege to the town—"

"Rendezvous," I blurted. Everybody looked at me and I felt my face get warm. I swallowed and then explained. "The name of that settlement is Rendezvous. Apparently it is some group from the valley that came over to get away from all the violence

118

on the I-5 strip." I hated how sheepish I suddenly sounded.

"Yeah...well they probably regret that choice," Jackson said with a shake of his head. "They are being pounded. But this group is not like anything we have ever seen. I have done a lot of ranging and been to damn near every community in the Northwest. I have seen towns that were almost like the old days in how normal they were. Heck, Island City was heading that way..."

My mind was trying to process what was being said. Could there really be places bigger than Island City? It just did not seem possible.

"That group surrounding Rendezvous is only a small part of the main body," Jackson continued. "I am being conservative when I say that they have to number over ten thousand. They have a camp set up at the old airfield."

"How do you know all of this?" Paula asked.

"Because they left behind one of their wounded."

Jackson did not need to say anything else. Obviously he had made the person talk. The idea of what that had to entail made me shiver.

"We need to go," a familiar voice said. I looked over to see Jim Sagar jogging up. His backpack looked a lot fuller than when he'd left us. "There is movement in the valley to the south by the airfield. I think these people are flushing rabbits from the hole."

That was something I understood. Jim was basically saying that this group, for whatever reason, was stirring things up. Then, when people came to investigate, they were hunting them down.

"You sure you want to stay, Cricket?" I asked. I don't know why, but I just liked the weird old guy for some reason.

"Like I said, Girly," the man patted me on the shoulder and smiled, showing off the gaps where teeth should be, "this is my home. I didn't leave way back when things started. I sure ain't goin' anywhere now."

We started off and I felt something grip my arm. I turned to see Cricket holding out his left hand. When he opened it, I looked up at him and shook my head.

"I can't," I insisted.

"You can return it to me next time we see each other if'n you don't fancy it," the man said in a gentle voice that was at odds with his ragged appearance.

I accepted the token and then started to go. I paused and turned back to give the man a hug...but he was gone.

We headed for the foothills. Unlike our trip here, we left a guard on our trail. Jackson and Jim found a spot that they could see most of the valley from while the rest of us continued home. We were within a few hours of home when they caught up to us. I already knew part of what they would report.

"They put La Grande to the torch," Jim said. I could see a tightness in his face that was so very out of place. And if Jim was upset, Jackson was much worse.

"They made sure the fires were burning way out of control...then they retreated to the airfield. They were halfway out of the valley by the next sunrise. By my count, they put five other smaller communities besides La Grande to the torch as well." With each word, Jackson was like a stone rolling downhill. By the time he finished, his voice broke off in a sob that was as out of place on him as a frown on Jim Sagar.

"But they were definitely not headed our way," Jim concluded. "They were headed south."

The rest of the journey home was in silence. Everybody was lost in thought. I had to wonder if this was the state of shock that I had heard so much about when people described how society handled the first days and weeks of the zombies. No wonder everybody got wiped out. I was numb.

Vignettes LVII

"We follow what was once called Glenn Highway." George pointed out the visible gash in the land where a highway once existed.

The harsh conditions and weather of Alaska had practically pulverized the road, but it would be a long time before nature could completely reclaim the land. Juan wondered what things might look like in another ten years.

George was one of the five Athna Athabaskans that would be escorting them on the first leg of their journey. They would pass through three different tribal lands on their excursion, and at each exchange they would receive a new escort. The various tribes knew where to cross the numerous streams, creeks, and rivers that sliced through the Alaskan wilderness.

A few members of the Athna Athabaskan had come to the settlement to offer up any last minute items that might need to be traded for, as well as to offer a few letters for possible delivery in Anchorage. While there had been no sign of any deaders around where Juan and his people lived, that did not meant they were not a possibility. And it was not the human version that Juan had to worry about as much as it was the wolves.

There were stories of packs of the deader wolves travelling in great numbers along the highway like it was a watering hole in the African Savanna. Considering it was probably the only place where they might encounter the wandering humans with any regularity, Juan supposed that it made sense.

At last, they were on the move. Juan still marveled at the idea of being on horseback. He glanced over at Mackenzie who was driving the wagon. She seemed a natural as she gave a gentle tug one way or the other to keep the team on the main trail.

By the time they stopped to make camp that night, Juan was sore, tired, and just a bit on edge. The excitement of the trip had turned up the knob of energy when it came to Della. She quickly grew weary of watching Rufus drift in and out just as Juan grew tired of hearing about it every single time the dog closed its eyes.

With the fires going and the perimeter trip wires set, everybody settled down to a dinner of venison stew and hard bread. Juan and Keith finished first and then went over to study the maps with George. They were making good time, but as of tomorrow, they would be in true wilderness country. There would be no known settlement or single living soul for the next few days. That meant that they would need to be at their most vigilant.

They were taking note of how many stream crossings they would likely be making tomorrow when a scream pierced the air. Juan knew immediately what the cause would be and had his belt knife in hand before he had taken two steps.

Sprinting to his wagon, he heard a raspy growl that made the hairs on his arms stand up. Why hadn't he just taken care of this before they had left? He knew that Rufus would die any day now, and the large, shaggy animal had been bitten at least a dozen times over the years.

Della and Denita were both scrambling out of the wagon as Juan arrived. It was too dark to see if either had been nipped, but the two were huddled close; both were crying, but not in a way that led him to believe they might have been bitten by the dog.

Juan reached the tailgate of the wagon just as Rufus' large head poked out. The smell was almost as jarring as the sight of seeing his dog join the ranks of the undead. With one swift move, he brought his knife up and under the dog's chin. The blade only hung up for a second before plunging through and into the brain pan. Juan gave a twist and a jerk to ensure that he finished the big dog off.

Just that quick, it was over. He turned to the girls as Keith and George moved in to remove and dispose of the carcass. Mackenzie was already hugging them both. She met Juan's gaze and her expression froze him. He could not bring himself to consider what her expression meant.

Instantly he intensified his visual examination of the girls. He saw no signs of a bite or scratch. And while there was not an abundance of light, they were close enough to the fire that he should have seen something if either of his daughters had been injured.

He returned his gaze to Mackenzie and saw the first tears drip from her eyes and roll down her cheeks. A sensation like being punched in the gut came on so sudden and strong that it dropped the big man to his knees.

"No." It was only a single word. But Juan struggled to get it to slip past his lips. His mouth was so dry, and he was afraid that allowing anything past would make it easier for the roiling sickness in his belly to find an avenue of escape.

Mackenzie stood and stepped away from the girls as Keith and his wife Mercy came up at a run. They took in the scene, and then turned their attention to Juan. He saw the looks of pity and concern.

"Come with me, girls." Mercy was the first to act as she stepped forward and took Denita and Della by the hand.

Once she was gone, Juan hurried to Mackenzie. Sure enough, there was a small rip on her left arm. In fact, it looked like little more than a nasty scratch. How could something so minor be the cause of his undoing, the end of the dream that his life had become.

***

As she watched the small boat come closer, Gemma shivered. Not from the cold, but from the memories. She could not recall when things had spiraled so out of control. Of course, she had no idea that humanity had slipped so far from its perch.

She and Chaaya were just exiting from a set of flats where they had been searching for food when the three men emerged from the shadows. They had huge swords in their hands and their belts were decorated with a variety of knives and axes. What they wanted was abundantly clear.

Chaaya shot a look in Gemma's direction and the two women actually stepped forward, placing all they carried on the ground. Raising their hands in a sign of surrender, the pair allowed the men to paw and maul them. Gemma let her mind drift to a place only she could reach. In that place, Chaaya did not exist, the man atop her faded into nothing.

She went so deep into her mind that she had no idea how long Chaaya had been shaking her. She blinked and looked around. The men had moved over to the things they had been carrying. Some of it they were simply tossing aside when it did not strike any sort of interest.

Gemma sat up and the men warned her to stay put if she knew what was good for her. She simply pulled her clothes on and sat with her hands in her lap. One of the men stood up holding her pack in his hand and dumped all the contents on the ground. He laughed as the other two men hooted and cheered.

It was sudden and jarring when the laughter ceased. She looked up and saw one of the men peering closely at another. His mouth was open and he had his head tilted to one side. Pretty soon they were clustered together and each one checking the other.

At some point, one of the men spun on the two women. Unfortunately for them, they had become distracted and careless. Gemma and Chaaya had scooted away and ducked around the corner of the closest set of flats. As they ran, they could hear the men cursing and screaming. The threats came in a torrent.

The men did not know that the women were often less than fifty feet away at times as the pair stayed to watch their handiwork. That night, one of the men decided that he did not want to become one of the living dead. Gemma was less than twenty feet away when he blew his brains out.

The other two appeared to be made of stronger stuff. They fought it until the end. At last they reached a point where they collapsed and could no longer go on. They chose—whether by coincidence or on purpose, Gemma would never know—the exact same flat that they had been coming out of when the barbaric men had found them.

Gemma crept into the room the men had chosen as their death bed and stood inside the doorway for several minutes listening to the two sick individuals as they struggled for each rasping breath. Eventually, she entered the room. Walking up to the first bed, she looked down with her best smile.

She stood there the entire time while the man first condemned her to the pits of Hell, then begged for her to grant him one favor and kill him. Gemma was unmoved by either speech.

At some point, Chaaya left. Apparently she did not have the stomach for this sort of thing. Gemma waited until the very end. When the first man began to shudder violently, an odd thrilling sensation rippled through her. She waited until he was still and then grabbed the huge sword that was beside his bed.

When the man's eyes opened, Gemma brought the sword up and then plunged it down into the man's chest, effectively pinning him to the bed. She then walked over to the other man who was unconscious but still alive. Once more she waited, but as she did so, she picked up another sword that reminded her briefly of the one that Harold used to carry.

Again she waited, and again she used the weapon to pin the man like a butterfly on a collector's palette. Leaving the flat, Gemma entered the world to her new life. One where she would use herself as bait to lure men to their deaths.

At some point, she became known to survivors in the area as the Black Widow. She knew that Harold would have thought it to be really cool. She also knew that Vix would not have approved.

For years, Gemma was the zombie apocalypse's version of Typhoid Mary, spreading her disease whenever and wherever she could manage. She stopped seeing the possibility of innocence. To her, all of humanity was guilty. At night, she drifted off to a tumultuous sleep plagued by nightmares of Harold's final moments.

As the weeks turned to months that became years, her mind did her the "courtesy" of blanking out the despicable things that had been done to her by her captors. All she remembered was Harold. She remembered the violence of his death. She could no longer remember why she was doing what she did, but she felt vindicated and justified for some unknown reason.

She was wandering the ruins of a village when she came across the Irishman and three of her fellow countrymen. Only, one of them was a woman. The closer she got to the group, the more she recognized the woman.

She was still staring when the woman's head popped up and she looked around, obviously feeling that she was being watched. Her eyes scanned like a hawk's and came to a halt on Gemma.

Suddenly frightened, and no longer having the heart to do away with any of these people, Gemma turned and ran. She could hear Vix's voice calling after her, but she only ran faster,

A few days later, Gemma ventured back to the same area. She had no reason beyond curiosity. She was surprised to discover a series of red ribbons tied to all manner of things. Each one had a note that read exactly the same:

Gemma,

I will return in two weeks. If you read this, please meet me. If nothing else, I just want to be able to talk to you in person.

Vix

***

Chad held a finger to his lips. He pointed to Ronni and then the new girl Melody Whittaker, then he hiked his thumb over his shoulder back toward where the cabin would be located.

Ronni's face darkened a little, but she nodded in agreement. Chad then pointed to Caroline and then to a high hide they had mounted in a cluster of nearby pines that grew close together. That was actually a fallback spot for them in the event that a herd of zombies came through. The hide was stocked with plenty of food and water in large jugs that they had salvaged from the cabin campground down by the lake that these strangers were currently searching through.

Caroline gave a nod and then started her climb. Chad was glad that he had insisted on putting a bow along with over a thousand range arrows up there.

Once he was satisfied that everybody was where they should be, Chad began to move quietly down the hill. They were prepared for more than just zombies. Chad had already dealt with more than enough monsters of the living variety to not have a plan in place for just such an occasion.

Moving slowly, he could see an occasional figure weave through some of the heavy growth that would probably obscure that cabin campsite from the world forever within the next few years. Already, a lot of the small wooden structures were leaning or had already collapsed due to the regular deep and heavy snows coupled with absolutely no maintenance or upkeep.

A pair of individuals stepped out into a small clearing and Chad felt his lips press tight. He had mistakenly thought that this group of searchers was comprised of exclusively men. However, one of them had pulled her knit cap free to allow her blond hair to cascade down past her shoulders. He brought up his binoculars to confirm that it was not just a delicate featured male.

"Dammit," he breathed.

And not only was it a female, but, if he was being honest with himself, she was quite attractive. She had a perfect oval face and a slightly upturned nose that was flawless in its small size and defined form.

"Well…can't be helped," he muttered as he moved over beside a small piece of twine that was tied off to a stake just under the cover of a group of ferns.

Pulling his knife from his belt, he took one last look down into the cabin area. Luck seemed to be on his side as three others joined the two he had just spied. If he and Caroline had been correct, that was all of them in this group.

He gave a flick of the wrist, severing the taut strand of twine. There was a moment's pause, and then a tremendous clatter. He was able to bring up his binoculars just as the entire group rushed in the direction of the sound.

"Five...four...three...two...one." Chad reached down and picked up the triggering device that was here as well. There was a loud "whump" and then a muffled explosion. Screams followed, and Chad popped up and scurried down the hill.

He could already smell the burning flesh through the acrid and bitter scent of burning wood. As he rounded the corner, he pulled up short. For just a moment, he felt a sense of horror and revulsion at what he had done. A single example of his handiwork was just a few yards away as if to pierce his conscience just a bit more.

A man was on his back, staring up at the clear blue sky. A piece of metal was jutting from his chest and his body was charred black and smoldering. He was missing most of the left arm.

Drawing his sword, Chad hurried over and drove the tip through the man's lidless left eye socket. Knowing there was at least one other group, he knew he would have to act fast. He wove through the blast zone, until he found the main parts of the other four intruders. Main parts was the key since none of them had survived the blast without losing a limb or two.

Obviously the woman had been closest, because her body had been blown in half. Her upper torso was a good ten feet from her pelvis and left leg. The right leg was another several feet from the main part of the lower half.

A few years ago, Chad had come across a military convoy that had been what looked like victims of a roadblock ambush. It was impossible to tell what had happened, and perhaps the only reason they had found anything still useful was the fact that it was so far from anyplace, that looters had apparently just never stumbled across it.

There had been two metal cases. Inside had been twenty Claymore mines each. Chad had always kept them deployed whenever he and Ronni stayed someplace for any length of time.

When they had decided to call this new place home, he had made setting up perimeter traps his top priority, even over building their home. Besides acting as a nasty surprise should they have to deal with the living, they could also be used to distract or re-route a herd of zombies.

Chad had been thrilled to discover an intact propane tank. Unfortunately, he had no way to tap its resources for home use, but it had been a great place to attach a single Claymore. This had been his most elaborate trap. Inside the ruins of the cabin where the propane tank was located, he had nailed a sheet of tin on the floor a few inches off the ground. The twine he cut had allowed a bundle of river rocks to fall on the piece of tin. When the noise prompted whoever or whatever to check it out, he triggered the Claymore.

He had no idea how big the explosion would be—or if it would even work—but it seemed to have done the trick. He finished off running his sword through the head of each corpse just to be certain. He had just finished the last one when he heard shouts coming from back up the hill.

**

Jody crawled on his belly. Thankfully, clouds had come in overnight and completely blocked any ambient light from the moon. It had the added benefit of keeping it gloomy even as dawn was about to break.

The turrets were all set up the same. The ground was scorched earth for a good fifty yards all the way around. There was a deep trench in close that served as a moat, mostly for defense against zombies, and a metal fence with razor wire coils on top that circled around on both the inside and outside of the moat.

Some had said it was overkill, but those who chose to make

these turrets their residence certainly appreciated the added layers of security when herds made their appearance. Living beings were also supposed to be easy to defend against. And that was the main reason for the scorched earth idea.

Reaching the edge of the overgrowth, Jody halted and scanned the area. Whoever these people were that had taken over the turret, they were not even using torches. The place was completely dark. He could still smell the stink of the bonfire that had been used to burn the bodies, but even that had gone to ash and was not even giving off the slightest curl of smoke.

There was a dark silhouette where the cage still hung suspended. Jody could not tell if there was anybody in it or not. He had to remind himself to take things one step at a time.

He rose to a crouch and then gave a low hooting noise to signal that he was ready and in position. One by one, he heard others do the same. When he heard the eleventh and final one, he started forward in a crouch-run. Out of his peripheral vision, he could see the others moving with him.

They reached the outer wall that surrounded the moat. George pressed in and produced a set of heavy-duty bolt cutters. Like a hot knife through butter, the man sheared the chain that kept the door shut.

"Everybody ready?" Pitts whispered.

Jody glanced over to the left. They were closer now and he thought he could just make out a dark figure in the cage. There was no movement, but he was pretty sure that he could see what had to be a body.

Person, he reprimanded himself. *Danny is fine. Maybe a little worse for the wear, but he will be alive and well.*

They pulled the gate open slowly, every creak of the metal sounding like the roar of a jet engine to their hyper-sensitive hearing that each of them possessed at the moment as adrenaline course through them like currents of electricity.

That had been just one more feature. While minor, they had ensured that every door open out instead of in. That allowed them to reinforce the jamb just that much more to keep it from being forced in by the press of a swarm of undead.

As the team slipped in, Jody could feel some of those old familiar senses of his trying to come online. Having been a soldier, he had trained for things just such as this. He had never thought he would be putting these skills to use on American soil.

Lowering down into the moat would be easy. It was the eleven foot walls that came at a reverse angle that would be the hard part and take a few moments to navigate. However, within just a few ticks, all twelve members of the team were up and on the other side.

Jody glanced up, but the turret obscured the cage at this point. Jody cursed himself for not taking just a few seconds while he was in that moat to try and get a better look. The murky dawn was upon them. They could actually make out each other's faces at this point.

The second gate was handled the same as the first, and then they were at the main door to the turret. This is where things might get dicey. If the massive oak door was locked, they would have to risk trying to use grappling hooks to enter through the windows. That would be noisy and almost assure them of taking casualties if not losing the entire team outright.

When the door pulled open, Jody let out the breath that he had not been aware that he had been holding. The next inhale was one that brought him welcome relief.

They entered the main entry chamber. It was a huge open room. This would be where the meals were cooked, served, and eaten. There was a set of wooden stairs that went up to the second tier landing. This was typically the arsenal and storage area. The top floor would be more storage as well as the sleeping chambers. Each turret had four bedrooms and two larders. They were only accessible through trapdoor-style ports.

George took the lead once they fanned out to ensure the ground floor was empty. Reaching the top of the stairs, he held up his hand with a clenched fist, bringing the entire team to a sudden halt.

Jody watched the big man draw his knife and then take the last three steps that would put him on the next level. He instantly vanished in the darkness, but a second later, there was a muffled groan and a soft thump.

George returned to the stairs and waved everybody up. Here is where things would get sketchy.

The occupants, while obviously somewhat negligent in their security, had at least displayed the presence of mind to pull up the ladder that led to the top floor sleeping area. Other than hoisting somebody up and jimmying open that trapdoor, making a lot of noise in the process, there was nothing they could do other than wait.

***

Entry Twenty-five—Oasis reminds me of Mos Eisley from *Star Wars*. It is a crazy place. More than one of the scars I sport came from here. It is not uncommon to see a fight in the streets. In fact, the people here step around them like you might do with a mud puddle.

When the caravan pulled in, I was not surprised that nothing was said about the "cargo" in the last wagon. People actually can sell themselves in Oasis. Seriously.

If you have never been, let me just say that you would do well to stay away from the gambling halls. Unlike the old days in places like Las Vegas where people were known to go into pawn shops and hand over wedding rings and other things in order to return to the tables to "just break even" or any of the other self-deceptive excuses they would use, the currency in Oasis has been known to include one's person.

Darwin Goodkind's gang is obviously in to resupply and search for anything "exotic" that they can bring out to the settlements that can be found. Most of the smaller communes that exist these days are typically self-sufficient. They trade with each other for some things. And when trading caravans like this one roll through, they can grab that odd or difficult-to-find item.

Traders are part of the landscape today. Like the snake oil salesmen of old, most of them are seedy and out to dupe the unsuspecting rubes they encounter along the way. They would actually embarrass the used car salesmen of old with not only their tactics, but in the way they strip people of anything valuable for something that seldom lives up to the promises made.

That is also why these traders have such short life expectancies. These days, folks ain't shy about chasing down a bad trader and having a good old-fashioned lynching. One town had a zombie in a cage hanging right above the entry gates. The zombie was under a sign that read: *The last trader to deal dirty with our town!*

Anyway, I have come up with a plan. Now to see if it will work.

Entry Twenty-six—Perfect.

That is really the best way to describe how things went off for me today. And now there are seven.

I only wish that the caravan was staying a little longer. I would have them handled in a matter of a few days even with the fact that they would probably become suspicious and maybe even a bit concerned.

What I do know from the one that I was actually able to question before I slit his throat is that Darwin Goodkind is really the guy's name (as far as they know) and that he hires on people through a third party that gives referrals. (That might be my next job once I deal with this piece of trash—find the person who runs a referral service for human trafficking.)

They do ride the normal trade routes, but they do not travel on a schedule. That supposedly prevents them from being tracked and taken down or robbed of their "goods." There is always a compliment of four mercs on the team. These guys are nothing but muscle and don't take part in the actual acquisition or trade, but they are granted liberties with any of the "cargo" they choose in addition to being well paid.

I guess Darwin will be looking to hire a new pair of mercs before he leaves Oasis, but that should not be a problem. This place is crawling with mercs, bounty hunters, and traders packing some of the most expensive and hard-to-find goods. I think a better name for this town would be either Sodom or Gomorrah. It is a den of iniquity beyond compare.

I really want to save Darwin for last, but I also know now that I will take him down if the opportunity arises. Sure, somebody else will just pour into that crack and fill it when he is wiped out, but that is why I will never be out of work.

Entry Twenty-seven—Back out into the wilds.

I was not surprised that the caravan had two new mercs by the end of the same day that their other two no-showed after what was supposed to be just a night out on the town to unwind. This guy runs his show tight.

I am now almost certain that I will never be able to take this bastard down out here. It will have to be when he rolls into a town or commune.

The weather is turning bad, so maybe I will get a chance in the next night or two. Heavy rain started falling early this afternoon. I am under a massive rock overhang just on the other side of a hill from the place where the wagons have stopped for the night. No perimeter barrels tonight; the rain is just coming down too hard. Not even a campfire.

I actually considered making an attempt tonight. I managed to creep within about a hundred feet of the camp when I got my first nasty surprise.

Crybaby zombies.

I would have to guess, but I think they had at least ten chained up at seemingly random intervals around the tightly clustered camp. Bastards almost seem to be able to see in the dark. A lot of people say that zombies are drawn to heat and sound. Some say that a zombie does not so much see in the dark as they sense your heat signature. I know it is just a bunch of guessing, but I do know I never even actually saw the crybaby that sounded the alarm when I got close. I also know that men popped out of those wagons in a big hurry and searched for at least an hour until they gave up.

Entry Twenty-eight—Well, at least now I know. They keep the crybabies strapped to the underside of the wagons. I guess that is as good of a place as any. It's not like they have to worry about dinging or damaging the meat sacks.

Seriously, that bothered me all night. I could not figure out where they had been keeping the crybabies. But it also shows me that this Darwin Goodkind has been at this for a while. He has contingencies that I would never have thought of when it comes to security.

I will need to be careful.

Dead: Reclamation

9

A Place A Geek Would Call Home

"Who sent you?" Kevin asked, his eyes locked on Darlene's. "You get one chance to answer, and then I am going to cut you just enough."

He did not need to explain the rest. Anybody alive today knew full well that the blood of a living infected person was just as capable of transmitting the zombie condition as a bite. Perhaps that was the reason behind these people's hatred for those who showed immunity.

However, that sword cut both ways, as was obviously the case with the people of Rock Ridge. If the rumors were true, they were about to embark on the modern day version of biological terrorism. They were going to contaminate the food or water supply of the other two settlements, and then gather all those who survived and try to create some sort of all-immune society. In that way, they were no better than these people that had come to exterminate those who did not turn.

All of this was simply the surface of the issue as far as Kevin was concerned. He wanted to know who was spreading the rumors; and who had found these extremists and notified them of the folks at Rock Ridge. This could all be a propaganda war. People had stopped being afraid of the zombies. Nowadays, it was actually more common to be afraid of the living.

If there was ever going to be any chance for humanity to survive, then they would have to start coming together. It really was that simple.

Darlene's lip trembled and she looked up at Kevin, her eyes glistening with tears. "We were sent by our commander...our leader."

"Okay, and where did you come from? Where is your camp."

Darlene's eyes hardened. "Go ahead...kill me. I ain't lettin' you folks go and wipe out my friends. So if you're gonna do this, then let's just get it done."

Kevin was at a loss. He had no idea what could have turned her so quickly. He felt her slipping away and needed to try and pull her back. "I don't want to kill anybody. In fact, here is a deal for you to consider."

He took a deep breath, not sure if this was the right way to go about things, but for some reason, somewhere along the way, he had decided that he wanted to call this place home. He and Catie could start their life here. If that was going to happen, he needed to pave a safe road for them. He knew there was no such thing as perfect these days; hell, there was no such thing *before* the zombies.

But if he was going to call this home, then he needed to eliminate what he considered to be the biggest threat. The plan was still forming in his head, and he knew that those sorts of on-the-fly things often went haywire, but he had to act if he was going to stay here and try to start a family.

"You and I will go to your people alone. Let me talk to them under a banner of peace." He knew that it was a half-cocked idea, but he was confident in his ability to reason with whoever these people might be.

"Your friends will just follow, and then they will poison us or do something else that turns everybody who ain't like you freaks into one of them dang zombies." Darlene shook her head.

Just then, the door flew open. "Kevin Dreon, you will do no such thing!" Catie was dragging Clint and another man behind her.

Clint made the mistake of getting behind Catie and trying to wrap his arms around her waist. She threw an elbow that caught the man in the face. A crunch and yelp of pain sounded and Clint fell back holding his hands to his nose as blood trickled through his fingers.

"Catie, calm down," Kevin said, turning and grabbing her by the shoulders.

"You aren't just going to hand yourself over to some group of whackos that are bent on killing anybody who is immune. Have you learned nothing over the years or from your stupid books and movies?" Catie was sobbing now, and her voice was strangled as she tried to make her point. "Religious fanatics are not ever going to listen to you as you attempt to reason with them. Their brains are fried."

"Let me ask you something," Kevin said, his voice calm and relaxed in stark contrast to Catie's. "You felt it the moment that we got here, didn't you? This is the place for us. This is where we can make our home and start our life."

"We can find someplace else," Catie insisted.

"And what will we find? Worse? This is it. You know it and you feel it. I need you to trust me."

"I trust you with my life, you idiot." Catie scrubbed at her face and then glared. "It is everybody else in the world that I don't trust any farther than I can throw."

"But if I can do this…" Kevin felt the wind leaving his sails. He could not explain why he was so suddenly enamored with this place. The truth was, he just felt it inside where it counted.

"Then I go with you." Catie folded her arms across her body and fixed Kevin with a stare that made it clear there would be no bargaining, discussion, or debate.

Kevin turned back to Darlene. "Take us to your people. Let me talk to them. I give you my word that I will release you to them no matter what. I simply want to speak to whoever is in charge. There must be a way that we can all coexist."

"I have to speak up," Clint bristled, barging farther into the already crowded room. "I really appreciate what you are trying to do—"

"If we do this, it is best for everybody." Kevin did not want to get into a long discussion; mostly because he had no idea why he felt so strongly about this place. For whatever reason, this was home.

"Y'all are crazy," Darlene said in a voice just loud enough to be heard.

"Maybe so, but there comes a time when a person has to choose to draw a line. I went through this once before. I won't do it again," Kevin insisted.

"But what is to stop another group and then another and another?" Cap had walked into the small room now, making it even more crowded and uncomfortable. "Wouldn't it be less dangerous to just find someplace safe...make a new home?"

"Until they find you again?" Catie scoffed.

Kevin turned to Darlene. "I only ask that you at least give me an idea of what I am walking into. How many of you are there?"

The woman chewed her bottom lip in thought for a moment. Eventually she looked up at Kevin. "Five...maybe six hundred."

An audible gasp escaped somebody, but Kevin remained calm. He turned to everybody and asked them to please leave once again. Catie crossed her arms and made a point of leaning against the wall. She returned his questioning look with a gesture of locking her lips, the rest filed out reluctantly. After the room was empty except for him, Catie, and Darlene, he sat back down.

"Can you tell me why?" Kevin asked, leaning back in his chair.

"Why what?"

"Why are you people so set on wiping out those who are immune?"

The woman sat for a moment, and after a long silence where Kevin was almost certain that she would not answer, Darlene spoke.

"It started a few years ago for us. We had a nice place just north of what used to be Parkersburg. We had the Ohio River on one side giving us all the water and fish we could ever want. It was really something to see. We even had lights after these really smart ladies came and helped build some sort of solar thing with all these panels and stuff. It was all going so nice."

Darlene closed her eyes and smiled. For the first time, Kevin could see a regular person sitting across from him, not an ignorant being that sought to kill what she did not understand.

"Folks started getting back to normal. Yeah, sometimes we lost somebody, but that was rare. Then this group of folks showed up. We let them in, they all seemed okay, and we didn't mind. The more the merrier. Plus, when you have a lot of people, some of the roving raiders tend to leave you alone."

Kevin almost laughed at the irony of her sentiment. However, she was starting to get on a roll, so he kept quiet, nodding for her to continue.

"One day, a few of our people got sick. They hadn't been out, and they was all in relations with folks who weren't infected. Everybody knew that you had to keep to your own, infected and not infected. That was why it was so strange. They turned and we had to put 'em down. Folks was really upset, then the kids got sick."

"The kids?" Kevin asked, unsure of what she meant exactly.

"Every single kid in the community…well, most of 'em. Of course a few turned out to be immune, or at least that was what we figured eventually."

"You are saying that these people came in and basically started poisoning you all for no reason?" Kevin asked with a hint of skepticism.

"That is what happened whether you believe me or not," Darlene shot back. "They would have gotten away with it to…"

"If not for those meddling kids," Catie quipped just loud enough for Kevin to hear. He shot her a dirty look and then returned his focus to Darlene.

"They didn't give any reason?" He leaned forward, his hands firmly planted on the table.

"They said that we was the weak link in humanity's chain or some such nonsense. They said that, for humans to have any chance of survival, the ones who could not withstand the sickness and then change into the walking dead needed to be eliminated." Darlene stared up defiantly, a tear welling up and then leaking from the corner of her eye. "I went through hell that first year…but I saved my boy. He was only three when his own daddy come in the door and tried to eat us. I beat him down with a frying pan and then ran. That year was…" Her voice trailed off and sobs began to wrack her body.

Kevin reached across the table to take the woman's hand with his but she threw herself back, eyes wide in terror. Kevin flushed as he realized he was still sporting an open and bleeding wound. Making a show of pulling the offending arm back, he patted her hand with the other.

"So you people basically flipped their idea and started hunting down those who were immune."

"It wasn't like that." Darlene shook her head, but Kevin could see the look of doubt in her expression.

"How is it any different?" Catie blurted. "You people are hunting and killing folks. In what world is that not exactly the same thing? If anything, you are worse."

"How so?" Darlene's voice changed to angry in an instant.

"You are taking the bible and perverting it so that you can give your cause some sort of holiness that it does not deserve. You are destroying the image of Christianity by becoming some sort of twisted stereotype. You all are no better than those old television evangelists that always seemed to be getting caught in seedy hotels with hookers that ended up in *Playboy* or *Penthouse* once the story broke."

Catie stalked around the table and stood over the woman. Kevin noticed that, even sitting, Darlene was almost as tall as Catie was standing, yet Catie seemed to tower above the woman at the moment, her anger seemingly adding to her appearance.

"Go ahead, mock our beliefs," Darlene shot back.

"Your beliefs!" Catie exploded. "Did you have these before? Or did they get instilled in you *after* that tragedy. Yes, I feel sorry for you and your people. What those others did was wrong, but for you to turn around and do the exact same thing? Where does it end? When there are none left among the living?"

There was a long silence. Finally, Darlene looked up at Catie. She made no effort to brush the tears that were now flowing freely from her eyes.

"My boy died...became one of those...those things. Not because he got bit, but because some people decided that he was not fit to survive. Do you have children?" Catie shook her head. "Then you wouldn't...no, you *couldn't* understand. They stole a part of me that will never be replaced. They did it based on no belief other than some sort of natural selection mumbo jumbo. Go ahead and see how you feel after that baby you are carrying comes into this world and relies on you to protect it."

"So you do it based on twisting the words in the bible to fit a belief that you know in your heart not to be true," Catie whispered. "I could actually respect you a lot more if you were just doing this for revenge. *That* I could understand."

"How far to your people?" Kevin asked, breaking the conversation up. "I would like to get you there as soon as possible."

"They will probably kill you." Darlene looked up at Kevin, and he could see that she was not trying to threaten, she was being perfectly honest.

"Well, maybe you can talk them out of it. Either way, this has to end. We can't keep doing this or there won't be anybody left." Kevin turned to the door, not surprised to find Clint and Cap waiting on the other side.

"You sure about this?" Cap asked.

Kevin looked at the man. Things had happened so quick that he really hadn't had the time to get a reading on the guy. It only took him a moment to realize that the man looked like a young John Travolta. He suddenly had the urge to ask the man to say, "I'm so confuuuuused."

"I want to stay here," Kevin admitted. "Something about this place makes me feel like I am home. That can't happen if we are at war."

"But you do realize there will always be another group," Clint spoke up. "That has been the way of things since we settled here. Fortunately, we have taken in enough folks that we are still here. Add in the other two...err...I guess one now. But add in the other communities and some of the outlying ones, and we have been able to fend for ourselves pretty well."

"That is all fine," Kevin gave a nod of his head, "but there comes a time for peace. I think that is in the bible also, right?" He turned to Catie for confirmation.

"Ecclesiastes," Catie confirmed. "There is a time for everything, and a season for every activity under the heavens: a time to be born and a time to die, a time to plant and a time to uproot, a time to kill and a time to heal, a time to tear down and a time to build, time to weep and a time to laugh, a time to mourn and a time to dance, a time to scatter stones and a time to gather them, a time to embrace and a time to refrain from embracing, a time to search and a time to give up, a time to keep and a time to throw away, a time to tear and a time to mend, a time to be silent and a time to speak, a time to love and a time to hate, a time for war and a time for peace."

"Wow," Kevin breathed. Catie blushed.

"I had to memorize a scripture verse each month in school," she admitted.

He suddenly realized that, with all their conversations and debates, the one thing they had never discussed was religious beliefs. He knew where he stood. He was not a believer in God, and he did not try to scrape his way along by saying that he believed in some "higher power" or some of the other nonsense that people used when they tried to skirt such an awkward conversation. He simply had no belief other than you were born and then died. In between, a bunch of stuff happened based on other stuff that you did or did not do to set things in motion. In a nutshell; life was random.

"I thought that was a song by The Byrds," Clint said, breaking the spell of the moment with a chuckle that died on his lips when Cap gave him an even darker glare than the one Darlene was shooting his way.

"It sort of was, that is actually why I initially picked that one. However, the teacher wouldn't let me sing it, so I got marked down." Catie admitted "Sort of like the alphabet." When curious glances shot her direction, she raised an eyebrow in return. "How often do you say the alphabet without sort of singsonging it the way you learned as a child?"

"Ever since that cop that failed me on a field sobriety test. Bastard told me I had to say it and not sing it to pass. Damned if I could do it," Clint admitted. Now it was everybody else's turn to laugh.

"Anyways," Kevin spoke up, trying to steer people back to the situation at hand. "If I am going to stay here, I need to deal with these people. I have a feeling that they will be coming back once their little band of riders does not return." He glanced at Darlene who nodded in confirmation.

Twenty minutes later, Kevin, Catie, and Darlene departed through the main gates of Falling Run. Once they were about ten minutes away, Kevin came to a halt. Reaching inside his leather coat, he produced a knife in its sheath.

"Here," he said as he handed Darlene the blade. "If we get separated for any reason, you shouldn't be without your weapon."

The woman looked at him with confusion. "What's to keep me from sticking you the moment that you turn your back?"

"Nothing," Kevin replied with a shrug. With that, he turned and resumed walking. A few seconds later, he heard Darlene rushing to catch up.

***

"Just beyond that bunch of trees you will probably be able to see it," Darlene said as the trio hiked up the gentle slope. "It is on the outskirts of what used to be Lexington."

"Kentucky?" Catie asked.

"West Virginia," Kevin and Darlene said in unison.

"The Virginia Military Institute was there along with another university that I can't recall." Kevin paused for just a moment to wipe his brow with his sleeve. The sun was directly overhead, having burned away much of the early morning clouds.

He didn't care what anybody else did, he refused to remove his leather jacket when they were out and about. He and Catie used to argue over it—Kevin insisting that she wear hers—but eventually he had given up.

"There is an island that looks like it used to be a big park," Darlene said. "That is where we have settled in."

Kevin had been surprised that Darlene's people were not mere nomads. From what he had learned, they had been happy and content in their last settlement before the incident. They had eventually moved because the painful memories were too great. Also, everybody was afraid to drink any of the water or eat any of the food.

For the past few years, they had tried one spot and then another. He had been surprised to learn that their reason for moving the past few years had stemmed from hostilities between other settlements. These people wanted much the same as he: a life of peace.

Despite Darlene's warnings, he felt that he had at least a small chance of reasoning with these people. He had also learned that their leader was a woman named Erin Crenshaw.

At last they reached the crest. In the distance, he could see the crumbling remains of Lexington, West Virginia. They would have to cross a lot of overgrown fields to reach their destination. He hated those the most because it was so easy for zombies to be hidden within. Many times over the years he had encountered zombies that had, at some point, wandered out into a field and apparently just stopped. Whatever had driven them obviously long since gone, it was as if they simply went into a sleep mode like a computer, waiting for a living person to come by and jiggle their mental mouse to put them back in motion.

"There is an old road to the south of us," Darlene offered.

Kevin was tempted, but the reality was that they were still venturing into enemy territory. It was possible that this Erin Crenshaw had a form of picket sentry in place around their position. He did not want to be captured and brought in as a prisoner. He wanted to walk in of his own free will and offer Darlene back as a show of good intention.

"We can cross to the north. See that mound?" Kevin pointed. "From there we should be able to see your camp. We can stop there for the evening and build a good fire. They should see it and hopefully send somebody to investigate."

"Does your mind always work like this?" Darlene asked.

"Yes," Catie answered before Kevin could say a word.

Kevin shrugged and they started down the slope. At the bottom was an expanse of high grass; just the sort of place Kevin hated. Fortunately, it was bisected by what had once been a major highway. They would have two such breaks as they made their way for the hill Kevin had pointed out.

It was not long into their journey through the high grass that they encountered the first zombie. Standing naked, its clothing long since deteriorated into nothing or simply ripped away over time, the zombie was as still as a scarecrow until the trio actually got to within a few feet. Its head turned, but the tendons and tissue had tightened to the point of that action being almost impossible. Instead, the zombie actually had to turn its entire body to face them.

It opened its mouth and something fluttered from it and vanished. Spiders scurried across it as webs were torn apart by the creature's movement. Catie moved in and spiked it in the forehead, ending a pitiful mewling sound; but seconds later, the grassy field was alive with echoes of the responses of other zombies.

"Damn," Kevin breathed.

"I told ya we coulda gone south to the road," Darlene whispered, unconsciously moving a step closer to Kevin.

"And be captured? No, that was not how I wanted to meet your people."

"Better than being eaten," Darlene quipped.

Kevin nodded agreement to her point, but he had no intention of being eaten. They would simply need to be at the ready from this point on. It was easy to get into a state of mind where you almost forgot about zombies. They were slowly gathering into larger and larger herds. The few singles out there seldom posed a threat...unless you were in a field where the growth was a foot or more above your head and so thick that you couldn't see more than five or so feet in front of you at any given time.

"Everybody stay close," Kevin said needlessly.

"I have our back," Catie announced, turning around and reaching back with one hand to hold on to Kevin for a guide.

Darlene drew her blade after casting a questioning glance at Kevin who simply nodded. They started to make their way through the tall grass. The biggest problem besides the lack of visibility was the fact that it was high summer and the grass was dry and starting to get crunchy. That, coupled with the newly "awakened" undead, and it was almost like back in the early days.

A zombie stumbled through the grass just ahead of them and Kevin drove his blade forward and through its head just as he heard Catie grunt as she swung her machete in a downward chop. With both of them engaged, Darlene had the perfect window of opportunity to make a run for it. She was considering just that when five more zombies emerged through the thick growth that surrounded them on all sides.

In an instant, she made her decision. With a low sweep of her left foot, she took the legs out from under the closest zombie, sending it tumbling into one of its brethren. Stepping forward, she twisted her wrist at the last second, driving the sharpened tip of the hilt of her big knife into the eye socket of the next zombie still standing. Snapping her wrist back, she twisted her arm out like an exaggerated gesture of a hitchhiker to plunge the blade into the temple of another.

She was freeing her weapon as Kevin swept past and dispatched the pair she had sent to the ground. A hand clasped her shoulder and Darlene turned to see a wispy haired zombie that brought to mind the Cryptkeeper from the old *Tales from the Crypt* television show. Its mouth was so close to her face that she wondered only briefly why she could not feel its breath on her cheek. Just then, a blade came down from behind it and split its skull.

"Zombies don't breathe," Darlene muttered.

"What?" Catie shot her a quizzical glance.

"Nothing...thanks," she quickly added.

The trio bunched up once again and picked up the pace. By now, moans and cries could be heard from all sides.

"I don't understand," Darlene huffed as they jogged along the uneven ground, each one trying his or her best not to turn an ankle. They had to keep Kevin's limping pace, but years of practice had made him pretty adept at moving with his prosthetic.

"Probably the remnants of a herd that passed through. They reached this spot and eventually slowed to a stop. With nothing to draw them, it is like they are on pause until something activates them again," Kevin explained.

"We've actually seen an entire herd parked in one spot on a huge open plain," Catie added. "Where was that again, Kevin?"

"Probably Wyoming," Kevin replied. "We were...oof!" His sentence was cut off as he tripped and landed hard on his stomach.

A creeper had snagged his foot and tripped him. He only had a second to be grateful that it was his good foot that got snagged. Had he caught on the zombie with his other foot, it might have unseated his prosthetic or even yanked it off. Even at his fastest, it took a few minutes to put it on and secure it, and that was time they did not have at the moment.

The creeper reached out with its claw-like hands, clutching at Kevin's sleeve and pulling his arm to its mouth for a bite. Darlene kicked it in the temple, causing the teeth to clack as they missed completely. The half-torso flipped over, leaving the thing momentarily helpless as it struggled to flip back onto its stomach. As its arms flailed, Catie moved in and chopped.

"Up ya go," Darlene grunted as she gave Kevin a hand up.

Once again, they were on the move. After a while, the moans faded behind them. At last, they reached the clearing where a highway had once cut through. While it was crumbling in many places and washed away in others, it was still relatively open ground.

They crossed and Kevin froze. The others were several steps ahead when they realized that he had come to a stop. Catie turned to see what had brought Kevin to a halt and her own eyes went wide.

"Mother of all that is holy," she breathed.

"What's the—" Darlene began, but the words stopped as

suddenly in her throat as Kevin had in this open clearing.

"That's one of the big ones," Kevin breathed.

"I've never seen so many," Darlene involuntarily took a step back. Despite the fact that this herd was a good mile or more away, it was still so large that it was impossible not to be overwhelmed by its sheer size.

"How does that happen?" Darlene asked, moving close to Kevin and Catie.

"Like a cartoon snowball rolling downhill," Kevin quipped. "But seriously, over time they just seem to have merged. One group joins another which joins another, and so on. Add in the noise they make…" He paused for effect.

The reason they probably hadn't noticed up to this point was that they were already hearing the moans of the zombies in that field. Couple that with basically running for their lives, and the mind can tune things out as it focuses on the simple act of survival. Now that they were in the clear, the distant low tones of a million moans seemed to vibrate in their skulls.

"They draw more and more of their kind over time until you have these massive super-herds. They are like a force of nature, leveling everything in their path and leaving a trail of destruction," Kevin finished, starting to walk again, urging his companions to join him.

"We have seen them flatten neighborhoods," Catie added as they hurried to cross the road and melt into the cover of the next field of high grass. Even if it was laced with zombies like the last one, that would be a blessing in comparison to what was headed in their general direction.

"Your community," Kevin said once they were well within the obscure and at least perceived safety of the grass. "Maybe we will have to push through to them. That herd is heading along the natural route created by the old highway. If your people are in Lexington—"

"But they are on an island," Darlene said, a hint of hopeful optimism leaking through.

"If they are where I think they are, it used to be called Jordan's Point Park. While it is technically an island, that one side is barely a ditch. While zombies have this thing about not just walking into water, the body might force the leading edge in. Before long they would be walking across the bodies of their fellow herd members like an unnatural bridge."

Darlene shuddered at the image this created. "But if my people know what you are..." She let that sentence die on the wind as the moan of a nearby zombie demanded their attention once more.

Unlike the last field, they were more alert, and thus, more prepared to deal with the situation. Kevin noted this as well and scolded himself for his previous carelessness as they crossed this field and emerged at the second road/divider.

To their right was the hill that he had originally wanted to head for and make camp. To the left, the framework of a small bridge could be seen in the distance. They were actually much closer to where Darlene's people had set up their new would-be home than he realized. That was made more apparent by the five individuals on horseback on obvious sentry duty at the head of the bridge.

"I guess we find out the hard way," Kevin sighed.

"Listen, just let me do the talking," Darlene blurted. "They don't know y'all is immune to the bite. You should be safe at least for a while. And since you aren't asking to join our people, there won't be any need for an exam."

Kevin did not like leaving his fate in somebody else's hands; especially somebody that he had been at odds with so recently. Sure, they had worked well together thus far, but how much of that was by necessity, he had no way of knowing.

"We don't have much choice at this point," Catie hissed, not moving her lips as she spoke.

Knowing what was coming just around the bend, it actually seemed to take forever for the riders to reach them. Kevin noticed that two of the riders hung back and allowed the other three to approach.

"That you, Darlene?" one of the men called as they got closer.

"Yep," she answered, stepping forward.

"Where's the rest of the group?" the same man asked. The other two were studying Kevin and Catie much like they might something that they stepped in.

"It didn't go well," Darlene said with a shake of her head.

"But we saw the smoke. Y'all lit that place up, right?"

"Oh yeah, we did what we were s'pposed to, but then we run into some of the folks from the other communities we was told about. Seems that the three settlements act like one if they come under attack."

"And these two?" The man pointed to Catie and Kevin.

Kevin held his breath. Now was the moment of truth. Either she would help get them to this Erin Crenshaw, or else she would turn on them and the fight would probably be short and unfavorable for him and Catie.

"These two helped get me home," Darlene said. Kevin felt his body relax somewhat. At least until she spoke again, "Which is pretty good considering they is both immune."

"Damn," Catie hissed, drawing her blade. Unfortunately, the three men on horseback all had crossbows, which they brought up to the ready. One of the two hanging back turned and spurred his horse for home, the other had his bow drawn and an arrow at the ready in an instant.

"Wait!" Darlene yelled. "They come in peace and want to talk to Erin."

The men exchanged knowing looks that Kevin did not like in the slightest. Perhaps they would do better to try their luck here and now, die quickly, and be done with it. The expressions on these men's faces told him clear enough that talking to this Erin Crenshaw might not go well.

"Also," Darlene's voice became even louder despite the fact that nobody was really saying anything, "there is the biggest herd that I have ever seen in my life coming right for us."

"So we just blow the bridge," one of the men said with a shrug while still training his crossbow at first Kevin, then Catie, as if he was doing a mental "eenie-meanie-miney-mo" to decide which one he was going to shoot first.

"Too many," Darlene said, and then turned to Kevin. "Tell

'em what you said about how they would just push the leading edge forward and walk over the ones that fell into the water."

Kevin raised his eyebrows at her and pressed his lips tight. If he was going to die, the last thing he would do is offer any help to these people.

"He wants to see the boss, huh?" the man who had done most of the talking said with a harsh smile. He shrugged and wheeled his horse around. "Well, I guess they brought you here alive. We can show them at least a little courtesy." He looked over his shoulder and winked at Kevin. "I'd be careful what I wished for, pal."

Kevin simply shrugged and pulled Catie beside him, taking her hand in his. They walked with a horse in front, one in back, and one to either side. Darlene walked beside the man leading the way and relayed most of what had happened to her group. Kevin did note that she left out certain details that might have cast him in a negative light.

Maybe there was hope after all.

10

Differences

"We made sure they were not coming this way," Paula repeated for probably the hundredth time.

The entire community was present for this huge meeting. I had not been allowed to go in and make any reports to the town council. Paula had told me that there was no need. We had all seen pretty much the same thing. But when she, Cynthia, Jackson, and Jim emerged, I could tell it had not gone well.

Two hours later, everybody was in the square. Even Melissa had left the apartment to be present. However, I think that had more to do with the fact that, when Stevie had greeted me upon arrival and I had refused to go home with him, he had run and told. I probably should have gone home at least to say I was back, but I had wanted to talk to Paula after she had finished with giving her report. And that is why I am now standing in a sea of people, still dressed in my field clothing, and thinking that we suddenly don't seem like all that many.

If I can smell me in all of this, I am pretty sure the folks closest are getting a real treat. It may just be my imagination, but I think I am being given a little more room than most.

"But why would they just raid the warehouses, and then burn Island City to the ground?" a voice bellowed. It was greeted by a chorus of approving shouts.

"I didn't stop them and ask."

Well, it seemed like Jim was a little bit closer to being back to normal. I would take that as a good sign.

"I realize that there are a lot of questions and concerns," Billy stepped forward and addressed the crowd. "Trust me when I say that I share them with you. However, as tragic as things might be for the folks of Island City, it would seem that we have been spared that terrible fate."

"And we are just going to leave it at that?" another voice yelled. I was pretty certain that it was Kayla Brockhouse.

"For the time being." Billy raised his hands as more shouts from the crowd started in earnest. "Folks, this meeting is over. Please…return to you homes or jobs. There will be a candlelight vigil for the poor souls of Island City and the other surrounding communities tomorrow night at dusk."

Slower than Stevie when he is told to go take a bath, the crowd began to disperse. I headed home with Melissa and Stevie. Surprisingly enough, there was no conversation at all on the way.

After a hot bath and some hearty stew that seemed to fill empty places that I had not even been aware existed, I went to my room and shut the door. I was tired, kind of sore—nobody tells you that your muscles do not take kindly to the strain of being out in the wild for a few days.

My eyes began to close, but I thought I heard a knock on the door just as I drifted off to sleep.

***

"Wow!" Stevie held the prize in his hand. He let the pendant drop and dangle at the end of the leather thong. He ducked his head inside it and then looked up at me with an expectant smile.

"It looks great," I said ruffling his hair. The pendant was a large piece of turquoise that looked sort of like a turtle.

"Where did you find it?" Stevie said with awe as he held the stone away from his chest so he could look down at it and admire it some more.

"Found it in Island City." Okay, that was only partially true. I had not actually found it; it was given to me by Cricket. I held on to a sliver of hope that the weird old man was okay.

"Thanks, sis," Stevie breathed as he gave me a hug and then hurried off to the gardens.

I always knew when he was feeling especially emotional. That was when he called me 'sis' instead of just Thalia or a host of other names that often did not bear repeating. We were as close as we could be considering the situation. The fact was that Stevie was the natural son of Melissa and Steve Hobart.

I had been Steve's daughter for the most part since the day he saved me and brought me along with him as he escaped the madness of those early days of the zombie apocalypse. When he died, Melissa seemed to be no more alive than the zombies. More than once, I went to stay with either Dr. Zahn or Sunshine when she broke down. During those times, it was like she just forgot that I was there. Stevie was her world. I didn't hold it against her...or him for that matter. It was simply the way things had always been for as long as I remember.

As far as I knew, Melissa had always been good to me for the most part. But when I got older, a few people let it slip that maybe she was not all there in the head. She had a history...

I only knew what I'd heard in stories since I was too young to really remember much. Also, so much happened in those first days that I doubt anybody really remembered things all that clearly.

Everybody except for Billy.

He seemed to be the one person who could tell you the most about how things went down those first few years. He used to tell me stories when I stayed over with him and Katrina some-times during those instances when Melissa would have her little breakdowns. Sometimes Stevie came with me, other times, only I was sent away.

Maybe that was why Stevie and I grew up so differently. Stevie was what I would call a caretaker. He took care of every-thing and everyone around him. I was a scrapper. I still remember the day that I was picked up from school. I had gotten into a fight with another girl.

Kayla had called me an orphan. I wasn't an orphan. I had Melissa and Little Stevie as well as Billy and Katrina, Dr. Zahn, Sunshine and even Paula sometimes. That was five whole families to her stupid old one. At least that was what I was saying as I punched her in the face over and over.

Stevie climbed the fence and vanished. Why that kid didn't ever use the gate, I had no idea. I turned and started over to the cabin. Folks called it a lot of things. At one time in my life, I had called it home. It was a huge log cabin atop a hill that was surrounded by a deep moat.

I was just reaching the top of the hill when the door to the cabin opened and Billy stormed out. His face was red and his fists were clenched. A second later, Dorian Watkins exploded out the door as well.

Dorian was tall and skinny. He had a face that reminded me of a rat. It was kind of squished at the cheeks and he had a pointy nose that looked like he could poke your eye out if he ran into you. I guess that was where his unflattering nickname came from.

"Screw you, Dicknose!" Billy snapped, spinning on his heel so fast that Dorian actually scuttled back a few steps.

"If we don't do it, somebody else will!" Dorian said in a voice that was just as pinched as some of his facial features.

"We have all we need. Our stores are fine. Sending anybody down there to pick through what may or may not be left is a pointless risk." Billy closed the distance between the two men and now towered over the much smaller man. The thing was, Dorian was not that much shorter. He was just so scrawny, and he carried himself in a sort of hunched over way that it made Billy seem even bigger by comparison.

"We are not that self-sustaining that we can afford to simply pass up this opportunity. When did we become too good to scavenge and salvage?"

"Since we built those ten greenhouses. Since we brought the wind turbines online. Since we completed that trench that circles the entire town. Since we completed the outer wall. Do you want me to continue?" Billy ticked off his points on his fingers until only the middle one was up. I knew what that meant, and I was actually impressed that Billy had the sense of mind in the midst of his anger to come up with exactly four very strong points so that he was left flipping Dorian the bird.

"Such a clever young man," Dorian said with a dismissive wave of his hand. He was obviously counting on the fact that Billy did not want to be put in the lockup.

"Here is an idea." Billy stepped up into Dorian's face so fast that I was willing to bet that the man peed at least a little. "Why don't you gather some of your little know-it-all buddies and *you* go down there?"

"The community can't—" Dorian began, but Billy cut him off with a loud snorting laugh that I am certain sprayed Dorian's face with a bit of spit. Probably not as much as the rat-faced jerk was trying to make it seem as he scrubbed at his face with both hands and flung them like gobs would go flying.

"Can't risk your mental capabilities?" Billy actually patted Dorian on the top of the head, making the man's face turn an ugly deep crimson. "Just like our supply situation, we have moved past the stage of such things being too much of a concern. I was here when this place was nothing but that log cabin that you guys have turned into some sort of make-believe White House where you seem to think that you are running things." Billy's voice got quiet, but I was still able to hear him. "You little brainiacs keep thinking that things revolve around your agenda, all the way up to the point where the walkers breach the walls and start ripping you apart."

I was afraid to say anything. I didn't want Billy to change his way of putting Dorian in his place because he thought that I might think less of him. And I didn't want Dorian to see me because he just plain old gave me the creeps.

"I have no idea how you pussies made it through that first year," Billy muttered as he turned and stormed off.

I ducked behind the corner post of the cabin's huge porch that wrapped around the entire front and a few feet around the corners on each side. I seem to remember a time when everybody that lived here could stand on that porch and carry on a conversation, but I might just be imagining things.

I waited a bit until I heard the door slam. As soon as I did, I took off after Billy. He was walking down along the huge moat, and I had to clear my throat twice to get his attention.

"Hey, cupcake," Billy said when he turned and saw me.

"Saw you having words with Dicknose," I said, trying to lighten the mood. It worked and Billy laughed.

"Nothing new there." Billy still smiled and gave his shoulders a shrug. "I swear...I really see no way that he and that band of geeks survived."

"So what was his deal this time?" I asked.

"He wants us to send another team down to Island City and the surrounding area to loot whatever is left."

I had heard Billy's argument against it, but I thought there was even more than just the risk factor. He knew as well as anybody that the teams were trained more in evasion that in actually taking on zombies. There was just no need any more to take that sort of risk.

"So what?" I finally said.

Billy's head snapped down to me and his eyes were wide. His mouth opened and he looked like he started to say something three or four times before his mouth finally figured out what to do.

"You were there, would you be okay with going back there?" he asked.

"If I drew the assignment," I said with a shrug.

"And you don't have any problem with it?"

"Why would I?"

Billy scrubbed at his stubbled head with both hands and let his breath out in a loud sigh. Then he looked at me and smiled weakly.

"I guess I am just being silly."

"How?" I asked honestly.

"I just thought we were past all that. I remember the days when we had to sneak in and out of houses to try and find each and every scrap of food. It always seemed so wrong...so disrespectful of the people who once called those places home. It always felt like stealing to me. I did it because we had to do what it took to survive. Only, things are pretty good here. I just don't see why we need to go and pick through the remains of the dead anymore."

I thought about his words. I guess I could see his point. The only problem that I had was that he grew up in a world that I could not relate to or fully understand. He had told me about things like movies, video games, and this thing called the Olympics where people from all over the world would come and run races and stuff. Some of the events sounded kind of weird. But the even weirder part was that people would stop everything and watch these events, and all the countries made a big deal about whose athletes won more.

He talked about being able to speak to somebody by just pushing a few buttons on a little device smaller than my fire starting kit. And you could actually talk live with somebody on the other side of the world right then and there if you just pushed a few buttons.

I'd seen cars and that sort of thing for myself now that I had made a field run. It just did not seem possible, but I had seen the proof for myself. And then there was the whole thing about flying!

"So let me and Paula make the run," I said. Billy opened his mouth, but I was too fast and kept talking. "We make the trip, use it as a chance to just scout the area and search for any possible survivors. We come back and say that there was nothing salvageable. It ain't like Dicknose is gonna go check for himself...and he sure won't argue with Paula."

"How old are you, Thalia?" Billy asked.

He knew darn good and well how old I was. "Gonna be sixteen in a few weeks."

"Jesus," he breathed. "Has it really been that long?"

I decided to keep my mouth shut. It was obvious that Billy was going somewhere with his thoughts. I could not help but be curious to see where it would lead.

"I was about your age when all of this started. Maybe just a little older, but not by much." He let out one of the saddest sigh that I think I have ever heard in my life. "Hell, when I was your age," he paused and looked at me with a smile that I had not seen on his face in a long time. "When I was your age, girls were not like you."

He paused again, but this time I saw him frown. He shook his head slightly and took three tries before he actually spoke again.

"Girls were interested in boys, malls, tweeting selfies, and Facebook." He made that statement like each of those things held some sort of deeper meaning.

I knew about boys, and sometimes they were even interesting. I had a few that I liked to go on walks with when they asked. I wasn't like Kayla, but I had at least kissed a few. As for malls, of course I had heard the stories. It still seemed so farfetched. At least it had until my field run. I could imitate a few birds, but I had never heard of a selfie, much less knew what it would sound like to tweet like one. As for Facebook…I had no idea what he was talking about.

"So are you gonna let me go on this or not?" I pressed when I realized that neither of us had said a word for at least ten minutes. In that time, we had managed to walk all the way around the moat and were at the bridge.

Billy stopped and turned to face me. He was all serious, so I made sure to put a lock on my mouth so I didn't say anything stupid that would mess things up.

"I am gonna do you one better." Billy shot a look over my shoulder. "But you have to promise me to do what I tell you and to follow my orders."

I nodded. *This was gonna be good*, I thought as I listened to Billy lay out his plan.

* * *

"So you are saying that it is okay for a fifteen-year-old girl to make this trip, but not you?" Billy leaned forward on the table with both hands.

Dorian Watkins had a good four feet of space between him and Billy, but it was apparently not enough. He leaned back in his chair, his own hands resting on the lip of the table like he was going to push himself back. He had certainly gone a few more shades of pale since this little impromptu meeting had begun.

"Are you certain that we can risk something like this?" Cynthia asked.

"My p-p-point exactly." Dorian was now showing a bit of pink to highlight his already pale face. He already reminded me of the belly of a fish when he *wasn't* scared for his life. Right now he barely resembled the Dicknose we all knew and hated. I almost felt sorry for him.

"We risk you, a medical person," Billy countered. "We risk Paula, our most experienced hand-to-hand fighter. We risk Jim, our explosives expert. And we sent our newest and youngest boot camp graduate on that last run. Besides, since this request came from his desk, I think that perhaps Mr. Watkins should be on hand to prioritize the haul."

I was impressed. You could not even tell just a little bit that this had been rehearsed.

"I c-c-can provide you with a detailed list," Dorian stammered. He was actually wringing his hands. I could even imagine the clammy coating that I just knew I would feel if he were to touch me with those gross mitts of his.

"Things change in the field." Paula shook her head and pressed her lips tight. Her almond-shaped eyes held a glitter that I knew Dorian was missing. Of all of us, I thought she might actually be the one to give us away if she did not wipe that smirk off her face.

"I think it would be great to have somebody so smart to come along and tell us what we needed," I added when Billy shot me the slightest raised eyebrow.

I needed to be careful. I was having such a good time watching Dicknose squirm that I was forgetting my lines.

"Then it is settled." Billy slapped one hand on the table making Dorian jump. "I will submit this list to the gate unless anybody here can give me a good reason not to do so. Show of hands?"

One by one, the council gave its approval by raising his or her hand. Dorian "Dicknose" Watkins was going on a field run. I could not swear to it, but I thought I saw the tiniest hints of satisfaction creep into the corners of the mouths on more than one council member.

This one was going to be different than before. We would be hitching a pair of wagons. Wagons meant noise. Noise meant zombies. Also, if there were any bad people, they would hear us coming from a mile or more away when we entered the pass. Sound carried in those winding, narrow cuts through the mountains.

I rose to my feet with everybody else who had been in attendance at this little impromptu meeting. On the way out the door, I heard Dorian pleading his case, but I could tell that even he knew it was pointless.

I stepped outside and pulled my cap from my pocket. I was going to need to get my hair trimmed before we left. It was not all fitting under my hat. Maybe Stevie could take care of it if he would tear himself away from the gardens for a few minutes.

I turned that direction when a voice called my name. I bit my tongue to keep my mouth shut. What in the world was Kayla doing here? And even more important; why was she carrying a field pack?

I watched the girl jog to where I stood. She had to be more oblivious than I imagined if she did not see the look of annoyance plastered on my face that I would absolutely not make an effort to conceal.

"Thanks," Kayla gulped as she struggled to catch her breath.

Okay, so I had been at the tip of one of the entry berms and made no effort to go down and meet her. Those berms are awful steep, and with a full field pack, I imagine they were difficult to climb. Maybe her weight in front helped offset the pack, but it sure didn't look that way when she almost toppled over backwards twice.

"What do you want, Kayla?" I finally asked.

Kayla was still bent at the waist with her hands on her knees, taking in great gulps of air. I had things to do, so she could either get to whatever it was that made her actually speak to me in public without it being some sort of nasty remark about confusing me for a boy, or I was going to go about my business.

"You are going back out." Kayla stood and brushed the hair from her eyes.

The straps of her field pack squashed her boobs together so that they were jutting out from her in a way that made me want to poke them with my knife and see if they would deflate. It was only made worse by the fact that her shirt was a few inches above her belt line, exposing her tanned and well-toned tummy with its perfect little belly button.

"Yeah," I said with a shrug, turning to go find Stevie.

"You are bringing a full foraging team."

So far she was not telling me anything that I didn't know. Yeah, I knew what she wanted, but I was going to have the satisfaction of making her ask me out loud so that I could tell her "no."

"That's what they told me."

I could hear her grunting a little as I started my hike up the switchback trail that led to the massive garden where I would find Stevie. I waded through a few low-lying branches that were just about shoulder height, making no effort to keep them from whipping back into place after I passed.

"You gotta tell Mr. Haynes to assign me to this run."

"I *gotta*?" I spun to face Kayla. She came to a stop suddenly and actually staggered back a step. "I don't *gotta* do anything!"

Her face was as smooth as a doll's for just a fraction of a second before the façade shattered. I was ready for her to yell at me. I was ready for her to belittle me and shift into her bullying tactics. I was ready for anything except what I got.

Tears.

Seriously? She was crying?

"What the…" I started, but my voice tripped up on the way out and I stood there with my mouth open and a stupid expression on my face. I was beyond confused.

165

"Nobody takes me seriously," Kayla managed through a sob that caused her to shudder. "They think I am some big joke. You don't think I have heard the cracks about how I would only be good for a river trip where my boobs could be used as flotation devices?"

Actually, I had probably started that one.

"You are like every field runner's wet dream," Kayla said with a sniff. She could have said it to sound snotty, but it actually sounded like she was envious. Of me? "You are the youngest person to graduate Paula's hand-to-hand school, you have been on a field run, and now you are going right back out. Please," her voice cracked, "please tell them to add me to the team."

"Kayla," I started, but that sense of smug satisfaction was gone, "I don't think I have that kind of pull."

"If you ask, tell them that you want me on the team, I just know they will listen. I will do anything you say, I swear. " She was actually begging.

A thought hit me, and I could not stop the words that came out of my mouth. "Do you have any idea what is out there? And you are nowhere near the regs with that long hair of yours. No hot showers, no warm beds. It ain't your kind of thing."

I turned to walk away. A hand grabbed my shoulder and spun me around. A part of my mind was actually impressed. I did not think she had that much strength. However, the majority of me was finally able to enjoy some righteous indignation.

"I can do this!" Kayla insisted.

I was about to rip her a new one and tell her that if she ever touched me again that she would pull back a bloody stump. The only thing that stopped me was the great big knife in her hand. Before I could say anything, she grabbed her braid and sawed it off, flinging it to the ground.

"I'll shave it all off if that is what it takes!" Kayla wailed, tears streaming down her face.

"You're crazy," I whispered.

"Please, Thalia." Kayla sniffed and grabbed my hands in hers. She looked me in the eyes and suddenly I didn't feel so righteous.

"I will ask."

Kayla's arms went wide and then wrapped around me. It took me a few heartbeats before I realized that I was just standing there like a doofus. Slowly, I brought my own arms up and hugged her back. That didn't necessarily mean we were going to be friends, but I was seeing a new side of Kayla. Maybe I was actually seeing the real person, not the version of her that I had built up in my head.

She had actual human feelings and emotions; who knew?

***

"Absolutely not." Billy shook his head without even looking up from behind his desk.

"Why not?" I pressed. "If this is *my* team like you say, then shouldn't I get some say in who comes?"

Billy looked up at me. His face was empty of anything that I could read. I had no idea if he was angry, annoyed, or simply curious. In any case, he was giving me all of his attention.

"I'm not an idiot," Billy said as he folded his hands in front of him on the desk like he was some sort of model student. The question was if he was studying me. And if he was, what did he see? "You and the Brockhouse girl have hated each other for as long as I can remember. And, in all honesty, she has barely squeaked past her field tests. She is not an asset. This mission is—"

"This mission is you rubbing Dorian's nose in it and giving him a long overdue kick in the ass," I interrupted.

"And that is what you want to do with Kayla?"

"Actually, no."

There had been something so real in Kayla's plea. By the time it was over, I had gone from despising every fiber of her being to feeling sorry for her. But now that I was standing here in front of Billy, pleading her case, I had to wonder what I was doing.

"You have been out there. You know very well what it is like and how fast things can change. And this run is perhaps more serious than I think we were giving credit. Going in to buildings is scary and dangerous business." Billy's eyes sort of clouded over and I could tell he was remembering.

"Everybody has to pull their weight." I knew it was risky, but I took the chance in parroting one of his mantras back to him.

The door flew open and Paula stormed in, interrupting everything. She shot me a look as she strode past and actually went around Billy's desk to get as close to in his face as she could; considering she was barely five feet tall and he was over six feet tall, it wasn't all that close. Good thing Billy was sitting.

"You can't be serious, Haynes!"

"About what?" Billy always amazed me at how calm he could be when things got nasty.

"Kayla Brockhouse?"

"What about her?"

"She is telling everybody that she is going on this operation."

"Actually, that has not been determined."

"Then let me help...no!" Paula spun to face me. "This is not a time to settle some petty score or grudge."

"Unless you are an adult?" I snapped back. "And just what are we doing with Dorian?"

"That is different," Paula insisted.

"Is it really?" I saw it in her eyes. I would not have to press this issue. Both she and Billy knew good and well what this run was about. It had nothing to do with scavenging. They were putting Dorian in his place.

"Thalia, I need you to step out for a moment," Billy said, finally breaking the silence. I could hear the seriousness in his tone and knew this was not really a request. He was being very grim.

I stepped outside and let the sun bathe me. Closing my eyes, I shut out the angry voices on the other side of the door. My mind was drifting when it suddenly grabbed hold of a memory.

I was at the entrance to an apartment complex. A woman was pulling me along when a zombie reached out from the bush-

es and grabbed her, pulling her to the ground. Two more clawed their way out of the thick bushes that looked black in the night. The woman was screaming for me to run...then she was just screaming.

I was helpless. The zombies looked like giants—I was just a little girl! I was terrified, but my feet refused to move. All I could do was stand there as the woman, my mother, was torn open. I saw dark clumps of her being ripped from inside her body.

I found my voice and screamed.

There was a bright light, and then a man appeared.

He was the only source of light in the darkness and seemed to glow brighter than the silver moon above. He took my hand and scooped me up. He carried me to a truck and put me inside with a gentleness that belied the horror of what was unfolding around us—

"Thalia!" Billy's voice snapped me out of the dream.

"Huh?" I shook my head to clear it, but that didn't do a thing for the lump in my throat and the tightness in my chest.

"Go tell Kayla to get her gear."

I started away, but Paula called after me. "She is your second. You two will be joined at the hip. This is all on you, Hobart."

Wow. I graduated to last name status. I knew from being around her so much that she reserved that as a show of equality. She saw me as one of the team. I was no longer her student. That made my stomach tingle.

I was one of the team!

Crap! That meant she would not be watching over my every move and jumping in to save my ass!

Yep, I was one of the team.

Dead: Reclamation

11

Vignettes LVIII

"What the hell were you thinking?" Juan snapped. He was kneeling in front of Mackenzie, losing the battle to keep the tears from his eyes.

They had been through so much, and to lose her this way felt wrong...unfair. But this had not been the first time that a dog had nearly cost him the woman that he loved beyond words. It was little consolation that she had been as adamant verbally as he had felt when it came to simply doing away with Rufus before they had started off on this journey.

"He almost got the girls." Mackenzie said those words like they should make him feel better.

That was the problem with a situation such as this one. The girls were fine. He could not mourn what *might* have happened. He could only feel the heart-rending pain of what *had* happened.

"Maybe we will get lucky," Mackenzie said with a forced laugh. "Maybe I will be one of the immune type."

Juan heard the lie in her voice. Worse still, the light of the fire was enough for him to see all he needed to see. He could almost swear that he was able to watch the tracers as they ran through the whites of her eyes. It had been minutes, but already she was demonstrating the first telltale symptom.

The Squiggles.

That is what they had come to be called; at least by Juan and those he knew. The best way to tell if a person was immune after a bite was to watch their eyes. The black traces in the capillaries usually became noticeable within the first several minutes.

Juan's expression gave away the truth. Mackenzie gasped, biting her lower lip to stop the cry from coming out. Tears now poured freely instead of the one or two that had fallen because of the physical pain.

"Oh, Juan—" And that was the best she could manage before her sobs overtook her and strangled her ability to speak.

Juan pulled her close and felt her sink into his chest. His mind told him to remember every detail about how she felt. He would need those memories in order to continue.

That idea struck him, and it was actually several seconds before he could break it down and truly understand it. The idea of continuing without her did not seem possible. Yet, for some reason, he would have to do exactly that.

Why?

The girls!

That thought exploded in his mind as if it had been shouted in his ear. It took him another few seconds to realize that those very words had indeed just been spoken.

"You have to take care of our girls," Mackenzie said into his chest.

He could feel the warmth of her breath through his clothes. He wanted to absorb it and keep that exact place on his skin committed to memory. He knew that he was in shock…grasping at straws. But the truth was simply debilitating. Emotionally, it was unlike anything that he had ever experienced in his life.

"Mr. Hoya?"

It was George. Juan turned to the man, making no effort to wipe the tears from his face.

"The…animal has been disposed of away from camp so that the little ones will not have to see. Do you wish to remain here for a few days until…" The man's voice faded, and he cast his eyes down.

"We will continue on as normal."

Juan jerked back around to Mackenzie. She had pushed away from him enough to be able to see George.

"But—" Juan tried to protest, but she put a silencing finger to his lips.

"We will continue on. It does no good for anyone if we simply sit here and wait for me to die." Mackenzie actually pushed away from Juan and rose to her feet.

"Very well," George said.

The man glanced at Juan who gave a slight nod. He knew better than to try and dissuade the woman if she was set on something. Once George had walked away, Juan turned to her.

"Before you say one word," Mackenzie said, beating him to the punch, "I have my reasons." Juan folded his arms across his chest and nodded for her to explain. "If we just sit here, the girls are going to be a mess. If we are on the move, there will be ways to distract them. Also, it will give me time to take each one aside and talk to her. They are not like we were back when we turned seven. This is a different world."

"Different world or not, they are losing their mother!" Juan said through clenched teeth. "No amount of time riding with them in a wagon is going to make that any easier. Especially for Denita? Did you even take a second to think what this might do to her? Already the girl does not talk."

"Don't you think I know this will be hard on them...you." As she spoke that last word, she stepped into him and wrapped her arms around him, resting her cheek on his chest. "And this is not going to be all that easy on me either."

Juan felt his knees start to turn to water. How could he be so insensitive? She was the one dying! He squeezed her tight, wishing that he could swap places with her.

"The girls will be better off with you than they would have if the situation was reversed and you were the one dying," she whispered as if she had read his thoughts. "You are a fighter and a survivor, Juan Hoya. You got me through this and gave me a better life than I ever knew possible. You took care of me...and you will in the end. You will do what I would not have been able to do if the situation was reversed."

Juan wanted to argue, but he simply did not know how. He did the only thing he was certain that he could do at the moment and not screw things up worse; he held Mackenzie.

***

Gemma was nervous. Her hands kept smoothing her ragged and tattered clothing or trying to brush a non-existent strand of hair from her eyes on this windless afternoon. She knew without having to look at her reflection that she was an absolute fright.

Being alone all these years had allowed her to "let herself go" as the old saying used to put it. She had seen nothing resembling a razor in years, and while her blades were more than sharp enough, she felt no desire to continue a practice that had been pushed on society by those bloody Americans. As the boat came closer, she noticed Vix lean down and say something to the figure manning the oars. Whoever that person was, they were wearing a stocking cap pulled down tight and bundled up needlessly on what was a gorgeous day.

She considered running. After all, what did she have to say to this woman? Besides that, she still had her latest catch back in the treehouse that she called home.

She never ceased to be surprised at how easy it was to lure in and trap the human male. Even in her near-feral state, all she had to do was strip naked and splash around in a nearby creek or pond. The male passer-by could not resist…mostly.

There was a fair share that either ignored her completely, most likely writing her off as a loon. Some even warned her that her actions were unsafe. The few that offered to stand watch until she finished were usually given the option of receiving a "special" reward. She was always surprised at how many of them politely refused.

The boat was almost to her now. She had to fight the urge to run. Suddenly this felt like a bad idea. She was fine all by herself. She did not need Vix or civilization.

"Why am I here?" she whispered.

The slapping of the oars on the water began to sound like thunder. Her heart began to race and her breathing became shallow panting like she had just run all the way to London and back.

The urge to run became overwhelming. Only, her feet seemed planted to the spot she stood; like they were encased in concrete. At last, the boat came to a halt, the bottom grinding on the shore.

Vix was to her feet and hopping over the side before whoever had been rowing even managed to pull the oars in. She hurried up to Gemma and threw her arms around the younger girl in a huge hug. It took Gemma a moment before she returned the gesture, her arms coming up slowly and then making an awkward attempt at an embrace.

"I just can't believe it is you!" Vix exclaimed through the tears. "I was certain that you had met your end back at that fort along with Harold."

Gemma said nothing. She bit back the words she wanted to say. She would not say that she wished she *had* died that day. Instead, she had become England's Black Widow. She was a cautionary tale and a story to tell children at night if they wanted a scary story at bedtime.

"You are alone?" Vix looked past Gemma, but only briefly, giving away the fact that she already knew the answer to that question.

"How have you managed all this time by yourself?"

Again Gemma did not speak. That question was providing more information for her to consider. Somehow, she knew that Gemma had been alone this entire time.

"You can speak, can't you?" Vix whispered. "I mean, being alone all this time hasn't ruined your ability to talk, has it?"

A smile curved the corners of Gemma's mouth. But it was a smile that made Vix take a step back. It was almost evil in its appearance.

No, Gemma thought, *I speak when I need to. If I need information I get much more if I just stay quiet for a little while.* However, she felt that her silence had reached its tolerable level;

175

much more of it and she would possible wear out her welcome. Not that she was looking for any sort of welcome. She had been fine all by herself, thank you very much.

"I can speak," Gemma said in a harsh rasp. "I just don't find much time for it since I have been on my own."

"You must tell me everything," Vix said. A second later, her face flushed and she quickly added, "You can certainly omit the part about Harold."

"Actually, he plays a big part in my life," Gemma said cryptically. "But a question first."

"Ask it."

"How many people are across this river on that little island of yours?" Gemma folded her arms across her chest and set her feet just a little further apart to signal she would not budge easily.

"Close to a thousand," Vix answered. It made Gemma gasp audibly. "And there are six more island communities within a day or two from here. We all trade with each other and help each other out if the need arises."

Gemma considered it. A thousand people? The days of being able to even remotely imagine those numbers when it came to living populations were long gone.

"And I can leave..." Gemma ended her statement with a slight uptick in her voice to indicate that this was a very important matter.

"Whenever you want," Vix finished. "You would be coming as a guest, not as a prisoner."

Vix's smile grew wider when it became obvious that Gemma was going to at least let it be considered. Gemma seemed to hesitate, but at last she stepped toward the boat. When she climbed in, her heart skipped a beat.

"Chaaya?"

***

Moving as fast but as quietly as possible, Chad made his way back up the hill. He got down on his stomach when he reached the top and could hear actual voices. It seemed that the other group had come on the run when they heard the explosion.

"…smells like bad barbecue," one of the men was practically shouting.

"And if'n they got blown up by whatever the hell that was, it is a damn shame. But going down there is out of the question," a second voice said with unusual calm for the situation. "Somebody up this way pinned Renny to a tree with a half dozen arrows. If you go tearing around in these parts, I do believe that whoever has laid claim to this area will do the same or worse to you, Butch. And splitting up is absolutely out of the question."

"Bidwell is right," another voice agreed. Then she shouted, "Hey! Whoever is out there, we don't want no trouble. All we want is Melody Whittaker. Little gal with blond hair, blue eyes, and a nasty bite on her face? We are willing to overlook the members of our group that you have already murdered. Just return the girl."

Chad wasn't buying it for one second. He saw no rational reason why a group would be willing to just ignore the fact that at least six of their number was dead.

The sound of rustling brush alerted Chad. From his position, he could see just a bit of Caroline from her spot up in the hide. Had he not been watching, he doubted that he would have heard the slight thrum of the bowstring as it sent another arrow flying.

"Over there!" the voice belonging to the one Chad thought to be identified as Butch shouted. That yell was followed by the crash of somebody tearing off into the woods.

"Butch!" Bidwell called.

"Let him go," the woman said. "He is as good as dead. And we will be as well if we stay around here much more. Fall back."

Chad could hear them moving away, but then they stopped. There was a long moment of silence. Then, the woman called out once more. "We will go for now. But you should know that the girl you are risking your lives for is evil. She infected seven of our people."

Chad heard them resume their retreat, but he stayed put for a few minutes to be certain. Caroline had a better vantage point, so once he saw her start down, he came out from where he was hiding.

"So…" Chad let loose with a big sigh. It was never good when he had to kill the living. Sure, he had done so on more than one occasion—each time he had justified it as a necessary evil—but that did not make it any easier.

"We need to get back to the cabin," Caroline said, shouldering her bow and drawing the twin axes she carried on each hip. "Something does not fit here."

"You get that too, huh?"

"Why would they say she killed a bunch of their people and she say that they were trying to kill her because she was one of the damned or some such thing?"

"And then there is the bite on her face," Chad reminded. "It is definitely old enough to confirm that she is not going to turn, but something about that does not add up with everything else we got going on."

The two started off at a jog back up the hill to their cabin. The entire time, Chad's mind was humming with all the possibilities. The more he thought it over, the more it did not add up in his mind.

They were almost to the cabin when Caroline grabbed Chad's arm and yanked him back and down. Before he could protest, he spotted what Caroline had obviously seen first.

A man, presumably Butch, was creeping along the side of their cabin. He had a wicked curved blade in his hand. He had come to a halt, froze in place with his head cocked to one side as if he might be listening to something.

Caroline was already unslinging her bow. Chad watched with no small degree of amazement as she grabbed an arrow, nocked it, drawing her hand back to her cheek. Her eyes blinked slowly and she let out a long, slow breath.

Thrum-hiss.

And just that quick, the arrow was loosed. There was a yelp and Chad looked to see the man pinned to the side of their cabin with and arrow in the upper left part of his chest. It had not pinned him fast, probably due to the arrow losing some of its velocity because of the distance it travelled, so, when Butch fell to the ground on his knees, the arrow came free from the wood.

Leaping to his feet, Chad rushed the man. Already, Butch had reached up and yanked at the shaft to pull the arrow free. However, this was not a range arrow, and the shaft was barbed. The man quickly ceased his actions and threw his hands up begging for mercy.

"Y'all don't understand," Butch was saying through tears of pain or frustration, "that girl is not the innocent one here. She is evil."

He could hear Caroline coming up behind him; he could also hear voices in the cabin. Still, he had one thing in mind. Chad never slowed as he approached the man and kicked him square in the chin, sending the man flying backwards unconscious.

The door to the cabin flew open with a bang, but Chad was still focused on the man named Butch, ensuring that he was out cold.

"Dad! Watch out!" Ronni screamed.

***

They had been waiting for almost an hour. The team was getting a bit restless, and Jody was having to shift around quite a bit as parts of him would start to tingle. At one point, while he sat on his haunches, both of his feet began to fall asleep. When he shifted, he lost his balance and began to fall. Margarita was beside him and actually caught Jody before he fell, flashing a dirty look as he sheepishly re-shifted his weight once more.

An abrupt shifting and creak of boards from above made everybody suddenly freeze. Most of the team unconsciously held their breath as all heads craned up.

Muffled voices could be heard. Jody's hand went to the hilt of his saber. Another surge of adrenaline hit and his mouth went dry. He was having a hard time waiting here and doing nothing while Danny may or may not still be alive just a stone's throw away. He shook his head.

One thing at a time, he told himself. The reality was that this outpost was more important to the big picture. They had worked very hard to create a place to live that was as safe as possible. He had been surprised more than once at how often Pitts deferred to him when it came to matters of planning the set up and merge of their two communities.

The reality was that Pitts and his people could have wiped them off the face of the earth. Instead, they had come to terms. And while he had been more than dubious when it came to the idea of exchanging women between the two communities like they were little more than breeding stock, it turned out that Pitts had been on to something. Now, a decade later, these two communities were the equivalent of a global super power.

By that logic, they could have simply come at these invaders with all their military might and hit them with a frontal assault. However, these turrets were sort of designed to counter that possibility. Thus, they had chosen this stealthy approach.

Jody still could not believe that these people had been so careless. They had made no effort to place watches with the exception of the one man who had apparently fallen asleep at his post.

This got him to thinking; he had not been to one of the turrets in a few years. Had this been how his people were taken out? Had people gotten complacent? Perhaps he would address that issue once things settled down from this event. The military had been all about drilling and preparedness.

A sharp elbow to the ribs snapped him back to the situation at hand. Once again, it was Margarita who was glaring at him.

"I don't know what is wrong with you today, but get your head back in the game. If I die because you are spacing out, I am gonna be really pissed," Margarita whispered.

Jody felt his face become warm. She was right. Why was he having such a hard time staying focused? He knew very well that any distraction in a situation like this could send you to the grave in a hurry.

"How come Morton didn't wake us?" a female voice called from above.

"Lazy bastard probably fell asleep," another voice responded.

"Somebody go wake the lazy bastard," a third yawned. "We gotta get that damn Irishman to talk. I got a feeling there are some more people in this area."

Jody could not help but raise an eyebrow. So far, he had heard nothing but female voices. It dawned on him that he hadn't even taken the time to get a look at the person George had killed. The body was fifteen or twenty feet away and he had paid it no mind.

The trapdoor groaned and Jody tensed. The ladder dropped with a deafening thud and a pair of legs lowered.

"Morton, you lazy bitch, get the hell up. I need you to help me lower that cage so we can get that smart mouthed punk to spill either information or his guts," a woman's voice called.

She was halfway down when George rose. Jody was still amazed at how a man that size could move so silently. In two steps, he was at the side of the ladder. Like a cobra, he struck fast. One hand shot up and grabbed a handful of hair, yanking the woman's head back. His other hand came across just as quick as he slit the woman's throat. There was only a single, short gurgle of surprise, but the woman was dead before George laid her on the ground and started up the ladder after making a "let's go" gesture with his head.

Everybody fell in, Jody finding himself somewhere in the middle of the pack. They would have to hurry and count on the fact that these people were not yet armed if they were going to get through this with little or no loss of life from their team.

A scream came, followed by a roar as George obviously reached the top and charged into battle. The sounds of feet thudding on the floor overhead came from all directions.

When Jody emerged to join, he saw one woman already sprawled in a pool of blood just a few feet away. The doors to all the bedrooms were shut except for one. Margarita came up beside him and pointed to the closest door.

"Let's get 'em," Margarita stalked to the door with murderous intent.

Jody was right behind her when she kicked the door open. A chorus of screams came; again, Jody noted that they were all women. Following on her heels, Jody rushed in with his saber and threw it up just in time to block a machete that clanged with enough force to make his hands tingle.

He kicked out at the half-naked woman that was coming at him with her teeth barred in angry determination. Something collided with his side and Jody found himself on the ground staring up at a woman who had a machete dripping with blood in her hands. She held it with both hands and raised it for the killing blow.

***

Entry Thirty-seven—Scratch one more.

Today was another good day for me. Besides the fact that I was able to slip away for a couple of days and drop a deer that should keep me fed for another week or so, I was also able to trade what I could not use with an elderly man that paid me with dried fish and some apples, potatoes, and onions that almost made me cry *before* I cut them.

You gotta appreciate the small things.

The caravan just slipped into one of those small communities that looks like it holds less than fifty people. Since I know they will stay for at least a day or two, I felt okay with slipping away.

I returned to find them still inside the walls of the tiny village, so I was setting up camp. I was not really doing much except for basking in a mild day and nibbling some dried fish when I saw somebody slip over the wall.

At first I thought it might be a citizen of the community. However, being curious, I moved in to just get a closer look. I was being careless and only had my belt knife with me.

The thing is, I have been stalking these guys for a while, so I know what they look like. By the time I recognized this as one of Darwin's people, it was too late, I was too close to the guy to go back and grab my favorite hand-to-hand weapon: a toma-hawk.

A few years ago I did a job for this great group of Native American folks. They paid me with some sturdy bearskins and oiled leathers that actually keep me pretty dry as long as I re-member to grease them every month or so. Sure...they reek like you would not believe, but dry and stinky beats wet and misera-ble.

Besides the killer clothes, they also gave me this honest-to-goodness tomahawk. I actually stayed a few weeks extra to learn how to throw it. I got pretty good by the time we parted ways. However, that baby also works great in a stand-up fight. It is heavy enough to damn near break the wrist of somebody who tries to deflect it with a sword.

But back to my latest contribution to society...

I managed to get within about ten yards of the guy. I think he was skimming some of the goods or something, because he was awful nervous when he plopped down behind a large rock and pulled a water skin from inside his coat. He unscrewed the top and, after another look around, he took a big drink.

People can be pretty nasty. Funny the things they do when they think nobody is looking. It reminds me of when I used to commute to work each day. At least a few times a week I would be driving and pass by some yay-hoo that was knuckle deep in a nostril. Oh yeah, women were just as guilty as the men. Maybe I did not see them as often, but more than a few gals got busted. More than once I would have to fight my gag reflex when that nose-nugget-coated finger would end up going into the mouth.

Yikes...gives me the heebie-jeebies just thinking of it.

I say that because my target apparently had some serious butthole itch. It was bad enough that he was shifting one way and then the other to gouge at his itchy ass, but to sniff his fin-gers after? Why...just...why?

The way I saw it, I was doing the world a favor on more than one front. This guy was nasty.

I waited for him to take a few more drinks. I could tell by the expressions he would make after each gulp that this stuff was some potent booze. (The sip I took later confirmed it when the stuff felt like it would burn through my guts and drip out the bottoms of my feet.)

When he laid his head back and shut his eyes, I decided that it was a good time to move in. For somebody my size—just over six and a half feet tall and about two hundred and thirty pounds—I move pretty quiet when I try.

I had the sun in my face, so he would not even get the warning of my shadow. When I reached him, I just stood there. I tried to look at this guy and figure out where he had lived his life, and what had given him the mindset that it was okay to do the things that he was doing. I came up empty. I guess I will never understand.

He started to snore, so I kicked him in the foot. I have a rule about killing somebody in their sleep. Basically, the rule is that I won't do it. I want the person to see me. I like the shock factor when they realize they have gone from victimizer to victim. It also helps that I have my face smeared black with charcoal except for the white smudges I have around my eyes.

Originally, I was going for a skull effect or some sort of Mask of Death thing. I don't think it came out nearly as cool as I pictured in my head, but it still became my thing, and I have been doing it since the first kill.

When he opened his eyes, he shouted and spooked me. That was unfortunate. It was simple reflex to bring my weapon down on the top of his head. He died not even knowing why I was there to kill him.

What a pisser.

12

Ghost from a Geek's Past

"Listen to me," Darlene hissed. "I trusted you, and now I need you to trust me."

"That is a commodity that is hard to come by these days," Kevin scoffed with a dismissive wave. "You already played your hand and showed us your cards. You gave us up the moment that you got back with your people."

"That's because I did not want to spring it on them later and have everybody freak out because we kept information back. In case you didn't notice, I tried to paint you in the best light possible."

Kevin continued to glower at the woman, but Catie elbowed him aside and took Darlene's hands.

"I heard what you said." There was a clear hint of gratitude in Catie's voice. "I also heard what you did *not* say. So did Kevin, he is just angry because his plan has a few bumps in it. He gets that way, but he is smart enough to figure out what you have done on our behalf." She had raised her voice just a little on that last bit to drive a point home for Kevin.

The flap to the tent opened and four men entered; each was heavily armed. Three of the men were strangers, but one of them had been the man on horseback that had obviously been in charge. Kevin was starting to think that this guy was one of the big shots here in the community.

"You," the spokesman pointed at Kevin, "come with me."

"I won't be going anywhere without her," Kevin insisted, nodding to Catie.

"Listen, she will be safe," the man replied. "I give you my word that nobody is going to lay a hand on her."

"And I would believe you why?"

"Kevin." Catie placed a hand on Kevin's shoulder and leaned into him. "I will be fine."

"And I will stay with her," Darlene assured.

Kevin shot the woman a withering glare. Was that supposed to give him comfort? She had turned on them the moment an opportunity arose. Yes, she had omitted certain things that could have cast him in a more negative light, but the fact remained that she had given them up right away.

"Here." The man pulled Catie's knife from his belt and handed it to her. He turned to Kevin. "I know that you have concerns, and I respect that, but you need to come with me, Kevin Dreon."

Kevin's mouth opened. He had made no mention of his last name. Obviously this man knew him...or at least he knew *of* him. Also, they were just giving Catie a weapon? Did they truly have no idea how dangerous that woman was without one?

"Go, Kevin," Catie insisted, accepting her blade and clipping it to her belt.

He hated doing it. His place was with her. Period. Finally, Kevin kissed Catie on the cheek and then stepped forward and took his place with his escorts.

"If anything at all happens to her—" he began, but the man silenced him.

"It won't...and don't waste your time with idle threats. You are not in any condition to make them, and they just sound silly."

"Silly?" Kevin muttered.

They exited the tent and began to weave through the camp. Kevin was at least happy to see that these people were taking the approaching zombie herd seriously. They were breaking every-thing down. He had half-expected these people to ignore his warnings until it was too late.

A group of teenagers darted across their path. They were playing what basically looked like some twist on "kill the man with the ball." Once you got tackled, you were "infected" and became a zombie. One of the teens paused to watch him pass and got "infected" by a girl with blond hair and long braids. Kevin looked over his shoulder just before he rounded the corner of a large military tent that had not been struck yet. The young man was still watching him all the way up until the girl got so tired of being ignored that she leaned over and licked the boy on one cheek. The yelps of disgust faded as he turned the corner and headed for another large tent with people rushing in and out.

They stopped at the entrance and the man held up his hand, sticking his head inside. "I have him," he called.

"He's here?" Now?" a female voice practically squealed. There was the sound of a flurry of activity. "Everybody out…go!"

Kevin was pulled back as a rush of people poured from the tent. All of them cast him inquisitive glances as they hurried away. He was growing increasingly curious. Whoever this was, they knew him.

At last, the voice from inside the tent called for him to be brought inside. Kevin was given a nudge, and he entered the tent. His eyes had to adjust for the sudden gloom, but when he could see clearly, he saw a woman standing at the end of the long tent, her back to him. He sighed inwardly. This person was obviously trying for some sort of dramatic reveal. He thought there were more pressing matters than whatever this person was trying to achieve.

"You and the men can wait outside, Loren," the woman said softly.

"But—" the man Kevin now assumed to be Loren started to protest, only to have the woman cut him off.

"I will be quite safe. Kevin wouldn't hurt me." The woman turned to him, a smile on her face.

Kevin held up his manacled hands to indicate that he was pretty helpless for the most part; at least when it came to dealing with people who were armed. This woman had a sword on her hip and a loaded crossbow on the table less than two feet away.

"Excuse me, do I know you?" Kevin asked once the room was clear.

"I think I am hurt," the woman said, easing into a chair and folding her hands in her lap.

"Not my intention." Kevin shrugged.

He studied the woman's face. There was something familiar about it, but that didn't mean anything. This woman was in her late twenties or early thirties. She had gone the muscle route and her well-defined arms were visible since she wore a sleeveless vest.

Her dark hair had been pulled back and braided into tight rows on her head that should have been unflattering, but with her perfectly oval face and still girlish features, it actually enhanced her appearance. Kevin was briefly reminded of some of the female MMA fighters he had seen on television. This woman would have definitely fit in with that crowd.

"I guess I can't hold it against you. It has been a long time, and when you knew me, I was more of a pain in the ass and a weight to be lugged than I was a help." The woman leaned forward. "But spend a few years with an all-woman army unit and you learn a few things."

"Erin Bergman?" Kevin gasped.

"It's Erin Crenshaw now," the woman corrected. "But I guess it doesn't matter. My husband is dead...and so is my daughter."

The woman's features began to change. While her voice was certainly conveying sorrow, her expression was showing anger and even a bitter hatred. Kevin had his doubts that this would be a happy reunion.

***

"You really think he will be okay?" Catie asked.

"That's the third time you've asked that question," Darlene sighed. "I am telling you, our leader knows your man. She actually described him to us...more or less. But it was clear that she was describing him. All the way down to how damn smart he is."

"I just worry about him," Catie admitted. "Sometimes he can make a good situation bad just by opening his mouth."

"I get that," Darlene said with a nod.

A commotion from outside the tent caused her to get up and look. Two horses were coming down the center of camp at a full gallop. People were having to literally dive out of the way to avoid being trampled.

"Grab what you can, they cut through that other field instead of sticking to the road!" one of the men shouted. "They will be here in less than an hour!"

"Crap," Darlene grumbled.

"We need to go get Kevin," Catie said, heading for the flap of the tent. Darlene turned and blocked her path.

"Our leader wanted to see him. She will have the same information, and trust me, she will be rolling up and moving out. Kevin will be escorted back. If not, we will meet up with him at the first rally point." Darlene grabbed Catie by the shoulders to stop her. She saw a look in the woman's eyes that made her let go in a hurry, but she remained in position to block the exit.

There was a tense moment of silence, and then somebody came in, easing Darlene aside in order to enter the tent. It was the man who had escorted Kevin to this mysterious meeting.

"You heard the rider, pack up," Loren told Darlene. He turned to Catie. "Here are your choices, you go with Darlene and stay by her side or we kill you."

"Wow, it's really all or nothing with you guys," Catie retorted with a sarcastic laugh.

"It wasn't how we wanted to do things, but the situation has changed." Loren gave a shrug of his shoulders as if to say that it was what it was and he couldn't help it.

"Given the choice, I will stay with Darlene." *For now*, she thought as an add-on to that statement.

The two women exited the tent. Catie looked around at the growing chaos. These people had not been prepared for this situation. That left her wondering just how scatter-brained their leadership might be.

They reached a tent that was already a hive of activity. Several other men and women were loading backpacks and placing footlockers into a wagon out front. With all this madness, she hoped to God that she and Kevin did not get separated to the point of losing each other.

***

"So, what made you leave that unit?" Kevin asked. He was struggling with trying to make this conversation as normal as possible. It had become increasingly difficult with the announcement that the herd was less than an hour away.

"Things got a bit out of control. At one point, there were three power struggles within a month of each other. We started becoming nothing more than a mobile raiding force. Also, they started taking the whole "no men allowed" thing a bit too far for my liking." Erin shot Kevin a wink that, despite the fact that Erin was a grown woman, made him feel a bit dirty. In his mind, now that he knew who she was, he still saw her as that little girl.

He seemed to recall that, even as a young girl, Erin liked the boys. It had become a problem more than once. Hell, just prior to the whole zombie apocalypse, the girl had been in all the tabloids. She had gotten knocked up by her pop star sister's manager. The scandal was triple-edged since, not only was she the sister of a relatively well-known celebrity, she was also the daughter of a United States Senator. Oh…and she was fourteen when she had gotten knocked up.

"Plus, I was never one of the soldiers in their eyes. I was always an outsider. Sure, good enough to go out on supply searches and to patrol the perimeter, but never quite one of the gang, ya know. After a while, that starts to grate on a person."

"So you just left…on your own?" Kevin asked, wondering where this conversation was leading. Erin kept flip-flopping between nice girl, and really pissed off woman who lost her family to a terrorist act by people who were immune and used their tainted blood to infect others,

"A few of the girls came with me, but I am the only one left of that group."

Kevin had to wonder how she had built such a devoted and large following. And where did religion come in to play?

"After a few weeks, we found a small community. The problem was that there were like thirty guys and only seven girls. They were really happy to see us. Until a bunch of them died in their sleep.

"But that was also when I met Tracy Crenshaw. He was an old Southern Baptist preacher...the real hellfire and brimstone type. I was gonna kill him, but he had preached that night, before the evening meal. He was telling the men to ease up on the ladies, that we were to be treated like something precious. That was also when I realized that he had never taken any liberties with any of the women as far as I knew.

"After we got rid of the riff raff, things got nice. That was when I got married, had a baby. I thought that I was going to move forward with my life, such as it was. And all the while, I would listen to Tracy speak and watch folks drink it up.

"He was also the first person to tell me about the End Times. This was all God's plan, and we were being tested, but those who were immune were obviously minions of Satan.

"You look confused," Erin said with a laugh that would do any evil villain proud. "Oh, this is absolutely priceless. I have confused the great mind of Kevin Dreon."

"I wouldn't be all that proud of yourself." Kevin shrugged his shoulders and did his best to smile in such a way that it wouldn't look like a grimace.

"But you always had the answers. You were always the one everybody said could figure out anything...do anything."

"I just never took you as the religious sort," Kevin finally said with a shrug.

"Oh...I'm not." Erin laughed wickedly and ran a finger under Kevin's jaw. "But I saw the power in it. Folks eat it up. I never bought into that whole thing about folks who were immune being demons or any of that nonsense…but other people sure do. And if you say all the right things, they will follow you anywhere and do anything you tell them. They become so blinded by their twisted belief that they don't even really know what they believe in anymore. They become puppets. And that is what I built…an army of puppets."

"But then you lost your husband and child when the immune people came to your community," Kevin pointed out.

"That was the easiest thing in the world!" Erin plopped back into her chair. "Don't you get it? I killed one of them after I found out what they were. You know how much blood is in a human body." She held a hand up despite the fact that Kevin made no move to speak. "Of course you do! Anyways, I did all of that. I put the tainted blood in the food and the water tank at the school."

"You killed your own child?" Kevin gasped.

"Wouldn't be the first time," Erin said with an evil laugh that gave Kevin chills. It reminded him of the laugh Reagan MacNeil had when she was possessed.

"I have no idea what happened while I was out there getting that medicine. And if I had known that something was wrong with your baby, I would have done all I could to get whatever she needed as well. That baby was just as important as anybody in the group, and both Peter and I would have done what it took if we'd known," Kevin said softly

"Who said there was anything wrong with her?" Erin asked in a whisper that seemed to drive into Kevin's head like a spike.

"I don't want to hear this," Kevin spat. "Whatever problems you have, they are not anything I did. I tried my best for you, your mom, *both* your sisters." Kevin made a point to emphasize the word 'both'. After all, he had initially devised his plan to raid The Basket because of Ruth.

There was a long silence, and then Erin pushed herself up from her chair and slunk over to where Kevin stood. Her moves were probably supposed to be graceful and sultry, but they just came across as dirty and whorish. Then it struck him; he thought that he might have figured out how she got her following. At least the men, and at least in the beginning. Although, from what he was seeing, perhaps in the latter stages as well.

"But you couldn't figure out a way to save my sister Shari, could you?" Erin had moved behind him, and she whispered that bit into his ear. "You let her die."

One of the hardest and most painful memories that he carried came back in a rush. She had no idea that it still haunted him to this day. He still remembered knocking Shari out with a sleeper hold and then covering her face before putting a crossbow bolt in her head.

He, Valarie, and Shari had been on the run. Having just escaped a crazy military dictator, they were trying to get back to the others when Shari fell and broke her leg. It had been an ugly break, with the bone jutting through the skin. She knew there was no way that Kevin could carry her for what might be possibly a day or two and still watch out for Valarie.

They had taken refuge in a house that was quickly surrounded by zombies. Shari had insisted that Kevin and Valarie make a run for it, but on the condition that he not leave her to die at the hands (and teeth) of the undead.

"You weren't there," Kevin whispered.

"Where was your incredible mind that day, Kevin? Were you too worried about getting back to that little slut of yours? Aleah, was it? And where is she now? Did you leave her to the zombies one day when she became too much for you?"

"Wow," Kevin breathed. He turned his head and fixed Erin with his gaze. "Where is all of this coming from?"

Kevin remembered the young girl Erin, and while she certainly had some problems, he would have never imagined that she could become this person that stood before him.

"You abandoned all of us for a retard...you hid while me, my mom, and my sisters were kidnapped and taken by a bunch of animals. And then...when the leader of the people who raped my mom and sister and left Ruth to die on a cross and turn into a zombie showed up, you wanted to forgive him and let him join us! It was me that killed that bastard, Shaw!"

Kevin felt the sting of her words, and while she was certainly simplifying and twisting the truth to suit her need, he could still see the grains of fact that she had sandwiched in amongst the exaggerated memories.

He considered for just a moment the possibility that perhaps he had minimalized those memories. After all, he had not been the victim in any of those instances.

"And now I discover that you are immune...just like the people that came to us a year ago. Just like the people that killed my husband, my child!" Erin was shrieking now and Kevin had a strong sense that this was going to go badly fast. The funny thing was that her outrage was strictly in her voice. She actually winked at him! This was all for show. It was for those people gathered outside the tent or passing by.

He now knew how she gathered all these followers. She was an excellent performer. She had slipped into the character of martyr with flawless ease. Only moments before, she had all but admitted to killing her own child, but that was not the story she had sold these poor saps that followed her. And there was nothing he could say or do about it. He was perhaps the only person who knew the truth of what Erin Crenshaw was...apparently what she had always been.

It almost made him curious as to what sort of person she would have been in the old world before the zombies. He was willing to bet that she would be one of those mothers that put her kids in a van and then let it drive into a lake like that crazy woman, Susan Smith. He had no problem imagining Erin standing in front of a bank of cameras, her mom the senator on one side, pop star sister on the other, and lawyer sister behind her as she looked into the camera and cried for her missing child to be returned. Hell, she would have probably gotten away with it.

What he was having trouble understanding, or grasping, was how she had found him? How had she known that he was immune?

"I don't get it," Kevin admitted. "I never did anything to hurt you. I took care of you as best I could. And Shari...your sister died a hero."

"Save it, Kevin!" Erin snapped. "I wish that I would have killed you that night when I heard what you did."

"Heard what I did?" Kevin was becoming more confused by the minute. What had she heard? Better yet, when had she heard it?

"One night, you and that cheerleader that had the hots for you...you were talking. You were still on a lot of pain meds after losing your foot, and you told that little skank how you shot my sister in the face with a crossbow because she had a busted leg or something. You chose to take care of that damned retarded girl instead of Shari!"

Tears were running down Erin's cheeks, but anybody witnessing them would be hard pressed to tell if they were from anger or sorrow. She was pacing back and forth, her hand drifting to the hilt of Kevin's knife that she wore on her belt. He had not realized that it was his until the third or fourth time she gripped it.

"I begged her to let me bring her, I told her we would stay together, but she—" Kevin tried to plead his case, but Erin was having none of it.

"You carried that boy all the way back that time...that stupid boy that ended up dying anyways!"

"There was three feet of snow on the ground!" Kevin fired back as the memories of that night with Shari and Valarie became clearer. He had wanted to carry her, but his feet were already destined for the cutting floor of a surgery tent. And, as Shari had pointed out, if he fell, then they were all doomed. He had done everything he could to make it as easy for her as possible.

"Your sister made the choice for the greater good. I have no idea when it happened, but that young lady became a selfless, wonderful person. She loved Valarie, and she gave her life to save others."

"I wish I had more time to consider this," Erin said with a sneer.

"Maybe we can have some sort of secret vote to decide if we take him with us or not," another voice called as the tent flap opened.

Kevin felt his insides turn to ice water. When Cherish Brandini walked around to stand in front of him, Kevin knew that Death's pale horse had to be near.

Cherish had joined up with him towards the end as he, Catie, and the others had travelled to South Dakota. Her actions had nearly gotten everybody killed more than once, and eventually, a vote was taken on whether or not they leave her behind. It had been almost unanimous. However, she had made nice and continued the journey to their eventual home just south of Sioux Falls in a town called Beresford, South Dakota.

About three years after their arrival, Cherish had apparently killed a woman in a fight over, no surprise considering her history, a man. She was exiled from the community—the equivalent of the death penalty back in those days.

How she had hooked up with Erin Bergman...or Crenshaw...or whatever she wanted to call herself, was anybody's guess. Of course, Kevin had been on the council that passed sentence on Cherish. He had also been the one that called for the vote that would have left her behind.

***

Darlene held the tent flap open for Catie. The two women stepped out and had to avoid a team of horses moving past, drawing a fully loaded wagon.

"Wow!" Catie said appreciatively. "You guys really have this whole pack and move routine down to a science."

"Erin makes us practice. She says that we have to be ready at a moment's notice for anything." Darlene looked around as if she were searching for somebody in particular.

"Maybe we should head over to her tent," Catie suggested.

"That's not a bad idea," Darlene agreed.

The two women hoisted their packs onto their backs. As they walked, Catie looked around at the flurry of activity. She noticed the calm attitude everybody seemed to possess. While they were obviously in a hurry, they were not frantic. She was so engrossed, that she almost missed seeing Cherish Brandini striding across the compound. She was headed for a large tent, and the look on her face was just a bit unsettling. She froze in her tracks.

"What's wrong?" Darlene asked.

"That woman." Catie made a slight nod of her head. Cherish had come to a stop at the big tent. She was talking to one of the guards posted outside. Actually, as she laughed and flipped her hair, Catie amended her assessment. She was flirting, as usual.

"What about her?" Darlene scrunched up her nose as she watched the woman lean into the man standing outside the entrance to Erin Crenshaw's tent. She knew the type, and she didn't much care for them.

Catie took a deep breath and started giving Darlene a rundown of the tumultuous history of Cherish Brandini. If she was here, and even worse, if she was aware of Kevin's presence, there might be a problem. If they were not prisoners, she needed to find Kevin and they needed to get the hell away from here.

"And now I discover that you are immune...just like the people that came to us a year ago. Just like the people that killed my husband, my child!" a voice shrieked from within the tent.

A few passers-by stopped, their heads turning towards the sudden outburst. Catie felt her stomach twist. She was pretty sure she had just found Kevin. However, it was the reaction of Cherish Brandini that had her more than a little concerned. While everybody else was drawn by curiosity, and the expressions were already turning dark on many, Cherish was smirking like the mean girl in school who had just pranked some poor wallflower and embarrassed her in front of the entire student body.

This was not good. Not good at all. She glanced over at Darlene who seemed to be considering something. Catie could not wait. And she had a feeling that every second she let slip by was one that added a steepness to the slope that would eventually dump her and Kevin into the fire. No, if she was to have any chance at getting out of here alive, she would need to act now. Her hand was going for the blade at her hip when Darlene spoke.

"This is starting to add up," Darlene said in voice that was pensive as she was obviously thinking something through.

"What is?"

Darlene looked around like she was afraid somebody might be listening in; whatever she was about to say, Catie had a feeling that it was big.

"There were a few folks that said something about one of them immune people goin' missing just before everybody got sick. And then, supposedly, one of our tower sentries was sayin' that he saw a few of Erin Crenshaw's personal security team carrying something out one of the gates late one night. But then that guy—"

"Let me guess," Catie interrupted. "He got sick with the zombie virus and died."

"How'd you know?" Darlene deadpanned.

Catie took a step forward, but Darlene grabbed her arm and pulled her back with a shake of the head. Catie glared, but she turned her gaze back and watched as Cherish was obviously listening in on whatever was going on inside the tent. As if she was waiting for a cue, she bobbed her head and then entered.

"We need to move," Darlene tugged at Catie's arm.

"I'm not leaving him." Catie spun on the woman, jerking free. She ignored the few heads that turned her way. Kevin was in trouble by the sounds of it, and she was going to help.

"If you want to help him, then come with me."

Catie turned back to the tent. Every fiber in her being wanted to charge in and just start taking down whoever she saw, but she wanted to see herself and Kevin through this alive. As difficult as it was, she allowed Darlene to lead her away. Stomping her feet, she eventually hurried off with the woman.

They wove through tents that were all in various stages of coming down. At last, Darlene slowed. She also seemed to be looking over her shoulder a lot. Finally, she stopped in front of a wagon where two men were busy loading it up. One was up in the bed and the other was on the ground, tossing up various duffels and boxes.

"I think we need to do something."

That was all Darlene said to the men, but both immediately stopped what they were doing and came to where Catie and Darlene stood. A few more heads popped out of the long, green military tent. In a matter of seconds, a dozen people had gathered around.

***

"Long time, no see, Brandini," Kevin said, trying very hard to keep his voice from wavering or cracking. But the truth of the matter at this exact moment was that he was more than a little scared.

"Oh, maybe for you," the woman laughed like she was at a fancy dinner party. In other words, with absolutely no sincerity; it was as fake as her breasts. "I've seen you many times over the years."

Kevin dismissed the comment. While it was possible, he doubted that Cherish had what it took to conduct actual covert surveillance.

"I was more than a little surprised to see you with that dyke soldier girl...Chrissy was it? I thought you were all hot and bothered for the gal who was missing part of her nose."

Kevin pressed his lips together. He was not going to give this pair of harpies the satisfaction of seeing him lose his temper. He suddenly wished he would have stayed back at Falling Run. If he had, then the herd of zombies would have done his dirty work for him, and these people would be long gone. Why had he gone on this fool mission that nobody had asked him to do? And worse still, he had brought Catie. Of course she would not let him make this trip without her; she'd made that clear...but still.

Was he losing his sharpness? Had he come to the point where he had dropped his guard so low that he had just walked foolhardy and headlong into something that he never should have undertaken in the first place?

"I would love to continue this, but, unfortunately, a massive zombie herd is coming. I want to deal with you personally," Erin said.

"What about his woman?" Brandini asked.

"No time. As it is, we are going to be cutting it close here. We can deal with her after the move to a safe place. I am sure she will come looking for him." She pointed to Kevin.

Erin walked over to the entrance to the tent and stuck her head out. Kevin heard her say something, and then she was back.

"I have had years to think about this," Erin whispered in Kevin's ear. She moved away and came to stand by Cherish. "I am only sorry that I won't get to enjoy it like I had hoped."

"Enjoy what?' Kevin did his best to try and sound brave, but he heard the slightest tremor in his voice. The smile on Erin's face told him that she heard it as well.

"You see, after some long, hard thought, I decided that you deserve the same fate you gave my sister Ruth."

Just as she finished speaking, three men entered the tent. One of them had a large beam that looked like a railroad tie. That was dropped unceremoniously to the ground and the other two converged on him. Kevin kicked at the first one to get close enough, but his attempted resistance was short lived when something crashed down on the back of his head.

Sprawled on the ground, he looked up to see Cherish holding a large machete in her hand. As his eyes cleared and his vision reduced everything back to single images, he was able to see a bit of blood on the very end of the hilt.

"Not too much damage," Cherish said when Erin shot her a nasty look.

"I want him alive," Erin scolded. "I want him to feel the pain and the horror when those things start tearing into him. I only wish that there would be enough of him to come back as a zombie. I think I would love to catch him and keep him in a cage."

"You're a sick bitch," Kevin said with a wince as one of the men kneeled on his left arm in order to secure his wrist to the railroad tie with huge zip strips.

"I must say," Erin turned to Cherish, "this is not as fun or fulfilling as I'd hoped. Actually seems rather...what's the word I am looking for?" She clapped her hands. "Anticlimactic! That's it."

"I feel sorry for you," Kevin said to Erin with a hiss when the man knelt on his right arm with a knee as he went about securing that one to the large beam.

"Why? You're the one about to be hung up as zombie bait." Erin threw her head back and laughed. Cherish joined in, reminding Kevin of a backslapping sycophant.

"You are going to live a miserable life—" he started to explain, but Erin cut him off with a kick to the ribs.

"But *I* will be living, you idiot!" She really drew out the word "I" as she spoke, leaning over and leering at Kevin as the men got up to reveal that he was now tightly secured to the heavy beam.

"Get him on his feet," Erin barked. "We don't have a lot of time. I want to get this done so it doesn't go completely to waste."

The three men complied, helping to heave Kevin up to his feet. When they let go, he staggered just a bit, but caught himself before teetering over. A hand in his back guided him toward the tent flap.

As soon as they exited, Kevin was hit with all the movement going on everywhere. He had to admit, as far as a breakdown evolution, these people had it down to a science.

"This way," Erin said, giving him another shove. Once again he teetered and came close to falling.

Already, a small group had stopped what they were doing to get a look. Kevin felt eyes on him and hoped to God that one of those sets of eyes were not Catie's.

They came to a halt where a group of four more men were putting the finishing touches on a hole that the tall pole sitting on the ground a few feet away would slip into with no problems, He was led over to the pole and pushed down to the ground hard. He cried out when he felt his wrist snap as he landed awkwardly on a rock. He was rolled over and the tie was attached by a large steel ring on the back to a bolt that stuck out from the pole.

"Hoist him!" Erin commanded.

13

Fallen

"They're so big!" Kayla gasped as she and I stood beside the silver bus that had come to rest on its side over a decade ago. "Four or five of these would be enough to move everybody in Platypus Creek."

She was right. That is why this smashed up train of eleven seemed so impressive. I climbed up onto the entry step behind her and my nose wrinkled automatically. There were a few mostly decayed and dried out husks of the dead. One stuck out from the rest in that it was missing just about everything above the chin. A dark stain gave evidence that this person had blown their brains out. I only briefly wondered what the person who had come and obviously relieved the body of whatever weapon it had used must have been thinking. Did they simply rejoice in the find? Or, did they give a moment's pause and consider the horror that had taken place here?

"C'mon, you two," Jim said as he walked past. He didn't even give this scene a second glance. How many times had he passed by this spot? Was this all so boring to him like he made it seem?

I hopped out, Kayla right behind me. She was being very well-behaved. That little scare had done its job. I still thought that Paula had somehow arranged it. That zombie had just been in too perfect of a place to not only give Kayla the scare of her life, but also for Paula to drop it with next to no effort.

We had moved to the south and were coming in to La Grande from a different route than we did the last time. I was having a real hard time acting like a "seasoned" veteran since so much of what we were seeing on the way in was just as new to me.

"Don't go sticking your head into places like that," Jim whispered as he allowed me to fall into step beside him. "It is a rookie move. You are supposed to be the example."

I didn't see the big deal. It was an empty old bus. All we did was take a peek inside. It wasn't like we had gone nosing around a roadside stop like he had done just this morning. Sure, when he did it, it was because he was looking for specific items in order to make one of his explosives. When I did it, I was being a rookie. It was starting to get under my skin how adults always had a pretty obvious set of double standards.

Of course, if Kayla was having it rough, then Dorian was probably never going to sleep through the night again for the rest of his life. Somehow, it seemed that zombies always came on *his* watch at night. And even worse, there was usually one just about an hour before his watch and then again about an hour after. He was probably not getting more than two or three hours of uninterrupted sleep a night. It was showing on his face and this was only the second morning away.

That was another thing. This route we were taking was almost twice as long. We would be out for over two weeks. It would take us four days to reach La Grande.

"Dorian!" Paula called out. I swear Jim snickered. "You and Kaplan get up that hill and see what is on the other side of the ridge. And keep your eyes peeled, there were a few small clusters reported in the area by the forward scouts."

When I heard Jim reciting the exact same words under his breath, I knew it was just another set up. We hadn't done anything of the sort on the run I'd made. She was sending him up and down hills as a form of punishment...or torture.

Kayla moved up close to me. "When are they gonna send us

on a ridge run?" she asked. I glanced over and saw that she was being serious. Since I did not want her doing anything stupid, I decided to let her in on the secret.

"That's mean," she huffed. "That poor guy is going to collapse or get himself killed."

"Yeah." I turned and shielded my eyes to get a look at him as he and Kaplan wove their way up the steep incline. In just the few seconds I watched, Dorian slipped and fell twice. "Well, he wanted this run."

There was a long silence, and I thought that the conversation was over. Then Kayla opened her mouth again.

"And so when will it be my turn?"

"What?" I actually stopped and turned to face her. I had no idea what she was talking about.

"When do you make a fool out of me? When do you start in on me like you all are doing with Mr. Watkins?"

"Why would we start in on you?" The pop-up zombie flashed in my mind, but I quickly stuffed it away.

"I didn't actually think you would be able to get me on this run. When you told me I was coming, I still did not believe it until the walls disappeared behind us." Kayla was near tears. I absolutely did not have time for this.

The scream ended the conversation.

I had spun with my crossbow unslung before I actually realized what I was doing. Later, I would allow myself to be proud of my reaction, but at the moment, something was wrong.

My eyes went to the hill and just up a bit from where I'd last seen Dorian and Herb Kaplan. Herb was probably the best field cook ever. You could bring him a handful of dirt and some leaves and he could probably make a feast that would make you ask for more. He was also the one screaming.

I brought up my crossbow. Not because I could do anything; Herb and Dorian were well out of actual range, but I could use my scope to get a better view. That was probably not the best idea.

From the looks of it, a small pack of zombies had managed to get up the backside of that hill. They had obviously seen the pair (or more likely heard Dorian's bitching). Zombies are not tacticians or planners; unless you believe all that you hear about the child versions, they simply act. These had fallen from a small ledge just above the unwitting pair. Even worse, another dozen or so were now at that same ledge and would be flopping down on their prey in the next few seconds.

There were two wrapped up with Herb. I could see the dark stain growing just under his chin. Despite all the protective gear, one of the zombies had gotten in under the chin strap of Herb's helmet and torn at the tender flesh.

Dorian was doing the only thing he was probably qualified to do: he was running and screaming. Actually, running is over-stating it. He was sort of jumping his way down the hill, using gravity and the loose scree to aid in his rapid decent.

"We have to help him!" Kayla suddenly started to scream over and over.

The thing was, I don't think even she knew which of the men she was talking about. One was basically a dead man walk-ing unless he was fortunate enough to be one of The Immune. Only, with the amount of blood loss, it was doubtful he could survive the attack. As if on cue, I watched as a solid series of pulsating jets of blood shot from what I had to assume was now the ruined throat of Herb Kaplan.

By now, Dorian was almost halfway down the hill. He took a tumble and was now coming head over heels. The detached part of my brain wanted to enjoy the humor, but a fall like that could be a bad deal.

"Thalia!" Jim barked.

I pulled my eye from the scope and looked. Crap! Kayla was running for the hill. She was still screaming like an idiot and actually managed to spook a team of horses pulling the lead wagon.

I let my crossbow fall to the end of its tether as I took off af-ter the stupid girl. I was closing when I felt something flash by my head. It was too quick to see, but with my senses heightened, I sure as hell felt it and dove, tackling Kayla. My hand was on the hilt of my knife almost before we hit the ground.

Rising up, I shoved the stupid girl's head down. Sure enough, two zombies had just stepped out of the thick brush that ran along what had once been a highway road and was now little more than a well-defined nature trail as the years of weather had buckled and washed away a lot of the actual pavement, leaving a huge scar in the earth that made travel just a bit easier.

The closest zombie had a bolt from a crossbow jutting from its chest. This was one of the ancient zombies. You could tell because they were almost impossible to determine gender due to the years of abuse, weather, and even vermin that whittled away at anything loose or dangly.

I hopped up and took two long strides, jabbing my knife into its eye, yanking my wrist back quick to avoid the weight of the fallen body snatching the blade from my hand. The second one obliged by stepping right up to be next.

By now, Dorian had stopped falling, and Herb had stopped screaming. Both were blessings in their own right. My pulse was pounding in my ears, which is why it took me a few seconds to realize that I could hear a moaning from the nearby brush.

"Don't move!" I turned and snarled at Kayla. She nodded vigorously, and I wondered if she was still as excited about her first field run as she had been just moments ago.

Knife at the ready, I held up a hand when Paula called for me. I knew she probably thought that she was the only one who could do anything, but I was closest to this sound.

Of course, by the time I had ducked into the foliage, I realized what I was hearing. I shoved a branch aside and stepped into a grassy patch where Dorian lay sprawled. Without even taking that close of a look, I could see that his left arm had a nasty break and his left foot was turned very awkwardly to the right much further than it should.

"Thalia," he moaned as I bent down to get a better look.

He had a variety of cuts and scrapes. His ugly nose was busted, and that gash on his forehead was turning his face into a crimson mask made all the more creepy when he opened his mouth to reveal more than a couple of missing teeth. He spat a wad of swirling crimson that had chunks that could be dirt and gravel...or teeth.

"Shut up and stay still," I hissed.

My head went on a swivel, searching for any signs of movement. There could be a few more zombies. Plus there were the ones that had stepped off the ledge. No telling how many of those had joined Dorian in the tumble down the hill.

On the plus side, if they suffered serious damage to their legs, they would be severely hampered. On the bad side, they did not need to recover from those injuries, they would simply start creeping. A few moans and cries from the woods told me that there were a handful that were close.

"I'm not supposed to move you." I reached under Dorian's armpits. "But if we stay here, we are in trouble."

I started dragging him backwards. I had only taken a few steps when Paula exploded through the brush. Without waiting, she moved to his feet and picked him up. To his credit, Dorian had not made a sound. I was impressed until I looked down and saw that he was unconscious.

"We make camp here," James was announcing as Paula and I carried Dorian's limp body into the midst of the flurry of activity.

"You sure being out in the open like this is a good idea?" Jackson White asked.

I had been glad when he insisted on coming along. In fact, with the exception of Cynthia Bird, we had all the same people from the last field run in addition to the others that brought our total to twenty; nineteen now with the loss of Herb Watkins.

"We will be fine for one day." James pointed out a place for the two wagon drivers to park. "We make camp here for the night and then we turn around and head back for home at first light."

"We are going back?"

Everybody turned to look at Kayla. She shrunk away from the sudden and intense scrutiny.

"And what would you have us do?" Paula asked as she and I laid Dorian down in the back of one of the wagons. "Dorian needs medical attention that he can't get out here. He will be lucky if he survives the ride home."

"But the salvage—" Kayla began, clearly not getting the gravity of the situation.

"Was a fool's errand to begin with," Paula snapped, cutting the seemingly clueless girl off. "We have no need to make this run. Platypus Creek is not in want of anything. Going down to Island City does nothing but expose us to the possibility of being spotted by that army and followed home."

There was a moment of silence. That is probably why we heard it. It had to be far away, but there was no denying the scream.

"Thalia, you and Jackson come with me," Jim Sagar said as he took off at a jog. A plume of black smoke could be seen to the southeast of our location. It looked to be just beyond two gently sloped foothills.

"James!" Paula called. "Whatever that is, it isn't our problem!"

I had fallen in beside Jim. Jackson was right on my heels. I started to slow down and felt the big man's gentle hand urge me to keep going. I had to sort of agree with Paula, but my curiosity was much louder and shut out the demands that were chasing us as we rounded the first bend that mercifully put itself between Paula and the three of us.

***

"Just down there," Jim whispered as he handed me his binoculars.

I looked to where he pointed. At first I didn't see anything. I was ready to give up when I caught just the briefest of movements in the midst of a massive blackberry patch that looked to have completely engulfed what Jackson said was once a trailer park; whatever those are.

Sure enough, seconds later, several dark figures scurried through a small clearing amidst the briar patch. It was difficult to make out exact numbers, but I had to guess there to be at least five individuals.

I let my scan drift to the right. Beside a small creek was a walled community of perhaps fifty. They were on full alert, but two of their buildings were burning out of control already.

"I don't get it?" I handed the glasses back to Jim.

"Tribal dispute," Jim said. When my expression made it clear that he had not helped any with his two word answer, he continued. "There are probably fifty or more small communities in the area. Tribes. For whatever reason, it looks like two of them are at odds."

"Which will be the downfall of both," Jackson added.

He was still looking to the south. A constellation of campfires gave away the location of what could only be the same army that had wiped out La Grande for whatever reason.

"Who are these people, and why are they doing this?" I could not hide my confusion and frustration.

I had heard all about Island City and some of the crazy stuff from way back when all of this started. Honestly, none of it made sense. Humanity was facing extinction and people were fighting and killing one another. If anything, I would have thought that this was the time to come together.

"Man is a selfish and greedy animal," Jackson said with a sigh. "It is a sad truth, but history has shown time and again that we will leave a path of destruction wherever we go."

"Whoever these people are, I think they are trying to take the entire valley and want to ensure there are none left to dispute their claim." Jim rolled onto his back and opened his pack. He handed me and Jackson a hunk of dried meat.

"Why?" I asked. That was simply not a good enough answer.

"Why not?" Jim shrugged. "This valley is excellent for farming. It has a multitude of streams, creeks, and small rivers. The mountains surround it and act as a natural barricade. This place is a paradise."

"But there was plenty of it that was not claimed or settled," I insisted. "They didn't need to come in and wipe people out. They don't need all of it."

Neither man spoke. I don't think they really had any answers. And who knows, maybe there wasn't one beyond Jackson's claim that man is selfish and greedy.

"So what do we do now?" I asked. Neither man had a chance to answer.

"Chelsea!" a voice called from a mound of rocks to our right.

I stiffened. Whoever this person was, they had managed to get within a hundred or so yards of our position without us seeing anything. That meant they were probably trying to stay hidden.

"Blake?" a female voice replied from the shadows of a clump of trees that were just below the lip of the ridge we were on. "Stay put, I heard somebody just a few seconds ago."

"How 'bout you come out and make this easier on all of us," there was a slight pause before the oily-sounding voice wheezed and finished, "Chelsea is it?"

There were the sounds of a struggle and then a meaty smack followed by a yelp. All of that came from the direction of the voice I had to assume to be Blake. Only, it was obvious that he had some company.

"Don't do it, Chel—" Blake's voice yelped, but was quickly muffled.

"That's right, Chelsea. You just stay put and let old Blakey here take some pain on your behalf." There was an evil laugh and then the sounds of violence.

"You can't just sit here while all of this is happening," I whispered into Jackson's ear.

"And what would you have us do? We don't know how many or what the hell we stumbled into the middle of. Ain't that right, Jim?" Jackson peeked over me. "Jim?"

I turned my head and was stunned to find Jim Sagar gone. How he had managed to slip away without me having felt or sensed it was astounding. We'd actually been touching at one point we were so close. I guess I had been distracted to the point where I had lost track of him.

"Dammit," Jackson swore, peeking up and over our little ledge towards the rocky area where Blake had been. "C'mon,

Thalia, we better move."

At first I thought that he meant to abandon Jim, but when he eased back down our little bluff and then started off in a crouch towards some cover that would get us close to those rocks where the beating was still taking place in between taunting calls from whoever it was that wanted Chelsea to "just stay put, Blake won't miss them pretty teeth of his one bit!", I felt a ripple of excitement course through me. This was way more than I had bargained for, but somehow, I was more excited than I was scared.

We ducked into some tall grass that cut into my exposed skin better than any razor sharp knife when I just haphazardly went to push it aside. From that point, I was more careful and made my way up beside Jackson who had caught up with Jim.

"Sheesh, what kept you guys?" Jim mouthed.

From our new vantage, we did not even dare whisper. We could see the man I had to figure to be Blake. He was on his knees. The man standing over him wore an oversized burlap glove that actually looked heavy like it was weighted with something. The two other men standing around were scanning the area in the direction we'd last heard the mysterious Chelsea.

"C'mon, Skins, give me a turn," one of the men practically begged.

The man doing the beating up to this point—presumably Skins—stepped back and let this Blake person fall flat on his face. He began to unlace the glove; quickly confirming my suspicion that the bulbous fist portion was indeed weighted.

I didn't need that much prompting to know this was our time to act. With as much stealth as I could manage in the tall, dry grass, I brought my crossbow around and slid the stock against my shoulder with a degree of comfort that was like hugging an old friend.

I felt Jim tap me and glanced his way. He gave me a stern look that I was not sure about. Since I did not know what he was trying to say, I just smiled and then sighted in on the one who was currently putting on the glove.

I felt Jim inhale and hold it. I did the same, and as soon as I felt him exhale, I pulled the trigger. My bolt zoomed through the air, nearly invisible as the shadows of dusk all met to bring darkness to the world as evening fell.

There was a yelp from my target as my shot was off by just a fraction and caught the man in the gut instead of the center of his chest. Before I could ask what we should do next, Jim and Jackson were on their feet, rushing in to meet the one man who was uninjured. That just happened to be the one we knew as "Skins."

I scrambled up and hurried in as well, drawing the long knife at my belt. I rushed in just as Jackson tackled Skins and the two went tumbling into some of the nearby blackberry bushes. Jim had stopped over his guy and toed him with his boot. My guy was on his side.

I hurried over and put my boot in his side to flip him flat onto his back. He looked up at me and I took a step back. He could not be any older than I was, but he looked like hell. He had scars on his face and his nose had been busted so many times that it sort of laid on his face because it had no place else to go.

"P-p-please," he begged, throwing his hands up.

"Finish him off." Jim had stepped over beside me and was standing there with his hands on his hips.

"What?" I spun, but he grabbed my shoulders and turned me right back to the boy on the ground.

"Don't ever take your eyes off of an enemy!" Jim barked. There was not an ounce of the mirth and humor I knew so well.

"He's not—" I started.

"You shot him. That makes him an enemy. And since we don't have the resources to take care of his injuries, you need to kill him. He will suffer horribly if you don't."

In a rush, I recalled our little conversation about killing a living person. He, Billy, and Paula had told me that it was not the same as killing a zombie.

I turned and looked down at this person. Everything else in the world seemed to fall away. I knew that Jackson and Jim were dealing with the situation around me. I thought that I heard crying and wondered when they had brought the mysterious

Chelsea out of hiding.

Then I realized that it was me!

The man was staring up at me with a gaze that saw nothing. There was a bolt through his left eye that I did not remember firing. Feeling strangely numb, I reached down and pulled the bolt free. When I did, there was a gout of dark red blood.

I turned as quick as I could so that my vomit would not douse the corpse of the man that I had killed. That would have been extremely rude. When I finished being sick, I wiped my mouth with the back of my hand and stood up despite my legs feeling like they were going to refuse to support my weight.

"You okay, cupcake?" Jim put an arm around my shoulders.

"Not really," I admitted.

Jackson was over with the strangers, Chelsea and Blake. I could not hear what they were saying, but the stern expression on Jackson's face told me that it was probably not good.

"There's no going back," Jim whispered. At first I thought that I might have imagined it. But then he continued. "I wish I could take it all away, but once you have killed a living person, justified or not, it changes you forever."

"What was I supposed to do?" I asked weakly. In truth, I was actually hoping that he had an answer I could cling to that would pull me out of the aching feeling that I felt in my heart and soul unlike anything I had ever experienced.

I knew what sadness and depression felt like. They are natural and normal. This was something of its own ilk; there was really nothing that I could compare it to in my limited experience. It was sort of like I had lost something that was a vital part of me.

"The only thing that you could have done is to never step foot outside the walls of home," Jim answered.

At first, I thought that he might have been making a poorly timed wise-crack, but his eyes were so cold, his lips so tightly pressed together.

"We have to go!" Jackson announced as he walked up, breaking the momentary spell of guilt and pain that I feared might never diminish.

"What's up?" Jim instinctively flipped open the cover to his pack where he kept his array of improvised explosives.

"That army is in fact moving in to settle the area. I guess they sent advance teams to Island City as well as the larger tribes in the valley. It seems they were down in Oklahoma or something. A massive drought wiped out their crops and put them on the verge of starvation. Apparently, they had some active trade with the folks in Island City. Since it was apparently the largest settled area in a location that was sustainable, they simply decided to take it for their own."

As I listened to Jackson explain things, I was at first confused, then I was angry. Was that actually their only option? To take what other people had worked hard to create and just claim it as theirs?

"If the people in Island City couldn't defend against these monsters, then how can we hope to keep them from taking us out?" I asked what I considered to be an obvious question.

"For one," Jim smiled, "the people of Island City did not have me."

"Plus," Jackson was much more serious, "they might not even know that we exist, and even if they do, there is really no reason for them to come up into the hills and try to root us out."

"They only want the valley," a man's voice rasped. At first, I thought that it was the man Blake that we had just rescued. "They don't know anything about you, and even if they did, they wouldn't care. We had plenty of smaller communities in Oklahoma that we traded with before the drought."

It was the man called "Skins." I peered around Jackson to where the man was lying on the ground, his wrists and ankles bound securely. I could not really make out his features that clearly considering that it was now almost completely dark.

"How could you even think to do something like this?" I pushed past Jackson and stood over the dark figure on the ground.

"When it comes to survival, it is you or them."

His answer was so simple, said with no malice, anger, or any real sort of emotion. It was simply said as a statement of fact. This man saw nothing wrong with wiping out an entire community in order to further his own survival.

At first, I just stood there staring down at Skins. I could not see his face. I guess that is why it was so easy. Yanking my knife free, I plunged it into the center of where I guessed to be the man's chest. I think I heard Jackson and Jim both yell at me, but it was really nothing more than background noise.

"How's that working out for you?" I hissed as I leaned down and put my face right in the man's.

I could smell his sour breath as it came out in a final rattle. A hand grabbed my shoulder and jerked me back roughly, tossing me to the ground.

"What the hell are you doing?" Jackson bellowed.

I didn't know. That was the problem. So much was swirling around inside me that I wanted to scream, cry…

"Well, so much for being able to question him," Jim said.

At some point, camp was made. Blake and Chelsea would return to their people in the morning. I was told that I would not be standing watch. Any time that I approached Jim or Jackson, they got quiet.

When I finally fell asleep, the nightmares came fast and vivid. Maybe it was that reason that the screams did not wake me right away. There were plenty of screams in my nightmare, so all I could figure was that they masked the real ones; that is, until somebody grabbed me.

14

Vignettes LIX

Juan sat quietly. Both the girls were in with their mother. This would be goodbye. Mackenzie had managed to hang on for two days. Over the years, the infection had slowed in its ability to turn, but it had not stopped being lethal. It was horrible watching her change from the vibrant, beautiful, energetic woman that he loved into this frail and sick shell of her former self.

They had spoken just moments before, and she had asked to see her daughters one last time. Juan could hear the harsh rattle of each cough as Mackenzie struggled to speak. He felt his heart turning to frozen stone, and he was helpless to stop it. He knew he had to be present for Della and Denita, but he could not find the strength.

"Daddy," Della called as she came out of the tent, "I think you need to go in there now. Mama is done talking."

Climbing to his feet, he entered the tent. The smell was a physical presence that coated his throat and nostrils in such a way that he almost believed that he would never be clean of it.

Mackenzie was on her cot. The bindings that secured her in place acted as a stinging but unnecessary reminder that the woman he loved would turn into a mindless eating monster, and therefore, she must be bound like the dangerous thing she could become at any moment.

"C-c-come sit beside me," Mackenzie coughed.

Juan took one of the small folding chairs and moved next to the bed. He saw Mackenzie's fingers wiggle slightly and he reached down to hold her hand. He winced at the coldness of her grip. He knew he should probably be wearing his gloves, but he would not miss the feel of her skin against his no matter how it felt.

"I just want you to know that I love you with all my heart, Juan Hoya."

Each word came with obvious pain. It almost sounded like the words were being ripped from her throat. He half expected to see blood start to trickle from her lips.

"I need you to look at me," Mackenzie rasped.

Juan brought his eyes up to hers. It was a struggle not to let the horror of what he was seeing show through in his expression. Her eyes were a nightmare and her skin was a waxy greenish-gray that looked like it would slough off her body. Her cheeks had gone hollow and her lips were nothing more that after-thoughts.

"I need you to promise that you will make it quick…as soon as I have taken my last breath." That entire sentence took what seemed like forever as Mackenzie had to stop more than once when she was wracked with harsh, hacking fits of coughing that were almost painful to hear. "I would ask you to just end it now, but I know that you won't."

"You can't be serious." Juan struggled to maintain his last shreds of humanity. If he did not snap out of this, his daughters would basically be orphans. He had to pull himself together.

Not for the first time, he wished that he could go back in time—hit a rewind button. He knew deep down that he should have done away with Rufus when the dog showed signs that he was reaching a point where he could die. In the past, hadn't people simply taken their pets to the vet and had them put down? Why had he allowed this risk to exist?

"Stop it!" Mackenzie managed through shallow, rapid breaths. "This is not your fault. If it is anybody's…it is mine. I told you we could handle Rufus when the time came."

Juan gripped Mackenzie's hand tighter. In his imagination, she squeezed back, but the truth was that she was simply too weak. He sat there with her in relative silence. The only sound was that of her ragged breathing. Sometimes it was in rapid pants, other times there were long pauses that made him sit up straight.

"I'm sorry."

Juan jumped and looked down to see Mackenzie staring at him, tears leaking from the corner of her eyes. They were wide but unfocused. He doubted that she was seeing him, and when he leaned down and her gaze continued to stare past him, he knew. He kissed the top of her forehead and looked over his shoulder. The tent flap was closed.

A tremor rippled through Mackenzie's body and her legs began to twitch. Juan stood, his eyes unable to tear away as the woman he loved with all his being began to go into the throes of death. Reaching down, he pulled the pillow out from under her head and placed it over her face that was now an unrecognizable rictus of pain.

"God, if you exist, you know that I have been a screw-up my whole life. I doubt you got a place for me up there, but please, if you are real...forgive me."

Drawing his knife from his belt, Juan placed the tip where he figured Mackenzie's forehead to be and shoved down hard. There was initial resistance, and then the blade slid down.

Turning, Juan felt his heart leap to his throat. Denita was standing in the entrance to the tent, her mouth in a perfect tiny "O." In her hand were a few straggly-looking wildflowers.

"Sweetie..." Juan's mouth tried to work, but he found that there were no words forthcoming. His brain had locked up.

"Has mama gone to be with Antonio?" Denita asked, stepping forward and trying to peer around Juan.

Juan shifted his body to block her view as he reached back and felt around for the hilt of his knife. Pulling it free, he kept his hand behind his back as he knelt before his daughter.

"You're talking," Juan blurted, unable to come up with anything better to say to his daughter.

"Mama said you would need me and Della after she went to Heaven to be with Antonio." Denita walked up to Juan and held up the wilting flowers. "Can I put these on her bed?"

Juan could only nod. He watched with tears in his eyes as his daughter who had not spoken in years stepped past him and stopped at her mother's bedside.

"Give Antonio a hug and kiss for me, Mama. Tell him I am sorry. If I was watching out like I was s'pposed to and not playing with my doll by the water, he wouldn't have had to fight that dirty deader. He wouldn't have slipped in the mud and got bit and then had to go to Heaven and wait for us."

Juan felt his throat tighten. He wanted to cry openly, but he knew that at this very moment, his daughter needed him. It had never been known how the zombie that bit his and Mackenzie's son managed to fall prey. His throat torn open, he had died from blood loss before Juan and Mackenzie had even managed to get to him.

Kneeling beside his daughter, he bowed his head as Denita recited the only prayer she knew.

"Now I lay me, down to sleep…"

***

"Gemma," the dark-skinned woman said softly, not rising from her seat.

"What…h-h-how?" the other woman stammered.

"I came here like you said," Chaaya replied with a slight bow of her head. "They took me in without hesitation. I have married, he shares my immunity, and we have a beautiful son."

"So you two really were together…" Vix stepped back from Gemma suddenly. "Then I need you to answer a question."

Gemma sighed, her shoulders slumping. With tired eyes she looked up at Vix. "Yes, I am the Black Widow. I have killed over thirty men in the past several years…however many it has been. So I guess my invitation has been rescinded."

Gemma turned to leave, but a hand on her arm stopped her. She turned to see an odd expression of her former travelling companion's face.

"I was going to ask you if you might be willing to share the story of how you survived this long on your own, and if there would be any hard feelings between you and Chaaya. Considering that she deserted you, a point she admits and has made public knowledge practically since she arrived." Vix gently steered the woman back to the boat.

Now Gemma was totally confused. Had Vix missed the part where she said that she had killed over thirty men? Not only that, but Chaaya had told people about her. So, at the very least, they knew about those first men that she killed. Yet, she was not only being welcomed, she was being asked if she had any problems with Chaaya in such a way that she honestly believed that the woman would incur some sort of imposed restriction or some such nonsense.

"I can share. Not much of a storyteller, but I can at least remember most of the details."

"Then it is off to New England!"

And just like that, they were rowing back across the channel. Gemma actually took a moment to enjoy the light mist on her face as they cut through the water. She could not believe her fortune. After all that she had done, she was being accepted into this society with open arms. If she was able, Gemma might have cried. As it was, her throat was threatening to seize up.

They were less than halfway across when Gemma noticed the first people starting to gather at the dock in anticipation as to her arrival. Her anxiety was building once more.

She glanced back at Vix and saw that the woman was all seriousness as she watched the land get closer and closer. As for Chaaya, she had her eyes on her feet. Gemma would have to talk to her later. She had not done anything wrong, they would be able to clear the slate and start fresh.

Yet, as she looked from Vix to Chaaya to the crowd gathering on the shore, she could not shake the feeling in her gut that something was wrong. When a hand touched her arm, Gemma just about tipped the boat.

"Are you okay?" Vix asked with a furrow creasing her

brow.

"Something is wrong," Gemma whispered. Actually, she hadn't meant to say that out loud. She looked plaintively at Vix. Her hands began to twitch and she could not stop her feet from bouncing.

"You have been away for a long time." Vix took the younger woman's hands in hers. "I know it seems like everything is tilted on its hind end, but you are safe now, Gemma. You can come here, clean up, and make a go at living a normal life."

"Normal." The word sounded bitter and dirty coming from Gemma mouth. Her lips curled in a nasty sneer and her eyes narrowed to slits. "There is no normal."

"That's what I thought," Chaaya eased up on her rowing just enough to speak. "After what we went through at the fort, I thought I would never be clean...never close my eyes and not be haunted by the horrors we were forced to endure. But you can make it to the other side, Gemma. You have a strong heart. It is obvious that you are strong and brave. Look how long you lasted all alone out in the wilderness."

Gemma looked from one woman's face to the other. A very tiny part of her was screaming for her to listen, but a larger part, the broken Gemma, that part was screaming for her to end this pain once and for all.

She had heard that voice before. Yet, she had always been able to suppress that voice. Over time, she learned to blank everything from her mind. She did not discriminate. She purged herself of anger, sorrow, and fear. Unfortunately, she also did away with happiness, peace, and joy.

In the days before zombies, she would have been hospitalized and heavily medicated. But now, now the voices had free reign. Gemma listened to the ministrations of that single loud voice that dominated. She even cocked her head as if the voice might be coming in on a breeze.

Before Vix could react, Gemma grabbed the large concrete-filled bucket that was tied to a single fifty foot piece of line. In a lunge that once again almost threatened to tip the boat, Gemma threw herself backwards. She landed flat on her back in the water hard enough to drive most of the air from her lungs.

With the extra weight from the bucket, she sunk fast. Her last vision was that of a pair of faces peering over the side of the boat at her. Their expressions were wavy and distorted by the water. The sound was muffled and quickly faded from her ears.

As she sunk to the bottom of the river, her body convulsed with the first big intake of water that poured into her lungs. That only made Gemma's hands clutch the barrel tighter.

A sense of peace came in the final seconds. Gemma would have let loose with a heavy sigh if she'd been able.

***

The girl they had saved was coming at him at a sprint. Out of reflex more than anything else, he swung a haymaking left hook that connected hard with Melody's jaw. There was a loud crunch and her feet shot out from under her as the force of the blow knocked her back. She landed awkwardly; out cold.

"Crap!" Chad shook his hand.

Ronni and Caroline rushed in, both trying to get a grip on his left arm and help get off his glove, but he pulled away. Using just the fingertips, he tugged the glove off. Already, the hand was swelling.

He glanced down at the unconscious form of Melody and mused briefly at the idea that the punch seemed to have done more actual physical damage to him than it had to her. At least one of his knuckles was busted and/or jammed back much farther than it should be.

"Well?" Chad turned to Caroline and his daughter. "I say we tie them both up. Something is wrong here, that's for certain."

Ronni and Caroline moved in, binding and gagging both Butch and Melody as securely as possible. They carried Butch into the underground meat storage dugout that they had made. Chad's hope was for the half of a deer hanging from the log rafter might unsettle the man when he regained consciousness. As for Melody, she was taken back inside the cabin and secured to one of the chairs, and then turned to face the wall.

Chad turned to his daughter. "Are you okay?"

"Yeah." Ronni was still looking past Chad, glaring at the back of the head of the girl tied to the chair.

"What the heck happened?"

"Everything was fine until she heard that man's voice outside. Then she looked at me all weird. I was just getting her some water from the barrel to clean her face when she shoved me out of the way and ran for the door."

"Just like that?" Caroline asked, peering around Chad at their prisoner with a raised eyebrow. "I think your dad is right. There is a lot going on here that we don't know. I am not comfortable with us being in the middle of all this nonsense."

"We can start questioning whichever one wakes up first," Chad said through a grimace of pain as he absently rubbed his sore hand that had started to purple up in addition to the swelling.

"I say we start now," Ronni growled as she grabbed the pan of water from the table that she had scooped up only moments before to help Melody get cleaned up and poured it on the girl's head. The girl shuddered and made muffled coughs and snorts. "Start talking, bitch!" Ronni pulled the gag down and jumped back just in the nick of time to avoid Melody's gnashing teeth.

With a booted foot, Caroline shoved the chair over, letting it topple. Melody landed on her side with a painful sounding thump as her head bounced off the hard, wooden floor.

"Try that again and I will shove a knife in the side of your head," Caroline whispered in Melody's ear as she and Ronni grabbed the chair from either side and sat it back upright.

"Now," Ronni tugged on the arm of the chair to turn it around, "you want to tell us what the real story is about why those people were looking for you."

Melody glared up at the three of them with a face twisted into a mask of contempt and hatred. It was made all the more sinister by the ugly, seeping bite mark. She pressed her lips tight as if in response.

"Fine," Chad shrugged, pulling the other two back, "let's go see if Butch is any more cooperative or helpful." Before Melody could react, he grabbed the wide leather strap and tugged it back over Melody's mouth.

They left the cabin. Chad was a little surprised that the girl did not react. He had expected her to have a sudden change of heart and spill the beans. He hoped that Butch would prove more cooperative.

When they walked in, Ronni made a noise in her throat and held her nose. "What is that smell?"

"The guy probably messed his pants. That happens sometimes when you get knocked out," Chad explained as he walked over to the man.

"But Melody didn't," Ronni pointed out.

"That is why I said *sometimes.*" Chad tilted the man's chin up and slapped him until he got a groggy moan. He pulled the gag down and stepped back, waiting for the man to regain his senses at least a little.

It didn't take long.

"Wha-what the hell?" the man groaned.

It took a few seconds for the situation to sink in, but when it did, Butch's eyes went wide. He had none of the defiance and anger that had shown on Melody's face. The only thing coming through in Butch's expression was fear.

"I am only going to ask this one time," Chad said, hand brushing the hilt of his saber. "What is the deal with the girl? Why did you guys have two groups searching for her?"

"She's a killer," Butch finally managed around the gumminess that had suddenly coated his tongue and throat making it almost impossible to talk.

"You have to be more specific." Chad knelt down to eye level with the man. He would try the "good cop" routine first. "We already know that she killed several of your people. What we don't know are the details and why she was running through the woods with a zombie bite on her face."

The man looked at the three people facing him. "I'll tell ya everything…"

***

There was a thud, and the woman straddling him had a sudden change of expression. It transformed from murderous intent to a distant, slack, and empty look. Her hands loosed their grip on the machete and Jody had to jerk to one side to avoid the point coming down on his face. That movement caused the woman to slide over and begin to fall.

As he pushed away, Jody saw the hilt of what looked like an axe jutting from the back of the woman's head. Whoever had just saved his bacon had not waited around for him, but instead, he could see two members of the team storming into the room across the hall. Turning around, Margarita was wiping off her blade and heading his way. She did not even spare him a glance as she elbowed past and rushed across the hall to help.

Looking around, Jody took in the carnage. He was still trying to make sense of the whole ordeal when somebody blew a whistle. That was the signal to regroup.

He walked out of the room, again not able to take his eyes from all of the bodies sprawled on the floor. He counted five. Between the four in the room he and Margarita had gone into, the room across the hall, and the hall itself, there were fourteen bodies; fifteen when he added in the one down below.

George emerged from the room diagonally across from the one in which he was still standing in the doorway; being shoved before him was a woman in her early fifties. Her hair was silvery gray and she had a hard look that only seemed more intense through the blood leaking from a nasty gash on her scalp just above the hairline.

"All the rest taken care of?" George called.

"Clear at this end," Margarita reported.

Somebody else shouted out that it was clear in the room across from George. Jody glanced around and wondered if he might be the only person on this team that had not registered a kill.

He didn't care. If things were all clear, then he knew where he needed to go. Not saying a word to anybody, he walked to the trapdoor opening and started down. Somebody called for him.

He was not sure if it was Pitts or George, and he didn't care.

The calls faded as he reached the second level and ran for the stairs. Hurrying down, he reached the ground floor and rushed through the door that was still open just as they had left it. He stepped out into a light rain and sprinted around the turret for the cage.

"Danny!" he called.

There was no answer, and Jody quickly studied the mechanism that controlled the raising and lowering of the cage. It was nothing more than a block-and-tackle pulley. The end of the rope was wrapped around an apple tree trunk and tied off.

"Danny O' Leary!" Jody barked. "Answer me, you stubborn sonovabitch!"

The form up above in the cage twitched. There was a low moan and Jody felt his stomach turn.

"I am so sorry," Jody whispered.

"About what?" a raspy voice called down from above.

"Danny!" Jody yelped, rushing for the rope. He began to unwind it to lower the cage when Danny called out again.

"Please don't do that."

Jody could hear the sincerity in the man's voice, and it made him halt immediately. He stepped back from the rope and looked up to see a very battered Danny looking down at him.

"Don't you want down?" Jody asked.

"Umm…yeah." Danny pulled himself up a bit, a wince rippling across his features. "But this thing is freaking heavy, dude. If you try to go it alone, it falls and I get to bounce around in here like a BB in a boxcar."

"Let me help," a voice called.

Jody turned to see Tracy Sasser approaching. Tracy was about the same age as Jody, deep into his thirties. He was also one of the people immune to the bite. If Jody remembered correctly, Tracy was next in line for a turret assignment. He would be the one moving into Turret Ten with his wife Leeann and their son Mikey.

Between the two of them, they managed to lower the cage. As they unhitched the rope, Jody looked up at the man and saw something in his expression.

"How come you aren't inside with the others?" Jody asked.

The man hesitated for a moment. At last he let out a long breath. "I know we gotta protect ourselves, but at what point do we become the bad guys here?" When Jody remained silent, the man continued. "They are doing some pretty bad things to that woman up there."

"You might want to save some of that pity," Danny called down. "They might all be women, but delicate they ain't."

"So two wrongs make a right?" Tracy mumbled.

There was silence as Jody and Tracy lowered the cage to the ground. As Danny came down to eye level, Jody had to work to stifle a gasp.

Danny was sitting because he could not stand. His legs were jutting out in front of him, but his feet were at hideous and awkward angles. Looking at them made Jody want to be sick.

"One of 'em was apparently a fan of *Misery*." Danny forced a laugh. "I really did think that they were bluffing…all the way up until that bitch swung the sledge hammer."

A sound of heaving danced across Jody's consciousness as Tracy spun and doubled over to spew the contents of his stomach on the nearby ground, but Jody was too transfixed on the horrific damage to Danny's ankles for it to register fully.

"She never even called me a doodie-head or Mister Man," Danny quipped.

***

Entry Thirty-three—Almost got myself killed.

Sometimes you can forget that there are still zombies out there. I'm no expert, and I don't really pay attention all that much, but it is widely known that the undead have been sort of gathering into larger groups.

Some people say there are herds of the things that number in the millions. If they pass through your area, it is a lot like the old days when hurricanes would hit the East Coast. The damage can be devastating.

So far, nobody has thought of a way to just get them all to walk into the ocean or something. (Okay, maybe not the ocean since they don't seem inclined to walk intentionally into water for whatever reason, but I think I made my point.) There are even some herds that have names if you can believe that happy crappy.

Anyways, it was not a herd that almost did me in, it was one single zombie. Even worse, it was only part of one single zombie.

Back when this all started, there was a lot of bad information out there. Who knew that it would be as simple as following the rules that were put out in the old Romero movies? You gotta shoot 'em in the head. A tank is an awesome machine, but against a zombie, it just acts like a lawn seed spreader.

Some of the folks I was with back in the early days before I lost my little girl took to calling the severed or blown off heads "snappers." It was sort of a play on the snapping turtle.

I know of this one bar called The Deer Hunter Saloon. They have a twist on the game of Russian roulette. There is this big wheel like from *Wheel of Fortune*. It has six metal boxes mounted on it. They put a snapper in one of the boxes and then a curtain goes up as the wheel is spun. People put their hand in one box, and if they don't get bit, they win. Crazy, right?

So, I am setting up camp for the night. I found a great spot in some tall grass beyond a ridge. It was going to be chilly, so I had dropped back so that I could at least dig a small Dakota Hole and have a fire to warm my hands over.

I did not even see the damn thing. It had one of its arms left and part of the upper rib cage and a few vertebrae that looked almost like a stubby tail. I was just on my back, staring at the sky, enjoying the warmth of the fire when the thing grabbed my arm. Before I could do anything it had latched on to the sleeve of my coat with its jagged, broken teeth. If not for the thick flannel pullover that I had on underneath my jacket, I would not be making this entry.

Most zombies these days have some pretty busted up chompers from all the years of gnawing bone, trying to chew through walls and doors, along with the general lack of oral hygiene. That allows them to tear through things better. I should have been wearing my studded leather; but NO-O…I wanted to be comfortable and star gaze.

After I spiked the thing, I had a rough time sleeping. Not to mention I had to sweep the area for signs of any more snappers. Sure enough, found three more. This little pod had probably once been part of a larger herd and got left behind.

We are a few days outside of Billings. Since that area has one of the larger settlements, I have to guess that is their destination. I will be happy just to sleep in a bed. I have not been to Billings in a while, I wonder if it is still the same.

For those of you who have not been…it is like a mix of ancient Rome and the Wild West. They have everything you can imagine, and a lot of things that you can't. I am willing to bet that Darwin Goodkind will sell his "cargo" there.

I think I have him figured out from what I have seen. This is his scam.

He stops outside of a town he targets. His mercs stay with the wagon of women and he goes in to town with the other men that he travels with. They sell goods, but the entire time, Darwin's men are seeking out women to seduce or proposition. They arrange a meeting outside of town the day they leave. The woman shows up expecting a little fling and gets knocked in the head and thrown in that cart.

Since I started following them, I have seen this play out in four settlements of varying size. If I am correct, there are at least a dozen women in that wagon now.

On the down side, I think this Darwin character is suspicious. He has lost a few men in a short time. That last one was sloppy. They found the body, and that prompted Darwin to hire four more mercs. I am going to have to either make my move soon, or give up on this one.

One way or the other, I will make up my mind in Billings. I would hate to give up on this one. The guy is scum and needs to be taken down, however, while I can certainly hold my own in a fight, only action heroes in the old movies can win when the odds are this stacked against them. In the real world, taking on over a dozen seasoned fighters would be my death sentence. And while I am not afraid to die…I am not willing to just rush into it enthusiastically.

Dead: Reclamation

15

Geek on a Cross

A small crowd quickly swelled to a large one as word spread that one of the "unclean" had been handed over to their leader for justice. Kevin heard the ropes strain and the pulleys whine as the men began to heave. Slowly, like the start to a roller coaster, Kevin began rising up.

With a few momentary pauses as the men re-gripped the rope and gave a pull, eventually Kevin was almost all the way up. There was a sudden drop that sent his stomach to his throat as the pole seated into the hole with a reverberating thud that sent pain through his shoulders as the weight of his body shifted.

His feet scrambled for purchase on the tiny block. When his heels found it, he was able to take some of the weight from his body off of his shoulders.

"My people," Erin called out, and the crowd went silent. "I have another of those that would defy God and resist his call to the grave when the curse set free from the vials and broken seals seeks to do its holy work."

There was a cheer, and Kevin looked around, hoping for, but not finding one face that was sympathetic. What he saw was hate and rage. These people were sheep being led by a wolf.

"This abomination would try to come and steal your soul before you have redeemed yourself and made peace with the most holy God in order to secure your place in Heaven. With his tainted blood, he would have you all infected and one of the soulless wanderers for all eternity."

An angry roar arose, and from somewhere, a rock sailed through the air and slammed into Kevin's chest. As if a signal had been sent, several more came. He could duck and bob his head somewhat, but his ability was so limited, and in seconds he felt pain radiate and his vision go to white as rocks found his face.

"Enough!" Erin bellowed.

Amazingly, the rain of stones ceased in an instant. Kevin could feel the warmth of blood trickling down his face. His vision remained blurry and it felt as if his right eye might be swelling shut. He spat out a mouthful of blood and was thankful that no teeth came along for the ride.

"This man will remain here as that wave of death comes. He will be swept away by them, and it will be he that loses his soul before he can redeem it!" Erin shouted, her voice becoming fervent.

The crowd cheered. Kevin looked down as Cherish began to string a long cord with hundreds of tiny bells around his legs. She tossed them up and over his outstretched arms. Every time that he moved, there was a jingle. When he re-positioned his feet, there was a cacophony of noise.

The men who had hoisted him up were now busy building a fire just about five feet away. He was going to be the decoy. It was common knowledge that zombies came to large heat sources. They were doing everything they could to bring the dead right to him.

Wagons were already in a line to cross the bridge and depart this small island that had once been a park that housed a soccer field on one part with a picnic area on the other end.

A group of men appeared and started dispersing the crowd. Erin remained with Cherish as everybody left. Kevin continued to struggle with keeping his heels on the tiny wooden block. Every time he so much as twitched, bells would ring like some sort of deranged Christmas ornament.

"I really hope that sound carries," Erin said, looking up at Kevin with almost no emotion on her face. "And don't you worry about that woman you were travelling with, I am sure that my people are keeping tabs. Perhaps there will be enough left of you that I can have your head on my desk when she comes looking for you once the dust settles, so to speak."

Erin turned and started off, directing her people and leaving Kevin as the last person on the tiny island. He wanted to hope that maybe the zombie herd might shift again. But, if anything, all the noise from this camp being broke down and on the move would only serve to pinpoint his location.

His feet slipped and the jingle of bells sounded. A second later, it was answered by a chorus of low moans.

***

"Well I didn't sign up for this kind of garbage!" a woman spat. "If she did what you are saying, then why don't we just kill her?"

"I plan on it," Catie mumbled. Darlene nudged her in the ribs.

"And you are certain of what you saw?" a man asked, standing up on his tiptoes to be seen.

"Absolutely," another man said calmly.

Catie had been introduced to Rob McKay. He and his partner, Sam Redding were like night and day...in more ways than one. Sam was tall, with dark skin. Rob had skin that was so milky white that it practically glowed in the dark, an enormous splattering of orange freckles and curly red hair that almost looked like a fright wig. But where Rob was muscular and had the look of a fighter to him, Sam was nerdy and stick thin.

"It's like Carrot Top and Erkel," she had quipped when the two men were out of earshot and it was just her and Darlene.

"Yeah, but you don't want to piss either one of them off," Darlene said with a frightening seriousness. "They have things floating around in their minds that make me grateful they are on our side."

She was curious, but it would have to wait. They had gathered in the shadow of the partially struck military tent. Catie counted seventeen people. They were all apparently "in" on the whole idea that their leader, this Erin Crenshaw, might not be all that she was trying to claim.

Darlene had been on the fence about it, but now she seemed to be committed. Catie had to credit it to Kevin. He had shown her the "monster" up close and personal. She had made her own conclusions and realized that those who were immune were not all evil just like all that were not immune were all good.

"You need to see this!" a man exclaimed as Rob was about to speak further on his plan to depose Erin Crenshaw.

Catie had actually chuckled at the use of that word: depose. What they meant was that they would kill her and somebody else would have to step forward. But now that would seemingly have to wait. The man standing just inside the tent flap looked like he had seen a ghost.

People started filing out, mostly out of curiosity in regards to whatever had this young man so rattled. Catie figured that the herd of zombies had finally made the scene. Honestly, it did not matter how often you had dealt with zombies in the past, a large herd could still put fear in your heart and make you stop and stare for at least a moment or two to witness the awesome power the zombies possessed when they were in such great numbers.

They had to weave around the people involved in the mass exodus of what had once been Jordan's Point Park. Word had been passed that the rally point was the parade grounds of the Virginia Military Institute. Once everybody was there, apparently Erin was going to announce their new destination.

Catie had decided that these people were the modern day and human equivalent of locusts. They came, ravaged anything and everything useful. Made themselves a nuisance to anybody who might already be in the area, then they moved on. She was pondering that idea when she stepped into the alley between a pair of the last remaining tents that were in the process of being taken down.

"Is this some sort of ritual?" Catie asked.

In the distance, she could see a man hanging from a cross. The sun was in a position that it was really nothing more than an amorphous and unidentifiable shape. However, a sick feeling began to grow as those around her had gone suddenly silent.

She turned to Darlene. "I'm serious, do you guys do this every time you leave. Some sort of offering to God or whatever it is that you believe in?"

"No, these are only done for the worst of the worst. The last one was over three years ago. Some guy went on a bit of a spree and raped three women. His last victim managed to tear his mask off. He beat her down and left her for dead outside of camp, but a roving patrol found her before a zombie did." Darlene shuddered. "The guy was strung up and then lowered into a cage of zombies as his punishment. Oh...and he was stripped naked. Guess what they ripped off first."

"He wasn't on a cross, though," Rob pointed out. "They put him on what was basically a giant 'X' and so he was left dangling...literally."

Catie shuddered at the thought and shielded her eyes to try and get a better look. She still could not see because of the way the sun was hitting, but a feeling was growing inside her.

A hand grabbed her arm, and Catie looked down to see it was Sam. He shook his head. "We gotta go. Everybody is rolling and that herd could be here any minute."

Catie pulled away. "In case you forgot, I'm not one of you. Maybe you are okay with something like this, but it seems rather barbaric to me. Why not just execute the poor bastard and be done with it?"

She started walking against the grain of the crowd. A moment later, she felt somebody beside her. She was not surprised to see Darlene.

"I have a bad feeling about this," Catie whispered.

***

Kevin tried to turn his head, but every time he did, he would slip from his perch and jerk to a halt, wrenching his shoulders something terrible. To compound things, all the bells would jingle and clank. The zombies were getting louder. This caused him to want to turn his head and the whole thing would start over. He was almost certain that he had dislocated his shoulder the last time he fell. The pain was white hot and constant from his left shoulder now, and even with his foot on the perch, the pain remained.

For some reason, the sun seemed especially bright and hot. He hadn't remembered it being quite so brutal, but his thirst was becoming almost painful in how unbearable it had become. Carefully taking the pressure off of the one heel, Kevin allowed that single foot being lifted to act as his center of focus. It was the only spot not engulfed in pain at the moment. He had to bite down to endure the agony in his shoulders, but it was just for a few seconds and then he wedged it back into place.

He took those few seconds to take stock of himself. He was certain that his one heel was terribly bruised, it would not allow him to stand on that tiny wooden ledge much longer. At some point when he'd been hoisted, his prosthetic had come unseated. Now it dangled impotently and useless, reminding him of his often ignored fragility. His head throbbed from the blow he had received at the hands of Cherish Brandini, and flies were starting to buzz around it which added to the creepy and unclean feeling that had him fantasizing of a giant wash basin.

He could feel a dull, hot throb from his one wrist. He could not bear to look over at it. His arm was straight and tied securely, but about halfway up the forearm, that horrendous break left what remained hanging limply. The radius and ulna were both snapped in two. He was certain the bone had come through the skin, but he was wearing a long-sleeved shirt and coat which prevented him from actually confirming that suspicion with his own two eyes.

Yet, none of this compared to what was coming, He could hear them; and by now, he could smell them. The dead were coming for him and there would be no miracle save. His credo of "This ain't the movies!" rang like an evil taunting chant in his head. The zombies would finally win.

He thought about everybody he had lost. Some he had missed terribly, others not so much. Hell, he was only human. He had never been much of a people person, and when he was being honest with himself, he knew that his know-it-all mentality was off-putting to say the least.

Yet somehow, through it all, he had met Aleah. They had been madly in love. It was not her fault that he was immune and she was one of the unknown. They had gotten drunk one night on some homemade blackberry brandy. She had actually suggested going out to find a zombie and letting it bite her. That way they would know for sure.

Kevin still hated the fact that he had taken a few seconds before coming to the conclusion that such a thing would be a bad idea. He had loved her so much, and while they could have tried to make a go of it, they both knew it was mere fantasy.

And then there had been the odd fling with Heather. Five years of being so close and more of the homemade blackberry brandy coupled with them both being immune had resulted in an odd romance. Kevin struggled the entire time with the fact that he had known Heather when she was still just a teenager. The fact that she was in her early twenties held no credence in his mind.

They parted under good terms and remained friends all the way up to the day that he and Catie left. In fact, Heather had been intent on coming along with her new beau, but the pregnancy nullified that possibility.

And then there was Catie. Their love-hate relationship had been one for the ages. Not once had she ever just accepted anything because it was his idea. Many council meetings were adjourned with those two going at each other over everything from matters of security to farming techniques.

One night after a particularly heated argument, it had been Aleah's insistence that the two meet and hash out their deepseated problems, whatever they might be. She had acted as moderator for the first ten minutes when she stood up and told Catie to simply kiss Kevin and get it over with. After some sputtering and hemming, she had actually kissed him. It had been done out of anger more than anything else as she vehemently denied any interest in him.

At some point, apparently Aleah had left. Kevin could not say when, because it was as if something in him had finally clicked into place. He was madly in love from that point on. The two became Beresford's first "power couple" as they steered the community to a prosperity and comfort that many believed they would never know again.

It was as if his mind had found its other half. Eventually, the town no longer needed their guidance to sustain itself. People had learned, paid attention, and offered their own contributions to making things better.

And then the nightmares came. He's had to know for certain about his sister and mom. He had to return to the place he knew they had gone and see for himself what had befallen them. He had actually considered slipping away and going alone. He loved Catie dearly and was afraid that such a trip would result in her death. He'd already sent enough of the people that he cared about to their graves. He did not want to be the reason Catie died.

But he knew that there was no way he could do something like that to her. She had made it clear early on that she would remain at his side forever.

"You're the first person smart enough for me to love forever," Catie told him one night as she lay snuggled against his side.

"And you might be the only woman tough enough to stand me that long," Kevin had said as he leaned over and kissed the top of her head.

It was in that instant as he hung on that cross, his mind doing everything possible to distract him from the pain, that he realized why he had felt so at home in Falling Run.

As a child, his family had owned that cabin up the hill. They had made the trip every year, sometimes as many as four different outings. It was his father's escape from the hustle and bustle of his work life. And while he had hated it as a teen, he realized that most of his best childhood memories had revolved around that cabin. This area was someplace that was imprinted on his mind as good...peaceful. Home.

Kevin screamed. Looking down, he saw that the first of the leading edge of the zombie herd had at last reached him. One of them had grabbed at his leg and tugged, causing the pain to shoot through both shoulders.

Through his blurry vision brought on by the tears filling his eyes, he saw more heads turn his way. Some that had passed by and perhaps not noticed were now very aware of his existence. He was an island of meat in a sea of undead. Already he was engulfed on all sides; the undead tens of feet deep.

Yet, one had noticed. That one had grasped and pulled, causing Kevin to scream. And so now...well...now they all knew. More hands grasped him and began to pull. Kevin bit it back for as long as he was able, but he could feel his shoulders being pulled to their limits of their abilities.

Teeth gnawed at his pants, and at last, one of them managed to create a rip in the fabric. The jeans tore, and flesh was now exposed. That first mouth closed on him. Teeth jagged from being broken on who-knows-what tore his flesh.

The pain was too great, and Kevin screamed again. This time, it was *that* scream. He'd heard it before. And part of his mind refused to accept that he was actually the source this time. He felt a chunk of meat actually tear away from his calf, and Kevin shrieked.

Hands grabbed and pulled. Kevin begged for unconsciousness, but it eluded him. He cursed his mind, because it was that part of him...the part that had been his savior, the savior of others, for so long. It was his brain that now became his enemy. It wanted to know. What would this be like? How would it feel to be torn apart and eaten alive?

A ripping sensation came, and Kevin screamed so hard and loud that blood seeped from the rips he inflicted on his own throat. His right arm actually gave first and his body tilted to one side. Kevin's eyes rolled up and he could see that arm still bound to the crossbeam of the cross. The nub of the bone where it had connected to the shoulder socket was a dazzling white to his exaggerated vision.

And then the other arm tore free and he was being pulled to the ground. A sea of faces looked back at him without seeing a thing of the person he was; they only saw something to consume. He meant nothing, and his agonizing screams fell on deaf and uncaring ears.

He looked down as hands tore at his clothes and then found the vulnerable flesh beneath. Every zombie movie he ever saw had to feature that one scene. It had been made famous by one of his first childhood heroes: Tom Savini. The scene at the end in the mall where a few of the bikers (led by a handlebar-mustached Savini) meet their doom at the hands of the undead. One in particular is surrounded, and then his belly is ripped open. The zombies begin to pull out the man's insides as he can only look on in horror and scream.

Now it was Kevin's turn. A part of him became the spectator…the kid he was that day he first watched the scene on a VHS tape with wide eyes and an open mouth. At some point, it had been Mike who said, "What a load of crap! That guy would have totally passed out from the pain."

Kevin was sorry to discover that was not the case. He saw parts of him pulling free and vanishing into the mouths of the undead that crowded around him to the point of blocking out the sun.

As the darkness came, both real and from his sensory shutdown that was now trying to catch up with the fact that he was dead, Kevin thought he heard his name being called.

"Kevin…I love you!"

"Mom?"

The words were formed by his mouth, but there was no sound. Kevin was already dead, and his lungs had been ripped from his body along with most of his other vital organs. He was ripped apart, and at some point, his head rolled down the slight slope that his cross had been planted upon.

Eyes stared blankly up at the cloudless sky for several minutes. Then…they blinked.

***

"No!" Catie screamed, but Darlene had her around the waist and both Rob and Sam had a grip on her arms.

She had seen the hordes of undead as they washed over that small ridge and engulfed the open ground around that cross. She had a momentary thought that she wished she was close enough to end that poor soul's misery with a crossbow. It was just a matter of time before the zombies realized there was a person within their grasp. Yet, for several seconds, the leading edge simply trudged past.

"Dogs don't look up, and neither do zombies."

That line was one that Kevin liked to spit out in his awful impersonation of an English accent. She had never seen *Shaun of the Dead*, but she felt like she had after all the times of hearing Kevin recount it, including some of his favorite lines. One day, he had told her that the part about zombies not looking up had been his own addition to the line, but for some reason, it tickled him to no end to say it.

For a few seconds, it looked as if he might actually be right. Then...one of them turned. She saw a hand reach up and grab the person by the ankle and give a pull. The person lost their footing and fell. In that instant, only being suspended by where he (she was guessing at that point that it was a male) had been fastened to the crossbeam, there must have been a terrific wrenching of the shoulders. That had been the cause of the man's (she was certain the instant she heard it) scream.

However, she also recognized something in that scream. Like a mother who can pick out her child's cry in a nursery full of children, she knew the owner of the gut-wrenching sound.

"Kevin." Her mouth made the word, but it was an act of her mental autopilot.

That person who was condemned to a horrific death was her Kevin! She knew, despite immediately searching her brain for even the slightest possibility to the contrary, that he was going to die. Saving him was an impossibility. Yet, she felt herself trying desperately to move towards him. Her arms reached out, but something was holding her back...pulling her away.

It all happened in the few blinks of an eye, but it seemed that she could live each frame-by-frame moment for an eternity. Her ears refused to allow the sounds of his screams to penetrate. Yet, they would forever exist in her nightmares where she would hear them almost every night for the rest of her life.

One side of him seemed to shift unnaturally, and then she saw his body tear free, the arm still dangling by the twine used to secure it. An arc of blood shot skyward in rhythmic pulses. Then, the other side came free. It was almost merciful as he vanished into that sea of undead.

In that instant, it was over. She knew he was gone. This was the end of Kevin Dreon. Perhaps it was fate being cruel and kind as was her wont. At least she would have no doubts as to if he might be alive somewhere.

There would be no rescue mission. No quest to save her lost love that ended with the fairytale kiss.

"This ain't the movies," Catie whispered.

Those around her had no idea what she meant. A few thought that perhaps she had lost her mind. Darlene knew different. Darlene was staring into Catie's eyes and seeing the depths of her pain. In that moment, she pulled as much guilt into herself as she could manage.

"We need to go," Darlene whispered. She knew that the woman was hearing none of it. She had shut down everything except the horror playing out a scant fifty yards from where they all stood.

Looking around, they were now the last people still on the island. They would need to head almost on a straight line due west and cross the small slough that separated this island park from the fringes of Lexington.

"Kevin!" Catie screamed at the top of her lungs, as if she were just now registering what had happened. "I love you!"

"We gotta go!" Rob urged.

Yes, Darlene thought, *we have to get moving right now.* The zombies had turned to this new sound and were now coming their direction. On the positive side of things, the zombie is a simple creature. They would reach the point where they would cross over and then be able to vanish into the woods. That leading edge would stop at the banks initially. The rear of the herd would soon force those in front to stumble forward and act as a bridge.

As they crossed the narrow channel, Darlene looked at her companions. None of them had actually met the man. To them, he was just another poor soul to fall victim to the undead. Their only emotional stake was that they were believers that Erin Crenshaw was a fraud; that she had possibly manufactured situations in order to get the masses to act in a certain way and do things to fit her agenda.

Basically she was government by fear.

They had two choices. They could take this opportunity and escape to form their own community, or, they could attempt to take Erin down and change the course of the large group of people who were following in Erin's footsteps.

When they reached the other shore and climbed up, Darlene cast one more look over her shoulder. The first zombies were being pushed into that little creek or stream. A thought came as she took Catie's hand and led the woman into the relative safety and obscurity that the trees provided.

"I am one of those zombies…"

***

"As grand as that gesture is, I say it is a fool's errand," Sam said sternly and with a shake of his head. "That woman has people eating out of her hand. She is the post-apocalyptic Jim Jones and they all drank the Kool-Aid."

"So we just walk away?" Darlene asked. She was not doing so to sway the group to change its course and go after Erin; she simply wanted some form of clarification. So much had been said for both arguments that she had lost track.

The group was hunched around their fire pit. They had made camp on the crest of a small hill that offered them a view into the camp of Erin's people. It looked to have once been a baseball field; now, it was a mirror of the stars—at least from this vantage point. From above, each of the little fire pits looked like the pinpoint light of a star. With so many spread out, a person could find a pattern if they looked hard enough.

Catie sat alone on the outer-most fringe of the small group. Darlene had brought her some water, but the woman had simply stared straight ahead and not even registered that another person was there. Her red puffy eyes looked even more frightful in the gloom.

"If we do this, it probably ends with us getting killed," Sam repeated his stance for perhaps the tenth time. "I say we hightail it outta here and just start over."

"I think we have talked about this long enough," Rob spoke as he stood. "We need to cast a vote, but before we do, is there anyone amongst us that will have a hard time following the consensus of the masses such as it were."

Nobody said a word. Truthfully, Darlene was tired of talking, she wanted to know what they planned to do. Either way, she would handle her business.

"Show of hands," Rob stage-whispered, "who is for taking the fight to Erin." One hand rose. His. "And for getting on with our lives and getting the hell away from here with our skin intact?" Everybody else's shot up fast. "So be it."

Darlene turned to Catie. "Are you gonna be okay with that, Ca—" The name died on her lips.

Catie was gone.

16

Captive

"Wake up, Thalia!"

My eyes opened and Jim was standing over me, blood trickling from a gash on his left temple. I sat up and initially was confused. When I fell asleep, there had only been the three of us along with Blake and Chelsea. Now there were a dozen people at least, and they were all decked out in some very serious body armor.

I finally found Jackson in the clutches of four men who were easily just as large as the man that had always been one of the biggest that I'd known in my life. The worst part was that all of these people were wearing dark face shields so that you could not see their expressions.

Somebody grabbed Jim and jerked him away from me. There was a struggle, but I was grabbed roughly and yanked to my feet by one of the faceless invaders.

"Hands behind your back," a voice demanded.

Still not entirely awake or aware, I guess I took too long. My left arm was wrenched behind me, causing me to cry out. The right arm was treated just as roughly, and I felt something being wrapped around them a few times before being cinched tight.

"Leave her alone!" Jim howled.

For his troubles, he was yanked back by his hair and punched in the gut. He slumped to his knees and began to cough. Jackson was faring no better. The men who had him were taking turns. One would hit him and he would spin or stagger into another that would continue the beating until he finally fell hard onto his back.

"Why?" I asked.

I never saw the fist. Everything flashed, and my vision went dark. Sound continued to come in through a muffled filter. When I could clear my head enough to see, I was looking up at one of the tinted visors that reflected what I hoped was a distorted image of my face.

"On your feet," the voice behind the mask ordered.

When I saw his fist clench, I struggled to push myself up. I saw Jim and Jackson both being hauled up. What I did not see was any sign of Blake or Chelsea. Either they were lying dead and out of sight, or they had run off into the woods and escaped. I was not sure which I actually hoped for.

"Alright," my captor hollered, "let's get back to camp."

I was shoved forward. Jim was a ways in front of me and I had to assume that Jackson was somewhere behind as we headed south towards the general direction of the La Grande valley.

***

All my life, I thought that we had a pretty decent amount of people living in Platypus Creek. There were even times that I felt crowded.

Three days ago, I was marched into an encampment that was easily ten times the number of people that we had back home. And, if what I was hearing in the bits and pieces of conversation that I managed to eavesdrop on was true, this was nothing more than the "advance" force.

I had not seen Jim or Jackson since we arrived. They had shoved me into a tent that was well guarded as I discovered the first night when I thought that I was being clever. I had feigned sleep when my meal was brought in and set on the small box that was my only furniture. As soon as the person exited, I had crept to the back of the tent and pulled it up enough to slip underneath. The boot that caught me in the side was hard enough to knock the wind from me. I was scooped up and unceremoniously dumped back inside my tent/cell.

I waited every day for somebody to come in and question or kill me. Honestly, both seemed equally as probable. Still, each day passed the same way. Two plates of vegetable mush was brought in by a person who was decked out in the armor and visor that my captors had worn. I was allowed to empty my toilet bucket each morning under escort to a deep trench that made me almost gag the first time I was brought to it.

On the fourth day, two guards entered. Judging by the light outside, it was just about sunset.

"On your feet." One of the men stepped forward with a leather thong in his hand.

"It takes two of you?" I snarked. That earned me a backhand that put me on my butt. I tasted the familiar coppery saltiness of blood.

"Hands behind your back," the man who hit me demanded.

I thought about making another sarcastic remark, but it was clear that these guys had no problems roughing me up. I was not stupid. I knew when I was in a "no win" situation. At least I certainly did after I'd been belted once to jog my memory. Once my hands were secured, I was blindfolded.

"Is that really necessary?" I asked. Big surprise, there was no response.

I was led along. There was a vibrant hum to this camp. With so many people, I had to wonder how they did not have every zombie for miles converging on their location. Even at night there was noise, and when we had been brought in, I had not seen any sort of barricade. I had been surprised that they had not simply moved in to Island City and maybe patched up the damage they had inflicted. It had to be better than just being out in the open.

And then there was the whole logistical issue. How were they keeping fed? I walked past a wooden pen and saw a pack of dogs. This only added to the logistical nightmare that it must be to keep this many people supplied while on the move. This was an army.

At last we stopped in front of a large tent. There was no real sentry or anything in front of it, but I was not exactly sure what I should be expecting. I had read plenty of books over the years, and in all of them, the evil villain always had an entourage of guards that sneered or made a general nuisance of themselves.

"Send her in!" a voice called from inside the tent. I was more than a little surprised to hear a woman's voice.

I walked in and looked around. It was nothing special. There was a cot against one side, and an arsenal of bladed weapons on a rack. There was a folding table in the center of the tent, and a woman was sitting at it with a few tubes that I had to assume held maps.

"Come on in," the woman beckoned, standing as I walked in alone. My escort remained outside the flap of the tent.

I might have gave a shrug, but I did as she asked and walked up to the table. She got up and came around, removing my cuffs.

"Who hit you?" she asked.

At first I thought it might be a trick. When she came back around and sat down, leaning forward with an expectant look on her face, I answered. "One of those goons of yours that escorted me here."

"Which one?"

"We never exchanged names."

"Chance, Randy?"

I heard a rustle behind me. "Yes, ma'am?" two voices replied with unveiled formality.

"Which one of you struck this girl?"

There was an uncomfortable silence. It went on long enough that I thought there would be no answer.

"It was me."

I glanced over my shoulder and took a better look. Honestly, I had made no effort to really learn anything about my captors. When I'd been smacked, it came out of the blue, and I hadn't really paid it much mind.

The man was nothing special. Maybe mid-thirties; just a bit older than Melissa if I had to guess. He had short, brown hair and was about as non-descript as a person could be. He could be a teacher, a farmer, or a cook. He did *not* look like an evil henchman. Just a regular guy.

"Report to the watch commander, Randy. Tell him you will have outrider patrol for the next two weeks," the woman behind the desk said with all the emotion of a snake. There was something in her voice that scared me. It was like you could hear the violence she was capable of just by listening to her tone.

"Yes, ma'am." I had no idea what outrider duty was, but I could tell it was not pleasant.

The two men turned and hurried out. I returned my attention to this woman behind the desk. She was actually very pretty. She had dark hair just touching her shoulders and eyes that were large and very blue which were made all the more striking in the frame of her almost perfectly black hair. I say almost because of the few strands of silver that were laced throughout. She was dressed in black (which reminded me that she was my captor, and therefore, probably the bad guy).

"My name is Suzi. I don't imagine you are quite ready yet to tell me yours?" She had tweaked her inflection at the very end of her statement just enough to hint at a question.

I was not ready to say a thing to her. One of the things that I learned when I was in training to be a field scout was the art of keeping quiet. Of course I had learned that lesson much earlier from the likes of Billy, Paula, and Dr. Zahn. I could not count the number of times they got me to tell on myself by just staring at me and not saying a single word.

"That's okay." Suzi leaned back in her chair and regarded me over steepled fingers. "So perhaps I can let you in on a few things. Maybe that will help you realize that I am not your enemy."

I made a point of keeping her gaze. I could not tell if she was trying to stare me down, or if she was just trying to figure me out.

"The first thing that you should know is that we did not engage the people of this area until they left us with no choice. If you are from one of the small communities around here, then you should know that we did not mean any harm, and we would not have launched an attack without provocation. Our patrols came under attack first. We simply retaliated."

As she spoke, this woman rose and began to pace. That did two things: first, it put me on the defensive physically; second (and I think this had to be her actual reason), it broke our eye contact. She was lying—if not outright, at least partially. I had seen with my own two eyes as this army had struck that smaller community just to the west and up against the foothills of the Blue Mountains. That had been a bunch of college kids that migrated here to escape the insanity of the valley corridor war zone. I believed Cricket over this woman that seemed to radiate a coldness that I could feel physically.

"When we arrived in this valley, we were delighted to find so much lush farmland," Suzi continued. "When we discovered that there were some settlements, we sent our emissaries to see if there might be a place that we could settle and call home."

"Where are my friends?" I blurted in the moment that she took a breath during what I was now thinking had to be some sort of rehearsed spiel.

I was not surprised when she did not turn to face me. If she was half as smart as she needed to be in order to be running an operation like this, then things like eye contact tells during a lie were probably common knowledge. However, the one thing I might be able to assume here in the moment is the fact that she has a visual tell in her eyes or on her face when she is being dishonest. I could at least bank that nugget of knowledge.

"They are all alive and well," Suzi said. She turned after that statement and her face held no emotion at all. It was entirely blank. I was getting nowhere with this playing cat-and-mouse garbage.

"Then prove it."

"You are a bold one," Suzi said appreciatively. That was perhaps the most emotion that I'd seen from her so far. "But maybe you can tell me why I should just give you what you want. What can you give me in exchange?"

"If you think I would ever tell you where my…" I tried to think of the correct word while still keeping it as generic as possible, "where my home is, then you are mistaken."

"And why is that?"

I actually laughed out loud. And it was not in a happy or pleasant way; nope, it was laced with all of the nasty sarcasm that it needed to have at the moment. I saw something flash in her eyes; it might have been anger, but it was gone too quick for me to be positive.

"Do you really need to ask that question? Maybe you should look out across the valley to what is left of Island City." I felt my anger build. The fact that she could even ask that question was just a little insulting.

"Are you so quick to condemn? Do you know the whole story?" Suzi was suddenly right in my face. She had not raised her voice, but there was a threat in it now that did not rely on volume.

"I know that killing the living is no way for humanity to have a chance. I know that I have heard folks say for years that maybe it was time we were gone as a species. I never understood such things…until now." I did my best to keep my voice from wavering. Inside, I was a bundle of nerves. I have heard Paula say more than once that a person can be brave and still be scared; now I understood what she meant. "Your people came in and killed women and children. Maybe you can tell me what threat they posed."

"How many children did you see?"

The question caught me off guard. At first I thought that it was a trick; then I realized that she was being serious. She was looking at me with an open concern on her face. Either she was searching for something, or she was actually asking me.

Suzi continued to stare at me with that raised eyebrow that indicated she was expecting an answer. I let my mind drift back. I replayed when we first entered the break in the barricade. Almost immediately we had come across a pile of corpses. I remember how something had seemed off, but that I was too overwhelmed to figure out what I was missing. Like a sack of rocks, it hit me with an almost physical force.

"Few…if any."

Making that admission was difficult for more than one reason. The first was that I had missed something so obvious; but then, so had the others. Or, if they had noticed, they had not bothered to point it out to me.

"Good, I was worried that my men might have lied. You just saved about a dozen lives, little girl." Suzi actually had an expression of relief on her face. For whatever reason, she had been concerned about the children of Island City. Still, that did not make okay what had been done to the people of not only that settlement, but the others that had fallen to these raiders.

"So what is the whole story?" I asked, taking our conversation back to the point she had tried to make earlier.

"Excuse me?"

"You said that I did not know the whole story, and that I was being too quick to condemn. What's the whole story?"

"How about you tell me your name first." A wicked smile curved Suzi's lips. It was not malicious or evil; it was more playful than anything else. That had me returning to the idea that this was some sort of cat-and-mouse game. I knew which one I was, and I knew how it often ended up for the mouse.

"My name is Thalia Hobart."

"Pleased to meet you, Thalia." Suzi folded her hands on the table. "Would you care for something to eat or drink?"

"I want to know where my friends are being kept and be sure that they are okay."

The last thing I was worried about was a snack with the person responsible for capturing and keeping us prisoner. I knew for a fact that Billy would be worried by now. This was supposed to be an out-and-back mission. We were to grab whatever supplies we could find, teach Dorian a lesson about how rough things can be outside the fence of Platypus Creek, and then get back home. We were long overdue.

"If I can show them to you and that they are okay, will you return to my tent with me? Will you answer a few of my questions?"

"Not if it has anything to do with where I am from." There was no need to lie. She was either going to do this or not, but there was no way that I was going to tell her where my home was so that she could launch an attack on it.

"Fair enough." Suzi rose and started for the exit.

I hurried to catch up. She walked with purpose and wove through this massive camp, making it a point to hail individuals by name as they called in greeting. I was impressed. It was clear now more than ever that she was running this show. It was also apparent that she knew these people. They were not just anonymous faces of her army.

We passed one large tent and a dozen children between the ages of four and maybe ten came rushing up. Suzi paused, kneeling in the dirt to hear what the little ones had to say as they all seemed to speak at once and at a million miles an hour. There was no fear, and I had to admit that they all looked rather healthy. This was starting to confuse me even more.

I knew very well that every story has two sides. Still, I had a difficult time being able to accept that the people of Island City deserved the fate that had been dealt. These people were raiders.

Pure and simple.

Right?

We stopped at a series of large wooden grates that were over a handful of deep holes in the ground. I was led to the first one and felt my heart flutter.

"Jim!" I leaped forward and collapsed on my knees at the edge of the large square cut into the ground.

It was at least ten feet deep, and it showed signs that Jim (or whomever else had occupied it before) had made attempts to climb out. There were gouges in the walls that gave evidence to the failed efforts.

As for Jim, he was a filthy mess. Not only was he bloody and visibly battered, but he was caked with dirt. Much of it had mixed with his blood, which only made him look worse. His normally curly hair was matted to his head, and I could make out at least two nasty gashes that had bled like only a head wound can bleed.

"Hey, cupcake!" Jim looked up at me and his face instantly broke into a huge grin that looked just a bit creepy coming through all of that filth.

"You look terrible," I managed around the growing lump in my throat.

"Yeah…I missed my day for shower sign up."

I wanted to cry, but hearing him still be able to make a wise crack was enough to give me the strength to push my tears back. As I gave him a closer look now that I was over the shock, I saw that he had one hand that was terribly misshapen; easily twice the size of the other.

"Are you okay?" I know that it was a stupid question, but I was at a loss. What could I say? How long would this Suzi person allow me to stand here and talk to Jim?

"I'm not making any new friends," Jim said with a shrug.

"Would you like to see the other gentleman?" Suzi asked, stepping up beside me.

"Hey there, gorgeous," Jim hooted. "Are you my reward for not beating the crap out of my guards the past two days?"

I had to stifle my smile. At least now I had some idea of why he looked that way. Despite his obviously beat up condition, I was feeling much better about things for some reason.

"If you behave today…*Jim*…" Suzi said with obviously fake sweetness, "…perhaps you will be allowed to clean up. A few of those wounds look nasty. Wouldn't want to risk infection."

I cursed myself, I had just given up his name, and judging by the emphasis she put on it when she said it, he had not given even that bit of information up to our captors.

"That would be awful swell, ma'am." Jim clasped his hands together and tried to bat his eyelashes. I imagine it would have come across better minus all the caked mud and blood. That, and if his right eye was not almost swollen completely shut.

I felt a hand on my elbow. Suzi was leading me away. I expected to stop at another of the pits, but instead, we continued until we reached a metal box that was about eight feet high and maybe three feet by three feet square. A single guard was standing at the latched door.

"How has he been?" Suzi asked the sentry.

"Same as always. As soon as he gets his voice back, he starts yelling until he loses it again. I imagine he should be able to muster up enough voice if you want to question him."

This did not sound good at all. What had Jackson gone and done? I braced myself for the worst.

"Open the door." Suzi gave a nod of her head. I saw a look of concern flash across the man's face. He looked around like he was expecting help from somewhere.

"Don't worry about him, he will behave." That coldness had returned to Suzi's voice. I felt my flesh pebble up; whether it was because of her or my growing fear over what I would see when that door opened, I have no idea.

The sentry undid the chain and let it slide through the latch. Hand on his large belt knife, he opened the door. The stench that rolled out from it made me think that maybe Jackson had become one of the undead. It was a sour mix of sweat and blood and human waste all mixed together and then heated.

Standing in the box, looking like he had been beaten with a sledgehammer, Jackson stared out through slits where his eyes should be. His mouth was swollen almost to the point of sealing off his nostrils; and it did not help that his nose was a flat smear on his face.

"Oh!" escaped my lips before I could silence myself. For some reason, I did not want to give any satisfaction to our captors in regards to showing how upset I was over the condition of my friends.

Jackson made a noise that sounded like a laugh. His face was simply too misshapen to tell if he was smiling or grimacing. I saw a twitch at the corner of his mouth and decided that he was trying to show me that he was okay.

I spun to face Suzi. "And just how do you think showing me this will get me to cooperate in any way with you for any reason."

"Because," she gave a curt nod and the door to the box was

shut, sealing Jackson off from me...the world. "They are both still alive, yes?"

"Is that what you call it?"

"In this world, absolutely. Now, I have been very patient with you, Thalia Hobart. So I am going to ask you a series of questions. You get one chance to answer."

"Or?" I knew the response was going to be unpleasant, but I was trying to stall in hopes that any idea at all might form and guide me through this.

"I guess that is for you to find out."

Suzi walked over to a wooden table and sat down, motioning for me to sit across from her. I had no other option. I spotted at least half a dozen men who were lurking around the perimeter of the area that I had to assume to be their detention block.

"How many others were in your group?" Suzi asked.

That was simple. I could answer that question without lying or giving anything away. I told her about Blake and Chelsea, making sure to emphasize that they were not with us. As I explained the details that made up that encounter, I saw Suzi's face begin to darken. It was a few seconds before I realized that I had stopped talking in mid-recount.

"Well, that would explain your reactions to me and my people," Suzi finally muttered somewhat cryptically.

I stayed silent. As far as I was concerned, I had answered her question. Sure, I left out the part about the rest of the team that I had traveled with, but I had been truthful by omission.

"Hunter!" Suzi barked suddenly, causing me to jump.

A man trotted up. He was in black much like Suzi. I guessed him to be an older guy; possibly in his late forties. He had a crew-cut and it was almost silver, but I could see hints of the dark brown it must have been when he was younger. He had brown eyes that seemed warm and friendly. I noticed when he shot me a glance that he actually smiled in a pleasant way that did not seem anything other than pleasant. I would guess him to be just under six feet and around two hundred pounds of lean muscle judging by the arms coming from the short-sleeved shirt he was wearing.

"Yes, ma'am." Hunter came to a stop and stood almost at attention. He was favoring his left side just a bit, and that was the only imperfection in his stance.

"I am not aware of a man who went by the name of Skins. Is there one?" Suzi asked with just a hint of anger starting to show in her voice.

"Not that I am aware." Hunter glanced at me after he replied, then his eyes went back to Suzi.

"And what became of the dead bodies that were found on scene when our three guests were apprehended?"

"Burned, ma'am."

"And were there signs of another male and female with the three that were brought back?"

"Not according to any of the reports."

Once again Hunter shot me a look. Now I was starting to get uneasy. This was coming down to my word versus that of the people who brought us back. However, that left me with some other questions and concerns. If Skins and his gang were not part of this group, then what group were they a part of?

Suzi turned back to me. "So…these men you killed were not mine."

"I don't know what to tell you." I felt my mouth go dry and my mind began to replay the images that I saw of Jim and Jackson. I hoped that I would be able to withstand whatever torture was in store for me. It was obvious, or at least I felt comfortable in the assumption that neither man had said a word.

"I do not doubt what you have told me, although it has been very little up to this point. Perhaps we should try again tomorrow."

With that, Suzi gave a nod of her head. Hunter stepped forward and ushered me to come with him. I glanced over my shoulder as I was led away. Suzi remained at the table we had sat at and was staring skyward in deep thought as she vanished from my view.

Hunter remained silent as he escorted me through the camp. I still could not get over all of the activity. There were children running and playing, people doing wash and hanging clothes up to dry. Basically, everything about this place screamed normal. Only, these people had sent scientists in to Island City. They had infected them with some terrible virus that they passed off as a cure or inoculation against the bite of zombies. They had wiped out a small community of college kids who were nothing more than farmers trying to make a home for themselves here in the La Grande Valley area.

At least, that was how I saw everything. Was I missing something? Perhaps Cricket had lied. How could I justify believing one person over the other? I was going on what I saw with my own two eyes.

Or, at least what I *thought* I saw.

"How old were you when all of this started?" Hunter broke the silence. It was in that moment that I realized that it was not an uncomfortable one. There was something about Hunter that I liked. I was oddly relaxed.

"Like five or so," I answered.

That was weird. I had never given it any thought. I grew up in a world of zombies. That was just the way things worked out. I actually felt sorry for some of the older folks sometimes. I would hear them talk about the way things used to be and I just could not imagine it. The world they spoke of was simply too foreign.

"...with your parents?" Hunter's voice inflection snapped me out of it and I managed to catch the last part of his question.

"A neighbor in the apartments I lived in saved me. I guess he found me while my mom was being eaten."

I had heard the story enough. Steve had obviously shared it with Melissa. It was actually one of the few stories about Steve that she had ever told me. I got more from Dr. Zahn and Billy when it came to Steve and a girl named Teresa.

"I was thirty-five," Hunter said with a crooked smile that reminded me of Jim in a strange way. "I was the manager of a movie theater. Not one of the big multi-plexes. We showed foreign films and artsy-fartsy crap. But on the weekends we showed this movie called *The Rocky Horror Picture Show*."

He went on to try and explain this movie. I didn't really get it. I would swear that he was making most of that stuff up, but his voice and the look on his face told me that he was telling me the straight truth.

When we reached my tent/holding cell, Hunter turned me to face him. His expression was serious, all signs of that wistfulness only moments ago was gone like it never existed.

"You are in a dangerous place, Thalia. But these people," he waved his arms to indicate the camp, "they are not the bad guys. I am not saying that you should just trust us. Trust is the most valuable commodity a person can give these days. What I am saying is that you might want to consider all your options."

"Did you make that same speech to Jim and Jackson?" The words were out of my mouth before I could stop them.

"I had nothing to do with anything that happened to them. I do know that they were…" He paused as if to search for just the right way to phrase his next words.

"Uncooperative?" I offered.

"That is one way of putting it."

"And what would you do in their situation?"

Hunter opened the flap to my tent and ushered me inside. I was surprised when he followed me in.

"All I can tell you is that the people here in this camp are good folks. I don't know how well you knew the people in that settlement, but we came in peace."

With that, he turned and left. I went to my cot and sat down. My head was spinning and I was so confused. Was this just more of their way to get me to let down my guard?

I fell asleep despite the fact that my brain was going around in circles. Maybe I was not as ready for being out in the field as I thought. Images of Jim in that pit and Jackson in that box came every time my eyes shut. They did not go away when I began to dream.

* * *

A light rain was falling, but it was still warm. I stood just inside the flap of my tent and marveled at the flurry of activity.

It had begun about an hour ago when it was still dark. It was only in the last few minutes that enough sunlight was forcing itself through the gray clouds above to allow me to see more than ten feet past my tent.

A group of heavily armed people rushed past. I noticed that the person guarding me was over by the fire pit talking with a few other people and did not seem to be paying attention.

It had been five days since I'd met Suzi, seen Jim and Jackson, and then been escorted back to my tent. In that time, I'd been fed, allowed to shower every other day with warm water, and even been allowed outside of my tent when it had been so hot that I was starting to get dizzy from the heat.

The thought came so fast that I was acting on it before I even realized what I was doing. My guard was intent on his conversation about whatever had this place in such a tizzy. He actually had his back to me.

I slipped out and around the corner of my tent in a hurry. As soon as I was out of sight of my guard, I had to fight every urge in my body to run as fast as possible. Despite the increase in activity in the camp, it was likely that I would draw attention if I just took off.

The first problem that I encountered was the fact that this camp was so massive. It was sprawled out across one of the huge open fields and sitting on a sloped hill.

Eventually, I reached a bit of a clearing between all the tents and was able to get a better look around. The ruins of La Grande were to the north of my location. We were on a slope that was close to the eastern edge of the valley which put us just on the edge of the foothills.

However, I now also saw what had the camp in such chaos. Coming up from almost directly south of our location was a massive herd of zombies. They were on the same side of the creek that ran sort of north-south through the heart of this valley. That put them on *our* side.

They were coming right for us.

17

Vignettes LX

"I don't think we can cross here," the guide said above the wind that threatened to almost blow the tiny man over.

A storm had come in the middle of the night. Juan had not been surprised. They were less than a week away from Anchorage, and other than the painful loss of his wife, the trip had been uneventful. They had not seen a single deader; wolf or otherwise.

The small wagon train was at the edge of just another nameless stream. The only problem here was that the water was roaring; whitewater rapids churned and threatened to smash anything that got swept up in the aquatic fury.

"Keith and I will range north and south from this spot." Juan had to yell to be heard over the chorus of wind and water. "No more than a mile or two," Juan said as he turned his attention to Keith.

"Agreed," the man said with a nod. "If we can't find a good crossing in that range, we might have to just camp and wait a few days for this to die down."

Juan nodded and wheeled his horse around. Both of his daughters were sitting on the bench seat of their wagon with Brianne Macintyre. She and her wife Stella had been the third family to join in this trip to Anchorage.

Brianne was a petite woman, but Juan had seen her spend a day splitting wood right in the midst of the men back at the old community. She was into things like yoga and jogging. Juan had tried the yoga once and discovered that he was about as flexible as a rock. And as far as the running was concerned, he had done quite enough of that during those first days of the deaders to know that he hated the very idea of it.

"You girls mind Brianne while I am gone. I won't be long." Juan held up a hand to halt the coming protests. "We have to see if there is a place that we can cross. The water is too rough here."

Brianne gave a nod, and Juan leaned over to accept the hugs and kisses from each of his daughters. Turning, he gave a wave to Keith and started off along the banks of the raging stream. Not more than ten minutes into his search, he spotted something up ahead that made him yank back suddenly on the reins. The horse shook its head in protest, but Juan did not notice; his eyes were glued on the scene a hundred or so yards ahead.

A huge bear—he assumed it was a grizzly since that was the only type of bear he'd ever heard anybody talk about since he'd arrived in Alaska—was surrounded by at least a dozen wolves. It was raining too hard to be certain, but Juan had the feeling that these were deader wolves. Most wolves would not actively seek out and attack a grizzly unless they were starving. With the absence of humans, game had come back in abundance, so he doubted that was the case here.

Staying back, he watched as two wolves moved in. Their slowness and absolute lack of fear when it came to the massive paws of the bear swiping at them was enough to confirm his suspicions. He knew that he should simply turn and leave, but he was inexplicably transfixed by the scene.

The bear never had a chance. It could not keep all of the wolves at bay, and since they were as single-minded as any deader, they simply continued to come at the massive beast despite any injuries inflicted. However, Juan did make note of one thing; the bear refused to bite at any of the wolves.

Even as it was dragged down and torn apart, the grizzly

would not bite them. At last it was over, and he turned to head back before being noticed by the pack of deader wolves. They would not be heading this way even if there were a crossing point. Also, he would tell the others to increase their vigilance.

He was riding up the hill to where the wagons were waiting when he heard something. Whipping his head around, Juan could see several figures slinking along in his wake. He had waited too long and the pack of deader wolves had obviously spotted him before he had gotten away cleanly.

Giving his horse a nudge in the ribs, he increased to a fast trot. It was dangerous to do in good conditions considering the uneven terrain, but in this horrible weather, it was verging on reckless.

When the horse took a tumble and the beast came crashing to the ground, Juan was not in the least bit surprised. He was upset. He was angry. But, considering things as they had transpired up to this point, he was not shocked. For some reason, he had apparently lost every vestige of common sense. This last time might be his undoing.

The horse screamed, and Juan thought he heard a terrible snap. However, the pain that shot up his right leg made him wonder if that sound had originated from him or the horse. Not that it would matter. Neither of them were going to be able to get up and run away. And while they were deaders, and they were still much slower and less coordinated than their living counterparts, deader wolves were easily as fast as a slow running human.

Juan closed his eyes and waited for death. The faces of his daughters came and he welcomed them. Unfortunately, so did the face of Mackenzie…and not the beautiful one that he knew and loved. This was her as a deader. Juan tried desperately to shove that image aside. If he was going to die, then at least he could do so with his final thoughts and mental images being pleasant ones.

***

Vix stood at the edge of the water. It had been over a week since Gemma killed herself. In that time, she had replayed the events over in her head a thousand times. She tried to figure out what she could have done different.

"It was not your fault," a voice said.

Turning, she saw Chaaya walking down the gentle slope. Her black hair was pulled back and she was wearing a sarong and blouse that looked all the more elegant because of the wearer. The woman had a delicate grace to her that made Vix wonder how the woman had survived the early days of the apocalypse.

"You know that, right?" the woman asked as she came down and stood beside Vix, looking out over the water.

"But maybe if I would have brought her in differently. If I had not had everybody on hand as a welcoming party. Perhaps she was just not ready…" Vix's voice trailed away as she dove back into her thoughts.

"She was broken."

The words made Vix snap her head around to regard the woman. Chaaya was still looking straight ahead, but a tear was rolling down her cheek.

"I saw it when we were out there. When she killed those men, that was the only time I had ever seen her smile. And it was an honest smile like the kind you would get if you see a dear friend walk through the door." Chaaya turned to face Vix. Twice she opened her mouth, but both times she snapped it shut.

"Go on," Vix urged. "You obviously have something to say."

"When we were crossing in the boat, were you watching her face?"

Vix thought about it and realized that she had been more focused on the far shore. She had been anxious to get Gemma home and have somebody to care for again. She had never allowed herself to develop a new relationship. The death of her husband had been it. And while she was in constant demand as a nurse in the community, she realized in that short span of time while they were crossing the channel back over to their community of New England, she was excited to have somebody to care for directly.

"No," Vix admitted.

"Gemma was terrified. She was seeing ghosts…something that wasn't there. For whatever reason, the closer we got to the other side, the more frightened she was becoming. I have no idea why, but she was petrified to her soul."

"So, what could I have done?"

"That's just it," Chaaya said with a shrug. "I don't think there was anything that you could have done. She was broken. She had become like some wild animal that can only survive in its natural habitat."

Vix considered that statement. It seemed so at odds with the young girl that she knew and had departed with from Basingstoke. But then it was as if the proverbial scales fell from her eyes. There had always been a certain degree of impetuousness about Gemma. And then there was all the madness from when they had at last reached the country home. Not to mention more than a few incidents when they had been on the road. Each time, she had dismissed it as the ignorance of youth and the hormones of teenagers.

The bell rang from up in the village, announcing that the afternoon meal was about to be served. The two women turned and started back up the hill. As was the custom, the entire community came together for the evening meal in the great hall that had been erected on what had once been a massive paved lot.

The meal was just coming to an end when Vix noticed a few of the children had wandered over to the fence that ran along the perimeter. This area looked out over where the River Medway broke away from the Thames. Across the river sat the ruins of an old industrial area that had been ravaged by fire a handful of years back.

Vix remembered it well. The fire lit up the sky for over a week and the fumes that came from it had made a number of people ill. Two women had miscarried.

Getting up, Vix wove through the tables towards the children. She could hear the excited tones in their voices. Climbing up onto the walkway that ran along the length of the perimeter fence, Vix felt a growing sense of unease.

"What do we have?" Vix mussed the hair of a boy no older than six.

"Lots of people." The boy pointed and Vix followed his finger, although she really did not need to.

It was clear what he saw and what had these children so excited. It dawned on her that none of these children had actually seen a zombie. They had all been born after, and since the island had been completely swept in the first two years after the start of this madness, the new generation only knew of zombies as the source of scary stories. Tales that were no more real to these children than they had been to her when she was younger and saw *Night of the Living Dead* at the late night cinema.

They had talked about this for years. The possibility had always existed, but as time passed, that talk had faded. And now…here it was right before her eyes.

Turning, Vix walked over to the hand-operated claxon. Grabbing the handle, she began to wind it. The shrill siren cut through the evening calm. Every head turned her direction. The looks of annoyance and confusion were slowly replaced by determination and a hint of fear.

The zombies were here. In numbers too great to count, the undead had massed at the water's edge. About a mile of water was all that separated what looked like millions of the undead from the community of New England

***

"She showed up one night in the rain," Butch said, his expression relaxing some as he let his mind drift back and dredge up the pertinent memories. "A dozen or so of the stiffs were on her heels. Nobody even thought about it. We just put them down and brought her into the gates.

"We only gave her a cursory look. She wasn't bleeding or anything, and that was our first mistake. When she showed up, she said something about some religious group offering her up as a sacrifice…"

Chad, Ronni, and Caroline looked at each other. This made Butch pause. He began to look unsure until Chad spoke. "That is the same thing she told us."

I guess it is easier to keep your story straight that way," Butch said with a nasty laugh and a shake of his head. "She was our poor little victim. We brought her in and everything was fine for a week or so. She was eager to help and do her part. At least that is what she was saying. I got my own suspicions about that."

When Chad gave a nod, Butch elaborated. "I think she was scouting us. And I imagine it is a hard sell now, but she was a hottie."

"Yeah, about that." Caroline moved in and gave Butch a tap on the shoulder.

"That little nip on the face? She's lucky she got off that easy," Butch snarled. "If it would have been up to me, I would have staked that whore to the ground and let the stinking zombies have a picnic."

"Whoa!" Chad barked, reaching forward and grabbing the man by his shirt. "Watch your mouth, pal. You are skating on thin ice."

Butch looked around as if suddenly remembering his predicament. He gulped once and let out a long breath.

"Are you saying that injury was inflicted on her by your people?" Caroline asked.

"At the trial," Butch said like that explained everything. When Chad gave him a rolling motion with his hands for the man to elaborate, Butch nodded.

"When all the guys at Jack's bachelor party came up infected, it didn't take a damn rocket scientist to figure it out. That gal showed up when the boys were good and drunk. From what we could put together before we had to end each one of those poor bastards, she just barged in and said that she wanted to do something special to show her gratitude. She did some sort of strip tease and had the boys lined up at the door in less time than it takes to shake a stick.

"Damn shame when the groom came up infected two days later. As each case popped up, it was pretty easy to put one and one together." Butch looked up at Chad, Caroline, and Ronni. The open-mouthed expressions gave him a touch of confidence. "Now you are getting it. That gal is one of them folks that don't get turned until they die."

"Jesus," Chad breathed. Caroline echoed the sentiment, but Ronni turned and darted from the room.

"Keep an eye on him," Chad told Caroline before turning to take off after his daughter. He had no idea what she might be up to, but he knew it could not be good.

He was at the door when he heard the crash. There was a slap and then a scraping sound.

Entering the cabin, Chad saw his daughter standing over Melody who was curled up in the fetal position on the floor. Ronni had a knife, but it looked clean, which indicated that he did not think that she had used it as a weapon…yet.

"Get up!" Ronni shouted. Bringing her foot back, she let loose with a kick that connected solidly with Melody's ribs. "C'mon, play that crap with me, you little—"

"Ronni!" Chad cut his daughter off and stepped the rest of the way into the cabin.

"She's evil!" Ronni spun to face her dad, all the anger showing like raging bonfires in her eyes. "And she was coming at you. All she would have had to do was get some of her blood on you and that would be it."

"First," Chad moved in carefully between his daughter and Melody, being careful to stay clear of the infected girl in the chair, "it does not happen quite that easily. You can't get it just by somebody getting a bit of their blood on you."

"And you know this how?" Ronni challenged.

"It just doesn't work that way. I would have to be cut or something."

"You don't know that, Dad." Ronni was starting to cry. Chad was becoming confused. "You are only guessing."

"But I am pretty sure." He reached over to pull his daughter into a hug, but she yanked away.

"And I am pretty sure won't give me my dad back if you are wrong!"

And there it was. Chad looked at his daughter, speechless and unable to counter her statement. She was right; he could not be absolutely certain. He was just making a guess, but how much faith did he have in it. Suddenly, his conviction was slipping.

"Sweetie—" he started, but she jerked away and cut him off.

"You are all that I have. I lost everything in the world except for you. And when you were sick back at Dustin's, I realized that I was very lucky. So many people have already lost everything. And here I was with my dad...and I didn't care. I felt terrible. Terrible for how I acted, how I treated you. And now you can just risk dying and becoming a zombie because you *think* you know how this works?"

Chad pulled his daughter to him again. This time she did not resist. She buried her face in his chest and cried. It struck Chad that he could not actually recall the last time his daughter had a good cry.

As he held his daughter, a million thoughts tried to crowd his mind. He shoved them aside. They stood that way for a long while until Caroline actually came to make sure that they were both okay.

Reluctant, but aware that they had some things to take care of ASAP, Chad eased away from his daughter and turned to face Caroline.

"Go cut that guy loose."

***

"Says her name is Jan Seiber or some such thing." George gave a jerk of his chin to indicate the woman crumpled on the floor with Margarita standing over her. He had his arms folded across his chest and did not seem to notice the droplets of blood that had splattered his face.

Jody looked around at the group. Not one single person seemed the least bit bothered. A couple had actually sat the dead bodies of a few of the women against a wall and placed their hands over their eyes, ears, and mouth in a twisted parody of "see no evil, hear no evil, speak no evil."

271

"Everybody downstairs now," Jody said calmly. When nobody appeared inclined to move, he added, "NOW!"

People jerked and Bill Pitts looked up from the pack he was poking through. All eyes had turned his way, but Jody would not shrink. Instead, he drew himself up taller.

"I said everybody out," he repeated with a hint of menace in his voice.

"What's your problem?" George challenged, clearly not happy with being told what to do, much less ordered.

"When did we become *these* people?" Jody asked, indicating the dead bodies and then pointing to the woman on the floor who was breathing in slow, labored gasps that hinted at a broken rib or two. "When did we become the bad guys?"

Pitts rose to his feet and Jody was prepared for a confrontation. Instead, the man walked over and stood beside him. After giving Jody a nod to continue, the man folded his arms across his chest and fixed a disapproving scowl on his face.

"We have seen plenty of this over the years. And sure, these people did something horrible, but is this what we have become now? Because, if it is, you can all count me out. I'll pack my stuff as soon as we get back, and I will take my family someplace else." Jody kept his tone hard, but did not yell.

"And what would you have us do to get information from these people…tickle them?" George asked. "And maybe you forgot that they murdered the people who lived here and then burned the bodies."

"We were simply coming for one of our own," a voice coughed.

All eyes turned to the figure on the floor at Margarita's feet. Jody winced at the woman's face. She struggled to move, but Margarita had her booted foot in the woman's back. Pitts cleared his throat and she stepped away with a sour twist of her lips that almost looked like a snarl.

"What do you mean?" Jody asked, stepping forward.

"A pair of our girls were scouting the area when one of them was grabbed by a couple of men. Her partner followed to this place before returning to get the rest of us. We were simply coming for our friend." The woman had pushed herself up to her knees.

"So, you want to explain what was done to *our* friend?" Jody asked.

"We were trying to find out where our girl was, and he was the only one left after we took this place," the woman stated matter-of-factly. "And before you ask, we did not set out to kill everybody when we got here. It just ended up that way once things got ugly."

Jody looked around at the bodies of his own group's recent handiwork before turning back to the woman. "And how did you get in this place to begin with?"

"A tower full of five men? Really?"

Jody shook his head. She had a point. But that still did not really explain Danny.

"And the man you people maimed and put in a cage?"

"He showed up late for the party, hell, that is probably what saved his life. If he'd been here with the others when we took this place, he probably be just as dead as the others."

"Listen...Jan...Sieber is it?" Jody knelt in front of the woman. "You aren't doing yourself any favors with your attitude. I can only keep these people back for so long. Can you tell me about the women from your group that was supposedly kidnapped and brought here?"

"Yes, my name is Jan, *her* name was Angel, and they dumped her in that pit like so much garbage after they did God-knows-what to her."

Jody did not know anything about a body in the pit. He looked around and got shrugs in return.

He considered things for a moment. He glanced over at Pitts, but the man had stayed silent and was offering no help. At last he told everybody to move down to the lower level. Danny was down there with Tracy, and he wanted to have everybody in one place. Also, the time it would take for everybody to get down there would give him time to think.

Once they reached the ground level, Jody had a couple of the group do a circuit around the tower to see if there was in fact a body. He also had a few others help Tracy carry Danny inside. He did not need the verbal confirmation when he saw the expressions on the faces of the two he sent when they walked back into the turret.

"I want this woman and Danny separated from each other," Jody announced. "Set each one up in a store room for now."

"Ummm, you want to tell me why?" Danny asked.

"Because," Jody announced, making his voice loud enough so that everybody could hear him, "we are going to return to doing things right around here. We have let things go long enough. It is time to start acting like civilized people. I think we are on that edge, and if we don't pull ourselves back, we are going to fall over and never be able to get back."

"What in the world are you babbling about?" Margarita huffed.

"We are going to have a trial."

***

Entry Forty-nine—We reach Billings early tomorrow.

I am determined to do this now. No more waiting…no more stalls. I forced myself to face the truth. For all my desire to do what is right, I am afraid. I don't really want to die, and I am frightened that this is exactly what will come of this should I pursue it to its conclusion.

Entry Fifty—They are outside the door.

I know that there is no escape, but at least I have done what I vowed to do, and that is make sure that Darwin Goodkind never again victimizes another living soul.

I woke early to reach Billings before the caravan. I was seated by the window in a saloon when the wagons passed by. I quickly followed, doing my best to keep my distance in order to minimize my being discovered.

It almost made me sick when I watched Darwin Goodkind walk into the nicest inn Billings has to offer. Seriously, each room comes with a tub and your choice of a young man or woman to keep the hot water refreshed as well as scrub you down and a number of other things that do not bear repeating.

He was greeted at the door by a man dressed in a white suit that looked at least two sizes too small and fell out of fashion six months after *Saturday Night Fever* hit the big screen. The man had greasy looking black hair and a scar from one temple to the corner of his mouth on the left side of his face that looked like it was put there with a big knife.

I am telling you all of this because of the fact that I know how this ends for me. I will not leave Darwin Goodkind's hotel room alive, and if I do, I will be taken someplace and killed there. So, when I finish this entry, I will throw this book under the bed and hope to God somebody finds it besides the people banging on the door right now.

But, back to Darwin...

When he entered the hotel, I found the first boarding house I could and checked in. I got cleaned up and then went to the market. Using everything I had of value, I traded for some nice clothes that would get me through the doors of the Billings Grand Hotel.

Once inside, I strolled with surprising ease into the lounge where I spied Darwin talking to the greasy hotel manager (or whatever the guy is). It was an animated discussion, and in the end, a satchel was pushed across the table to Darwin. He promptly excused himself and exited.

I followed, making my way up the stairs. I arrived at the fifth floor just as the door was closing. Waiting for a few heartbeats, my hand grabbed the knob and turned it as slowly as I could manage in an attempt to minimize any noise.

When I opened the door and peeked down the hall, I did so just as Darwin stepped into a room and shut the door. I hurried down the empty hallway and pulled up on one side of the door. I could feel my heart trying to pound its way out of my chest, but my goal was so close that I could taste it.

I was just trying to decide what to do when the door from the stairwell I had exited flew open to reveal a pair of men who were brandishing spiked bats. A second later, the door at the other end of the corridor opened to reveal two more.

With no other choice, I kicked open Darwin's door and rushed inside. He was simply sitting in a chair like he was expecting me. Turns out he was. This is my best attempt at recreating that dialog.

"When exactly did you start following us? I told my men that it was somewhere around Park City." Darwin folded his hands in his lap and leaned forward just enough so that I could see his eyes as he peered at me over the tops of his tinted glasses.

"I'm here to stop you from hurting anymore people," I finally said, ignoring his casual remark and accurate guess.

"Oh goody, a crusader." Seriously, the only thing missing was an English accent to make this guy sound like the evil villain that I knew him to be.

Pulling my knife, I saw the first glimmer of concern cross his features. But it was quickly erased when there was a solid thud against the door that I was currently leaning against.

"You will do no such thing, and...you will have the added benefit of dying a painful death for your troubles."

Another slam into the door I was braced against caused me to lurch forward an inch or two before slamming back into place. I would not be able to hold these guys off for long, then my eyes made a connection: there was a table just inside the door against the wall to my right.

I endured another solid thump against the door and then reached over and yanked the table to me, spinning around it and then wedging it cockeyed so that one corner of the table was right under the doorknob and the kitty-corner was just inside the entrance to the small closet on the right hand wall. I knew it would not last for long, but I didn't need too much time.

When I turned, knife in hand, I saw the fear in Darwin's eyes. He was on his feet and had drawn a long slender blade at his side. I was willing to bet he hadn't had to pull that thing in a long time. It looked awkward in his hands and he wielded it with the uncertainty of a novice.

My backhand caught him across the face and sent him flying. I was on him in a flash. He started to try and make deals, but I had no desire to hear it and I quickly pulled out one of my gloves and shoved it into his mouth. I heard a couple of teeth break in the process as the large steel studs held up better than his teeth did. A piece of leather wrapped around his head once and tied tight ended all but his gurgles.

I was not going to have all the time that I wanted to make this animal confess or even really get into detail as to why I was here to kill him.

I will die knowing that he had no doubts as to what had brought me to his door. Sure, he might wonder which specific person he had hurt was the reason, but his eyes told me that he was aware of his wrong doings.

I wish I had the time to share more, but the door is giving. They stopped trying to break it in and are now smashing in the top half. I will give them a good fight, maybe take one down on the way, but I know that I will be reunited with my loved ones soon…and that will have to do.

Dead: Reclamation

18

The Geek's Girl

"If we do this, it probably ends with us getting killed," Sam repeated his stance for perhaps the tenth time. "I say we hightail it outta here and just start over."

"I think we have talked about this long enough," Rob spoke as he stood. "We need to cast a vote, but before we do, is there anyone amongst us that will have a hard time following the consensus of the masses such as it were."

Catie didn't need a vote to know what these people were going to decide. These weren't soldiers or warriors. They were just people. None of them had any reason at all to take this fight to the person responsible. They'd obviously seen this sort of thing before.

They would all run and hide, using some sort of excuse like this Erin was too difficult to get to without putting themselves in grave danger. They would slink back into whatever cracks they had oozed out of until somebody else came along to lead them. They would follow for a while until they got their panties in a bunch over something, and then…they still wouldn't do anything except maybe run away again.

This world was full of followers but very few real leaders. One of the best leaders she had ever known was dead. The only man she believed worthy of her love had been taken. Somebody had to pay.

Catie slipped into the shadows. She glanced back just as the vote was being taken.

"Show of hands," Rob stage-whispered, "who is for taking the fight to Erin." One hand rose. His own. "And for getting on with our lives and getting the hell away from here with our skin intact?" Everybody else's shot up fast. "So be it."

Big surprise, she thought as she allowed the shadows to take her into their embrace.

***

Catie moved in the darkness. Her mind drifted back to the last time she had actually been alone. It had been the day that she decided to walk away from that all-female army unit and follow Kevin and his people.

She had known right away that he was different. However, he only had eyes for Aleah at the time. She didn't begrudge him that; the girl was a natural beauty. It is not every woman that can lose part of her nose to frostbite and still be gorgeous.

Sadly for the couple, Kevin would eventually discover that he was immune. And while it was possible that Aleah shared his immunity, the only way to be sure would be if a zombie bit her. Once things settled down after the arrival at Beresford, they had to eventually face the harsh facts.

Kevin had known long before, but as is human nature, he held on to some hope until the last strands of it were peeled away. When the couple parted ways and vowed to remain friends, Catie had wanted to finally make herself known to this man who had wedged into her heart much like a popcorn kernel between the teeth.

Something just kept her back. Every time she would start to build up the nerve, some job or another would need doing, and if she was not elbows deep in getting it done, then Kevin was heading it up in some capacity.

Then the "Heather" thing happened.

She kicked herself a while for waiting to the point where

Kevin felt his only choice for companionship was that silly girl. And that was the perfect way to describe Heather Godwin. Yes, she had her moments, but Heather was a girl. Once the walls of Beresford went up, once the illusion of safety and security had been cast, (because Catie knew that it was nothing more than an illusion as long as one zombie existed) Heather returned to being concerned about her hair, nails, and if a pair of pants made her butt look big.

It had been a rainy night when somebody knocked at her door. She was not surprised to open it and discover Aleah standing there. They had remained friends over the years. What she was surprised about was the topic of conversation.

Kevin.

"Why aren't you going after him like you do everything else that you set your mind on?" Aleah had asked.

Catie had not insulted the woman by feigning ignorance. Instead, she had simply stared at her and not said a single word. That had always worked on people in the past. If she sat there and said nothing, then they usually got intimidated and changed the subject. She should have known better than to try that with Aleah.

"Kevin has never seen me as anything but a soldier. I have been his muscle, I have been his enforcer, and his sheriff. What I don't think I have ever been in his eyes…" Her voice had faded as she simply could not bring herself to say the words.

"A woman?" Aleah had no such reservations.

That had opened a floodgate. The women had cried, laughed, and come to an understanding. The next day was that fateful argument where, out of the blue, Aleah blurted, "Oh, just kiss and get it over with!" Or something to that effect. They had kissed. And in that moment, the world melted away. Their romance had started slow, but it had burned hot and steady ever since.

Even when they argued, there was something about it that was wonderful. And as the years fell away, it was clear that she had everything she wanted. Only, she began to realize that Kevin still had a hole. When the realization came, Catie almost broke down and cried. Kevin had been largely responsible for bringing her home. He had helped her create this safe place for people to live. But how could she not have seen sooner that he needed the very same closure that she herself had craved so desperately all those years ago?

And that was why she began gathering supplies. On his celebrated birthday (he refused to say how old he was, but Catie believed he might have actually forgotten) she had all their friends come over to say good bye. He was going to have closure in this part of his life one way or the other.

The trip had been an adventure of its own. In fact, Kevin had started to keep a journal. He said that maybe he would write a book about their adventures. He enjoyed the irony of the idea of being an author of post-apocalyptic fiction during the post-apocalypse.

As the journey went from weeks to months, the two saw the best and worst of what had become of the country, of humanity. There had been a field in Iowa with bodies stacked like cord wood for no apparent reason. They had walked one stretch of highway where bodies were hung every hundred or so paces—each one with a placard around his or her neck announcing their supposed crime. On the other end of the scale, there had been the wedding they witnessed in the shadows of an old stately courthouse that was a verdant green from the vines that were climbing and wrapping around every surface. There was the morning they woke to a strange sound and watched as a massive herd of buffalo stampeded across an expansive plain. There were all those sunrises, many witnessed as the two simply held hands and took in nature's beauty. Catie loved sunrise, it was a colorful promise of the potential awaiting in the new day.

And now, she was alone again.

Catie moved down one slope and followed the banks of whatever river ran through this area. She could hear the sounds of the camp as she drew closer and closer. People were going about their night with the blindness of sheep trusting their sheppard.

Catie pressed herself into the ground when she reached the

edge of the faint and flickering shadows created by this many people camping on an open parade ground. While they did not have bonfires or anything of that nature, there were a few lanterns or torches lit inside a handful of tents. Those would be the people who considered themselves to be in charge. Leaders that gave themselves a different set of rules than what everybody else was expected to follow.

A figure was less than ten feet away. Judging by the way the person was moving with a deliberate slowness, she had to assume this was some perimeter security. It was that person's misfortune to have drawn a watch shift in this location and on this night.

Catie's hand went to her hip and the knife she had. At the moment, it was her only weapon. She still could not believe that these people had handed her one. If they'd only known…

Quick and quiet, she rose to a crouch and scuttled up behind the person. In a flash, she came up, wrapped an arm around the person's face, effectively covering their mouth, and then drove her blade up and into the kidney. There was a muffled cry that died as the pain seized the person and made any sort of noise a near impossibility.

Catie felt a bit of sticky warmth on the hand that held the blade. Once the person was still, she lowered the body to the ground and dropped back into a crouch. She never even bothered to look at the face to see if it had been a man or woman. She didn't care. At this point, they were all sheep, and she was the new wolf in the field.

As she reached the first tent, she paused. Inside she could hear a muffled voice. It had the steady cadence and supplicating tone of a man in prayer. Slipping down the side of the tent, she decided that it would do her some good to perhaps find a backup weapon. She cursed herself for not searching the sentry. She would go back if needed, but it could not hurt to check here first.

Hugging the inky black of the shadows that had devoured the fringes of this camp that were farthest from that small cluster of tents with lights inside giving off a dull white glow, Catie moved with caution and paused at the entrance.

"…and bring strength to our leaders as they steer us through these trials. Please forgive my sins and accept me into your kingdom when my time on this earth is finished…" the man was whispering fervently.

Catie slipped in, covered the man's mouth and slit his throat. This time, a geyser of blood sprayed, making a wet splat sound as it met the taut wall of the canvas tent. Letting the body drop, Catie briefly wondered if he had gotten the answer to that final prayer as she went about searching for any sort of weapon. She was happy when she found a bow and quiver of arrows. It was not the best quality, but she did not need anything special. In addition, she found a machete. Its rough construction told her that it had been made as some sort of batch weapon. Again, low grade, but capable of what she needed tonight.

She left the tent and fixed her gaze on the cluster of tents that were lit. She did not care how many people she had to go through, but she would do it tonight; she would avenge Kevin and kill Erin Crenshaw.

She tried to remember all she could about this girl. She remembered that she had been with Kevin's people. She also knew everything from what Kevin had shared about how he had come to meet the Bergmans. The problem was that most of his stories were about the eldest sister Ruth, and then Shari. Erin's name seldom actually came up except as a side note. The only story centered on her was the one involving the loss of the girl's baby and the guilt Kevin carried for not having been able to save her.

She recalled the girl staying when Kevin and his group left. She had not paid it much mind. Whatever had happened between now and then was a mystery. However, she decided that she did not care what she knew or didn't know about this girl and her past. If all went well, she would be dead by morning.

If it worked out that she was able to take out Cherish Brandini, that would just be a bonus. Catie moved silently through the camp. She had discovered over the years that large groups of people eventually fall into a false sense of security. This seemed to be the case here.

Of course, they had just side-stepped a herd. When she had

evacuated to that hilltop, she had seen that Erin was smart enough to send trailers on the heels of that herd to ensure that they continued on a course away from the camp they had made in the parade grounds of the Virginia Military Institute.

As she passed one tent after another, she was actually finding herself becoming more and more angry. While it was unlikely that every one of these people had seen what happened to Kevin, she knew that plenty had watched it firsthand. Also, she had no doubt that word had spread. These people felt nothing in regards to that death. Well, perhaps they would feel differently when she was finished.

A part of her wanted to slip into each and every single tent. One at a time, she would kill them all. But her rational mind forced her to dismiss that fantasy. It only needed to go poorly one time to stop her from her ultimate goal.

At last, she was at the edge of the glow provided by those tents in the center of this sea of canvas. As she expected, there were armed sentries. The problem was that they were at the entrance to not one, but three of the tents. She would have to either risk playing a lethal version of the shell game or hope for a miracle where Erin would simply pop out for some trivial reason and reveal her location.

Her mind allowed Kevin's voice to filter in and remind him in that way he had. "This ain't the movies." She could not and would not hope for such a miracle. Then she heard a laugh.

It was familiar. She knew the sound of a flirtatious Cherish Brandini when she heard it. That laugh was coming from the tent on the far left. If things were in a logical pattern, she would expect Erin's tent to be the one in the middle. She would pin her hopes on that.

Dripping back into the shadows, she circled around. Every so often, she would stop and check the sentries. Were they being vigilant, were they talking to one another? These were all things that she would need to know in order to give herself the best chance for success.

At last she had worked her way around to the rear of the large tents. She waited patiently and was rewarded when the roving sentry walked past. She counted with a steady deliberateness to try and gauge the timing. Once she reached a hundred, she no longer cared. She doubted there was some kind of elaborate scheme where the guards came by at staggered intervals to eliminate somebody being able to time an attack. Hell, she was almost willing to bet that there was enough arrogance here that these people did not actually even expect one to ever occur.

Knowing that she had at least two minutes, Catie waited for the sentry to pass before scurrying to the tent. She held her breath and listened. There was no conversation. That could be a good thing. If Erin was in this tent, and if she were to be alone, then this might actually work.

Taking out her knife, she slowly worked it into the seam at the base of the tent. Once she had a good four or five inches, she laid down flat and tried to peer inside. Her heart slammed in her chest as adrenaline flooded her.

Sitting with her back to where Catie had made the cut was her target. Even better, Erin was alone. She was seated at a small desk writing something. Catie knew her time was almost up, she crept back to her hiding place and waited for the sentry to pass once more. As soon as he or she rounded a corner and vanished, Catie returned to Erin's tent.

"…will become a light in this time of darkness. I invite you to join me, and together we can ensure that we never again suffer such a heinous attack. I realize this will test some of you, but just remember our lost children. And not just my own, many of you feel my pain at this moment as the wounds of that loss are still fresh. We have taken down one of their leaders, but we must not stop there…"

Catie had heard enough. The woman was rehearsing a speech that Catie wanted to be certain was never given. She made a mental note to be sure and grab those pages as well. She would not want them to be discovered and used as some rally cry for these people.

Her knife cut through another several inches of the base of the tent. Catie had to retreat once more, but she knew that she would need to make her move on this next trip. That slice could be discovered if Erin turned her head.

As soon as the opportunity presented itself with the passing of that rover, Catie crouched and scurried to her handiwork once more. She laid flat and looked in again, using her index finger to just barely lift the tent. Erin was still at her desk, and currently bent over. This was where she would either succeed or fail.

Lifting the bottom edge just enough, Catie held her breath and pushed her head in. For a split second, she considered just thrusting through and attacking wildly. She would never escape alive, but she would still have enough time to kill this woman with her own hands before help arrived.

No, she was going to live. She was going to kill this woman and then return home to tell the others of his fate so that they could honor Kevin in a way he deserved. She knew that the people of Beresford would want to do that. Kevin had been well liked, if not loved, by the people of that community.

Instead, she moved as slowly as possible so as to not bring attention to herself. Erin continued to write at her desk just about twenty feet away. Catie wondered briefly why a single woman needed such a large space and decided that it really did not matter. She was almost all the way through the cut she had created when Erin stopped writing. Catie had been watching her intently, looking for any sign that the woman might sense her presence or become aware that she was no longer alone.

When Erin set her pencil down, Catie tensed. If need be, she would change tactics and charge this woman. There was no way that she would get this close and then fail.

Catie was all the way in now, and Erin remained at her desk. From her vantage point, it now looked as if the young woman was reading her speech. Catie rose and shifted her location just slightly in order to be exactly behind Erin. She did not want the woman to catch sight of her in her peripheral vision.

Knife in hand, she crept forward, one silent step after another. It took all of her self-control not to just charge and be done with it. Why was she being cautious? What did she have to live for? But she knew the answer to that question. It had been her final secret. One that she had intended to share after they made it official as to where they would settle down. She had not wanted Kevin's mind to be clouded. She wanted him to make his choice based on his usual logic. Unfortunately, things had not worked out as planned and she had blurted it out when they had been captured.

She only wished that she was far enough along that she could feel it kick or something. All she knew for certain was that she had a child inside her. Sometime in the last several weeks, maybe one night when they made love under the stars that lit the sky in a way that a person had to see to believe. It was a sight that she never tired of, and the fact that they had spent so many of those nights together these past several months was a consolation, although it did nothing to mitigate the loss she felt.

She was two steps away when the woman set the pages down and stood. Catie had to act now. She closed the last few feet just as Erin turned. Before the woman could scream, Catie reversed the hold of her knife and punched the shocked woman in the throat, killing any possibility of sound that might have escaped as the voice box crunched under the blow.

Like a viper, Catie struck again to be sure and used that forward momentum to grab the woman in her arms and guide her to the ground, sprawling on her with her body acting as a restraining weight. Catie brought a knee into the midsection as hard as she could. There was only a slight whistle of air escaping, and Erin's mouth opened as if to scream, but not even the slightest squeak came from the effort.

"Remember me, bitch?" Catie breathed in the woman's ear.

Erin just stared up at her, tears now leaking from the corners of her eyes. The confusion was enough of an answer. She had not made the connection yet. Well, Catie did not want to waste time. As much as she would have loved to make this woman suffer agony for a thousand hours and then a thousand more, she needed to act and then get out.

"I am Kevin's wife!"

Realization flashed in an instant, but was only allowed to remain for a second before pain and fear shoved their way back into Erin's expressive eyes. Catie smiled the smile of satisfaction and then brought her knife in and up. She felt the heart muscle resist for just a second before the blade pierced it. When Catie withdrew, blood came in a rush and Erin's feet twitched furiously.

Catie rose and looked down into the wide open and now empty eyes of her husband's killer. Leaning over, she snatched the pages of the speech and stuffed then into her shirt. With only slightly less caution, Catie peered out into the darkness. She knew her night vision was wasted by the brilliant glow of the lanterns in the tent, but she waited long enough that she eventually heard more than saw the roving sentry walk past.

Slipping out of the tent, Catie melted into the shadows. The laughter of Cherish Brandini tempted her, but she had done what she set out to do. Now it was time to go home.

DEAD returns

April 15, 2015

But turn the page for a sneak preview of

DEAD:Snapshot—Portland, Oregon

Coming soon…

1

It Begins

"…as reports continue to come in, we will do our best to keep you informed," the pretty blond talking head on the television said.

Ken Simpson was not fooled in the slightest. He opened his hall closet and pulled the long, black case out from behind his array of coats, jackets, hoodies, and windbreakers.

Walking in to his living room, he glanced out the huge picture frame window to the street. It was just getting dark and there were no signs of kids playing or joggers pounding the sidewalk. He was about to return his attention to the case when something caught his eye. It was the Calloway dog.

Brandy or Bailey or some other alcohol related name. He never cared enough to remember, and that was a good thing. If Ken Simpson knew the name of a dog in the neighborhood, chances are it usually ended up with a pellet in the ass. This dog had never used his yard as its personal toilet. Of course that spoke more of the owner, Ken knew that. But, since he would probably have ended up in jail a long time ago if he'd been shooting the dogs' owners instead of the dogs—

The dog stopped suddenly and craned its head back over its shoulder. The animal bared its teeth, growling loud enough to be heard in the house. Ken moved to the door and opened it. The

Golden Retriever paused and turned his direction. Its collar and leash were on, but the chunky balding man who he always saw at the other end of that bright pink leash was nowhere to be found.

A low moan made Ken look down the street in the same direction the dog was looking. What he saw actually made his knees buckle just a little. The owner of the Golden Retriever was headed this way.

***

Rose Tinnes followed the winding road as it took her deep into Washington Park. She loved her evening runs even more now that she had shed almost two hundred pounds of useless fat: her husband…make that *ex*-husband Frank. The last straw had been when she caught him following her in his car.

Frank had been certain that her running was nothing more than a rouse to hide the fact that she was having an affair. He had said that it provided the perfect alibi when she came home drenched in sweat. Maybe if he'd gotten his fat ass off the couch on occasion he would understand that a person can sweat if they actually performed some sort of physical activity that did not involve holding the controller to an Xbox.

At almost six feet tall, Rose was a slender young woman. Twenty-six years old in a week, she was in the best shape of her life physically. The divorce had taken some emotional toll, but she knew she would recover from that in no time. Her shoulder-length hair was brown, but got just a shade lighter in the summer to where she could pass for sandy blond. Her athletic figure had been a source of disappointment when she was younger and many of her girlfriends were starting to look more feminine, but now she was almost grateful. Breasts were a pain when it came to running. Besides, it kept men's eyes on her face; unless they were fans of legs and buns.

Her earbuds were pumping some nice classical as she pushed herself just a bit harder when she reached the steepest hill of her run. Some folks might like to jam the hard stuff when they ran, but Rose found that classical took her away from the world and almost made her forget that she was running.

She came to a sharp switchback turn and knew that she was hitting the toughest part of her trek. It was sheer reflex that allowed her to leap just in the nick of time to avoid the figure sprawled across the narrow road.

Her hands swiped at the thin cords, yanking the earbuds free. Out of habit, she had already hit the button that paused her run tracking app. She hated nothing more than being timed while she stood waiting to cross a street; it completely screwed up her average per mile pace.

"Hey?" she called softly. She took a tentative step forward and realized that the dark shadow on the road was from a slowly growing pool of blood.

Plucking her phone free from the armband she wore, Rose quickly called 9-1-1. After a few seconds as the signal bounced its way to a tower, there was the blessed sound of ringing. After over a dozen rings, Rose glanced at her display to ensure she had dialed correctly.

"You have reached the City of Portland Emergency Dispatch Center...all lines are currently busy..." the computerized voice droned.

***

Jason Johnson stepped through the gate. It wasn't much, but in that single step, he had gone from being an inmate and "guest" of the Oregon Department of Corrections to being a free man. Well, sort of anyway. He still had a parole officer to report to, but he knew that was going to be temporary. He would be walking the straight line this time.

This latest stint down had cost him everything. Apparently that had been what it took for him to decide that he needed to make some major life changes. He'd walked away from the gang inside. That had been tough. The subsequent assaults to try to get him to change his mind had been futile. If nothing else, they had convinced him that he was on the right path.

The large city bus pulled up to the stop and he climbed aboard. The driver gave him *that* look. It was obvious. The old version of Jason would have said something nasty to the obscenely overweight man who had given him the stink eye as he swiped the state-issued card that would provide him with bus fare for the next forty-eight hours. This version simply smiled politely and walked to the rear of the bus.

Sitting down, he took a moment to look around. It had been seven years this time. An old home invasion he had actually committed before his last stretch had come back to haunt him. One of the guys on that ride had been busted for some major shit. He had dropped dimes on everybody in the crew in order to get a deal put on the table that would not see him strapped to a table and given the lethal needle.

Jason stared out the window as the bus rumbled past a strip mall. He spotted a coffee shack and his mouth began to water in response. Then he saw something else that made him question his eyesight. Reaching up, he tugged the cord that rang the chime indicating the driver needed to stop at the next bus stop.

He jumped up as the bus slowed. The driver seemed to give the brakes an extra hard tap which sent him lurching forward. Jason's eyes shot up and locked on those of the driver as he scowled in his big rearview mirror.

"Not worth it, pal," he whispered to himself.

The doors opened with a hiss and Jason gripped his small carry bag and jumped off. He would catch the next one. He still had a few hours before he needed to be at his PO's office. He had seen something, and if he saw what he thought he saw, maybe he would start off on a good foot with whoever got his case. Besides, when he got on that next bus, it wouldn't be right in front of the Columbia River Correctional Institution. Maybe the driver would just treat him like every other passenger.

Jason ran across the lot and headed for the alley that ran alongside the strip mall. There was a dingy cinder block wall that made an alley along the side of the mall and allowed just enough room for a pedestrian or bicycle.

As he got close, he could hear something odd. It sounded

like wet slurping or smacking, like somebody with really bad table manners. That had him puzzled. He rounded the corner and froze.

He had believed that he had spotted a possible rape in progress. He had seen the figure grab the other and drag it down. Jason had just assumed...

"My God," he breathed.

A body was, in fact, sprawled on the asphalt. There was a dark pool spreading out from it. However, the attacker was not raping the victim. In fact, the attacker was a woman. But her face was a dark mask. He knew it was blood despite the early morning hour preventing any real light as gloomy shadows struggled to maintain their foothold for just a while longer.

The victim was on his back. Despite the relative darkness, Jason could see that the man had been ripped open at the belly. The woman had had her face buried in that ugly tear until he arrived on the scene. Now, her head was up, something dark and thick dripping from her mouth and landing with a wet splat on the concrete.

Jason backed up and turned to run, but a bright flash of white light blinded him momentarily and caused him to halt. The light blinked off and an older lady emerged from her car. She eyed Jason with suspicion. After all, it was barely six in the morning, and here he was at the edge of the alley running alongside the strip mall, caught in the headlights just as he was obviously about to flee.

"I don't want any trouble," the woman warned in a shaky voice. Her hand went into her pocket and emerged gripping a phone.

"Call the cops!" Jason exclaimed.

He glanced over his shoulder just as the woman in the alley was taking her first steps his direction. But then the man on the ground sat up, his insides spilling from the hole torn in his gut. The older lady with the phone looked confused.

"Call them...NOW!" Jason spun and backed up, his eyes not daring to leave the sight of the pair heading his way from that dark alley. He heard an audible gasp as the pair emerged.

Good, he thought, *now maybe she will call—*

The thought vanished when he heard the thud and a soft clatter. He spun to see the woman lying unconscious on the ground, her phone a few feet away where it had skittered after her hand relaxed and let go.

Without giving it another thought, he ran to the woman, scooped her up and carried her to the car. The driver's side door was still open and he shoved her in, pushing her awkwardly over to the passenger's seat.

As he put the car in gear and stomped on the gas, he had the briefest thought. *Maybe I would have been safer in prison.*

MAY DECEMBER
Publications

**The growing voice in horror
and speculative fiction.**

Find us at www.maydecemberpublications.com
Or
Email us at contact@maydecemberpublications.com

TW Brown is the author of the *Zomblog* series, his horror comedy romp, *That Ghoul Ava*, and, of course, the *DEAD* series. Safely tucked away in the beautiful Pacific Northwest, he moves away from his desk only at the urging of his Border Collie, Aoife. (Pronounced Eye-fa)

He plays a little guitar on the side...just for fun...and makes up any excuse to either go trail hiking or strolling along his favorite place...Cannon Beach. He answers all his emails sent to twbrown.maydecpub @gmail.com and tries to thank everybody personally when they take the time to leave a review of one of his works.

His blog can be found at:http://twbrown.blogspot.com

The best way to find everything he has out is to start at his Amazon Author Page:

http://www.amazon.com/TW-Brown/e/B00363NQI6

You can follow him on twitter @maydecpub and on Facebook under Todd Brown, Author TW Brown, and also under May December Publications.

Made in the USA
Middletown, DE
16 March 2019